A
Bicycle
Built for
Sue

Daisy Tate loves telling stories. Telling them in books is even better. When not writing, she raises stripey, Scottish cows, performs in amateur dramatics, pretends her life is a musical and bakes cakes that will never win her a place on a television baking show. She was born in the USA but has never met Bruce Springsteen. She now calls East Sussex home.

daisy.tate92167

@DaisyTatetastic

www.daisytatewrites.com

Also by Daisy Tate

The Happy Glampers

A Bicycle Built for Sue

DAISY TATE

HarperCollins*Publishers*

HarperCollins*Publishers* Ltd
The News Building
1 London Bridge Street
London SE1 9GF

First published by HarperCollins*Publishers* 2020
1

A catalogue record for this book
is available from the British Library

ISBN: 978-0-00-832275-5

Set in Minion Pro by Palimpsest Book Production Ltd, Falkirk, Stirlingshire

Printed and bound in Great Britain by
CPI Group (UK) Ltd, Croydon CR0 4YY

MIX
Paper from
responsible sources
FSC™ C007454

This book is produced from independently certified FSC™ paper
to ensure responsible forest management.

For more information visit: www.harpercollins.co.uk/green

*This book is dedicated to all of the Mind,
Samaritan and 111 call handlers. You save lives.
Thank you for being there.*

Incident No – 38928901
Time of Call: 11:43
Call Handler: SUE YOUNG

Call Handler: You're through to the NHS 111 service, my name's Sue and I'm a health advisor. Are you calling about yourself or someone else?

Caller: Yeah, hi. Ouch. Ooo. Buggerbuggerbugger! [Groan of pain]

Call Handler: Sorry, umm . . . sorry, hello? You're through to the NHS 111 service. Are you calling for yourself?

Caller: Yes. [Sharp inhalation]

Call Handler: I'm Sue. May I have your name please?

Caller: It's Carol. [Muted swearing]

Call Handler: Hello, Carol. How can I help?

Caller: Not sure.

Call Handler: Do you believe you need medical care? [No response] Carol? Can you hear me? Carol?

Caller: I'm here. You alright?

Call Handler: Oh, phew. I thought the line had gone. I'm well.

1

Thank you for asking. Carol, can you tell me why you're ringing today? Are you suffering with your breathing at all?

Caller: No.

Call Handler: Do you require a doctor?

Caller: I might.

Call Handler: Can you explain why you are ringing today?

Caller: I've stubbed my toe.

Call Handler: Oh, I'm sorry to hear that. Have you stubbed it badly?

Caller: No, but it's sore.

Call Handler: I'll bet it is. Is there anyone there with you Carol?

Caller: Yes.

Call Handler: Good. Can they help you if you require any assistance?

Caller: It's my cat.

Call Handler: Okay. Well . . . Carol, is there anything I can help you with now? [No response] Carol, perhaps it would be a good idea to make an appointment with your GP? Are you registered with someone locally?

Caller: I just wanted someone to know I was in pain.

A Bicycle Built for Sue

Call Handler: I understand.

Caller: Do you? Do you really? [Ends call]

Call Handler: Carol? Oh. She's hung up. Are we meant to ring them back if they hang up? What? A stubbed toe. Okay. I'll leave it there then. What's that? I've not ended the call? I thought I'd pressed the— Ah. This one? You'd think I'd've got the hang of it by now, thank you. Raven was it? Raven. Good. I'm Sue. Sorry? Yes. Of course. I'll just push—

Incident No – 5938272
Time of Call: 17:23
Call Handler: SUNITA 'RAVEN' CHAKRABARTI

Call Handler: You're through to the NHS 111 service, my name's Raven and I'm a health advisor. Are you calling about yourself or someone else?

Caller: Yes, hello. Umm . . . sorry . . . I'm calling about myself. I've just had my tea . . .

Call Handler: Okay. Are you alright?

Caller: [No response]

Call Handler: Can you tell me your name please?

Caller: It's Reg.

Call Handler: Alright, Reg. What can I help you with? [No response] Reg, do you require a doctor?

Caller: I was hoping I might have a slice of cake.

Call Handler: Sorry?

Caller: Yeah, well . . . I've had my tea. Is it alright?

Call Handler: Is what alright?

Caller: I was wanting to have a slice of cake.

Call Handler: I'm sorry, Reg. I'm not understanding what you're asking. [No response] Reg? Is there a medical situation I can help you with? [No answer] Reg? I'm just going to put you on hold for a moment. [Muffled laughter]

Caller: [Angry noises] I TOLD YOU! I WANT TO HAVE A SLICE OF CAKE!

Call Handler: Alright, mate. Okay.

Caller: I'm not your mate. I'm asking permission to have a slice of cake!

Call Handler: Are you a diabetic?

Caller: No.

Call Handler: Is there any reason you shouldn't have the cake?

Caller: I ate my vegetables.

Call Handler: Well done. What type of cake is it?

Caller: Chocolate. With sprinkles on it.

Call Handler: I'd say go for it, then.

Caller: [Silence]

Call Handler: Reg? Reg are you there?

Caller: [Sound of china and cutlery]

Call Handler: Buh-bye, then. Welcome to 111, may I take your order please? Would you like me to super size that, sir? Oh, shit. I thought I'd— Cheers. Normally I press the mute button before I—

Incident No – 5278374
Time of Call: 19:11
Call Handler: FLORENCE WILSON

Call Handler: You're through to the NHS 111 service, my name's Flo and I'm a health advisor. Are you calling about yourself or someone else?

Caller: Yes, sorry. This isn't technically an emergency, but I think I might need an ambulance.

Call Handler: Those are usually 999 calls, love, but let's see if I can help. Are you calling about yourself or someone else?

Caller: It's for my husband.

Call Handler: Is he breathing?

Caller: No.

Call Handler: Is he conscious?

Caller: No. As I said, it's not urgent. But it's quite . . . umm . . . I am pretty certain I will need an ambulance.

Call Handler: I'm going to transfer you to one of our on-site clinicians who will talk you through giving CPR. What's your name, love?

Caller: Sue. Sue Young.

Call Handler: Sue? Blonde hair, lovely jumper with the spangledy heart on it? It's me, Flo.

Caller: Sorry, I—

Call Handler: It's Flo Wilson, sweetheart. I took over your desk at shift change.

Caller: Oh, sorry. Yes hello. The turnover there is so fast, I— Did I leave everything alright? The headset was acting up a bit earlier—

Call Handler: Sue, love. It sounds like you should've dialled 999. I think you might be suffering from a bit of shock. Was it a familiar voice you were after, Sue? [No response] Sue? Sue, do you know how to give CPR?

Caller: Yes.

Call Handler: Are you giving compressions now?

Caller: I – no – I— [Rapid breathing]

Call Handler: Sue, darlin'. Stay calm. We need to focus on resuscitation. If you can, start giving him compressions. Do you remember the video we saw? [Sings] Staying alive . . . staying alive . . . I'm waving like a mad woman at the clinician. He's just wrapping up another call and can see I need him urgently. [Strange noise from caller] Oh, struth. It sounds like you're having a bit of a panic, there, love. Take a deep breath. We'll do one together. That's right. Keep taking those slow deep breaths while we wait for him to jog over.

Why not think of that lovely coffee cake you brought in earlier? So beautiful, all of those delicate little flowers you made. I'm all store bought, me. Not a talented cooking bone in my body. That's right. Deep breaths. Here we go, duck. He's heading this way now. While he gets his headset on, why don't you tell me what's going on so we can get you some proper help right away?

Caller: It's Gaz. My Gary, he—

Call Handler: Are you giving him compressions, Sue?

Caller: No.

Call Handler: Is there someone there who can?

Caller: No. It's just the two of us. Always has been.

Call Handler: Is there any reason why you're not giving him compressions, darlin'?

Caller: Well . . . He's dead.

Chapter One

'Let's wrap these up, shall we? You might want them for your tea.'

Sue's mother nodded in that perfunctory, no-nonsense manner she had perfected through the years. A quick nod, a press of the lips and a follow-up nod that settled the matter.

For the first time in her life, Sue wanted to slap the look right off of her mother's face. A bit of a shocker considering she generally preferred it when decision making was taken out of her hands, as it had been for most of her life. *Not those curtains, Sue, they'll show the dust. A call centre? Oh Suey, you wouldn't want to work there, what would people think? Marry that Young lad? Honestly. You'd best be shot of him. He'll bring nothing but sorrow, Suey. Nothing but pain.*

For the past three weeks her mother had been hard at it. Making decisions for her. Apparently that's what happened when planning your husband's funeral suddenly seemed too much and you moved back into your parents' and had always been the lesser of two children, her older brother Dean having taken the role of favoured child quite some time ago.

You'll sleep in Dean's old room, but try not to change things about will you? I've turned yours into my sewing room because of the light. If the little ones are needing it for a sleepover, we might shift you to the pull-out in the lounge.

You won't want to watch that programme, duck, it'll depress you.

11

You'll not want too fancy a coffin seeing as it'll be burnt straight away.

Yes, sometimes her mother's bossiness was useful. Today it filled her with rage. She'd just been widowed. She didn't want limp, pub wake sandwiches to take home for a midnight snack. She wanted her husband back.

Just as quickly as the instinct to lash out flared, it sputtered and disappeared. Who was she to make grand pronouncements on how someone should and shouldn't behave? Her mother's fussing always escalated when she was uncomfortable and having a son-in-law who'd ended his life was certainly pushing a lot of buttons. Sue, like her father, became more still, as if the prospect of having to select one solitary choice out of the thousands of options available rendered her inert. Like choosing what clothing Gary would like to wear in perpetuity. She'd let her mother pick in the end.

'I'll put the white bread ones aside for you, shall I?' Bev was already plucking out the white triangles from amongst the brown triangles. 'Your father doesn't have the stomach for it. Dean never was one for sandwiches and Katie won't let the children touch white of course, so . . .'

'Oh, I—' Sue stared at the triangles of leftover sandwiches her mother was already piling onto the fullest aluminium tray.

There were so many of them. Barely touched, really.

Sue looked at her mother.

Bev.

Neat, shock-white hair, tidy lipstick, bright blue eyes, not at all red-rimmed as hers were. She looked well in fact. Her skin was still tanned from the trip to Florida where she'd taken to her role as 'nanny granny' with Dean, Katie and the children like a milkmaid to a butter churn. Hardly a surprise. In fact, many folk were surprised to hear Dean had a sister at all. Once Sue had married Gary, Bev had lost hope that her daughter might, one day, blossom into something wonderful and promising, ultimately giving in to the poorly disguised fact that Dean was and always would be her favourite, along with his 'catch of a wife' and their two children.

Today, Bev wore a simple black dress from Wallis that she'd bought when Sue's Uncle Jake had passed about ten years back. It still fitted. Mostly. In fact, very little had changed about Bev through the years, save the colour of her hair. Suffice it to say, she'd not taken the journey from chestnut to white gracefully.

Sue's eyes skidded off of her mother's impatient expression and landed on her Uncle Steve. He was whistling in admiration at something on her brother's phone who, when he noticed Sue looking, shot her a guilty look and pocketed the phone. Gary would've laughed and shouted across the room, *What's the score then, Dean-O?*

Gary would've handled a lot of things better about today if it hadn't been his funeral.

Sue tugged at a hangnail she hadn't remembered having. 'Perhaps we should leave the sandwiches out a bit longer. In case anyone who missed the service shows up.'

'Sue, love.' Her mother's expression left little to the imagination. There'd be no one else showing up. 'The agricultural show committee have the room booked from three-thirty and after that it's Silver Surfers Book Club, so . . .' Her mother was a member of the Silver Surfers and hadn't enjoyed the latest book. Something depressing about a girl in a religious cult in America, she'd said in the car on the way here. One of those 'worthy' reads Carly Beacon always insisted everyone read when it was her turn to choose. Between that and her 'endless quiches' despite the decision to fine tune the meal to the book's overriding theme or location, Carly Beacon was frequently the recipient of the sharper end of Bev's tongue. Bev nodded at a smaller pyramid of sandwiches she'd briskly constructed. 'These will make a nice meal later on. Filler anyway. Two meals even now that . . . well . . .'

Now that Gary was gone.

No one had quite managed to say it yet. Then again. He'd only died three weeks ago. It had passed in the blink of an eye. What with the shock and the paperwork and the scrambling to book the Royal Oak's function room at such late notice, no one had had much time to wrap their heads round the fact Gary was dead, let alone absorb the surprise that he knew how to tie a noose.

If his father had been alive, Sue supposed he might've helped with the arrangements. Managed to find a way to contact Gary's step-mum, who was off working on the cruise ships now, completely unaware he was gone. Perhaps if his father had been alive, this might not have happened at all.

Why were there so many leftover sandwiches?

She would've expected it at her own funeral. A small crowd. Fickle appetites. No shows. Oh, she had friends and such, this wasn't a pity fest. There would've been some people. But she'd never had a large crowd she went around with. Not ones who'd fall apart at the seams if she died, anyway. When it came down to it, she and Gary had been a perfectly self-contained unit and that had always been enough. Perhaps they'd been a bit too self-contained. Outside of Gary's football mates, they'd never really needed a 'squad' like Dean and Katie had. Ones they invited round for spontaneous barbecues and such. And anyway, Sue'd always thought they'd die at the same time. Of old age. Hand in hand. Not a care in the world about how many people did or didn't show up at the crematorium and then, after, at the function room down the pub.

Sue scanned the faux 'olde worlde' oak-beamed room. It was the same place they'd had Gary's fortieth. There'd been silly balloons and jolly handmade posters and shouting. All sorts of shouting. Jokes mostly, about the plumbing trade and Zimmer frames. They'd had hot food then. Mini fish and chips rolled up in newspaper cones and chicken wings with a guacamole type dip that had had a bit of a zip to it. There'd been quite a turn-out for the birthday. More than had turned up today after the service, anyway. Cake and ice cream, she supposed, were a far better lure than hushed, awkward conversations over triangles of egg and cress.

Her sister-in-law, Katie, strode over from the small huddle of men she'd been presiding over. Katie never walked. She strode or jogged or, once, on her wedding day, glided. She pinched a sandwich between her fingertips then put it back down again, tipping her frown of displeasure into a benign smile as she gave Sue's arm a fingertip squeeze. 'Sue, love, this is a bit awks, but . . .' she made a wincey face and then, 'Are you still alright to look after the girls on Thursday?'

Sue frowned. Thursday. When was Thursday?

'It's just that it's been a bit of a struggle to get paid help in at such late notice and now that . . . well . . .'

Now that Gary's funeral was over? Was that what Katie was trying to say? Now that Gary's funeral was over could they get back to normal please?

'Of course,' she said without entirely pinning down where Thursday fell in the realm of days beyond her dead husband's funeral. She had work one of these days, but when exactly—

'I completely understand if you're not up to it, but I've got a regional meeting up in Manchester and Dean's—' Katie flicked a glance over in Sue's brother's direction, did a comedic little eye roll and laugh then, 'getting here today was quite the feat. Not that we wouldn't have shown. Obviously. But you know what this time of year spells for Dean, don't you?'

As it happened, Sue didn't have to imagine what this time of year spelt for Dean because on the ride to the crematorium, Katie had filled them in on just how busy his accountancy recruitment agency was from January to April. The *end* of the financial year. Not quite as busy as Katie's construction recruitment business was at the moment, but that was because *her* business picked up at the *start* of the financial year which meant, between the pair of them, they were always *terrifically* busy.

'Excellent. Thanks so much, Sue.' Katie was already turning to leave then, as an afterthought added, 'If you feel like spending the night—'

Sue didn't.

'—we're always happy to make up the sofa in D's office.'

'Thank you,' Sue said. She'd rather gouge her eyes out and that was saying something because she had always struggled with gory things. Whenever Gary wanted to watch a film with a certain amount of bloodshed, he'd had to do it on his own. Her heart felt hollow as it lurched off of her ribcage. Had that been the problem? Leaving Gary to confront all of his fears on his own? 'I think I'd prefer to stay at home, if you don't mind.' Perhaps then she could figure out why her husband had killed himself. The Support Officer who had come over to her parents' a handful of times had tried to explain that the 'circumstances' of Gary's death weren't unusual. She simply couldn't wrap her head round that. They were definitely unusual to her. After all, she'd only put together tea, called her husband to join her and found him hanging from a rope just the once.

'Of course,' Katie said a bit too quickly. 'You don't have to stay if you don't want to.'

'It was very kind of you to offer.'

Katie obviously thought so too and went off to tell Dean the good news.

If Gary were here she would've added the story to their catalogue of Katie-centric tales that he told the lads down the pub – this pub – after the football. *Remember the time at my funeral when Suey was freshly widowed and Katie checked to make sure she'd still be raising her children for her?*

Oh, how they'd laugh.

And then Sue would go and do it anyway. Everyone's favourite little helper.

She glanced down at the wilted sandwiches. Perhaps the pub had changed management since they'd had Gary's birthday. The catering genuinely had slipped. She made a mental note to put an addendum in her will (when she wrote one) that there should be minimal catering at her wake. Zero, in fact.

No wonder no one had wolfed them down. They didn't look at all appetising. Untidily cut brown bread, then white. Soggy tuna bleeding into the cheese and onion. Neon coronation chicken. Some rather lacklustre looking roast beef.

She watched as her mother teased a bit of egg salad out of one of the more generously filled sandwiches then popped it into her mouth with a furtive look that suggested she'd be lying to her Weight Watchers app later.

Gary had been loved hadn't he?

She'd loved him.

Obviously not enough given the circumstances, but . . . she'd loved him in her own way. Quietly. Without too much fuss, but . . .

Anyway.

She blinked against some approaching tears. The last thing on earth she wanted was to be comforted. Or cry. Crying would be akin to admitting that this was all deeply, unmanageably, irrevocably real. She scanned the smattering of people glancing at their watches and relocating their winter coats from the backs of the stackable chairs.

Was this all her husband's life had amounted to?

Barely a dozen people remained (there'd been more at the beginning but there'd been a mass exodus about forty-five minutes back when one of the wives 'suddenly' remembered their babysitter had a doctor's appointment). They were mostly family now – hers – making awkward chit chat over their phones until the next booking pushed them out the door into the wintry gloaming.

Perhaps she should've dug out Gary's phone and made some calls. He'd been much more social than she'd ever been. Footie with the lads down the playing fields come rain or shine. Any position they'd needed. He'd run a 10k for the local hospice for the past four years back. Raised a few hundred pounds for them each time, he had. Spent years – his entire adult life actually – building up his father's plumbing business. Installing hundreds of toilets and showers all over Oxfordshire. *And* Berkshire. Fixed her parents' toilet heaven knew how many times. Gratis. His grandad's shower. Her brother's hot tub. He'd done countless kindnesses, her Gary, and *this* is how people repaid him on a day when he needed them most?

She fretted at the hangnail again. Perhaps she should've made a bit more of an effort when he'd been alive to be their friend, too. One of those wives who knew just when to dip in and out of their laddish bantz. Knew when to pull out a tray of hot sausage rolls or a cheeky bottle of rum. To be perfectly honest it had never once occurred to her that there might come a day when Gary wouldn't be there.

'Sue, love.' Her mother was holding a tray out to her. 'Will you be taking the sandwiches or shall I give them to someone else?'

She stared at the handful of people left in the room. Weren't any of them *hungry*? Couldn't one of these people show a bit of appreciation for her husband by eating a tiny triangular sandwich in his honour?

She looked over to another table where the hot water urn was being replaced by a fresh set of tea and coffee jugs. A better grade of chinaware from the looks of things. The Agricultural Show folk appeared to have ponied up for a higher level of catering.

Flo, the woman from work who had taken her call, was already in her winter coat. A bright red, knee-length, puffy down number that made Flo, a woman who definitely looked to be in Bus Pass range, look very . . . *vital*. As if both Flo and her coat would cling to every last vestige of life they were afforded. She held a small square of (stale) Victoria sponge in one hand and was asking for a cup of the freshly brewed coffee. The catering woman was shaking her head no, the fresh brewed was for the Agricultural Show.

A surge of white-hot indignation rushed through her. Denying a woman a cup of coffee at a wake? What on earth did this woman know about anything?

Perhaps Flo had a condition and required coffee. Perhaps she needed sobering up before she drove off home where, no doubt, she had a large, loving family waiting for her with a hot shepherd's pie. Or a stew. Perhaps she was enduring a bereavement of her own. She didn't know, did she? No one did. Not unless you asked. Just as she should have asked Gary when he came home from work how he was *really* feeling instead of running through the same conversation they always did.

Alright, love? Nice day at work?

Yes, ta. Dinner ready soon?

Pop the telly on and I'll call you when it's ready. Coveralls in the laundry basket, please, Gaz. I'll put them in the wash overnight.

Fair enough.

He had, as instructed, put his coveralls in the laundry basket. Just as he had every weeknight. He was as predictable as rain, her Gary. Monday to Friday, he'd come when called. Sat down at their tiny little table in their homely little kitchen. He'd talk her through his day when prompted. She'd tell him about hers if he looked tired. Saturday they ate out. Here, at the Royal Oak. Sundays was roast dinner in rotation between her parents', her brother's and Gary's step-mum's when she was about. Their tiny two-up, two-down row house had long since been too small to contain all of the Greens and Youngs.

Three weeks ago Thursday she'd made toad-in-the-hole. She'd popped it into the oven, realized they were out of ketchup, called out to Gaz that she was going to nip out to the shop to get some while it baked, then, once back, table set, telly still burbling away in the lounge, *Neighbours* wrapping up its jingle in the kitchen, she'd set out the ketchup and called to Gaz that his tea was ready. He hadn't come.

He'd been hanging in the stairwell. Quiet as a mouse.

Bog standard suicide, one detective had whispered to another. As if her Gary was just one in a crowd of thousands of men casually heading up to the loft to end it all before their tea. The detective had said a couple of other things as well. Things she simply wasn't ready to take on board just yet. She supposed this particular detective had yet to attend sensitivity training. Which reminded her . . .

She marched over to the coffee table, aware of her body moving with a different voltage. It was purposeful marching. She'd not marched anywhere except, perhaps, in Girl Guides? Had they marched in Girl Guides?

Flo was pulling her handbag onto her shoulder, alongside another girl Sue recognised from the 111 Call Centre. Indian, perhaps? Dark hair, dramatic make-up, and tall. A good head taller than Sue, as were most people, but this girl seemed to own her height in the same way Sue shrank into her petiteness.

As she closed the space between them, Sue wondered if Flo thought her a bit simple, calling 111 as she had when it was clearly a 999 call. The simple truth was, she had known at the time it wasn't an emergency and she hadn't wanted to make a fuss. It wasn't as if an ambulance racing over could have done anything. In the end, of course, an ambulance had come. Not until after the police had deemed it alright to move Gary and the Technical Coroner had taken whatever notes she'd needed for the inquest. It had sounded so suspect, having an inquest. But apparently that too was bog standard.

The paramedics had waited their turn, then stomped their boots outside, their reflective clothing glinting in the streetlights, and, after struggling a bit with the stretcher in the stairwell and commenting on how warm it was in the snug little house, revealed some rather tired looking coveralls. Apparently it had been a busy day what with the unseasonal amount of black ice on the roads and, of course, flu season. All of it had been conducted briskly and businesslike. As if they'd come to measure up the stairs for a new carpet, not cut her husband down and take him away in a body bag.

The Indian girl – Raven, if she remembered correctly – refused a cup of coffee with a wave of her hand and crinkle of her nose. She was a quiet, big boned girl, but Sue couldn't picture her a different size. Or, frankly, at a different volume. Something about the defensive way she carried herself wouldn't have suited a chatty, willowy girl. Such an awful lot of make-up. It was impossible to tell if she was naturally pretty or crafted to look so. The pitch-black eyeliner did show off her rather mystical-looking eyes to great effect and today, she supposed, it was appropriate.

'Sue, love.' Her mother announced across the near-empty room. 'I'll wrap these up before they go completely rancid.'

Sue looked at her mother who gave her a *what* look in return. She turned back to Flo and gave her arm a quick pat. One she hoped said, *I'm going to sort this little coffee situation out for you.* She needed to sort something today. Just one, solitary, thing.

'Give my friend a cup of coffee, please,' Sue said to the catering woman catching Flo's startled look out of the corner of her eye.

The catering woman stared at her as if she'd spoken Swahili.

In all honesty, she felt as though she *was* speaking Swahili. Sue didn't give commands. She took them.

When the woman did nothing, Sue's ire rose with an unfamiliar, volcanic fury. 'Could you please give my friend here a cup of coffee?' The words marched out in staccato bites.

'She's been through an ordeal today and coffee is the only thing that will make it better. Fresh coffee.' In all honesty, she didn't know whether Gary's funeral had upset Flo in the least, but white lies didn't seem to matter so much in the face of an absence of civility.

'I'll pack the coronation chicken up for the children, shall I?' Sue's mother said to no one in particular.

'I wouldn't mind it in a takeaway cup if you have it, love.' Flo shot Sue a cheeky smile, 'If that's alright.'

The woman nodded and went back to the kitchen. The Indian girl looked away. Shy? Embarrassed? Difficult to say with all of that make-up.

'Katie will take the roast beef no doubt, although I wonder—' her mother tapped her chin as she looked out to the back garden where her daughter-in-law was having a cheeky cigarette – she normally vaped – with Sue's father, their two heads bent together conspiratorially. They glanced back together, as if they'd rehearsed it, then guiltily looked away, grinding out their cigarettes underneath the heels of their good shoes before heading back into the function room.

'Thank you for coming,' Sue turned back to Flo.

'Oh, love. How could I not? *We* not,' she added, nodding at the Indian girl. 'Raven here was at the station next to me when I took your call. I was ever so fluttery afterwards. Just couldn't focus. She had to make me a hot chocolate in the end.' Raven nodded as if confirming an alibi. Flo winced apologetically. 'You don't mind me saying I was a bit upset after you rang off, do you, love? Normally, I don't let them get to me, the calls, but . . .' She finished the sentence with one of those shakes of the head that said, *I'm only human.*

Her reaction hit Sue straight in the heart. Flo had cared. It meant more than she could express. This virtual stranger had come to her husband's wake when only a few of his mates from the football had come to the funeral then left amidst a smattering of mumbled apologies that they had to get back to work. All of them? Not that she knew what she'd say to them, but at least it would've meant fewer sandwiches for her mother to fret over. Made the room feel less bare.

Her niece and nephew had been kept away. As if Gary's death was some awful, humiliating secret she'd be forced to keep for the rest of her life.

'Sorry for your loss,' Raven said, breaking the silence that followed.

'Thank you, Raven,' Sue said, meaning it. 'Thank you for coming.'

Raven. It wasn't a very Indian name. Then again, her accent and style choices weren't either, so perhaps Raven had been born to a family of British warlocks. A distant cousin of that goth from *Bake Off*. Who knew? Who knew anything these days, the world being the way it was. Chaos everywhere. One minute you're making toad-in-the-hole and watching *Neighbours* on catch-up, realise you're out of ketchup, and think *that's* the calamity. So you get the ketchup, race back to the kitchen because the timer's going on the oven, pull it out in the nick of time, catch your breath, problem solved, only to find yourself in the stairwell looking up at your husband's feet. Was this Gary's fault because he wouldn't eat toad-in-the-hole without ketchup?

'Right, we'll see you at work sometime soon, then?' Flo prompted.

'Yes, I'm – I'm due in next week.'

'So soon?' Flo looked shocked.

'It'll be good for me,' Sue said. 'Getting back to the routine. Keeping busy.'

Flo pressed a hand to her forearm and gave it a compassionate squeeze. As if she somehow knew that none of Sue's debit cards were working. That she'd had to ask her father to pay for the funeral until she sorted it out. That she'd told him she'd muddled up the security codes when she'd been to the florists, but the truth was, there wasn't any money in their joint account. It seemed Gary had been quite the plumber, but not so talented at book keeping. Not that she'd looked into things with any great detail. Three weeks in and she'd still not been back to the house, called the bank, gone through his paperwork. Nothing. All she knew was that the account she thought had their life savings in it was empty.

'Here you are, love,' Beverly triumphantly presented her daughter with a bent aluminium tray of cling film-covered tuna and sweetcorn. 'Take these. They'll see you through until tomorrow.'

Gary's favourite. There was no chance she could have them in the house. Not tonight anyway. Perhaps tomorrow she'd regret not gorging on them as if she were reclaiming some of the time she'd never have with her husband, but tonight . . . No. She couldn't face it.

'It's alright, Mum. You take them.'

'What? You know how your father is with tuna in the fridge. He'd go daft.'

Sue looked at her mother as if seeing a complete stranger. Couldn't today be the one day her father pretended not to mind? The one day her mother championed her daughter over her son?

'I'll take them, love.' Flo took the platter. 'My Stuart'll eat them. I'll pass on his thanks in advance.'

Sue smiled gratefully and watched them go. She liked Flo. Barely knew her to say hello, but perhaps at work, if they were on the same shift, she'd take the time to ask, 'How *are* you?'

Chapter Two

Flo stood behind her husband and, just as she had the previous four mornings, held her hands out to the vulnerable, exposed length of his neck where it tipped down over the puzzle page . . . and pretended to strangle him.

No. Check that. She hadn't done it yesterday. Not with Sue's husband's funeral to go to. That would've been tasteless and lacking in gratitude. So. Only three times this week. It was becoming quite the habit. Fake strangling her husband. Not that she wanted him *dead* dead. Quite the opposite in fact. What she wanted was to shake some get up and go into the man. Here he was, healthy, fit and not even a splash of Alzheimer's on the horizon and Stuart's favourite thing to do was sit. Sit and read the papers. Sit and do the puzzles. Sit and ignore the morning telly. At least it freed Flo to pick the channel. She always plumped for *Brand New Day* in the mornings. A garish, chirpy Mr-and-Mrs-led affair that felt interactive. Unlike her husband, who was busy sitting.

Their Irish Wolfhound, Captain George, who was usually at Stu's feet or hers (if she was sitting, which was rare), was wolfing down the remains of the white bread tuna sandwiches.

She let her hands drop to Stu's shoulders, tweaking his shirt collar out of his jumper and trying not to notice just how thin his hair was becoming as a new segment began on the telly across the kitchen.

'Would you look at that!' Flo said when the piece had ended. It had been about Africa and taking advantage of inexpensive flights. She gave her hands a squirt of moisturiser. All of that bright blue sky, combined with the high heating Stu insisted upon this time of year, made her hands feel dry. Stuart looked up from his paper, bemused. Flo tipped her head towards the telly. 'Kev's trying to convince Kath to go on a safari in South Africa. Last chance to see the white hippos.' Or was it black? They hadn't actually mentioned the hippos, but wildlife was always a good way to get her husband's attention. David Attenborough boxsets were a Christmas staple in their home.

Stuart's forehead crinkled as his gaze returned to the paper. 'Who's doing what?'

'Kev!' Flo said as if she'd just been discussing one of their children and not a morning chat show host. 'Off the telly. He wants his wife to go on safari with him. South Africa.' She enunciated the name of the country sumptuously as if she were Marilyn Monroe saying di-a-monds.

Stu nodded without looking up, but . . . ohhh . . . there it was. He cocked his head to the side and she could almost hear his pilot brain whir into action. Maybe this time . . . ?

'They'd be best avoiding Jo'burg. Cape Town is safer.'

Flo bit back an irritated humph. *Safe schmaif.* Didn't he yearn for an adrenaline rush? The thrill of wondering . . . will this be the time I tempt the fates?

She gave him a meaningful stare.

Nothing.

Stu had really lost the knack for picking up her dropped hints these days. A safari would make such a nice change to their quarterly trips to the villa. It was spoiled to complain, but if they went back to Portugal one more time . . .

So what if Jo'burg was a bit dangerous these days? They used to fly in all of the time, no problem. Go out on the town. Find some great little shebeen to enjoy music and shots of stomach-scalding hooch. She loved those little . . . what did they call them? Those spicy barbecued shrimp. They'd near enough set Stu's mouth on fire the last time they'd been. She'd wept with laughter as he'd guzzled glass after glass of milk. Oh, those had been the days. Back when she'd wielded the power of persuasion.

Stuart's pencil hovered above his puzzle. Lowered. Lifted again. Taptaptap against the table before the process began again.

It drove her mad. The pencil tapping. And why didn't he man up and use a pen? Would it really be the end of the world if he couldn't fix a mistake? Take a bit of a risk, man! Use ink! Fly into Jo'burg! There was no appreciating the ups without a few troughs on the old heart monitor, was there? Unlike most of the other flight attendants, she used to enjoy a bit of mid-flight turbulence. Great stories to recount at the bar later on with the rest of the crew. Toupees taking flight. Cocktails spilt in awkward locations. Hands grabbing things they shouldn't. She was running rather short on them now. Hair-raising stories for Saturday afternoons when 'The Golf Gang' all sat down to order their grilled chicken or steamed fish at the club.

She tuned back in as Kev finished a tedious bit on winter tyre safety. He turned to Kath and told her how lucky she was to be married to him, a man who could change a tyre without having to call the AA.

Good grief. He was ever so fond of his own voice. Rattling on, never giving the poor woman a chance to reply, unless, of course, he was using her as the butt end of one of his ridiculous jokes.

Flo was half tempted to tweet in with a Kath and Kev challenge. Get the pair of them to change a tyre right there in the studio. Or better yet, out in the rain. Flo would happily bet cold hard cash Kev was more vain than capable and that Kath would win hands down.

She jabbed the remote at the telly and turned it off. 'That poor woman,' she clucked.

'Who?'

'The one we've just been watching, Stu. Kath off the telly. Married to Kev?' Nothing. She pointed to the wall-mounted screen. 'On *Brand New Day*.'

A blank look met her expectant one.

Astonishing. It was the exact same show she had on every weekday morning ever since she'd gone off that smug, baby-faced lad on the ITV. She liked that they recorded it up the road in Birmingham and the fact that it was on Channel 4 made her feel as if she was still tapping into the edgier realms of morning TV. The edgier realms of herself. 'Anyway,' she said, unable to resist pressing her point. 'It's a shame. The way he always has to get one over on her.'

'Why watch it if it upsets you?'

Oh, Stu.

It didn't upset her. It got her fired up. In a good way. The same way wearing short skirts and being called a slag had in the 70s. It made her want to *do* something. *Change* something.

Besides, *Brand New Day* was bright. Fun. Downright silly at times which made sense for a couple who'd met doing freestyle disco dancing in Blackpool. Or was it ballroom? Either way, they didn't put on airs and graces and watching it made her feel young. Apart from the little bits they did on old folk's homes. She muted those bits or did the breakfast dishes. She'd send herself off to *The Best Exotic Marigold Hotel* before her children booked her and Stu into some miserable 'retirement community'.

She sniffily continued her defence of the better 'alf of Kath and Kev. 'That husband of hers doesn't know how lucky he is.'

She stared at the top of her husband's bent and balding head, pencil hard at work next to the newspaper. Taptaptap.

She wondered if he considered himself lucky. Being married to a woman who not only knew how to change a spare tyre, but who also knew how to recharge dead batteries, unplug a blocked toilet and clear out the u-bend under the kitchen sink. Perhaps not, seeing as Stu had been the one to teach her 'just in case'. If ever anyone deserved a motto it was her Stu. She could almost picture the headstone: Here lies Stu . . . just in case.

And just like that she pictured that poor girl, Sue, looking utterly shell-shocked as her husband's casket disappeared behind that scrappy old velvet curtain Flo had been seeing a bit too much of lately. Susan's Derek had passed just before Christmas. Heart attack. Tom's Deborah, just after. Cancer. Now this poor lad taking his own life. One worth saving if the brief eulogy was anything to go by. The pains she went through to find a reliable plumber.

She moved on to another thought with another click of her tongue, pulled on the bright red puffer jacket her daughter had mocked for being 'too young' and shouldered her handbag. She and Stu weren't anywhere near death. Not yet anyway.

Chapter Three

'It's Sunita, isn't it?'

Raven looked across at the boy around her age who'd rushed in from the latest onslaught of sleet and perched next to her at the bus station.

Weirdo.

People didn't just *talk* to people at the bus station. Particularly when one of them was exuding back-off vibes.

It was one of her finely honed crafts. Few, that they may be, but she could pull off 'radiating with leave me alone' at the drop of a hat. She hoped it looked cool rather than what it actually was: standard practice for a five foot nine, overweight, Indian goth who was rapidly losing control of her whole entire life and was too shy/ friendless/insecure to talk to anyone about it.

She shot him a swift side eye.

He had on a striped slouchy beanie. It was artfully tugged down to meet his patchwork stubble and the collar of his thick puffer jacket. Tufts of blond hair stuck out the front of his hat. Trendy kicks and dark, mud-splattered trousers completed his outfit. He looked familiar, but this was one of those out of context meets she was never very good at, seeing as avoiding eye contact factored high on her day to day survival skills. Judging by his age and the fact he knew her given name, it had to be college. No one called her Sunita apart from her family and her teachers. Strangely, they hadn't taken

30

to her new goth name. (It wasn't strange at all. Her name actually was Sunita. Raven was a fairly new development, but she lacked the sulky panache with which Telisa Wadhurst had swiftly managed to get the entire universe to call her Twist. Perhaps one day she'd be able to deliver dark, dryly ironic bon mots without sounding angry and, as a result, get people to do whatever she wanted. A girl could dream.)

Raven didn't have the slightest clue what the boy's name was.

If she was being brutally honest – something she generally avoided in life but not at the call centre because, hello, no one could actually see her – she tactically forgot people's names in the hopes that it made her appear aloof rather than at risk of being ignored if she were to bounce up to someone she might actually want to talk to. *Hey Twist. How's tricks?* Bleurgh. As if. Not popular by choice was always a better option than the achingly painful gratitude some of the other girls glowed with when popular looking boys like him deigned to speak to them. Which was why this was totes awkward. Sporty, popular looking boys like him did not talk to fat Indian goth girls like her.

Particularly if they were glowering.

She was proactively glowering.

It was what happened when one's life was backed into a very small corner.

She shook her head. Her parents . . .

Her parents were *crafty*.

Of all the attributes she would've credited them with – punctiliousness, predictability, pernicketiness – crafty definitely wasn't one of them.

'Sunita, right?' he tried again.

Not really good at reading invisible auras, this one.

'Umm . . . It's Raven, actually.'

He did the chin lift thing guys always did instead of answering back then pulled out his phone. Good. That was that done, then.

She'd started calling herself Raven at college some eight or nine months back to just about no effect. Not really having any friends had a way of making a name change less effective. The new name had more sticking power once she began her first gap year job at a now-defunct taco bar. It wasn't her fault really. The name change. She'd been forced to reinvent herself. Take herself out of what had become an utterly toxic morass of teenaged hell and start afresh. With darkness.

Goth darkness, so there was some light (they could be *funny*, and not just Noel Fielding funny. So goth I was born black? Brilliant. Discovering the goths of colour was like finding a promised land of dark humour and above par personal aesthetics). To be fair, it had been the dark clothes and back right the fuck off auras that had first drawn her to the gothic side. She'd needed it after that horrible, soul-destroying, nerve-wracking last year of college. Half of her peers had become the most vile versions of themselves (bullies, really) and the other half had realised their worst fears (anorexia, anxiety, depression, and in one particularly awful case that Raven was still struggling to absorb, a complete and utter reliance on self-harming). In the end it had been easier to keep herself to herself. Less shy, more . . . proactively wary of anyone with a pulse.

What better moniker, then, than the poor, misunderstood Raven. Most people saw the bird as a portent of doom, but if anyone ever bothered to read anything properly, which they didn't, they would actually know that the raven represented prophecy and insight. Security. Wisdom. And, if anyone cared, which she was sure they didn't, the raven was the Royal Bird of Bhutan.

One of the few plus sides of working at the call centre meant that she could be or say or appear whatever way she wanted because the turnover was so rapid, no one ever noticed to comment. 111 was a way station for most people. A halfway house between working for 999 (which people thought sounded cooler but was actually freakier) or getting 'a proper job'. Staying longer than six months was unheard of. For most people anyway. Raven needed to stick it out for nine thanks to Parent-gate this morning.

She dabbed at her eyes, praying her eyeliner wasn't running. It had taken about a hundred years on Brown Goth Pinterest sites to get that right and sad clown goth was definitely not the look she'd been going for when she'd done her make-up at the Costa just down from the bus stop. Her mother's lecture had been so long-winded she'd had to leave bare faced. Crazy-eyed more like.

She still hadn't entirely registered her parent's ultimatum. Intern at her uncle's law firm in Birmingham or pay for her own university fees? They had a desk all ready and waiting for her. And a room she could share with her cousin Aneesha.

Intern for ambulance chaser Uncle Ravi? Nine months of sleepovers with Awfully Affected Aneesha?

Not ruddy likely! Why couldn't they get it through their heads that she didn't want to be a lawyer? That gazillions of teenagers had no idea what they wanted to do for the rest of their lives after they'd finished college. She was taking a GAP YEAR, not 'destroying her future' as her parents continually insisted upon calling the handful of months she'd asked for to sort herself out. Those last few months at college had been fraught with so much turmoil. Not so much in her life, but it was like the whole of sixth form had become a Netflix series intent on showing just how dark the teenaged heart could become. Hard to study and figure out the bright side of life with so much drama squeezing the joy out of everything. Not that she'd told her parents that. They'd been told she didn't want to be a lawyer. Which she didn't. Not the Uncle Ravi sort, anyway. Nor did she want to become a lawyer because it was mandated. As much as she loved her brother and sister, who became exactly what her parents had said they should (doctor, finance whizz), she did not want to grow up to be them. Or her parents. Or have another round of 'We would've leapt at these opportunities if we'd had the chance. Didn't Sunita know how difficult it was, working day and night, saving, moving a family halfway across the world, parenting, running a business, wanting more for your children?'

It had been difficult not to remind her mother that both she and her father had been born in Leicester when that particular lecture reappeared, as it often did.

'Raven. Hunh.' The guy next to her popped his phone back into his pocket as if they'd carried on chatting and not been completely ignoring one another. 'That's cool.' He looked confused for a second then did the chin lift thing again. 'I'm Dylan. Dylan Riley. I was in your chem class with Mr Houlihan. I used to watch you draw those cool, um, you know those skulls with the—' he pinned his fingers into bunches and put them in front of his eyes.

'Roses,' she filled in for him. She liked to do sort of a cross between Frida Kahlo and goth art. Mostly because it was the only thing she could draw, but it was better than doodling swirls or squares like Sara Richardson who sat next to her had. Sara was at uni now. English or Media Studies. No doubt making someone else's life miserable with that finely tuned look of contempt of hers. Raven dug her nails into her hands. She should've said something.

'Yeah, that's right,' Dylan nodded as if she'd just told him she'd actually created the flower varietal herself. 'Roses for eyes. That was some cool shit.'

She looked down at her shoes, too embarrassed to accept the compliment and saw that they were, annoyingly, spattered with mud. February was a messy month. Mud puddles. Rain. Sleet. Slush. Parents wanting to micromanage the whole rest of your entire life making you choose between one suffocating roof over your head and another. And then, mercifully, right before she fell apart in front of Dylan The Almost Stranger and told him absolutely everything she was going through, the bus arrived.

Chapter Four

Kath moved her eyes towards the autocue. She'd fine-tuned it to a craft, having her make-up retouched, not moving a millimetre and absorbing whatever was on the *Brand New Day* prompter before the cameras were back on her.

This was a new one, though. Touching her up as they played a ninety-second piece on a woman who knitted jumpers for her pets. Usually they waited until the commercial break. She couldn't bear this new make-up girl. Bridget. *Bridie.* For some reason the younger they got, the more their adorably quirky/old-fashioned/whimsical nicknames annoyed her.

'No lip pursing, chica,' Bridie chided as she put another layer of powder on Kath's upper lip. 'Lines.' Bridie's eyes shifted to Kevin's for just a moment and Kath knew in that instant that Kev had organised it. They must have some sort of signal. A 'the wife's looking a bit saggy' finger flick.

Kath's eyes slid back to the autocue.

K & K: AD LIB ON JUMPERS FOR PETS 30 SECONDS

She smiled, shook Bridie away and began to laugh as studio camera two lit up. 'That *face!* Precious. And what a lovely way to brighten up a grizzly February day, don't you think, Kev? A chihuahua in a zebra jumper?'

Kevin, who rarely looked at her off air anymore, looked her straight in the eye and laughed along, 'How could I not?'

Wanker.

After twenty-five years of performing together she knew subtext when she heard it.

Bloody ridiculous, he was saying. Only a simpleton would find that funny. If only their devoted fanbase knew the derision he had for them. The contempt. She'd read *Wolf Hall*, too. Didn't mean she couldn't find a gussied-up dolly dog adorable. In fact, of the pair of them, she was pretty sure she was the one with a handful more brain cells. Compassion anyway.

'Maybe we should get Humphrey a jumper. Stacy?' Kath waved to their producer in the gallery. 'Can we get a picture of our dog up? He'd look good in the one with pom poms, don't you think?' She winked conspiratorially at the camera.

Kev shook his head and gave one of those twinkly eyed wry smiles of his. The type that had won her over all of those years ago when he'd first held out a hand to her to dance. At the time she'd thought his cobalt-blue eyes held a hidden wisdom. An understanding of the depths of her soul. Now of course she knew that it was actually a finely honed ability to patronize without the recipient being vaguely aware of him being anything other than charming.

'Just so long as you don't try to put me in a matching one,' Kev said in a way that implied he knew he'd end up in a matching one on tomorrow's show. 'I'm sure Humph is willing to go along with anything. What do you think viewers? Is our Kath mad enough to try and get me and Humph into the same threads?'

'Listen to you!' She gave his arm a play swat. 'So down with the kids. You and your threads.'

Kev's smile brightened, which meant she'd annoyed him. 'Are you trying to say I'm an old codger, Kath?' He always ramped up the Liverpudlian twang when he was trying to endear himself to the audience.

Kath feigned horror. 'Never.' She felt herself losing the invisible audience so she threw a wink to her husband. 'You'll always be my toyboy.'

'Atta girl.' Kev gave Kath's knee a brisk pat and they both turned to the centre camera, expertly absorbing the next prompt on the autocue.

KATH: LEAD UP TO TEASER FOR CHARITY RIDE – TWENTY SECONDS

Kath's heart tightened and her smile dropped away. 'All of which brings us to a reminder about just how important it is to look after ourselves. Not just outside, but inside too.' She tapped the side of her head, then her heart and folded her hands together on her lap so no one could see them shaking as she continued. 'Some of you may remember I lost my brother, Ian, a couple of years back after he lost his battle with depression. Since then, I've become an ambassador for LifeTime – a mental health charity.'

Out of the corner of her eye she caught Kevin nodding soberly then suddenly unleashing one of his bright smiles. 'I'm afraid that's all we've got time for today. Don't forget to join us tomorrow when we do a special on luggage. I know we'll be needing an upgrade before we head off on safari in South Africa. And by safari, I mean a Cape Town wine tour! Save some Chardonnay for our Kath. Rowr!' He clawed a hand at the camera then gave it a warm smile. Warm, now that he was back in control. 'From all of us here in the studio at *Brand New Day* . . . we wish you an *epic* one until the *next* one . . . which we hope will be even better. See you again at six. Bye for now!'

Kath smiled, waved, 'Bye all.' Through gritted teeth she asked, 'Why'd you cut me off?'

Through his freshly whitened smile, Kev used his old ventriloquism skills, 'It's bloody depressing, that's why. No one gives a toss.' He gave the centre camera one of those hand opening and closing waves that looked a little bit like a salute.

'Bye all,' Kath leant into Kev to give him a kiss on the cheek, their signature 'close of show' move. His cologne stung her nostrils as she whispered, 'I'm leading with it tomorrow,' then turned back to the camera and waved, 'Buh Bye!'

Chapter Five

Sue loved her niece and nephew, but some days, like today for example, she wasn't one hundred per cent certain she liked them very much. Which did tend to make things awkward.

This Thursday, much like any other Monday or Thursday afternoon, began with Sue's phone pinging just as she'd turned off the security alarm inside the back door to Katie and Dean's Tudor-style detached house in 'one of the nicer villages' outside of Bicester. She didn't read it immediately because she didn't need to. There would be a reminder of Jayden's sensitivity to milk, wheat and a 'suspicion' about peanuts that they had not yet fully explored. (There was a doctor on Harley Street that had been recommended. He had *such* a long waiting list, but going to anyone else would really be a waste of time.) When she did glance at the text she saw there was an additional line. 'Would you mind hanging on for a bit of a chat?'

Sue didn't really fancy it, but, as Katie never asked her to stay once she'd whirled back into the house charged with another day's high of recruitment successes, she thought she should make an exception. Perhaps Katie had realised she might owe Sue a bit of an apology for implying that taking time off for Gary's funeral had put a spanner in their childcare plans. That, and Sue still had yet to begin to go through Gary's things. The previous two nights she'd simply sat in the diner kitchen, too anxious to go anywhere else in the small house. She sat and stared blankly ahead of her until, when the clock finally made it to ten, she headed upstairs and went to bed.

As she did each week (save the last three), she'd arrived thirty minutes before the children were dropped off so that there'd be time to make them a *hot* drink and a *nutritious* snack before they did their homework (Katie was very exacting about her children's intake, insisting *temperature* played a *vital* factor in their digestive process).

Now that they were both deep into primary school, Jayden (7) and Zack (9) had a proper 'home from school' routine. Return home, place shoes in the appropriate section of the shoe locker, hang coats up on the rustic, but decorative wall hooks, book bags into the 'children's recreation and study room' and into the kitchen for a snack before homework. This, apparently, went like clockwork for Katie, her mother Mallory and, on the rare occasions her brother was home on childcare duty, Dean. Not so much on Sue's watch.

Door banged open, shoes kicked off, coats dropped where the child stood, book bags deposited wherever and straight into the kitchen for a noodle round to see if there was something good to eat (usually Katie's hidden stash of chocolate for 'afters' which she claimed were solely for emergency, but, Sue had noticed, were regularly replenished). And then the demands began. Auntie Sue, this chocolate isn't hot enough. It's too hot. Mummy wouldn't make us eat this. Mummy would make us something good. Mummy lets us watch television before we do our homework. Can you find my iPad/PlayStation/remote?

When Sue had first agreed to look after the children quite a few years back now, she'd absolutely adored it. The cooking, the cleaning, the caring, the nurturing, that warm, sweet child scent when one or both of them would clamber up onto her lap to hear a story over and over and over again. She loved it all, convinced it was a precursor to the days when she and Gary would be able to do the same with children of their own. But, of course, things hadn't panned out quite the way she'd thought. Their children never materialised, Sue poured her affections into her niece and nephew, and the leniency she had afforded them as a loving Auntie had turned into a presumption that they could behave however they liked and that she'd smooth over the edges so Mummy never had to know they had been little terrors moments before they morphed into little darlings when Katie blew in after work.

She could've established her own rules, of course, but Katie was so *specific*. If Gary was here, she'd ring him up and tell him Katie had been making more rules and he'd say something to make her laugh or feel a bit braver as he had when she'd once admitted, after one too many glasses of Zinfandel, that she was a little bit afraid of Katie. The 'sugar cereal incident' was burned so vividly into her psyche she daren't go off piste again. So, she muddled along the best she could, fixing, refixing, heating, cooling, finding, tidying, searching, wiping, unravelling, sweeping, wiping again and popping a smile on her face when Katie's headlights filled the kitchen as she whipped her BMW into place next to the house.

'Right! Good,' Katie said once she'd kissed her angelic children who were diligently sitting at their desks finishing up some homework. 'Are you alright for a little talk?'

'Of course,' Sue took off the pinny she sometimes wore when she was there and, like a domestic servant, waited until Katie had seated herself before she, too, sat down at the long wooden kitchen table (Irish elm, the last of its kind apparently).

'Right, Suey.' Katie clapped her hands together and looked her straight in the eye. 'We all know you've been through a tough time and now that you've had a few weeks to, you know, cry it out or whatever, I've taken it upon myself to rip the plaster off, as it were.'

Sue quirked her head to the side. Plaster? What plaster?

'We think it's time you started looking at other income streams, considering . . .'

Considering what? That her husband was dead? That the cash machine had eaten the last of her cards? That she hadn't yet divined a solitary ounce of courage to enter Gary's office and find out if there was something, anything, to explain why he'd done this.

The idea of one more tea with the missus . . . sometimes they just don't have it in them. Shame's too high. Spirit's too low. Whatever.

That had been the other thing the tactless DCI had intoned to the other when they hadn't seen Sue standing behind them.

Didn't have it in him to what? Wait for her to get ketchup so he could have his tea the way he liked it? Bear the relentless rain of February? Book one more Sunday lunch with her increasingly exhausting family? They were wearing, she knew, but was that any reason to end it all? Love her? Was that it? Did he not have it in him to love her anymore?

Katie glanced towards the children's recreation room where the television was now on (Katie had okayed some Disney Channel until bath time), then redirected her considerable focus back on Sue. 'Your father mentioned about the debit card situation.' She whispered the words 'debit cards' in the way one might whisper 'prostitution'.

Sue's flush went every bit as hot as if she *had* been found turning tricks out on the Bicester gyratory. She looked at her hands. 'I thought I'd look into things this weekend,' she said, cringing at her own lie. 'I'm sure it was just some sort of mistake.' Where were all of these hangnails appearing from?

Katie tapped her on the knee and drew Sue's eyes back up to hers. The gesture made her feel like a child who'd been caught stealing from mummy's handbag. 'It's time to reset the tracks, Sue. What we were thinking, your parents, Dean and I, was that perhaps you could pick up the slack for my mum.'

What?

Katie put on her 'explaining' voice. 'Mum's getting on, as you know and with the children being so active, we thought perhaps you might like to come along every weekday from three until six. We give Mum a bit of money—'

They did?

'. . . so we were thinking we could do the same for you.'

A strange light-headedness overtook Sue. They'd been paying Katie's mum for her afternoons with the children? Sue had been doing this for three years. Longer, actually. Ever since that lovely Swedish girl they'd had had run off with a young lad from the nearby BP garage.

'How much?' Sue heard herself ask, a little pleased to see Katie look appalled. 'How much do you pay your mother?'

'A hundred pounds a week. It's the going rate,' she hastily added.

'Other than free,' Sue said, wondering where this rather bolshy woman living inside of her had come from. Had she been there all along? Or had circumstances brought her to Sue like a tiny, lippy, post-trauma fairy godmother?

'Free? Well. Oh dear, *Suey*!' Katie's laugh was more high pitched than normal. It was strangely satisfying. 'Suey, we thought you enjoyed your time with the little ones so much we didn't think you wanted paying. Not with you and Gaz not having any of your own. We thought you thought it was a *privilege*. Having so much time with your niece and nephew.'

She had. For a bit.

'Paying you would've felt . . . well . . .' Katie looked up to her artful display of glass Kilner jars decorously filled with pulses and grains Sue didn't even begin to know the names of. 'Oh, Sue, darling. Paying you would've felt *gauche*. Given the circumstances. Now, though . . .'

Her insides churned with indignation. Katie and Dean's children were little terrors! Bi-weekly (thrice if you counted Sunday lunch) reminders that she would never have little ones of her own to marvel at. To spoil. To teach proper manners to.

The indignation turned to that fearsome rage she'd felt at Gazza's wake. The money she would give to be able to whip an invoice out of her pocket and present it to her sister-in-law demanding back pay for the last three years . . . Everything she had. Which, at last count, was zero. 'Of course, Katie. They're a delight.'

'Good! Well. A hundred pounds can go quite far these days so long as you're careful.'

A hundred? Wait. Wasn't Katie's mother getting that for three afternoons?

'Would you like a day or two to think about it?' Katie stood up, conversation clearly over. 'Let your manager or whoever at the call centre know you'll be needing to be on those split shifts or the very early morning shifts from now on?'

Sue blinked at her. *What?*

If Gary had been there, she would've been resisting the urge to throw him a look. He would've laughed and told Katie Sue would be doing no such thing, she'd be carrying on as normal – in fact, minus the childcare, because they were quite happy as they were thank you very much.

'Suey,' Katie was chock full of compassionate looks today. 'I know it's tough, but Dean and I did a bit of maths last night on your behalf and it does look like you're going to need all of the hours you can get. Of course we'd love to offer you more, but—'

Sue stopped her, her light-headedness shifting to nausea. She had to get out before she crumbled into a weeping pile of disbelief right here on Katie's freshly sanded and polished oak floor. Could her family not have waited a few days for this? A week maybe, before ripping off the plaster and giving her a new cause to 'relay her tracks'? She knew they'd never approved of Gary, but this was a dose of disrespect she didn't need.

A coolness she'd never felt before came over her. 'Yes, Katie. I think I would like a few days to think it over. I'll let you know which direction I'm planning on taking . . . now that I'm relaying my tracks.'

When she walked out the door and sat down in her car without so much as inhaling or exhaling, Sue realised with a startling clarity that, for the first time since she'd met Gary all of those years ago, she was well and truly alone in the world.

Chapter Six

Incident No – 38928901
Time of Call: 08:43
Call Handler: SUE YOUNG

Call Handler: You're through to the NHS 111 service, my name's Sue and I'm a health advisor. Are you calling about yourself or someone else?

Caller: Someone else. Oh, god. Ugh. Hang on. [Vomiting sounds] Sorry. A little bit me, too. [Coughing] No, it's cool, Angie. I've got your hair. Hi. Hi, I'm back.

Call Handler: Hello? Can you tell me your name and the name of the person you're calling about please?

Caller: Hello. Yeah, sorry. I'm Jools and the one I'm also calling about is my flatmate, Angie. She's right unwell. Not from booze or anything. I think we might have food poisoning but we didn't know if we needed an ambulance.

Call Handler: Have you tried contacting your local GP?

Caller: They're closed for some mad reason. Anyway, Angie's only just moved in so she's not registered and I don't like my GP. He's dead judgey. [Retching noise] Sorry. Sorry. I made a welcome supper last night as a thank you. Some dodgy prawn thing I'll never make again. But I owed her. I were running right low on cash and she got me out of a tight one. Boyfriend just upped and moved out without paying the rent, didn't he? Oh, wait. Hang on. No, no, Ange – why don't you sit on the toilet and I'll get the bin? Hey. Hi. I'm back, so . . . it's coming out both ends now. Should I be bringing her to hospital or anything?

Call Handler: How long have you been unwell?

Caller: About an hour now, but it's dead gross. I'm not too bad, but Angie's actually, literally, green.

Call Handler: Our advice is to stay hydrated and get plenty of rest and the symptoms should pass. Do you or Angie have a fever?

Caller: I don't know. Sorry, Ange – do you mind if I touch your fore— I know. I know. Just your forehead, babe. [Vomit sounds] It is disgusting, but . . . [Laughter] This is a pretty intense way to get to know one another, am I right? Happy Valentine's Day to the single girls! [Weak laughter followed by retching noises] I totally promise an alcohol-only girls' night out after this. [Giggling and coughing]

Call Handler: Jools, if you and Angie can do your best to stay hydrated that would really help. Take paracetamol if either of you are in discomfort.

Caller: That's it? There's no, like, magic pill or anything we can take to make it stop?

A Bicycle Built for Sue

Call Handler: No, I'm afraid not. Umm . . . let's see . . . they do advise avoiding fruit juice or fizzy drinks as they can make symptoms worse.

Caller: Blimey. Yeah, okay. Sorry, just leaving the bathroom for a second, babes. Ohmigawd. Worse? I just gave her a Coke. Ange! Put the Coke down. Bums. I'd feel like *such* a wanker if it got worse. Do you think she'll move out? I mean – she's just moved in and now sploosh! Food poisoning. Mind you, she might lose a couple. I might lose a couple! Everyone loves losing weight even if it's utterly foul, am I right?

Call Handler: Oh, I'm not sure we can say. Sorry. I'm sure it'll work out. If you or Angie have any new symptoms or either of your conditions get worse, changes or you have any other concerns do call us back.

Caller: Okay. Absolutely. She's bloody brilliant, you know. [Crying noises] I've only known her for one night, but it's so good to have someone here. Someone who *understands*.

Call Handler: That is important, Jools. Call us right back if you need to because, umm . . . we're here, too. For you. For both of you.

Caller: Okay. Cool. Happy Valentine's Day.

Call Handler: Oh! Is it?

Caller: Yup. That's why we got so ruddy pissed last night. I mean – it was the prawns, not the booze.

Call Handler: Yes, well, I'm sorry.

Caller: What are you sorry for? It was me who made the bleedin' things, wasn't it?

Call Handler: Nothing, I – Happy Valentine's Day. Thank you for calling NHS 111.

Chapter Seven

Raven rubbed her hands together and gave her feet a little stomp. The wind seemed to whistle straight through the bus stop. What did it matter, though? Unless she came up with a plan quick smart, she was going to be riding in the back of Uncle Ravi's Jaguar on the way to her first day as his intern in a few days' time.

Her parents had well and truly upped the ante on crafty parental tricks.

One week. One more week until she had to either find a way to pay for her entire higher education or become a slave at Uncle Ravi's law firm.

Ugh.

Birmingham.

Double yuck.

Sharing a room with her cousin, Aneesha.

Triple vom.

It'd be like living in someone else's Instagram feed and if there was one thing Raven was sure of – she wanted ZERO social media in her life. Zilch. Nada. Nul.

A swish of movement caught her eye.

Dylan. The lad from the other day.

He glanced at her as he settled against the leaning seat, but was thumbing a message on his phone at such a rate of knots, it must've blurred the rest of the world out of existence, which, of course, totally proved her point that social media overrode absolutely everything and was to be held in complete and utter contempt.

When she'd deleted all of her apps she thought it would be completely curative. Life without having to account for her every waking second to a world that may or may not be watching. #WakeUpFace! #BFFsDoingItRight #LivingTheDream

Instead it ramped up the FOMO to high anxiety levels.

All of those things happening 'out there' that she wouldn't know about. Was it better to know the enemy or pretend they didn't exist?

'Had your results?' Dylan asked as if they'd been mid-conversation.

She shot him a look. They'd all had their results. Months ago. Last year actually. In August. She'd been offered three places. ULAW (Birmingham Campus; too close to Uncle Ravi's office). LSE (next to her sister's office and three stops away from her and her neat freak husband's flat which had a box room with her name on it). And Oxford, where her brother was a paediatric surgeon. Obvs. All within a stone's throw of one Chakrabarti or another. They were everywhere. Her family. All lying in wait for her to fulfil her destiny as a Law Lord. She'd never known belief could feel so suffocating.

'That your briefcase?' Dylan pointed at the retro Pan-Am flight bag perched on Raven's knees. She'd bought it off of eBay in an ironic attempt to show she was the mistress of her own destiny. 'Do you work in a bowling alley?' He laughed at his own genius, but in a nice kind of way instead of the judgey way loads of teenagers laughed. At you. Never with.

'No.' She pulled it in closer. She kept her purse, her eye liner and the ridiculous bright yellow polo shirt she was forced to wear at the call centre in it. The staff were colour coded. Like robots. Street light yellow for the call handlers (read: not flattering). An eye-catching red for the clinicians (a bit better but still not black). Dealer's choice for management.

Dylan stuffed his hands in his pockets then pulled out the linings. 'I don't need a thing to work at the palace of pleasure!'

Raven gave him an ooo-kay look. Weirdo. Weren't teenaged boys meant to be mute with discomfort or totes ignoring fat, awkward girls like her? He looked like the sort who would totally blank her if another lad walked in. So, what was the deal? She doubted he was lonely. Her mind pinged to Aisha Laghari and The Social Media Incident. She'd not been directly involved, but she could've said something. Done something to get the girls to stop. Then again, who can stop a person from posting something vile about someone else? No one really.

Raven's tactic had always been to keep out of everyone's way. It was the easiest way to avoid trouble.

'I work at Curry's,' Dylan continued as if she'd just asked, wide-eyed, about his place of work. 'Computer section. Sometimes they put me in AV but mostly I do the PCs.'

'Ah.' He was obviously very gifted at acronyms as well.

'Good staff discount.' He stuck out his leg and unearthed a shirt sleeve from his puffer jacket. 'Check out my jammy uniform.'

Black. Head to toe.

Jammy indeed.

She did the raised eyebrows thing and caught him doing a little double take. People did that sometimes. When they bothered to look at her eyes. They were this sort of weird mossy amber colour and when she did her eyeliner properly they popped. Sort of . . . reverse goth. Handy seeing as she'd never have alabaster skin which, from where she was sitting, seemed a total pain. Freckles, endless sunblock, zits unbelievably visible. She was quite happy with toasty cinnamon thank you very much. At least she had another thing she liked about her physical self. Eyes. But that's where her body self-love peaked. She liked her cerebral self just fine, but it was a bit . . . isolating. Not lonely exactly as online could be a friendly place to be if you knew where to go, but wishing you were invisible in real life was never really indicative of being in a happy place, was it?

'So,' Dylan stroked the stubble on his chin. 'Let me guess. If it isn't a bowling alley, you work for . . . McDonalds? Starbucks? MI5?'

'I work at a call centre,' she finally admitted.

'Cool.'

'Sometimes.' She shrugged, tactically keeping the part about it being 111 to herself. 999 was far more aspirational. The calls into 111 were usually so . . . *meh*. No one really cared if you took twenty-three calls from mums worried about their baby's cough. There had been, of course, the day Sue had called in and told Flo her husband was dead. That had got her adrenaline flowing. Even Flo, who didn't look like she'd bat an eye if tanks rolled into the call centre, was flustered. The call had made everybody think. Especially her. Which was why she had agreed to go to the funeral. She'd wanted to under-stand what it would be like to simply disappear into death. Not forever, obvs, but . . . every now and again?

To be honest, she hadn't come out any the wiser on that front. It had felt like being a voyeur into someone else's misery. When she'd got there . . . *Fuuuuck*. Even her finely tuned levels of detachment were rendered useless. Sue, a woman she'd totally dismissed as 'nice' and, at forty-something, 'old', had looked utterly shell-shocked. As if a tornado had whipped into town, picked her up and deposited her in an alternate universe. Her family had looked embarrassed for her rather than sympathetic. Going through the motions of there there, it'll be alright, another cup of sweet tea, love? Packing up the sandwiches before everyone had left so as not to leave any trace that they'd been there at all. As if death by noose was the most humiliating way to go.

If it wouldn't have been the weirdest thing in the world to do, Raven would've happily filled them in on a ream of much more embarrassing ways to go. Falling off a cliff on a Segway when you were the owner of a Segway was one. Taking a selfie on live train tracks as the *scheduled* train approached was another. Death by Viagra, eyedrops, water and the list went on. (Google was full of it.)

All of which culminated in Raven acknowledging that even the prospect of an eternity at Uncle Ravi's law firm wouldn't make her top herself. Which did beg the question, why wasn't she eagerly swotting up for her law degree like a good little Chakrabarti instead of taking a year out? She knew the answer of course. She didn't want to be a lawyer. She wanted to go to Newcastle Uni. And she wanted to study Art. Or maybe History. Or . . . and therein lay the problem.

Chakrabartis don't follow dreams. They pursue goals.

'No contact with the general public,' Dylan said. 'Sweet.'

Raven was on the brink of pointing out that working at a call centre was entirely about interacting with the general public but Dylan pulled out his phone and began to thumb through what looked like an Instagram account. He abruptly stood up and strode out into the sleet. He made a miserable face and did some weird twisty things with his fingers as he popped out a few selfies on his phone. 'Gotta keep up with my peeps,' he said back in the bus shelter. 'Let the lay-deez know I'm ready for some Valentine's action tonight.' The way he said it made Raven smile on the inside. He knew he was being a dozy poser. She wondered if the strangers who saw his post would think he was being ironically chavvy or just think he was another self-obsessed social media twat. If he hadn't spoken to her last week and again today, she definitely would've gone with the latter.

If she ever were to go back on social media she'd want to be an Instagram influencer who hit that perfect note between darkly ironic and wise beyond her years. A Raven.

She squinted at Dylan when he became properly engrossed in his phone again. Even though he'd said they were at college together, she still had yet to properly place him. He definitely looked familiar, but . . . She flicked her brain into etch a sketch mode and tried to picture him in the evergreen jacket, striped tie and white shirt all the boys had had to wear at college. She erased his slouchy beany hat and filled it in with a head of blond hair. She added braces. A few zits.

Bingo.

He'd been in her computer programming class. He was good at it. Duck to water sprang to mind. Had to be a gamer. She was just about to ask what games he played when she remembered she had yet to tell him what her results were.

All A*s.

She'd not told anyone outside her family. It was embarrassing.

Her brain found learning easy.

But using it to go to law school? About as stifling as the drop-down scripts they had to follow at work. Still . . . at nearly ten quid an hour . . . one year at Newcastle Uni was only 438 hours of 'You're through to the NHS 111 Service' away. And then a mountain of debt for the rest. She hated the idea of debt. Starting your actual, real life already in debt to the man. Her parents hated debt too, which basically meant their ultimatum wasn't actually a choice at all. It was go to work with Uncle Ravi – and that was it.

The bus pulled up and she got on without acknowledging Dylan again. Talking meant revealing more things about herself. She'd already seen how seemingly innocuous facts became terrifyingly elastic on the social media super highway and Dylan was obviously one of its players, 'keeping up with his peeps' and all. She closed her eyes for the rest of the journey and pictured herself getting off of the bus in Newcastle. It was her Oz. One day, with any luck, it would be her reality.

Chapter Eight

'Never lets her get a word in, does he?' Flo straightened her husband's dressing gown collar then glared at the telly. That Kev was always talking over Kath. She would've told him to put a sock in it years ago. She tutted to herself.

It was always easier to know what she'd do if she were in someone else's marriage. That poor Sue, for instance. Looked half dead yesterday on shift, poor thing. How was it someone could live with another person for twenty years and not have the slightest clue they were planning to take their own life? She would've had that Gary sitting down with a strong cup of tea and said we're not leaving this table until you tell me what's going on—

Would she, though?

She gave Stuart's shoulders a final smoothing sweep. When was the last time she'd really paid attention to him? Listened to what he was saying to her? For that matter, when was the last time they'd had a proper conversation? All they seemed to do these days was pass on information. Times. Schedules. Where and what his sandwiches were for the day. His soup. She clucked again. Best not to judge Sue, or anyone for that matter. Glass houses and closed doors and all that. She turned off the telly and unhooked her winter coat from the rack.

Stuart looked up from the paper, his white hair still a bit mussed from the pillow, the puzzles she could see, only half done. 'Off already?'

'Bright and early sings the lark!'

'Will you be back for lunch?'

'Not today, love.' She was on a ten to seven today. She could come home for lunch, but the breaks weren't that long and besides, that poor Sue. She'd be in again today and Flo was dead certain that the poor girl wasn't ready for it. All of that complaining and whining coming down the line. Half of the callers were lonely. The other half attention seekers. Most of them needed a bit of sense knocked into them, was all. Not a pull-down menu offering options. She'd always found flights where they'd run out of the chicken or the beef ran much more smoothly than the ones where people had a choice.

Saying that . . . perhaps the menu would be a handy crutch for Sue. Offer her some insight as to where it might have all gone wrong. The poor lass had been in a daze at the funeral and hadn't looked too much better yesterday. As though there'd been a loud explosion and she was still trying to orient her senses after the blast. That glimmer of fire over the coffee, though. It showed the girl had some zip in her somewhere. It had been nice to see. Normally she was so . . . *pleasant*. Not that being pleasant was a crime, but it sat a bit too comfortably with *mild* and Flo didn't do *mild*.

'What will I do for my lunch, then?' Stuart asked.

She wiggled her fingers towards the refrigerator. 'There's some of last night's beef on a plate. Have it with the rest of that soup you had yesterday. Top shelf, next to the Actimel. I can do something hot for you tomorrow.'

Stuart liked something hot for his lunch in the winter, but increasingly, there was a part of her that wanted to scream, *you can fly airplanes! Surely to god you can figure out what to have for lunch!*

'Stu? Will you be alright taking Captain George along to his hydrotherapy?'

Stu nodded, then twisted round to look out of the conservatory which gave a broader view of the elements than the kitchen window. His brow furrowed. 'It's horrid out there, darling. Wouldn't you be better staying in today?'

Flo pretended she hadn't heard him. He was always trying to get her to stay home. Over forty years together and the man still couldn't get it through his head that she liked the work. Loved interacting with people. Needed the . . . the . . . the *rigour* of human interaction. Mixing things up. Keeping life jazzy.

She glanced out towards the conservatory. Stu was right. It was a wretched day. The entire week was meant to be like this, straight through to the weekend. Perhaps she'd sign up for some extra shifts. 'You'll be at the club this Saturday, won't you?'

'Of course, yes. The lads and I are due to meet the Pro at eight thirty.'

'Oh! A group session.' She smiled as if it were fresh news and stepped over Captain George as he stretched out on the floor between the boot room and the kitchen. Loveable old goat. She adored that dog. Couldn't bear to think of the day when he'd—

She'd take him out on one of his favourite walks this weekend if the weather brightened seeing as Stuart would be at the golf club, which was more often than not, these days. Now that the club had that new indoor robot thing that corrected his swing. There were three other retired pilots' wives who could say the same. The same three wives who met for coffee 'down the village', talking on and on about how difficult it was having their pilot husbands home, underfoot all the time, messing up the lounge, the boot room, the ensuite. Flo couldn't bear it. The predictability of it all. It was why she actively sought out jobs that required Saturday help.

Three months back, after the charity shop she'd worked in had been forced to close its doors, she'd thought of retraining as a therapist, but Oxford traffic was becoming too tricky to negotiate. Even more so now that the optician had bullied her into wearing the varifocals. She'd tried one of those on-line courses for counselling but found the lack of human interaction tedious. No one *spoke* to one another anymore. No one *listened*. Even their cleaner wore headsets. All of which left Flo with precisely nothing to do round the house now that they weren't breeding the Wolfhounds any longer (too much time in Portugal made that awkward, plus the neighbour girl had gone off to uni to study accountancy rather than veterinary sciences – not got the grades – but she'd always been such a help during whelping), so what on earth was she meant to *do* with her time? She was hardly on the brink of death! When she'd seen the advert for 111 call handlers, she decided she may as well help people who thought they were.

'Darling,' Stuart set down his pen and gave his wife one of those gentle smiles that meant he was going to try and reason with her about something. 'If this is about you having more pin money . . .'

She held up her hand. It wasn't the money.

She had her pension and Stuart was always very generous, having done very well at BA. So well he'd 'earned the right to sit and read the paper all day long' if he wanted to.

For twelve years?

Honestly.

She'd die of anxiety reading about all of those people out there in the world *doing* something with their lives.

She tugged the zip up on her coat.

The man was *too* reliable.

She'd liked it at first. His predictability. After all, you wouldn't want a madman behind the controls of a jumbo jet would you? She'd ached to be a teenager in the Sixties. Went proper wild when the saucy Seventies bloomed. Love-ins and flower power were all the rage by the time she'd realized her future was not in a factory or behind a type-writer and had been taken on as an air hostess in the mid-Seventies. When Stu started joining her at the bars in Swingapore, Rio and Cape Town, it had been like having a straight man to her mad trolly dolly. The King's right-hand man to her Princess Margaret.

Now it was just a bit tedious. Wasn't he interested in throwing caution to the wind? Making good on the years-old promises to properly explore the world? To *live*? He'd done all the boring bits. Made the right investments, built a healthy pension, owned their house *and* the villa in Portugal, but oh, the *tedium*. There was not enough gold in the world to relieve the *ennui* that came with being married to a man who relished his retirement. Her very own cover boy for *Saga*.

She did love him. And the children. But she and Stu were getting older, not younger, so why waste all of this valuable time doing puzzles while they were able bodied?

One shift at 111 would light a fire under him. She was sure of it. Discovering just how *old* folk could be. How frail. How *helpless*. On the other hand, there was always the risk he'd be comforted by his routine. Confirmation that it 'kept him out of trouble'.

All of which meant speaking to hysterical strangers on the telephone added that gritty bit of frisson to her life she needed to stay smiley.

It made her feel terrifically guilty, of course. Whining about having a perfectly lovely life. Especially with that sweetheart Sue finding her husband dangling from the loft. It must've been terrifying. Flo's husband might not have much zest for life but at least he enjoyed having one.

She stripped her tone of snippiness. 'I'm just doing my part for society is all, darling.' She blew him a kiss then dug into her handbag for her keys. She never could find the ruddy things.

Stuart leant back in his chair and tapped his pen on the folded newspaper. 'You've not forgotten we're out tonight, have you?'

'No, love. I've got it clocked.' She tapped the side of her head, then continued to forage for her keys.

They went out for Valentine's Day. Every year. Flowers. Dinner for two down the hotel (the one nice restaurant in the village but not so far that they had to worry about having a glass or two).

They'd inevitably discuss when they'd next head to Portugal (already booked) and debate whether or not they should invite the children along (decided). She regularly voted 'no children', hoping for a bit of an adventure whereas Stuart loved the close access to the golf course the gated community offered and knew inviting the children meant they would be tied to the villa. He loved it. Loved it all. Reading the same stories to the grandchildren over and over, going to the same restaurants, watching little Lily and Jakie jumping off of the diving board again and again until Flo's oldest, Jennifer, or, more likely, her husband William, insisted the children get out of the sun and go inside to watch some telly. *Quietly.* Jennifer hadn't been born with much of a nurturing gene. Then again, Flo had found her own children utterly tiresome until they'd started developing little personalities and could be persuaded that Daddy's way was the boring way. Then, of course, the tables had turned again. Jennifer had become an efficiency expert of all things and now Jamie just did exactly what his extremely ambitious Australasian wife told him to, including setting up home in Australia, so . . . so much for apples falling close to her tree.

Taptaptap.

It was the soundtrack to their mornings.

Taptaptap. Pause. Taptaptap. Sip of tea. Taptaptap.

Flo was tempted to march across the kitchen and grab the pencil out of Stu's hand and snap it in two. Everything he did was irritating her lately. She needed a project. So she said as much.

Stu surprised her by offering a suggestion. 'Why don't you help out Linda Hooper? She's always looking for someone to help her.'

Flo whooped a laugh. 'Down the village hall? I'd go mad, Stu. I've never seen more people make a bigger fuss over fresh J-cloths and cleaning liquids in my life.' Linda Hooper was also one of the 'golf widows' and would've tried to rope her into coffee time.

Stuart's eyebrows went up. 'Cleaning liquids?'

'Oh, you remember, Stu. As a "cost-cutting measure" Linda wanted us to start measuring out the bleach we were using to clean the hall after puppy training class. I brought in three enormous bottles of the stuff to get her to stop. But did it? Not a chance.'

Stuart clucked and gave her a loving smile. 'Not everyone's as fortunate as us, darling. Able to solve problems with money.'

'Precisely,' snipped Flo, popping on her Akubra, brought back from Australia when she was young and interesting. 'Which is exactly why I must get to work.' She gave him a quick kiss on the head, Captain George a long, deep hug then waved her goodbye over her shoulder as she walked out the door. She'd use the car ride to come up with a project much better than working with Linda Hooper. Surely to god there was something that would capture her imagination.

Chapter Nine

'That's right. Only a few more seconds. You can do it. I believe in you.'

Kath let Fola's rich voice flood through her like a healing tonic as she forced herself to do three more burpees to the dying strains of 'Roxanne'. She'd never realised just how many times Sting said that bloody woman's name. Burpees, it turned out, had a way of punctuating the obvious. A bit like her husband. What on earth had possessed him today? Saying a bungee jump in South Africa might be a cheap way for her to get a face lift. The man wouldn't let up. She'd half a mind to tell folk about his haemorrhoids tomorrow. As if she'd dare. Mind you . . . ratings were slipping and the advertisers would love it.

She pulled herself up for the final jump and clap and caught a glimpse of herself in the mirror.

'*Crikey,* Fola! Why didn't you say I looked like the back end of a donkey!'

'What?'

Fola's smooth forehead crinkled, genuinely confused. Perhaps they didn't liken things to the end of a donkey in Nigeria.

'No. No, Katherine.' Her trainer gave her shoulder a reassuring squeeze. Everything he did was reassuring, the way he said her name as if it was a flower, the gentle way he guided her through her workouts, but his *touch* . . . finally she understood what it meant to have sparks and glitter bombs and confetti flickering through her system. Yes, she'd felt something when she'd fallen for Kev, too, but this . . . this felt more real. Less hungry.

Yes, that was it. When she'd met Kev, she was *hungry*. For fame, for validation, for attention. And he'd showered it upon her. Until, one day, all of that amazing, doting, glorious attention had turned into micromanagement. Which was where they were now. Publicly micromanaging one another. Gaining, then conceding, fractional bits of kudos in the form of ratings pops, magazine mentions (god bless *Woman's Weekly*, because she was always ahead on the magazine front), glitterati photos in any paper really (which worked better for Kev than for her as they had a softer touch with men's aesthetics and laser-sharp talons when it came to a miniscule weight gain or eye crinkle or, God forbid, an annoyed glance at her husband as they left yet another party early because 'someone' had overindulged). It had made her a master of the jolly flow of excuses as Kev stumbled towards the car. (*Oh, we had an early morning call was all. You know how it is. The alarm clock's king in our happy home!*)

They were beyond being grand. Desperate was what they had become. Desperate to stay on air while they frantically resisted the inevitable. Being replaced by the next young thing.

Fola took both of her shoulders in his large, rather gorgeous hands and gently turned her so that they were both facing the wall mirror. He was a good foot taller than her. Broad shouldered (all muscles of course), lean. Athletic, really. Quite unlike her short, stout husband who used to twirl her round the dance floor as if she were made of air.

'Look at you,' Fola said. 'Do you not see what I see?'

Her eyes met his and fizz pop! Good heavens. Her va-jay-jay was obviously not as crippled by menopause as she thought it was. She looked back at herself, tilted her head to the side and tried to make an effort. Honestly? All she saw was a woman desperately trying not to launch herself at her personal trainer's knees and thank him, endlessly, for making her feel better about herself. She'd never cheat, of course, and nor would Fola (there was, tragically, the occasional mention of a girlfriend). But . . . oh, the frisson when his fingers touched her pale skin . . .

She forced herself to look in the mirror. Properly.

What *did* she see when she looked into the mirror?

All of a sudden she was blinking back tears.

What she saw was a woman who no longer turned heads.

A woman who had aged considerably since her dear, sweet, lovable, overemotional brother had died.

A woman straining to find some validation in a world that thrived off of other people's misery. (She was mostly talking about *Love Island* and *Celebrity Big Brother* here, but honestly. Hadn't they had enough of mocking people for their weaknesses, when, in actual fact, what the world needed more of was celebrating all that was good?)

'Do you know what you do every day?' Fola asked her.

'Get up far too early, make a prat of myself on the telly, then come to you praying to keep all this from jiggling?' She held her hands in front of her belly, looked up at Fola and saw him shaking his head sorrowfully.

A deep shame filled her that she had answered the question so blithely. So thoughtlessly. Fola was one of the most genuine people she had ever met in the world. He had been asking her a genuine question expecting a genuine answer and she'd belittled it by being blasé in response.

She looked up into his eyes.

'The truth is, Fola, I'm not sure anymore. I feel like candy floss. Utterly decadent nonsense that only causes rot in the end.'

Even her children wouldn't come home for Christmas anymore. It was that soulless. A home that couldn't even offer Christmas cheer.

'You, Katherine,' Fola countered, '. . . bring joy. Every day you bring joy and sunshine and hope into the hearts of everyone who watches you. You remind people of the good things. Kindness. You are made of strength and commitment and beauty. And that is what I see every time we meet.'

Kath's chin began to quiver, her eyes darting from her own reflection to Fola's and back again.

Yes, she was sweating like a pig. Yes, she looked as if she'd been shoved through a wind tunnel backwards, but strangely, at this very moment, she felt beautiful.

Chapter Ten

Sue stared at the screen hanging from the wall. They were dotted all over the place in the huge warehouse-style complex, flickering and blinking. Tallying up the incoming calls they had. This particular screen was playing normal television channels. Presumably to make the Hot Drinks Station a bit more homely. A pair of sofas, some throw cushions and a coffee table with a spread of trashy magazines probably could've done it to greater effect. But then, Sue supposed, less work would get done, fewer calls would be answered and people might actually enjoy themselves. As her mother was fond of saying, it was called *work* for a reason.

Though it was still a few days away, Sue was already dreading Sunday lunch. Katie and Dean wanted an answer to their 'kind offer'. They also wanted to make an announcement. Excuses weren't accepted when announcements were on the cards.

The television was tuned into *Brand New Day* and had a little ticker tape running along the bottom of the screen filled with tweets from viewers about whether or not they thought this was Britain's worst ever winter. It wasn't going very well for Sue. She found herself raising her hand in agreement with Kath. It had been bad. Very bad, indeed.

'You alright, hon?'

Sue turned around, startled to realise there was a small queue behind her at the Hot Drinks Station. She looked back up to the television screen. The image had changed to a man standing at the end of a pier wrestling with an umbrella. Why did they do that to these poor weather people? Shove them out of doors into the thick of things. It didn't seem right. It was as if, unless the viewing public witnessed someone being bashed about in the elements, they couldn't possibly believe it was extremely windy and immensely unpleasant outside. In February. When it was traditionally windy and unpleasant. She lowered her hand. Perhaps it was time she started to look at things from a different angle. Not just 'go along with the crowd' as she usually did.

As she watched the poor man lose his battle with the wind, the umbrella all but yanking his arm out of its socket, the look on his face reminded her of when she was learning to drive. She'd been terrified of the gear stick. Gary had thought it hilarious, her squeals of terror each time she'd lurched into a different gear, only to shudder to an ungainly halt. She'd felt as if the car was in charge and her knuckles had turned white clinging to the steering wheel, all the while hoping, praying, she could keep it under control, a bit like a wild horse. And then, one day, almost as if by accident, she'd done a gear change and realised she'd been in charge all along. Was this one of those life-changing moments when something, anything, might bloom in front of her, suddenly allowing her the 20/20 aspect she needed to realise she was actually in charge of her own life?

It definitely didn't feel that way today.

Not with her mother dropping unsubtle hints about selling up 'that house that had never amounted to much anyway.' Katie and Dean's peculiar offer. Her manager, Rachel, slipping a pamphlet about 'discreet counselling opportunities' onto her work station when she'd sat down this morning. Perhaps she'd been a bit too vacant on that first day back.

But there was so much to think about now that she was the sole decision maker in her life.

She'd had to dip into their holiday spare change pot today. The coins were in an old green glass flagon Gaz had found years ago out on a job. They religiously put their spare coins into it, only tipping it out once a year before they headed off to Benidorm for their annual get-away with Gaz's best mate from school, Mark, and his wife Shelley. (They'd come along to the funeral and had popped in to the wake, but had slipped out quite soon after as Shelley's mum, who was in their care, needed her meds.)

She guessed she wouldn't be going to Benidorm this year.

Anyway, she'd taken the coins because she hadn't got any food in the house and thought, perhaps today would be the day she'd be hungry. She might pop into the Asda after. The one off of the roundabout where her mother didn't work.

'Are you alright?' The woman asked again, giving a pointed look at the Hot Drinks Station where Sue realised she was now standing and, from the looks of the dribbling hot water, making a drink.

'Yes, sorry, I—'

'Your cup's melting. You have to double up if you use those.' When Sue's response wasn't instantaneous, the choppy-haired woman bustled her to the side and swiftly shifted Sue's wilting plastic cup to the sink with a couple of poorly disguised swear words. She reached into the cupboard, took down one of the mismatched mugs that presumably belonged to other call handlers who'd been more prepared, and fixed Sue with an impatient look. 'Was it tea you were having?'

Sue looked at the mug, then at the hot drinks machine with its array of choices. She usually picked whatever there was the most of because she knew some people really cared if they were out of cortado. Whatever that was.

'What do you want?' the woman asked again.

Sue wanted her husband back.

Before she could answer, the woman threw an impatient 'do you see what I have to deal with' look over her shoulder, huffed out a little sigh, grabbed a pod from the tower, shoved it in the little pull-out drawer, clapped it shut, then jabbed a button before throwing a look back at the queue with a 'Don't worry, I got this' look.

Normally, Sue would've been mortified. She hated causing a fuss. Today she was relieved. She obviously wasn't up to the task. Thank heavens for the drop-down menu dictating the advice they gave the callers. Otherwise, who knew what she'd end up saying? *Don't ask me, I just muddle along with the crowd.* Not entirely reassuring when your child had a fever outside of surgery hours, was it?

Another stream of liquid, brown this time, drizzled down into the ceramic mug.

Why hadn't he left a note? Wasn't that part of the whole thing? Making it clear why he'd done what he'd done? If he'd gone out to the pub and not left a note she'd be properly cross with him. And here he was, never coming back and there was nothing. Not even a scribbled 'out with the lads' on the stack of unicorn-shaped note-lets by the phone. For some reason, her sister-in-law was completely convinced Sue had a thing for unicorns. They were lovely, unicorns, but not necessarily her favoured item for home decor. She didn't need unicorn notelets, oven mitts and drinks mats. She especially didn't need a unicorn throw rug. Perhaps Katie thought an abundance of mythical creatures made up for the fact she and Gary had never had children. Perhaps it was easier than thinking about what Sue might actually want when obligatory gift-giving was required. Gary thought the whole thing so hilarious he'd started buying her items, too. As a joke, of course. She particularly liked the bedside lamp that sent dancing unicorns round the room at night. And the toothbrush.

Her sweet, darling, full of life Gar-bear. Had he really meant to see it through? Perhaps he'd hoped she'd hear him futzing about with the rope or cut him down before it was too late? No. He wouldn't have trusted her on the ladder up to the loft. Never had. She wondered again about a note. If he'd left something in the office. The thought struck that perhaps he'd posted her something.

Perhaps the envelope was sitting in the kitchen now, tucked up alongside the post she'd yet to open. A mixture of sympathy cards and bills from the looks of things. She wasn't a hundred per cent sure what she was waiting for. Not to shatter into a million unfixable pieces, she supposed.

'Here you go,' the girl handed her a brown drink that came halfway up the mug then noisily went about popping another pod into the machine making sure everyone knew *she* would be quick about it, unlike *some* people.

As she stood to the side, a sudden, searing pain burned Sue's ribcage. Was there nothing she could do properly? Nothing that made a difference? Gary hadn't even waited to have his toad-in-the-hole. Not that ending one's life on a full stomach was standard practice (as if she knew), but it felt like an additional, unnecessary slight on top of a sledgehammer of a message:

I couldn't trust you with my deepest fears. I couldn't trust you with the smallest ones. I couldn't trust you at all.

Definitely not with those final crunchy bits of Yorkshire pudding he knew she loved. Had that been it? His final present to her? All of the toad-in-the-hole to herself? Surely not. She would've shared. She always shared. He was her Gar-bear. Lord knew she'd never, ever eat ketchup again.

Perhaps the truth was a more simple one. He'd simply not been thinking about her at all. Not in a selfish way, because that had never been Gary, but . . . what was toad-in-the-hole when all one could see was darkness? It had been rather good that week. Puffy and crunchy in bits. Doughier in others. The same highly peppered, sagey sausages he'd eaten without complaint for the past . . . fifteen years now. They'd been married fifteen years ago this May. The same year as the Sainbury's had opened down the road and, out of some sort of misplaced loyalty to her mother, she'd gone to the butcher's instead (she'd bought her onions and flour from the Asda; they weren't *made* of money). Should she not have gone to the butcher's?

Should she have stuck to the supermarket brand he'd eaten before she'd 'gone all posh' at the butcher's (Morrison's Cumberland, but the Morrison's had closed, so . . .) Perhaps he hadn't liked her toad-in-the-hole at all. Said it was his favourite because he knew she loved it so much. Perhaps her entire married life had been an exercise in pulling the wool over her eyes. Ha ha ha! Look at poor, gullible, Sue. Thinking she was loved and safe and secure. Ha ha ha! Silly mouse.

If that were the case, it had worked a treat.

The thought made her feel as naive and ridiculous as Katie often made her feel. 'Oh, *Suey.*' *tsk, tsk, tsk* 'You know the children have *far more* valuable opportunities to express their inner child than at a soft play centre.'

Express their inner child?

They *were* children.

In exactly the same way Gary had been a plumber. Not a 'water and piping development engineer' as Katie had told people at the odd barbecue she and Gaz had been invited to in their immaculately manicured back garden.

Gary was – had been – a plumber.

People paid good money for an excellent plumber and heaven knew Gary had never wanted for work.

An image of her debit card disappearing into the hole in the wall flickered up.

People had been paying him. Hadn't they?

She stared at the darkening foam forming round the top of her coffee.

How was it that everything could look the same? *Exactly* the same as when the man she thought she'd known best in the world had taken his life and she hadn't a clue why.

A painful twist of guilt squeezed out a jackhammering of heart-beats.

She'd yet to go into his office. For some reason she thought there might be clues in there. Indications. She'd been so tired at night and would obviously need bundles of energy to go in. Like an explorer would before they entered a dark cave. Not that the room had held any particular intrigue before, but he did hide her Christmas presents in it.

She wondered if she'd find any in it – presents for next year. Sometimes he did that. Saw something he thought she'd like in the sales, buy it, put it in the small cupboard she'd been instructed not to look in at any time of the year. Perhaps there were all sorts of things in there she wasn't meant to find.

In truth, fatigue hadn't been delaying her, terror had. After she'd found him, she'd run round their tiny house and pulled all of the doors shut as if seeing what was happening out in the stairwell would hurt the rooms as well.

She supposed she would have to go in one of these days. See if there was anything that would offer her some insight. Any more clues. Any passwords to secret bank accounts that did work.

She knew she'd never be called clever, but she'd seen enough telly to guess that the refused debit cards might have something to do with Gary's trajectory of despair. Either that or he'd been life hacked. Identity hacked? Perhaps he had an entirely separate family he'd been supporting and loving as well as her. A nice, bouncy wife who asked all sorts of questions about how he was feeling. Children they'd had without any problem whatsoever. A no-fail recipe for Yorkshire pudding.

Her brain hummed with the white noise that had virtually consumed her over the past few weeks. She hadn't dared mention the cashpoint eating her card to her mother, now that she knew about the crematorium bill. It was bad enough knowing the husband her mother had always predicted would disappoint had.

And yet . . . the sun still rose, the traffic was its usual snarly mess at the roundabout by the school and the heating was still far too hot in the entryway to the large anonymous building that housed the call centre staffed with people reading scripts meant to have that personal touch. A personal touch not unlike this awful, tasteless, coffee from a pod.

Flo appeared next to her and without so much as a hello peered into Sue's coffee cup. 'Oh, darling,' she said. 'You won't be wanting that. The coffee here is hideous.' She took the mug, dumped the contents into the sink then pulled a couple of packets out of her handbag. 'Here,' she waved them in front of Sue with a smile. 'Why don't the two of us make these and have a bit of a natter before we plug our headsets in, eh?'

Chapter Eleven

Incident No – 5278374
Time of Call: 18:22
Call Handler: FLORENCE WILSON

Call Handler: You're through to the NHS 111 service, my name's Flo and I'm a health advisor. Are you calling about yourself or someone else?

Caller: Yes, hello. Are you there?

Call Handler: Yes, hello. This is Flo. What's your name please, darlin'?

Caller: It's Emma, but I'm ringing about my boy, Jamie.

Call Handler: Is Jamie alright?

Caller: He's got a bit of Lego stuck up his nose— Jamie! Put your hands down. Don't press on it. Oh gawd, for fu—

Call Handler: Is he breathing and conscious, Emma?

Caller: Yes, he's fine, but a bit blotchy maybe? Bloody expensive bit of Lego to stuff up his conk. He keeps sneezing and sort of— Jamie, stop that! He keeps sneezing and then kind of choking, like.

Call Handler: Is he breathing alright?

Caller: Sort of. I don't really know. He's had a cold since Christmas and it's bloody impossible to tell.

Call Handler: Is there any discolouration to his lips or face?

Caller: Like I said, he's got some red blotches on his face, but I think that's because of all the sneezing. Or eczema. His skin's bloody dry, no matter what I put on it. Coconut oil, that vitamin E nonsense from the chemists. But his lips aren't blue or anything. [Sound of pained coughing]

Call Handler: I think you better bring him to the nearest A&E, Emma. Is that possible?

Caller: Can an ambulance take him? I'm a bit tied up right now.

Call Handler: No, love. You'd need to go with him—

Caller: Yes, but there would be attendants on the ambulance, right?

Call Handler: Yes, but he would need a parent or guardian along with him. I can see here there's an A&E about five miles down the road from you. I'm afraid it's a busy night for the emergency services. It might be faster to bring him there yourself.

Caller: Yeah, there is. [Muffled swearing] *Love Island* was going to be starting in a bit and— Jamie! Put your hands down!

Call Handler: Emma, are you able to get your son to A&E or shall I call an ambulance for the both of you?

Caller: Yes. Fine. I'll go. I'll have to watch it on catch-up. Fookin' nightmare. Anything else?

Call Handler: No, love. If Jamie has any new symptoms or his condition gets worse, changes or you have any other concerns call us back.

Caller: Jamie! Hands down! [Call ends]

Call Handler: Struth. The future of Britain looks bright indeed – oh! Bugger.

Chapter Twelve

A sense of dread washed through Flo as she glanced at the large wall-mounted clock. Ten minutes and her shift would be over. Over 1500 calls the team had answered that day. Over 1500 lives helped. Hopefully. She did worry about them. The callers. Wondered if little Jamie's bottom would feel the heated wrath of his mother's hand when and if she'd missed winter *Love Island*. Flo tried not to judge, but she was inclined to draw the line at someone who prioritised observing other people's lives (fictional or otherwise) over the actual life they were meant to be living.

Ha! Who was she kidding? She judged all the time. Or, as she preferred to call it, *pre-flight character assessment*. Nearly forty years in a flying sardine can had given her lightning-sharp assessment skills. Who would be difficult. Who could be relied on to sleep through the entire flight. Who the talkers were and what type (the kind best avoided or the funsters who'd relish a mini-tour of the aircraft and end up exchanging addresses . . . oh, the *villas* they had been invited to).

She looked across her section to the far end of the room that served as their kitchen area. The Staff Leisure Area. Oh, dear. There was that poor girl again. Sue. She was staring at the staff notice board in a way that suggested she could walk away and not name a single item on the board.

Poor love. She'd offer her another coffee but it was well after tea time and she would lay down money Sue wouldn't be sleeping well. Not if she was sleeping in her own house, anyhow. Coffee was not the antidote to her sorrows. Not tonight, anyway.

Flo closed her eyes and tried to imagine what it would be like walking into her house minus Stuart. No. She couldn't do it. Completely impossible. He was like one of the taps or the doorframes. A fixture. They'd moved into the modern bungalow after Stuart had retired and, rather to her astonishment, had convinced her to retire as well. Their bolt-hole, he'd called it. Their launchpad, she'd called it. In a way, both of them had been right.

She'd fled the confines of the house the moment she figured out Stu was never going to leave it. Taking job after job, trying to fill the void a life of travelling the world had filled. Rearing the Wolfhounds had been a highlight. Right up until they'd sold their last litter a year back. That day had been weighted with heartbreak. Seeing the last of the pups scooped into a child's arms and, without so much as a backward glance, driven away to a brand new life filled with heaven knew what.

When Flo opened her eyes, she saw Sue was still staring. She rose to go to her, her head catching as her headset cable snagged on the edge of her cubicle. A red number caught her eye up on the Scoreboard, the television screen that told them whether or not people were waiting. Then she saw Raven, the lovely girl she'd gone to the funeral with heading over towards the Staff Leisure Area. Nice to see a young woman showing a bit of compassion. The younger generation these days seemed to be all me, me, me. Her parents had obviously raised her to be a cut above the rest.

Flo's gaze moved back to Sue, lost as she was, in a world of her own. Back a week after she'd laid her husband to rest. Didn't she have family insisting she take some time off? Children to comfort? Parents to move in with who would bring her a hot water bottle and an endless supply of tissues? Battling all of that grief and bewilderment on her own? Horrid, horrid, horrid. Flo willed Raven to offer her a comforting word or two. It wouldn't be much more, the girl barely spoke, but . . . sometimes a word or two did the trick. It was why she, herself, had trouble sticking strictly to the script lately when she took her calls. She'd already had a telling off (two, actually) since she'd joined a few months back, but the managers changed so frequently, she didn't mind going off piste when the situation called for a more personal touch. After all, life was nuanced. Why shouldn't advice be?

She sat back down again, her eyes on the Scoreboard. She'd not been wrong. The calls were flooding in now that teatime/bathtime/storytime was over. The surgeries were closed. Babies, youngsters and oldies were meant to be in bed by now and if they weren't . . . She popped on her headset and pressed a key on her keyboard, 'You're through to the NHS 111 service, my name's Flo and I'm a health advisor. Are you calling about yourself or someone else?'

Chapter Thirteen

Incident No – 5628323
Time of Call: 18:27
Call Handler: SUNITA 'RAVEN' CHAKRABARTI

Call Handler: You're through to the NHS 111 service, my name's Raven and I'm a health advisor. Are you calling about yourself or someone else?

Caller: Honestly? I'm calling about my husband, but you will be helping my sanity.

Call Handler: Could you tell me your husband's name please?

Caller: His name's Robert and I'm Claire.

Call Handler: Hello, Claire. How can I help?

Caller: We need you to settle an argument for us.

Call Handler: I'm sorry?

Caller: Which is better for a toothache – paracetamol or ibuprofen?

Call Handler: I'm sorry. Does your husband have a toothache?

Caller: No. He does not.

Call Handler: Do you have a toothache?

Caller: No. No one has a toothache. You're missing the point here, sweetie. I'm trying to prove to my micromanaging husband that he isn't *always* right. That sometimes other people know things! Like actual, genuine facts.

Call Handler: Oh, well . . . this might be something your GP might be better able to handle. Or your dentist?

Caller: Well, what good are you then?

Call Handler: I'm sorry?

Caller: All I want to know, so for once in my life I can feel a little morsel of fucking validation, is whether or not paracetamol or ibuprofen is better for a toothache.

Call Handler: Don't you have a dentist you could ask?

Caller: [Heavy sigh] No, love. It's after hours, isn't it? [Screams] Why can't you do this? Why can't you do this one simple thing for me? All I want is an answer beyond what bloody Google says. Ibuprofen or paracetamol?

Call Handler: Ibuprofen I guess. It's an anti-inflammatory. Paracetamol if you're allergic.

Caller: Boom! You hear that? You. Hear that babe? I told you it was ibuprofen. [Muted: Babe. She said paracetamol if you're *allergic*. Ibuprofen is the better choice overall.] Here. I'm putting you on speaker so you can hear it yourself. The doctor says ibuprofen is the better choice.

Call Handler: Umm . . . I should say that I am not a health professional. It would be better—

Caller: What? You're not a health professional?

Call Handler: No.

Caller: What are you then?

Call Handler: Umm . . . a call handler?

Caller: Oh, jaysus. Fucking hell. The one time I'm bloody right and now you've gone and fucked it up by being a nobody. Thanks for nothing. [Call ends]

Call Handler: Thank you for calling 111! And a special thank you for depleting my self-worth. Please do call if your sysmptoms worsen or you have any other concerns.

Chapter Fourteen

With the television off, the house was far too quiet. Sue tried humming a little tuneless number as she washed up her mug and folded the tea towel on the edge of the sink. She hummed a bit louder as she headed up the stairs, but doing so reminded her too much of the ridiculously naive women who wandered straight into the face of danger in all of those horror films Gaz had liked watching. A part of her wondered if the films would frighten her now or if she'd roll her eyes, astonished that someone could be panicked by something as everyday as the dark. There were far more horrifying things to be frightened of. War. Famine. Walking into the stairwell of your own home with a spatula in your hand only to discover your husband had had enough.

She probably shouldn't have had that extra coffee at work today, but Flo had kept bringing the hot drinks round to her desk like clockwork. She'd never had them before. The packet cappuccinos. Australian, Flo had said. From her son. They were surprisingly moreish and had a strangely exotic taste about them. One had definitely had vanilla in it. Another had seemed a bit coconutty. *Cardamom*, Flo had explained without having to be asked when Sue had caught the scent of the third one. *Cardamom*.

Cardamom! Gary would've laughed, and not because she would have stumbled over the word. He had never made her feel small, her Gary, though he did tease. She could picture him clear as day laughing as she told him about the lovely older woman from work who was handing out flavoured coffees. 'Cor, look 'oo's posh now with her cardamom lattes.' He would've said the word perfectly.

'Cappuccino,' she would've giggled, wanting to be just a little bit right. (Having an older brother whose statements – true or false – were taken as a given had made her nervous about insisting she was right in front of anyone apart from Gary.) 'It's a *cappuccino*, Gaz.' She'd only just learnt the name cappuccino came from Italian monks who wore white hoods and brown robes. Kath off of *Brand New Day* had been on about it after Kev had asked what was wrong with plain old coffee, wondering aloud just how much money Kath had spent over the years on fancy coffees. Tens of thousands of pounds, he'd speculated. Tens of thousands.

Gary would've agreed with Kev. That the fancy coffees were a waste of money, but he would've liked the bit about the monks. She'd meant to tell him about it over dinner. The toad-in-the-hole. She'd not be able to wow him with that little titbit now. She'd loved doing that. Bringing home quirky little nuggets of information he could use at work if the person who had rung him to unblock this or de-drip that was hovering. She could picture it perfectly. Telling him about the Capuchins and the cappuccinos. Her smiling a bit too proudly when he pulled her into a hug and called her his resident brain box. No one else in the world had ever called her that. A brain box. Now, she supposed, no one ever would.

Sue resumed her trip up the stairs, her eyes glued to the steps. It was the safest way. If she looked up she'd see the hatch to the loft. She'd always thought it too dangerous being as close to the stairs as it was. It wasn't as if their tiny little two-up, two-down row house afforded ample space to locate a loft hatch elsewhere, but honestly. The top of the stairwell? She'd always said it was a deathtrap. Again and again she'd said to Gary as he wobbled up the retractable ladder with one hand on the ladder, another clutching a box (most recently after New Year's when they'd put the Christmas decorations away),

'It's far too easy to fall out of that thing if you get your footing wrong. Straight down the stairs. You could break your neck. Just like that.' Then she'd snap her fingers though there was never a noise. She wasn't much of a snapper.

The lead weight in her gut grew heavier.

She hadn't given him the idea, had she?

Her brain fuzzed with white noise then cleared. No. Absolutely not. They'd been happy. They'd talked and laughed. Confided in one another. At least she'd thought they had. He was the only person in the world who knew her secret wish to be a prima ballerina like Darcy Bussell. A mother dead set against airs and graces and 'a stumpy torso' had put short shrift to that dream, but even so, one Christmas he'd bought her a tutu. She'd worn it round the house when she did the hoovering until one day it had got caught on the kitchen door handle and tore. She'd told him about it, gutted that his gift had been ruined. He'd laughed, said never mind, and suggested as he poured her a glass of zinfandel that maybe it was time for a new dream.

The only thing she hadn't told him was just how much she disliked Terry's chocolate oranges. He wrapped one up for her each and every Christmas. He always looked so pleased with himself when she opened it, she hadn't dared put him straight. She wondered if he had felt like that about his entire life. Regularly swallowing down the things he really wanted to say, desperate to keep the smile on her face. Unable to choke through one more toad-in-the-hole to the point where *snap* he'd simply had enough. A rush of nausea washed through her. She wouldn't have minded. Would've changed meal plans in an instant. Didn't he know she was easy to please? That his smile was enough to keep her smiling? That anything he had to say she would've happily listened to?

She stared at the door in front of her. Gary's office. Still unopened since she'd violently pulled it shut the other week, the handle level with his ankles . . .

She reached out to the handle, hearing the minor chords from a film soundtrack as she did. Ridiculous, of course. Her life didn't come equipped with a soundtrack. And it wasn't like she was going to find him in there. Or a secret family. Or, heaven forbid, a body. When the police and the coroner and heaven knew who else had been round that Thursday (she must send Flo a thank you note for calling 999 on her behalf), they'd checked everywhere, as if she might have all sorts of men hanging from the ceiling. Nope. Just the one. The last person on earth she would've ever believed would take such drastic measures. And just like that, her hand dropped away from the handle.

Maybe tomorrow she'd see to any tidying it might need. Yes. That would be fine. Tomorrow she'd go into his office and start tidying up. Tomorrow would be a brand new day.

Chapter Fifteen

Dog walking services. Not one but two health and safety workshops. A reminder to wash your hands after you went to the loo. (Gross. Wasn't everyone old enough to have worked that one out on their own?)

Everything under the sun was on the work notice board apart from a blinking room in a blinking house to blinking let.

Raven's skin went prickly. Was she really making the right decision? Moving out to give herself some headspace? It seemed like the only option. Live with Uncle Ravi or endure a nonstop commentary on her poor life choices? Hmm . . . yeah, neither of those were sounding divine. Yes, moving out would eat into her savings, but it would also afford her time away from the Disappointment Faces her parents wore so well. She'd mulled and mulled and mulled over it and somehow it was already Friday morning, the clock ticking with the urgency of a tell-tale heart. As if her mortality was on the line. (It wasn't as if she was going to go My Little Pony about things at this point in her life.) It was strange feeling guilty for something she had yet to do.

Sure, it wasn't murder she was plotting. She was, to all outside appearances, a truculent teen throwing up two fingers to a life of assured financial security and professional respect. As such . . . it was a psychological form of murder. Every bit as stabby and complicated and, yes, darkly romantic (if everything ultimately turned out well). Could complete and utter destruction of her parents' dreams for her have a happy ending?

Would she like to become a Law Lord?

Sure.

What self-respecting baby goth wouldn't, with a job title like that? The business cards alone would be worth the slog, but . . . would she rather write a graphic novel about an Above-the-Law Lord who defied parental expectations so that she could make good on an innate ability to protect life's more vulnerable earthlings?

Maybe. Once she learned how to draw. Or figured out how to get the computer to do it for her.

She tried not to think too much about the fact that writing a graphic novel about a Law Lord would entail actually learning about the law, but, hey. That's what Google was for, right?

She'd left the house as her mother had begun pointedly pre-packing the car for the trip to Birmingham on Sunday afternoon. A blanket in case of a breakdown. A box of energy bars in case a blizzard blew in (it was snowing in Scotland so, of course, her mother wanted to be prepared for all eventualities). An up-to-date first aid kit. Natch. Her parents ran a chemists so they were never knowingly under-prepared in the medicine cabinet department. Lucky, she thought, that she didn't have an addictive personality. It'd've been far too easy to become a secret sniffer or drinker or, like Aisha . . . a cutter. Raven had bandages and antiseptics on tap. The one thing she wasn't so keen on was pain, so. Defying her parents with a gap year had been her crack . . . right up until they'd called her bluff. And now it was crossroads o'clock.

She looked to her right and noticed Sue staring at her so immediately looked away. Sue had been up here at the notice board at least once a day this week as well. Perhaps she needed to move house, too. Raven couldn't blame her. She didn't know if she could live somewhere where someone had – you know – done something so *definitive*.

Then again . . .

She looked back. Sue was staring at the board now, but staring in that blurry kind of way that suggested she was somewhere far far away. She knew the look well.

Most college students had that slightly hazy look softening their features at least once a day. Drifting off with no actual thoughts in their head as the hormones took over. Raven caught herself doing it all of the time in the bathroom. Staring at herself, wondering who the hell the person staring back at her was, only to shake her head a few moments later and realise she'd lost track of time just staring into the abyss of her future.

Today, in the Costa where she'd taken to putting on her make-up before she hit the bus stop, she'd actually almost kind of liked who she'd seen. She'd given her ebony hair a strident royal blue streak. Her eyeshadow feature colour was a glossy burnt tangerine with a hint of glittery gold (it made her freaky eyes look mad weird and she would never admit it but she liked the double takes she got when people noticed them).

Dylan had been at the bus stop again. Not much of a surprise seeing as it was his regular stop and not hers, but with her mother being so micromanagey, leaving the house without an ounce of make-up, dipping into Costas and then going to the bus stop was the easiest way to keep the peace and feel a modicum of power over her own life until she made up her mind about a life of indentured servitude with Uncle Ravi or one of penury with a splash of mental freedom. Dylan had asked if he could take a picture of her eyes for his Insta page but, mercifully, the bus had come and she didn't have to figure out how she was going to lie about giving up social media for the year.

A bustle of movement beside her made her turn. It was Sue pinning a notice to the board. She scanned it before the blu-tack backing had a chance to take hold.

Room to Let, it read. She took in the amount, the location, her savings and how much it would dent her monthly income with lightning speed. Before Sue's hand had returned to her side, Raven had swiped the card off of the board and said, 'I'll take it.' And then she remembered what had happened there.

Chapter Sixteen

Kath brushed her hand along her shoulder as she stared at her reflection in the well-lit dressing room mirror. Trying to recapture the feeling she'd had the other day in the gym was proving impossible.

She did it again, this time giving each of her shoulders a soft caress.

No.

None of that fizzy sparkle.

There was, however, a tad less self-loathing. She was pretty enough for fifty-three. Even prettier for fifty-eight, her real age. The one solitary secret Kevin had managed to keep about her. It felt weaponized. The secret.

Dave, the floor director, popped his head into her room. 'Alright, Kath?'

She pinned on a smile. 'Absolutely. Are we still keeping in the piece about Hadrian's Wall?'

If she called it the mental health piece, it always got axed.

'If there's time. Tight schedule today.'

She waited for him to go until she let her smile drop. Dave and Kev were drinking buddies. Kev had no doubt 'had a word' yesterday afternoon whilst Kath was with her trainer.

Her features softened. Wouldn't Kevin be absolutely furious if he knew how much she loved her training sessions? All of that passive aggression in the wake of putting her knee out on that ridiculous indoor snowboarding segment gone to waste. So she'd gained a kilo or two. At the time she'd been humiliated. Now, she was grateful that her comfort eating had brought her some actual comfort in the form of Fola Onaberi. Trainer to Birmingham's glitterati. If only Kev knew just how rehabilitative her time with Fola was.

Kev, of course, wouldn't consider Fola a threat for a second. To put it simply, he wasn't famous. He didn't have a book, or an Insta page or a Twitter following. All of which made him staff and Kev wasn't one to pay attention to staff unless they could do things for him or he could brag about them (like the one solitary time he did a ten minute workout with Gwyneth Paltrow's trainer whilst she was on a book tour).

A blessed relief, considering Fola Onaberi was the kindest, most generous, loyal and – yes, she'd admit it – utterly breathtaking man she'd ever had the privilege to meet.

Apart from his solid career as a personal trainer and physio, he was also, quite simply, a good man. When he wasn't keeping his client's tummy fat below the government-suggested guidelines, he coached children's sports in poor inner-city neighbourhoods. Sport had given him a boost up and out of his own impoverished life back in Nigeria. He'd run the 300 metre race for Nigeria in the 2008 Summer Olympics in Beijing (in his first pair of brand new shoes, no less) and had run .002 seconds short of a bronze medal. Instead of taking up a series of lucrative sponsorship deals with questionable companies, he'd retired from competitive sport and moved to the UK so he could earn some honest money to send to his family.

They'd never been anything other than completely professional with one another, but he'd elicited something in her no one had in a long, long time. An ache to be her very best self. Her kindest self. Her honest self.

As such, Kath had a decision to make. Leave her husband – the fame, the money, and all of the other trappings that went with being the other 'alf of Kath and Kev – or spend a lifetime being consumed alive by her cowardly option to stay. No, those weren't her only options. She could always have a stab at going solo, but morning television really did like a Mr and Mrs pairing. Maybe she could spin a twist on the magic combo of Holly and Phillip? Cast a younger man to be her sidekick rather than the other way around (the more likely route the network would take if she announced a separation). She did know one thing for certain. Things couldn't stay as they were. Mid-life crisis?

Maybe.

Another glaring reminder that life was short and being miserable was of no use to anyone except, perhaps, Kev?

Her brother's death had hit her hard. Kev had been all tea and sympathy at first, but after a week or so, he'd counselled 'snapping out of it'. A long face wouldn't change things unless she was going to lose some 'proper weight' and 'look haunted' which she apparently wasn't doing up to spec, so the best she could do was move on.

How could she? Her little brother was dead. While there was nothing she could do to change that, she could change herself.

She'd never cheat.

No matter how many women's tits or bums he'd ogle, she knew Kev wouldn't either. He couldn't bear the headlines more than anything else.

KATH FULLER'S OTHER 'ALF TAKES MORE THAN HIS FAIR SHARE (*The Mirror*)

KEV'S FULLA SOMETHING (OR SOMEONE) ELSE (*The Sun*)

Or, for Kev, the worst one of all:

RATINGS PLUNGE AS KATH AND KEV CALL IT A BRAND NEW ENDING (*The Mail*)

It meant the world to Kev. This show. She loved it, too, of course. It had been hard won. Years of blisters, performing in nearly every talent show they could enter and, eventually winning the public's hearts in a Royal Variety Show after placing second in the World Disco Dancin' Championships that had catapulted a pair of virtually unknown Butlin's dancers from holiday camps to children's TV, on to prime time and now a level of fame and, yes, fortune, she'd never dreamt of. (The show producers had quickly distanced them from their 'kitschy dance past' and whitewashed Kev's fleeting run as a ventriloquist in Blackpool, but for all intents and purposes, it was their kitschy/disco ball, Blackpool/Butlin's past that had got them to where they were.) But her passion for the light, bright, morning fluff they created for 'ordinary Britons' heading out to work or getting their children ready for a *Brand New Day* of school had definitely waned.

A knock sounded on the door. 'That's your five minutes, Kath.'

'Stacy,' Kath waved their long-term producer in. 'What do you think about leading with the Hadrian's Wall piece?'

Stacy's eyes shot to the door. Kev sometimes came in at the five minute call to run Kath through the segments he really wanted to push. The exec producers were all firmly in Kev's court, meaning Stacy had to bend like the willow when Kath requested specific segments.

Stacy's mouth rectangled into an apology smile. 'Kev thought it'd be fun to do another bit on your trip to South Africa.'

Of course he would. She wondered if Stacy knew the plan. The real plan.

They'd go to South Africa, try to get Ben Fogle or someone like that along to big up a conservation project. Maybe fly in Bill Nighy to talk to the meerkats. She'd hang around for that. Something about the meerkat's quizzical expression reminded her of her brother. Hopeful. Ever hopeful. Until, of course, he wasn't.

'What is he suggesting?' Kath asked.

'Something about a bungee jump?'

Ah. So he *was* trying to build it in. The 'back story'.

'I didn't know you always wanted to go on a bungee jump.' Stacy looked genuinely surprised.

Kath didn't. Never had. Her idea of a complete and utter night-mare actually. 'Oh, you know. One's got to grab life by the horns at some point or another!' Or the back of the ears as Kev had suggested when he'd first showed her the Uplifting Safari Tours online brochure. Nip Tuck Tourism with a plausible cover story.

Kev had come up with 'the bungee jump incident' when she refused point blank to go under the knife in front of their entire viewing public. *It'd be a fascinating experience for our audience*, he'd said.

Oh, it would that alright. It would also betray everything she believed in. That beauty came from within. That public acceptance of plastic surgery exacerbated the already perilous relationship young women had with their bodies, their faces. That acceptance of the person you truly were was critical if a full, rich, happy life was the goal. It was why her brother had only found comfort at the bottom of a vodka bottle. He couldn't believe anyone would or could love him after all of the things he'd done as a soldier. He was loved. So very much. The only one who couldn't believe it was him.

Whereas, Kevin's main worry in life seemed to be that his wife was developing jowls.

Lying about her age was fine. And the fact they had someone make them calorie-controlled meals instead of cooking from the stacks of freebie 'fitness first' cookbooks lining their gargantuan kitchen shelves. Even actively ignoring the fact they had grown children was okay. For some reason jowls were where he drew the line. Lip wrinkles were one thing (make up was magical), but the first hint of a softening jawline? Call in the devil to whip out his paintbrush and palette! *No one wants to watch a face made for radio, Kath,* her husband had said, with the sobriety of a doctor warning an alcoholic – like her brother – about cirrhosis of the liver. *Least of all on a woman.*

'Stacy,' Kath gestured for the producer – a permanently exhausted single mother of twins – to close the door behind her. 'Can I let you in on a little something?'

Twenty minutes later Kath sat back in the sofa as they hit their first commercial break.

'Happy?' Kev asked, that sparkling white smile of his stuck in a Joker-like leer.

'Very,' Kath replied, terrified at what she'd just done, but strangely calm as well. 'I think the audience are really going to love seeing His and Hers Hols. Especially,' she added, 'the day when you go bungee jumping. It's bound to be a ratings bonanza.'

She looked up into the control booth and saw Stacy grinning away, giving her a big thumbs up.

Girl power, when properly harnessed, was something to be reckoned with.

Chapter Seventeen

Flo applauded. 'Good on you, girl. About time you showed him what you're made of.' She whirled round triumphantly to Stu. 'What do you think of that, then, love?'

Stuart looked up from his morning paper. 'Sorry, pet. What was that?'

Frustration rattled through her. Of all of the golden opportunities to get Stu to light a blooming firecracker under his retiree bum . . .

'Kath!' she snipped.

'Who?'

'Kath! Her off the telly.' Flo pointed at the screen. They'd just cut to some poor weather girl being buffeted by the North Winds. She was up in the Shetlands no doubt, poor thing. It always blew a gale this time of year in the Shetlands. A sudden, bone-deep urge to go to the Shetlands, stand on the beach and see how she stood up against the elements swept through Flo with such force she shuddered. It felt exhilarating. Perhaps that's why the weather girls did it. Subjected themselves to the not altogether dignified on-air reportage. It made them feel *alive*.

Stuart glanced up at her. She must've been glowering because he raised his hands up in the surrender position. 'Sorry, love. I was away with my puzzles. Lost to the land of Sudoku.'

He gave her a smile and touched a hand to his temple, his white hair still a bit damp, strands aligned in the exacting rows the comb had drawn through it. What was left of it anyway. Stu's features had softened. Not the tiny, endless, folds of wrinkles his mother's face had shrivelled into when she hit her nineties. But they were soft enough to make cheekbones she'd once likened to Cary Grant's appear just that little bit more vulnerable rather than virile.

Flo felt a flicker of something she hadn't in a while.

Compassion.

He was such a good man, her Stu. Proper old-fashioned. He was an excellent father. A great provider. He'd literally flown her around the world and they had the home decor to prove it. Rugs from Marrakech. Carved wooden giraffes from Vietnam. A bloody great onyx chess set from Mexico City they'd never got round to playing. She put hors d'oeuvres on it sometimes. At the holidays. If the kiddies spilt on it, it didn't matter much as one quick wipe with a J-cloth cleared it away and the chances of them ever using it were increasingly slender.

All of that *stuff*. Stuff acquired to prove they'd once led an exhilarating life.

Her compassion flicked back to irritation as she swallowed back a recurring and unwelcome thought: a nervous, growing dread that their high-flying lifestyle had been a mask for weaknesses in their relationship. Should she have married him at all? Had he really been her soulmate? Ever so quickly their global shopping list had shifted from silk quilts in Shanghai, leather jackets in Bombay and tall, awkward-to-handle didgeridoos from Australia to over-the-counter antibiotics in Bangkok, pool cleaner from Jo'burg (for Portugal), nappies from America (first for her children and then her children's children). If she was still flying, would she be buying adult diapers next? Would they ever take a trip to Australia outside the regulation alternate years programme? (Jamie came to the villa every other year with the children to 'give his wife a break.' From what exactly? The tedium of marriage? Come to think of it, her Jennifer always took a week off – usually somewhere on the continent – with her gal pals from back in uni. Loved it. Said she never felt more human than when she was away with the girls. Flo, being of a certain age and not having that close mother–daughter relationship she knew so many others shared with their offspring, had never been invited.)

Oh lord. Flo flicked off the telly. She didn't want to be old.

'She's already earnt forty-five thousand pounds towards a charity cycle ride she's doing.'

Stu made one of those interested noises that meant if she were to ask him about this later he would have zero memory of the conversation.

Flo couldn't help herself seeing this pointless conversation through. 'She's putting her money where her mouth is, Stu. She's actually doing the ride along with the group.'

'Group?'

'Volunteers. Charity raisers. Whatever. People who ride their bicycles along Hadrian's Wall for charity. The point being, Stu, she's doing it on her own. Without her husband.'

'Oh, that's nice.' Stu was back in position, pencil tapping along the little squares of the puzzler. *Taptaptap.*

'Yes,' Flo said, perhaps a bit insistently. 'It *is* nice. She's doing it for her brother – the one who died after all that time in the military. She's asking for folk to join her if they like. Kev's off to South Africa to do some daft thing with meerkats.'

'Oh?'

Taptaptap.

Had he even heard her? She'd just said that Kath of the utterly inseparable Kath and Kev was going on a cycle ride across the blinking country *without* her ever-present husband. For a charity, no less. The most she'd ever seen the pair of them do for charity was some mad ice bucket challenge and one incredibly awkward run on *The Great Sport Relief Bake Off* when Kev's soufflé failed to rise on the first show and he was voted off. She'd not felt an ounce of sympathy for the man. Those teeth! Whiter than Matt

Damon's had been in that war film of his. Private Ryan Gosling, was it? Something like that anyway. She hadn't remembered much from the film, just that the lad's teeth had been terrifically white. Honestly. As if teeth stayed that white during a war.

Taptaptap.

Another surge of exasperation took hold. She yanked her coat from the hook in the corner (wrought-iron pineapples bought in Fiji). Why couldn't Stu break away from the blinking puzzles long enough to chat with her? He was the one always complaining she wasn't home. That they didn't do enough together. So why, when they *were* together, was he such a slave to his routine? She scraped her keys out of the little lacquered bowl (from Japan) she'd been trying to programme herself to drop them into. She could narrate the blessed thing without the benefit of witnessing it: Alarm at six. (He didn't need it. His body was conditioned to rise.) Right arm out to turn it off. Same arm flipped off a triangle of bedding and one-two-three there we go, Stu's sitting up in bed, stretching his arms to the ceiling to start another day of exactly the same thing as he'd done the day before unless, of course, it was a Saturday or they were in Portugal where the routine altered insofar as there'd be no dog walk (they tended to leave Captain George at home, too hot) and sometimes, and this was only an occasional some-times, *sometimes* he set the alarm for 5:30 so as to catch an earlier tee-time. Bless.

Taptaptap.

She fought the urge to yank the pencil out of his hand, throw open the conservatory doors and shout, Look! Look at the world out there. All of the *life* happening around you! Don't you miss it?

'Darling?' He looked up from his paper and gave her a warm smile. It was filled with love, that smile. Warmth and love she knew she should appreciate more than she did.

'Yes, duck?'

'Have you left any lunch out?' He nodded at the coat she was pulling on, then patted his tummy. 'Wouldn't want me languishing away while you're out saving lives, now, would you?'

'No, love. Course not.' She opened the cupboard, grabbed the first tin of soup she could see and put it on the counter next to a small pan, a bowl and a spoon, the movements as familiar to her as her husband's were. She shouldered her handbag, wondering how on earth he'd survive if, say, she were hit by a bus and never came home again. He needed a project. *She* needed a project to stop herself from going mad. Perhaps she should take a page out of Kath's book. Pick something to do on her own. It wasn't as if there was a law that couples had to do *everything* together. She glanced back at Stu, one hand patting the dog's head as the other returned to the puzzles.

Taptaptap.

Then she stepped out into the rain, relishing the sensation as it lashed her face with icy reminders that she was still alive.

Chapter Eighteen

'It's a certain path to failure.'

Raven held her sharp inhalation in her mouth, not wanting to give her mother the satisfaction of an 'adolescent response to common sense'. AKA – a sigh. Sighs, apparently, were now a sign of disrespect and, even more reprehensibly, immaturity. Silliness wasn't really a thing in the Chakrabarti household. Earnestness ruled over all.

She pushed a stack of black tops into her duffel bag and zipped it shut, thanking her lucky stars that her father had gone into the shop early. Who knew a girl could be grateful it was flu season? A two-pronged attack would've been unbearable. It wasn't as if she *wanted* to move out. They were making her move out. Sort of. If you used her logic anyway.

'A call centre,' her mother repeated in an ominous tone.

Raven double blinked. Seriously? Her mum was more cross about the call centre than the fact her youngest daughter had just announced she was moving out?

Shouldn't she be bursting into tears or something?

Raven waited for something, anything, to flicker across her mother's immovable features. Nope. Nothing. Fair enough. Hysterical pharmacists weren't really a thing. 'I can't believe you are turning your back on a promising future in law for a *call centre*.' Her mum spat out the words as if Raven had announced drug dealing was her chosen career path.

She squelched a sting of hurt. Did her mother not care in the slightest what Raven wanted for her life?

It wasn't as if she was planning on making her life's work answering 111 calls. It was a way to pay for uni. Ooo. What a crazy way to rebel against your parents. Pay for her own degree, just like thousands of other students do when their parents don't/can't/won't cover their student loans. And second of all, this wasn't exactly a surprise. Her mum knew she couldn't bear Uncle Ravi; his ambulance-chasing mentality wasn't even close to the type of law she wanted to practise; if she did want to practise it, which she wasn't sure about because living here was so ruddy claustrophobic it was difficult to get a solitary thought of her own squeezed in amongst her parents' detailed spreadsheet plans for her. In fact, the more she thought about it, moving out was definitely the right decision. Having one's life thrown into chaos always seemed to work out in the movies. Not so much in *Game of Thrones*, but she was going to go with the positive angle and pray it didn't colour her parents' opinion of her for all eternity. Memories like elephants. The pair of them.

'It helps people, Mum,' she muttered, dragging the tote off of her bed and onto the floor. 'Besides. It's not like I'm taking calls about someone's Freeview not working.'

Her mother was so angry the barbed comment didn't even land. Her Uncle Shonal ran a huge call centre in Calcutta and, by all reports, lived rather well off of it.

Her mum's hands and voice pitched upwards again. 'Who? Who is it helping? People who aren't clever enough to make a doctor's appointment? People unable to find a chemist? People who want your permission to have a slice of *cake*?'

Raven frowned. She knew she shouldn't have told her parents about the cake call. Whatever. It's not like they understood anything about real life in the real world anyway. How could they? They'd been entirely programmed from the day they were born. Her mother's parents had endured the hardship of immigration and racism and poverty (and selling countless copies of the *Daily Mail* and Fruit and Nut bars) so that their children could live lives untouched by dust storms and brown-outs and civil unrest. Her father's parents hadn't been too different. Substitute the corner shop for civil servants in the foreign office and Ghandiji was your uncle. AKA the man, the myth, the legend that her parents had chosen for her to aspire to be like when she failed to live up to their expectations. (Unlike her dutiful older siblings who, in order of birth, had to live up to Alexander Fleming – *why merely practise medicine when you can change it?* – and, for her sister, International Monetary Fund legend, Christine Lagarde – *why manage other people's money when you can oversee the world's?*) Her own 'motivational speeches' seemed to dig deeper into her psyche than they ever had with her brother and sister. Or maybe they'd been better at hiding it.

Do you think Gandhiji changed India by not doing his homework?
Would Gandhiji have eaten biscuits in his bedroom during his fast?
Gandhiji loved the law. And look where that got him. On all of India's legal tender!

No pressure, then.

Funny how any mention of Gandhiji making a roaring success of himself by living his life *against the grain* didn't go down a storm. Gandhiji, apparently, could only be used to point out a child's reluctance to do exactly what her parents told her to.

'Mum,' Raven hoinked her bags up, faced her mother, her arms straining against the weight of her belongings (books, make-up and her entire collection of black clothes). This was a make or break moment. Every fibre in her body was vibrating with fear but she knew if she didn't say it now, she never would. 'I love you. I want to make you proud. But I don't want to be an ambulance chaser. It is not, nor will it ever be, anything I want to do with my life. I don't know exactly what it is I do want to do and the whole point of this year was for me to explore options so as not to waste anyone's money when I finally do go to university. If I go at all.'

She swallowed. *Gosh.* She couldn't believe she'd added that last part. Of course she was going to university. She wasn't completely mental, but . . . crikey. She'd actually said it. To her mother. She didn't know what she wanted to do when she grew up.

It felt scary. As scary as deleting her Facebook page. Her Snapchat account. Her Insta site. Her Twitter handle.

Her whole entire cyber identity eradicated with a few taps and swipes of her index finger.

Her mother's face went puce. Maybe the no uni thing had been a step too far.

'Your Uncle Ravi is *not* an ambulance chaser,' her mother bit out. 'He is the *Vice . . . PRESIDENT . . .* of The Society of Clinical Injuries Lawyers.'

Oh, for fuck's sake. Seriously? Hadn't she, for one solitary second, fought becoming a pharmacist? Wanted to . . . she didn't know . . . become a life model or a singer or food truck owner (she made uh-mazing pakoras).

Her mother gave her the You Better Apologise Now face.

Nope. Apparently not.

'Mum.' Raven suddenly felt very, very grown up. As if she were finally, after years of biting her tongue, delivering a long-overdue home truth. 'Uncle Ravi isn't a bad man.' He wasn't a particularly nice man either, but she wasn't going to push it. 'But I think you would agree, he isn't the best of mentors. And even Gandhiji wasn't perfect.' Her mother's lips thinned, but Raven continued, 'He was *forty-five* when he went to India and began to do his work there. I'm nineteen. I have some elbow room to work things out.'

Raven turned sideways, eased herself past her mother, then walked down the corridor and out of her parents' house to an entirely uncertain future.

Chapter Nineteen

'It looks as though this trip of Kath's is going to have to happen now!' Kev wouldn't meet Kath's eye despite the fact she was sitting just a few inches away from him. 'Fifteen grand to ride across the country? She's got a lot of generous fans out there.'

Kev was particularly rankled by this. As if the donations that had been pouring in for the LifeTime Coast to Coast ride were approval ratings for Kath alone. Which, in a way, they kind of were. Making it so much more fun to rub it in.

'I'm still in shock,' Kath gushed to camera three which she knew cut Kev out of the shot. '*Forty-five* thousand pounds for something that hasn't even happened yet!' She blew a kiss to camera one which was always set to a two shot. 'Thank you all. Truly. From the very bottom of my heart. LifeTime does some amazing work. Who else out there wants to join me?' She crooked her arm and arced it, 'C'mon. Fit or not – we can do this. One hundred and seventy-four miles from the Lake District, all the way across Hadrian's Wall to my home town of Newcastle. We've still got room for more riders. Just log onto our website for all of the details.'

Kevin, without so much as a glance in her direction, turned to address the camera on the opposite side of the studio. He was in a right royal huff. Not only was her 'completely boring, depressing, uninteresting charity ride' garnering press attention, she'd also told him point blank she wouldn't get a facelift. People got through life perfectly fine without them. Even famous ones. Sharon Stone. Emma Thompson. Judi Dench. Proof, as if she needed any, that beauty ran so much deeper than any microdermabrasion treatment.

The part of her that marinated in insecurity rose to the surface. Sharon, Emma and Dame Judi also had 'character' on their side. Talent. Kath had a bright smile, a sparky two-step and a willingness to be made a fool of publicly. That was about it. She forced herself to focus on what her cherished other 'alf was saying.

'. . . it'll be a right laff seeing how the weatherman sees the bank holiday panning out. It's not as if the UK exactly has a track record for sunny ones, does it? Helmet head. Rain. No access to a blow dryer.' He shuddered. 'I don't fancy Kath's chances. Ha! Anyhow – let's get back on track with something we're all interested in.' He turned to the camera they both knew was on a one shot of him. 'I hope you'll all be tuning in tomorrow when the Prime Minister joins us to address the question on everyone's mind: Will he be wearing a red nose at Question Time along with the rest of the Conservative party? Always nice to see a charity that *truly* gives back to the British public.' Kev gave his invisible red nose a honk, smiled into the camera directly in front of him, his freshly whitened teeth sending incisor-sized flares of light up into the control booth, the dimple in his right cheek a bit deeper now that he'd gone back on the carbs.

Idiot. He may as well wee on the camera. Mark his turf the old-fashioned way.

This was his power move. Dominating the cameras no matter what the floor directors and, more importantly, their producer was trying to achieve. He adored talking eye to eye with 'his audience'. *They love it, Kath,* he'd say whenever she, or their producer, suggested more coupley interaction. *They lap it up, the one-on-one thing. Gives 'em an intimate feeling. A hint of what it'd be like to be you.*

She always let that one slide with a 'lucky me' smile.

Today, of course, the move had an added bite.

Today, Kevin's nettly behaviour wasn't about outranking *Good Morning Britain* or *BBC Breakfast*. It was about sticking one to Kath.

Hell had no fury like Kevin scorned.

She'd not warned him that her JustGiving page had cracked forty-five grand. He'd held the record on fundraising with the ice bucket challenge he'd done out on the Birmingham City pitch, but . . . for heaven's sake! This wasn't about him. It wasn't about his ego, or his pride or the fact she'd finally pushed back and said no to his completely unreasonable request that she get plastic surgery. It was about her brother and the legacy she was trying to build for him. A man who'd devoted himself to a career in the military only to come back like a jigsaw puzzle missing a few crucial pieces, as if he'd literally lost bits of himself on each of his tours.

Why did everything with Kev have to be so damn competitive? When had they stopped being a team?

She watched as he truncated the autocue script teasing a feature on last-minute holiday insurance and bled it into what he liked to call 'a splash of extemporaneous chat'.

'Speaking of holiday insurance . . . I don't know how many of you are lucky enough to have a wife willing to send *you* off on safari with the lads—' Kev stopped, gave his head a little shake as if something brand new had just occurred to him and gave her a sidelong look. 'Unless this is all some clever plan to get rid of me?' He twisted round on the sofa and gave Kath one of those sly dog smiles of his. 'Is that it, petal? Hoping the lions pounce at night? I'd like to see 'em make a meal out of this!' He feigned a little Arnold Schwarzenegger muscle pose, squawked out his rendition of the opening notes of *The Lion King* then clapped his hands together between his knees and launched into 'a surprise announcement'. Kev, it appeared, had managed to bewitch Team GB's women's beach volleyball team to come along with him. All in a lead-up to the Commonwealth Games. Of course.

Sly bastard. She hadn't seen that coming. Cute, though, that he thought he could make her jealous.

'How 'bout that then for a treat, eh viewers? A bit of ba-da-bing, ba-da-BOOM!' He mimed hitting a volleyball. 'A perfect antidote to the winter blues. Seeing our girls representing England enjoying some off-site "spring training".'

He loved using air quotes, her Kev. Never in the right spot, mind, but inaccuracy had never been a huge deterrent to throwing them out there.

It's coming up to 'half term'.

There was no other name for it. The break in the academic term was actually called half term.

Do what you can to join me on the beach in Cape Town as I give the girls a run for their money during 'training'.

That's actually what it was, Kev. Training.

Our Kath's turning 'fifty-three' this year!

She wasn't, but that's what they'd told everyone, so, perhaps in that case the air quotes had been merited, if not a bit of a giveaway.

He finally met her eyes, no doubt to see if his little surprise had had the desired effect.

'I have no doubt you'll give them a run for their money, love,' she cooed. 'Ladies, be warned: the legs on this man! Pure muscle.' She leant in to give him a kiss on the cheek, careful not to let his make-up smudge hers.

Bless. He thought the idea of him surrounded by twelve fit young women would drive her spare. It would never once have occurred to him that, at fifty-three, he'd be just another leering man trying to score some cheap jokes at the expense of their hard work and athleticism. Not much of a feminist, her Kev.

Kath smiled warmly as she read out the teaser for the next piece – a ninety-second taped bit on a therapy dog who had saved a woman from cracking her head open when she had an epileptic fit in the middle of a busy Sainsbury's. The dog would be coming into the studio next week. The woman, she'd just been told, proved too much of a health and safety risk.

As the piece began to play, and the camera lights turned from red to black, she tilted her head up to Bridie (*just smoothing out the edges, Kath*) as Kev had his forehead dabbed by Dee (his latest make-up girl). Kath silently wondered how many of their viewers had noticed the chill that had crisped up their exchanges ever since she'd announced she was going on the LifeTime cycle ride whilst Kev headed off to South Africa.

'Alright you two?' Stacy asked the pair of them through their earpieces. Her bright tone suggested she knew precisely what was going on. Stacy noticed everything.

'Great,' Kath gave the thumbs up.

'Never better,' Kev said, giving his hands a brisk rub.

Dave signalled them in from the epilepsy dog segment and the light on camera three lit up red. Kath swivelled to the right and looked down the lens. 'That's about all we have time for, folks. Once again I'd like to thank everyone who has donated to LifeTime already and would invite you all to join me on my new Instagram account . . . details below, if you want to get any snaps of my training sessions.' She pointed her fingers downwards knowing their producer would pop the details up on the screen as she recited them from memory. She threw Kev a cheeky smile. 'Kev's already seen a few pictures of me trying to get fit for the ride. I'm sure it's nothing compared to what'll be coming your way from Cape Town, but with a few more of my PT sessions whipping me into shape, perhaps one day I'll be able to take on the Men's Volleyball Team!'

'That's right, Kath,' Kev pulled her in for a strangely painful half hug. 'A girl can dream.'

Two hours later, Kath was still steaming. Normally her workouts deflated her increasingly frequent spikes of 'emotional turbulence'. The menopause expert Kev had insisted she visit never called anything by its actual name opting, instead, to give each distressing, awkward and increasingly difficult 'phase' she was going through a pastel-coloured hue. Sometimes she wished the woman would come out with it and call a spade a spade. She wasn't going through emotional turbulence. She was having a marital crisis and a hormone overhaul.

Kath swung the kettle bell one final time then released it with a light 'whooof!'

'That was brilliant, Katherine.'

As she met Fola's eyes for the first time in the hour-long session, the prickly remains of her anger left her. She loved his voice. The way he said her full name, his voice rounding over the vowels as if they were each a piece of precious, perfectly ripe fruit. Better than Kev's Liverpudlian accent anyway, or her own, media-softened Newcastle twang.

She put the kettle bell on the rack, watching him in the mirror as he tidied up after one of the other trainers who always left sweat soaked mats and weights lying around after his sessions. That trainer had a book and YouTube following. Seized by an urgent need to know whether what she was feeling was real or not, she whirled round and asked, 'How do you fancy coming along on a bike ride as a support rider and physio? It's for charity.'

Chapter Twenty

'Hey roomie!' Raven dropped her two large duffel bags with an involuntary grunt and gave Sue an uncomfortable wave. There was a blossoming of droplets along her ebony hairline that Sue was fairly certain had come from exertion rather than the rain she'd just scuttled through to get into the large foyer of the call centre. Raven huffed out a couple of steadying breaths then grinned, 'Ready for our first sleepover? I've brought my own pillow.' She threw her thumbs up, but, Sue noticed, there was a slight tremor to her smile.

Sue's eyes dropped to the large, drenched duffel bags then back to Raven. 'Ummm . . .'

Raven's casually ironic air evaporated, revealing a deep, permeating aura of anxiety. Make-up aside, it felt like looking in the mirror.

'You said today was cool, right?'

'Today?' Sue repeated, her eyes doing a strange blinky thing as her mind fuzzed with the increasingly familiar static. She knew this was going to happen. She'd agreed to it. Not less than twelve or so hours earlier. So, why was she acting as if it had come out of the blue?

Raven's smile faltered, then quickly, as if an idea had struck, she dug into her shoulder bag. The retro flight bag reminded Sue of a bag her mother had once had from British Airways. When she threw it out a few years back she'd told Sue she'd brought it on their honeymoon even though they'd taken the ferry and not the plane (too expensive) across to Ireland where they'd spent three damp days in Waterford trying not to break any crystal, before getting back onto the ferry whereupon she'd become terrifically seasick (she'd discovered she was pregnant with Dean shortly thereafter) and vowed never to travel by sea again. The day after they'd returned, her mother took a job as a checkout clerk at Asda (which she still had) and her father went back to his job at the council (which he still had) and they'd not travelled by anything but car or train since, bar Bev's trip to Orlando which, according to Bev, didn't count as Katie and Dean had paid for it. She'd thrown out the bag without so much as a second glance. Her fault, her mother said, for mistaking a man with a reliable job for one with ambition.

'What's this for?' Sue stared at the bills Raven had just pressed into her hand.

'Rent,' Raven clarified, as if she were regularly in the habit of plunging into her bag and handing people money. 'It's still alright to move in today, right?'

'Yes, of course.' Sue over-egged her smile. It was something her mother always chided her for. Appearing to be delighted when she was, in actual fact, completely mortified. Ironic, considering her mother was the most frequent recipient of the smile. Well. Maybe it was a tie with Katie. 'It's wonderful. Perfect. Moving in today is *exactly* what I was hoping for.'

'Phew,' Raven feigned swiping the sweat off of her brow, leaving a few crinkles of concern behind.

Sugar.

For some reason, Sue hadn't foreseen this. Raven actually moving in.

'Alright there, girls?' The jolly chap who did 'security' (read: sat at the front desk, drank coffee and cadged any and all cake/biscuits that came in) bustled in out of the rain, took one look at the large duffel bags pretty much blocking the reception area and reached for them. 'Anywhere I can help move these big boys?' He gave them one of those knowing winks. 'Health and safety, girls. I would've thought you 111'ers would know all about that.' He pointedly placed a bright yellow Caution triangle in the centre of the entryway as if the two of them were the hazard that needed to be circumnavigated.

Sugar, crumbs and duck bums as Gaz would say.

There was no chance she'd be able to whizz home and make it seem as if she'd spent even a minute whirling round the house like Kirsty Allsop, zhushing this and fluffing that, quirking a throw pillow into a jaunty angle on top of an artfully arranged (but seemingly casual) collection of other throw pillows all in anticipation of Raven's arrival. She'd not ironed any sheets. Bought a small bouquet of seasonal flowers. Made a warming pot of stew or even a Victoria sponge. She'd done absolutely nothing to prepare for a visitor, let alone a housemate. She hadn't expected anyone to actually want to move in. Putting up the notice had felt more of a symbolic move. A sign that, despite every outward appearance that she was ignoring the fact her life had changed irrevocably, she was trying to move forward. And pay the mortgage.

'You said it was alright—' Raven's voice was edged with the same panic Sue's was.

'Yes, I— Of course it's alright.' Sue reached out to give her a reassuring pat at exactly the moment Raven crisscrossed her arms over her chest, her hands overlapping at her throat where . . . was that a skull pendant she was wearing?

The entryway was getting busier. A steady stream of people shaking the sleety rain off of their coats, following Colin's instructions (the security man had put his badge on now) about where to leave their sodden brollies. People going through their daily routine without so much as a thought that one day, it might all change forever.

What had she been *thinking*? Asking someone to move in.

Her stomach churned as she tried to imbue herself with the power to explain this had all been a horrible mistake.

She didn't have room in her house.

She didn't need a flatmate.

She just wanted to be able to pay her mortgage, was all.

'Sue? I'm not really getting the vibe that you want me to move in.'

Sue goldfished for a moment, light-headed with indecision. This was worse than the time she'd smoked one of Katie's menthol cigarettes, only to throw up all over Katie, and that had been pretty bad. Worse, even, than the time she and Gary had gone to Portugal with the lads and their wives and she'd been the only one gullible enough to be tricked into eating snails. She should've known they weren't cockles, but she hadn't grown up by the sea, had she? Or the time she'd worn her swimsuit inside out. Those times had, of course, eventually become funny. Gaz had a knack for it. Getting her to laugh at moments that had filled her with mortification. It was one of the reasons she'd been attracted to him. Watching him josh around with his friends in the school corridors. Propping up the side of the newsagent's with his foot and his back as he and his mates cracked one another up. He'd leap up from his post to open the door for the old women or mums with children. She'd liked that, too. He'd been a teen, and then a man, completely at ease with himself. Or so she'd thought.

Last night, just as she'd done every night since the funeral, she'd walked up the stairs, stood outside Gary's office, fully intending to go inside and make up the small twin bed for Raven. Instead, she put her hand up, watched her trembling fingers bounce and jig closer and closer to the door handle.

Shellshock, her mother had said over and over in a stage whisper when she'd stayed with them in the weeks leading up to the funeral. *P-T-S-DEE. That's what they call it now.* Her mother loved a good armchair diagnosis. Particularly when it was a *psychological* trauma. She was always calling out to the police detectives on the crime shows she devoured, 'It'll be a mother issue with that lad. Can't let go of the apron strings.' Or, 'Most likely scarred by a kiddy fiddler,

115

she was.' Or, 'Parents must've let her run circles round them as a child. Never knew boundaries.'

The only boundary Sue had ever crossed was marrying Gary. Her mother had disapproved. Her father, who had never seen anything wrong with marrying a tradesman – particularly one who had his own father's business to build upon and expand as Gary did – had never openly objected; but her mother had never missed an opportunity. *He'll always smell of someone else's 'business', Suey. You'll be washing filthy coveralls until the day you die.* Or, Sue's favourite, *At least he'll know whose shit smells of roses.*

It had never once occurred to Sue that she might be right. A raw, painful ache twisted the oxygen out of her lungs. Her mother wasn't right. She didn't know the whole story. No one did. Not even her.

Which was why, instead of cleaning out Gary's office and preparing for the flatmate she knew would be coming, she'd stared and stared at the handle to his office willing herself to take hold of it and twist until, eventually, shaking from the exhaustion of her already over-stretched imagination, she took the few short steps to her own room, lay down on the bed and fell into a deep, dreamless sleep.

This morning when she'd woken up she'd gone through the motions. Alarm off, make the bed, shower, dress, blow dry her hair, then down to the kitchen for a cup of tea. The routine was built into her like breathing. It just happened. It had felt like any other day apart from the fact her husband was still dead, the joint bank account was still mysteriously empty and she had a housemate she'd never properly met moving in without knowing which way she took her tea.

But the mortgage was due shortly and she wouldn't ask her parents for help (or Katie and Dean for that matter). Not after the fiasco with the refused debit cards and the crematorium. She knew her father wouldn't press for the money, but she also knew (because he'd told her) that the money had been earmarked for taking her mother on a forty-fifth wedding anniversary cruise round the Mediterranean this November coming in lieu of a sapphire which she would, by her own admission, inevitably lose. He'd need to be putting a deposit down sharpish if it was anything like the cruise Katie and Dean had taken the children on last year. Booked in a matter of minutes. The entire ship. Some five thousand passengers – snap! – planning their holidays months in advance, completely secure in the knowledge that their loved ones would be there.

Forty-five years. Imagine.

Sue would never have a forty-fifth wedding anniversary. Not with Gary anyway. Marrying someone else and constructing an entire, brand-new life seemed completely inconceivable. Particularly if a forty-fifth wedding anniversary was the aim. At her age . . . well. Forty-two wasn't that old, but to court, get engaged, marry and live another forty-five years? Right now, getting through the day felt like a triumph.

She wondered if that was how Gary had felt. Exhausted. Too worn out from it all to wait and see if a bit of toad-in-the-hole might perk him up. The community support officer who'd called in to her parents' a couple of times said sometimes, when a person had made the decision to kill themselves, they waited until they believed their loved one was happy. She'd been watching *Neighbours*, which made her happy. Singing along with the theme song, which made her happy. Making her husband his favourite dish. Or maybe least-favourite dish. She'd asked his pillow at least a thousand times which it was and it never answered back. Not when she asked it nicely, cried into it or even the time she punched it. It awed her . . . the scope of things she didn't know. Wouldn't know unless, of course, she went into his office and went hunting for clues.

'Can I, ummm . .' Raven looked over her shoulder as an ever-increasing stream of employees lumbered in, shoulders hunkered down as if the winter weather bore actual heft. 'Is there any chance I could cadge a lift to yours after? You have a car, right?'

'Yes, I—' She did have a car. A tidy little red two-door sports Ka that Gaz playfully called the basic model runaround. It was full of clothes she'd cleared out of their once over-full wardrobe the day after the funeral. Her one burst of activity. In early January, she'd unsuccessfully tried to get Gary to downsize his Marvel T-shirt collection so, the day after she'd watched her husband's casket disappear behind a red curtain, she'd weeded out clothes she was unlikely to wear instead.

Widows didn't wear crop tops. Widows didn't wear mini skirts. Even that jumper she'd bought just after Christmas in the sales with the bare shoulders seemed inappropriate.

It hadn't even occurred to her to clear out Gary's things.

She would. Of course she would, but . . . had enough time passed? Were there time limits for these things? Mourning periods for threadbare coveralls?

'So long as you're sure,' Raven said.

'Positive,' said Sue. Which, of course, was entirely untrue. Where on earth was she going to put the poor girl?

There was only one solution for it. She'd give Raven her room. It made perfect sense.

She always kept it tidy. Had 'trained' Gary to keep his things in the spare room. Not that she was a neatnik or anything, but yes, she was house proud. Not in the way Katie was of their sprawling detached house with an acre-long garden that abutted the country-side. Nor was it the 'contemporary village community' her parents had moved into a couple of years back. 'To be closer to the grand-children,' had been the party line, but Sue had grown up listening to her mother go on at her father about wanting to live in a modern, brand-new house that someone else hadn't had their 'grubby mitts on' before she'd got a hold of it.

No, Sue and Gary's home was nothing out of the ordinary. A modest two-up, two-down they'd bought as a 'starter kit' en route to another where, one day, they'd hoped to raise a family. The family and the housing upgrade had never come to pass, but she loved the cosy row house almost as much as she'd loved Gary. It was a symbol that everyone had been wrong about them. About Gary. That he could provide. That he was a good man. That they did have plans to have a family of their own one day.

The baby thing had obviously never panned out, but, courtesy of Katie and Dean, she spent a lot of time with her niece and nephew (deterrents these days, more than heartbreakers) and then could come home to her own, very tidy, just-so house.

Sue had never lived with anyone who wasn't Gary before. She'd not gone to uni. Or been flatmates with any one of the girls she'd gone to beauty college with. Not moved out of her parents' house until Gary tempestuously said to her one day after they'd been to the pictures, *Let's do it. Let's get married.* He'd twisted the pop-top off of a can of fizzy pop and slid it onto her ring finger as she'd flushed with pleasure.

'If you're absolutely sure,' Raven said, her eyes darting past Sue as if hoping for someone else, a proper grown-up to come and sort the two of them and all of this awkwardness out. And then, as if by magic, Flo appeared.

'Of course I'm sure,' Sue quickly said.

'What're you sure about?' Flo gave her arm a squeeze, her warm demeanour already adding a bit of much-needed calm to Sue's over-wrought nerves.

'About giving Raven a ride home.'

'You moving back in with your parents, love?'

Raven's eyebrows templed. 'Umm . . . out of, actually.'

The poor thing looked about five years old. As lost as Sue felt. Perhaps there'd be solace in having her there. Two lost souls finding comfort in their mutual discombobulation. When they felt more comfortable, perhaps Sue would offer her some advice on colour streaking her hair. It wasn't quite the right blue for her complexion and, if she was really being fussy, the attention to detail at the roots was sketchy. Nor had she brought the streak all the way to the tips of her long, dark hair.

The practical thought gave her a bit of a boost and, more to the point, enough courage to bite the bullet. Though it still wasn't true, she insisted, 'Honestly. It's just perfect. I'm sure we can get your bags into the car.'

Raven nodded warily. 'If it's easier I can take the bus.'

'Oh, no. Don't take the bus.' A strange protectiveness washed through her and with it the tiniest flicker of belief that one day, she might feel vaguely like her old self again. Caring for Gary, keeping order in their small, relatively unremarkable lives, had been at the heart of her life. She was good at it. Looking after him. At least she thought she had been. Perhaps if she looked after Raven with a bit more care, a few more *questions*, she would figure out where she had gone so terrifically wrong with Gary.

'Would it be of any use if I offered to drive one or both of the bags?' Flo asked.

Sue and Raven turned to her, relief flooding their features, each of them nodding near emphatically as Sue said, 'Yes. Yes it would.'

Chapter Twenty-One

Incident No: 5938272
Time of Call: 15:23
Call Handler: SUNITA 'RAVEN' CHAKRABARTI

Call Handler: You're through to the NHS 111 Service, my name's Raven and I'm a health advisor. Are you calling about yourself or someone else?

Caller: Myself.

Call Handler: Can you tell me your name please?

Caller: Hailey.

Call Handler: Hello, Hailey. What can I help you with?

Caller: I think I've just messed up.

Call Handler: Sorry? Would you be able to be a bit more specific?

Caller: I only meant to cut a little bit.

Call Handler: Hailey? Can you please specifically tell me what you are ringing about? [Muted: Do you remember how to transfer to the police?]

Caller: [Barely audible] I think I might've hit an artery.

Call Handler: Oh. Ummm . . . Hailey – are you talking about yourself here? Do you need an ambulance?

Caller: I don't want my parents to know. Can you help? Hang on. I need to get a towel. There's too much blood.

Call Handler: I think you need to talk to someone else, a manager. No. The ambulance guy. Ummm – *shit monkeys*! Sorry, sorry. My bad. Hailey? Is there anyone there with you?

Caller: I normally do it lower, but this time I went higher. [Sobbing noise] Why did they have to put it on Insta? *Everyone* had had too much to drink. *Owwwoooohh*, shit. I'm pretty sure there's an artery in your inner thigh.

Call Handler: I don't know, I – ummm, are you applying pressure? Wrap a tourniquet. It should stop if you apply pressure and wrap a tourniquet above . . . no . . . wait . . . below. Tie the tourniquet below – hang on a second. Sorry. Let me check and see if there is an A&E near you. Is there anyone there with you? Are you able to drive?

Caller: [Crying] Normally it bleeds a little but this time I can't get it to stop.

Call Handler: Oh, god. Hailey, you need to – wait a minute – Hailey? Can you just . . . I'm just going to put you on hold for a minute to speak to one of our health advisors because I think we need to call you an ambulance. *Fuck.* Why isn't she applying pressure? Fucketyfuckfuck. What the fucking fuckety fuckmonsters pull-down fucking menu shitface— Where the fuck is that *bloody* man? Hailey? I've taken you off hold. Are you there?

Caller: I wasn't on hold.

Call Handler: Oh, god. I'm so sorry. Look. It's going to be alright.

Caller: [Crying sounds]

Call Handler: Hailey? [No response]

HAILEY!! I need to pass you over to our onsite clinician who can recommend what to do while I get an ambulance – Hailey?

[No response]

Hailey, are you there?

[No response]

Shit!

Chapter Twenty-Two

Raven tried and failed to steady her hammering heart. Blood roared through her ears, her pulse pounded at the base of her throat, lurching, now and again, towards her gag reflex. Her tongue was dry and her body felt as though it was being filled with cement. She was a panic attack waiting to happen. With any luck the on-site clinician would notice her slumped, quivery wreck of a body if she fell into a state of shock.

Protocol freaking bit the big one.

This time anyway.

It had been almost ten months since The Incident at school. Ten months of pulling herself back from her friends, social media, her future . . . all in an effort to wipe the memories away and start afresh. She'd thought if she could make it past the year mark, it would be like resetting the clock and then, ping! Off she'd go to uni, her ideals back in place, her spirit strong as a wild pony and her parents puffing with pride that they'd raised a child who chose to follow the beat of a different drummer or, in her case, bass guitar.

She tried some yogic breathing to see if that would drown out the chaotic thoughts pin-balling round her head.

Normally she was good at this. Raising detached to another level. It wasn't just a goth thing, it was a Chakrabarti thing. She'd taken not one, but THREE heart attack calls last week and had sorted them out without so much as the blink of an eye. She'd calmed down dozens of panicking mums (croup was hitting the under twos in a big way this year) and convinced one very lonely old man that talking back to the telly as if it were real wasn't necessarily a sign of Alzheimer's as most people did it, ageing or otherwise.

She pushed herself back up and stared at her screen, psyching herself up to take another call.

The scoreboard was blinking red. The number of calls taken was flicking ever upwards. It was after three, which meant school was out, and most GPs had been booked up weeks in advance so mums tended to call 111 to see if their extreme level of agitation (and need to get tea on the table for the other children) was enough to get them to send a doctor over. It usually wasn't. Normally she wrapped up the call with the usual advice: go to the chemists, call and make a proper appointment with the GP or head to the nearest A&E if the symptoms worsened.

This time, though . . . this time protocol left her feeling completely helpless.

She'd done the three call backs. Left the 'if the symptoms worsen please call back' message on Hailey's phone, but something deep within her knew it wouldn't matter. A person could only hear what the voices in their head were telling them and it sounded as though that girl's head was full of demons.

Intellectually, Raven knew she wasn't meant to take any of this personally. It was a job. Like a complaints line but with actual life and, in this case, possibly death, on the line.

Why hadn't she said something *useful*? Something *kind*?

Was Hailey dead? Alive? Best case scenario was that she had simply been fed up with Raven's inability to help and respond like a human. A compassionate human. It was all anyone really wanted, wasn't it? Someone to listen to them. To really listen and say, *yes, yes I hear you.*

The bloody script wouldn't let them! The bloody script didn't know what it was like to want to reach through the phone line and pull 'Caller' into a hug and say I know, I know it hurts, but it'll be okay. Whoever or whatever is saying bad things about you, they're not true.

Sweat was trickling down her back. The cold clammy kind. Her heart was lurching all over her ribcage. Her stomach hurt. Everything in her was cramping with a weird sort of inert exertion. More so than this morning when she'd refused Dylan's offer to help carry her bags onto the bus. She'd thought he'd done it because she was fat and she'd stupidly wanted to prove that fat people could do things too, so like a huge, lumbering walrus, she'd refused his help, hauled the bags all the way to the end of the bus wondering if the excruciating pain she was feeling was, in fact, the beginnings of a heart attack. It was the one thing they had received really good training for with 111. Vision narrowing. Lungs unable to suck in enough air. Cheeks turning a bright, horrifying scarlet.

She didn't feel the stabbing pain shooting down her arm, though. Or any of the other things that would've meant she was having an actual heart attack and, if she were to give herself the tiniest of breaks, she wasn't *that* fat. The morbidly obese kind. More the could do with eating fewer crisps in her room and doing a bit of exercise kind. Big bones had a lot to answer for. Thanks Auntie Anu. For absolutely nothing.

Why hadn't she pressed the bloody hold button? Said something positive that would've made Hailey realise no amount of cutting would take the real pain away. Kids were shitheads. Especially at school.

Not that she'd even got to the part where she asked Hailey her age or anything.

She'd frozen. Just like last time.

She'd just stood there all of those months ago. Stood there with the rest of the sixth formers gawping as Aisha Laghari was wheeled out of the girls' loo into the waiting ambulance and on to the hospital where she had been easily persuaded by her mother to close down

126

her Instagram account. Her Snapchat account. Her Twitter, her Facebook and all of the other ways kids tortured other kids – especially the different ones – to the point that they ended up trying to slice out the pain. And Raven had done absolutely nothing about it even though she'd caught Aisha in the changing rooms at the gym one day, a drop of blood trickling down her leg below her huge bath towel she'd brought in specially, presumably to cover up the scars that never quite healed.

'Sunita?'

'Raven,' Raven automatically corrected as she wheeled around, startled by the touch.

'Sunita? Alright to join me for a chat?'

Bums.

Hands loosely woven together, eyebrows raised, and 'concern face' ratcheted up to *very, very concerned*, Rachel Woolly was standing behind her like an over-cheery spectre.

What a nightmare. Rachel was everyone's favourite manager to hate. Rachel didn't just *love* working for 111, she *believed* in 111. It was her *calling* to provide *ground up* healthcare advice to *ordinary* Britons at their *most vulnerable* moments.

It was quite obvious from the way Rachel talked about their callers that Rachel hadn't ever actually spoken with 'an ordinary Briton' or ever dealt with the bloody pull-down menu when asked whether or not she believed elves were real. What Rachel *was* renowned for, was 'dipping in and out of the calls for quality assurance.'

Micromanaging.

Rachel nodded at Raven's headset. 'How about you unplug for a minute so we can go somewhere a bit more private?'

Raven silently followed behind, the weight in her gut churning round and round, growing heavier and heavier with each step.

She could not get fired. Please oh please oh please god, do not let her get fired. The last thing she could do today was go home.

Chapter Twenty-Three

Incident No: 601321
Time of Call: 16:48
Call Handler: FLORENCE WILSON

Call Handler: You're through to the NHS 111 service, my name's Flo and I'm a health advisor. Are you calling about yourself or someone else?

Caller: I am calling about my boyfriend.

Call Handler: Is he breathing?

Caller: Yes. I suppose.

Call Handler: Can you check, love?

Caller: No. He's not here.

Call Handler: Can you tell me why you're calling about him, then please, duck?

Caller: He's given me nowt for Valentine's Day.

Call Handler: I'm sorry?

Caller: He's not given me nothin' for Valentine's Day. It were over ten days ago now. Didn't pop in either. Not for a shag or nothin'. He were out with the lads. That's what he said. [Puts on a deep voice] *Sorry, love. Been out with the lads.* Do you think I should dump him?

Call Handler: Darlin', this is a health line, not a dating line.

Caller: I know, but it's actually, physically hurting my heart?

Call Handler: Are you feeling physical symptoms in your heart?

Caller: Aye. Definitely. One minute I love him so much I feel my heart is going to burst, the next I want to take the biggest bloody knife I have and—

Call Handler: I'm going to stop you there, love. As a health advisor I can suggest making an appointment with your GP or, if you're concerned you need immediate health care, I would head to the nearest A&E. I can see there is one about three miles down the road from you.

Caller: [Bitter laughter] Already been, haven't I?

Call Handler: Sorry, love. Have you been to the A&E or your GP?

Caller: GP. He's bloody useless he is. Never has appointments. Always busy. Just like Dan-o, innit?

Call Handler: Is Dan your boyfriend, darlin'?

Caller: You tell me. If coming round for booty calls at two in the morning after being out on the lash with the lads means he's mine, then yeah. He don't come round every night. What if he's seeing other women? Got two or three of us on the go? Do you think I should confront him? Ask him what he's playing at?

Call Handler: Perhaps you should give your GP another ring. Most surgeries are open until five or six. Why don't we end this call and see if your GP can sort something out for you?

Caller: Like what? See if he can find me a man who pays me some proper bloody attention? They don't listen right when I go there. Not any of the GPs. I've seen 'em all. They're all anxiety this, bi-polar that. Stop drinking. Can you imagine? Not having a drink when I'm this bloody stressed over my man?

Call Handler: Are you feeling unwell now, love?

Caller: I bloody well am. My boyfriend's given me nowt for Valentine's Day, hasn't he? Never picks up after himself. Wants a hot tea if he deigns to come before midnight. No warning. Just comes in, where's me tea? It bloody hurts, it does. All over.

Call Handler: Are you feeling any physical symptoms that are giving you cause for concern?

Caller: Yes.

Call Handler: Can you describe the symptoms, duck?

Caller: Hungry.

Call Handler: You're hungry?

Caller: Aye.

Call Handler: Right then, darlin'. Why don't you go into the kitchen and make yourself a nice bit of cheese on toast. That should help. And some tea. Can you get catch-up on your television?

Caller: Aye.

Call Handler: Put on *Love Island*, take note of how self-absorbed and unimaginative the men are, then ask yourself, do I really want a boyfriend who ignores me? You think about how you want to be valued and ask yourself, honestly, is Dan the man for me? Sorry . . . I'm just going to . . . you want me to end the call? Rachel, I'm just – oh alright. Just handing out a few home truths— Darlin', are you there?

Caller: Yeah. Are you in trouble for telling me to eat cheese on toast?

Call Handler: No, not as such. A little, maybe. Is there anything else I can help you with?

Caller: No. Thanks for listening.

Call Handler: My pleasure. Please be sure to ring back if the symptoms worsen or change. Thanks for calling 111. Now, Rachel—

Chapter Twenty-Four

'Fired?' Raven looked shocked.

Not as shocked as Flo was, but it was good to know she wasn't the only one who'd been blindsided by the 'little one to one' with that prissy manageress, Rachel Woolly.

'That's right, duck,' Flo nodded, trying to keep the swarm of conflicting emotions in check, eyes glued to the watery beams her headlights were throwing on the back of Sue's little red Ka a few metres in front of her. 'Although Rachel called it a "voluntary redundancy" so that my record'll be clean for whoever's lucky enough to employ me next.'

Raven's eyes widened.

'Not to worry. I wouldn't be surprised if I found something new tomorrow.'

With any luck.

Flo was doing her level best to remain cheery, but the truth was, she was absolutely fuming. Fired for offering that poor girl a bit of advice? She obviously hadn't been quite right in the head and needed some guidance. Some proper perspective. It was half the problem with the world these days. Children coddled and assured and cotton wooled to such an extent no one had any survival skills anymore! How on earth were they going to tackle all of the world's insurmountable problems? War. Famine. The extinction of polar bears. It wouldn't happen by calling a time out or putting Putin on the naughty step!

She had half a mind to turn the car round and offer that Rachel Woolly a piece of her mind.

Voluntary redundancy.

As if anyone in Flo's immediate circle would believe for a split second she'd left a job voluntarily. She'd been all but pushed out of the airplane when, at sixty-five, BA had deemed her too expensive to keep around. Oh, they'd said it was something to do with the vision test, but she knew a spade when she saw one. They'd called that voluntary redundancy as well.

Bloody pack of liars. She would've happily flown round the globe with them until she was dead. Wasn't that what glasses were for? The thought pulled her up short. Short-sightedness, she supposed, was her problem. Everyone, apart from her, could see the pearly gates looming. But honestly. Being let go from 111? Was she really unable to 'embrace a modern approach to health care' as Rachel had suggested?

Bollocks to that. What that girl had needed was a bit of sound advice—

'Oh, crumbs. Would you look at that?' Sue had gone through a traffic light just as it had turned amber. Flo had considered flooring it, then, remembering she already had six points on her licence, lurched to a stop. Sue probably wanted a bit of me time before Raven moved in anyhow. Perhaps a stop off at the off licence for a bit of fizz would be a good idea. And some nibbles. Maybe a balloon or two might be in order. Fresh start and all that. For Raven. Obviously. And Sue.

How on earth was she going to go home and tell Stuart?

She couldn't. Not yet. She barely had the capacity to admit the unexpected 'window of freedom' terrified the daylights out of her. Yet another chance for Stu and Jennifer to harangue her about finally hanging up her hat, sinking into the other, as yet unused recliner, for a life of sedentary observation. No. No. She simply could not sit back and watch the rest of her life pass her by. It was bad enough bearing witness to Stu slowly being absorbed by the beige surrounds of retirement.

She was going to have to do something. Something big. Something that made an impact, like that Kath off the telly. Maybe she'd join her. She was asking for people to sign up every day. Said the donations were rolling in, but not so much the riders. Perhaps this 'window of freedom' was, in fact, a window of opportunity.

Yes. *Yes.*

The idea was settling in, in the way a lovely pool of gravy did round a Sunday lunch. Warming.

'I'll not be a minute, love.' She gave Raven's knee a pat. 'Thought I'd get us some bubbles to celebrate your big move.'

Flo let the idea blossom and grow as she shopped.

How long had it been since she'd gone out exploring? In Britain, no less. And for a worthy cause. Even Stu couldn't balk at that, raising money for a mental health charity that actually *did* let callers listen and call handlers give advice on something the caller actually wanted advice on.

She sniffed a bit indignantly. Imagine. A thirty-something snip of a girl telling *her* how the world worked. She'd definitely have to put the plan in place before she told Stu about her change of working circumstances. If he had even a whiff of a window, he'd be booking another trip to Portugal. The wi-fi there was awful so job hunting would be difficult, and the exercise classes at the 'village centre' were too bloody boring to blow off any steam. Chair Zumba! Silver Swimmers! Not on your life.

After she'd zipped back to the car with a bottle of something fizzy and pink, Flo suddenly remembered seeing Raven in Rachel's office as well. Double crumbs. She hadn't been nattering on about being fired when the same thing had happened to Raven, had she?

'What was your chat with Rachel about, love? Anything nice?'

'Oh, it was . . .' Raven's fingers worked overtime weaving themselves together in different patterns as Flo pulled the car out into surprisingly busy rush-hour traffic. 'She just wanted to tell me about the counselling they had after . . . umm . . . difficult calls.'

'Oh, did you get a bad one? I'm sorry to hear that.'

'It probably should've been 999,' Raven wouldn't meet her eye.

Just like the call she'd had from Sue, then. Interesting, Flo thought. No one had pulled her into an office and offered her a sweet cup of tea after her call. Why hadn't they offered Flo counselling instead of slapping her with a red card? Sure. She may have had two warnings already, but no one had ever suggested ways to offer these poor, emotionally challenged people who rang in, hearts on their sleeves, loneliness pouring out of them like water, some actual useful advice. A listening ear was all they wanted. Someone to care.

Targets. Deadlines. Scripts.

Life didn't ruddy work to a pull-down menu, did it? After forty-odd years of flying round the world in a sardine can, the stories she could tell. Saw people at their best and their worst, she had. Dealt with them all in her own inimitable way *whilst* adhering to health and safety. Going off script didn't mean she was an idiot. It meant she solved problems.

'Thanks for driving me, anyway,' Raven said, suddenly lunging forward, both hands on the dash as Flo took a turn a bit later than anticipated. 'Sue looked a bit stressed.'

'The poor lass is going through a lot right now,' Flo said distractedly, then, 'It's a pleasure to lend a hand.' It was also a rather convenient way to buy herself some time to come up with a good cover story as to why she wouldn't be on the shifts she'd told Stu about.

Flo shot Raven a quick glance, saw her eyebrows were drawn close together and gave her knee a pat. 'You alright, duck? If it's moving to Sue's you're worried about, don't be. Any experience, good or bad, just adds zest to your experience as a woman of the world.'

Raven's forehead creased. 'Yeah, no, I just . . . I'm sorry about . . .' she flicked her hand towards Flo, then hesitated.

'Oh, love. Don't feel bad about me. I'm resilient. I'll get another job. I'm just cross because the call they cited as "strike three" wasn't exactly a matter of life and death. It were more a case of a pants boyfriend needing the axe, but . . .' She exhaled heavily. 'I guess it wasn't my business.'

Raven stared at her hands, then out into the traffic.

Flo slammed her hand on the steering wheel. 'Of *course* it's my business!'

Raven jumped.

'Sorry, duck. I'm a bit more worked up than I thought.'

'Well,' Raven drew the word out as she stroked a streak of blue-black hair as one might a teddy bear when they were nervous. 'It's not like we're robots, right?'

Flo slapped the steering wheel again. 'Exactly, right. We're not robots and the people who ring in aren't either. We're flesh and blood and need to be able to respond to the odd curveball life throws our way. Even if it does make us feel uncomfortable. That's what life is. A big, jumbly, uncomfortable mess that we have to treat like it's a big, gorgeous trifle. We should all want to dive right into the centre of that gooey, fruity, fluffy mess. Not cling to the hundreds and thousands as if they're life rafts. Isn't that right, duck?' She caught Raven considering the question even though it was obviously rhetorical. Poor girl. She looked a bit lost. Not too unlike Sue, who had been ever so flustered when they'd all climbed into their cars and had set off from the call centre. Flo quickly pulled the car into a little shopping centre. She'd pick up a couple of housewarming style items to give Sue a slightly longer window to regroup before they arrived. Bless. Raven and Sue. Her two new unexpected friends. Little ducklings, more like. The pair of them needed a mother hen to tuck them under her wing and . . . an idea struck.

'Raven, love. How do you feel about cycling?'

Chapter Twenty-Five

'You think you might like that? Raising some money for charity?'

Flo looked so hopeful as she pulled up to the kerb on Harworth Lane it would have actually been painful to say no. Raven shrugged and made what she hoped was a noncommittal *mmm* that went up and down an octave before fading away.

'Luhhhvely!' Flo clapped her hands, clearly taking the shrug as a yes, then pitty-patted the steering wheel as she sing-songed, 'Get on yer bike, Rachel Woolly! We've got something better in mind!'

Raven winced. Flo did know Raven wasn't going to quit her job to go bike riding with Flo, right? It was, like, *winter* out. That. And she didn't have a bike. Even so, this was the happiest Flo had been on their entire journey which had comprised of not one, but three stops at the shops to 'pick up party supplies.'

Kicking herself out of her family home and moving into the house of a woman who needed a flatmate because her husband had just killed himself in it didn't seem much cause for celebration to Raven. Maybe Flo had been buying 'Just got fired' party poppers. Who knew? Flo was a trip. Not like any seventy-year-old she knew anyway. If she was vaguely interested in riding her bike across the country, which she wasn't, she would want to do it with Flo.

In fact, riding a bicycle at all fell pretty firmly in the 'not gonna happen' category, but so did moving out of her parents' to avoid working for Uncle Ravi during a gap year that was rapidly drawing to an end. Perhaps there was room for a bit of elasticity in what she did and didn't go for now that she was, in Flo's words, a 'woman of the world'. Flo, who'd given her a lightning-speed autobiography in between running in and out of the shops, hadn't had parents who felt morally obliged to micromanage their daughter's entire future. In fact, they'd celebrated when she'd got a job and moved out. *In my day, university was one of those things for posh folk and nerdy types. They were right chuffed when I cleared off and started fending for myself. Best day of my life, come to think of it. The freedom!*

Flo, still lost in her daydreams about the cycle ride, laughed and gave a happy sigh. 'I can guarantee you it'll be an adventure. I can't say I'll be very speedy. I've not ridden a bike in . . . oh . . . when was it?? Rio? Maybe Santa Monica. Adelaide? Somewhere on the beach and quite a while back. Years, must be.'

'You've been to all of those places?'

'And more, duck. Courtesy of a spiffy uniform and British Airways. All over the globe.' The happy sigh turned wistful. 'I was a trolley dolly for almost forty years. Started well before you were born. Back when we were allowed to be trolley dollies anyway.' She flashed Raven a wicked grin that gave Raven a glimpse of what Flo must've looked like back then: glamorous, fun-loving, the life of any party.

Raven had no idea what it was like to be any of those things, let alone feel a splash of the glee Flo glowed with. She'd had hits of enthusiasm when she thought of being at Newcastle, and once when she'd got her eye make-up just right she'd felt the tiniest bit pretty, and, obviously there was the weird, ghoulish satisfaction of watching her blood pour into a bag whenever she donated, but . . . no, she'd never felt anything close to what Flo was radiating. Pure, all-consuming happiness.

Still putting the pieces of the Flo jigsaw together, she asked, 'And yet you live in Bicester, the epicentre of all that was trendy and stylish in the world? Last season.' Raven clapped a hand over her mouth. She hadn't meant to be rude, but . . . c'mon. Bicester, home of discount designer wear and an ever-increasing amount of pop-up, new build 'communities' was hardly the centre of the universe. For some reason Raven had pictured worldly people as big city dwellers. The type of urban Oz big enough to have their own *Time Out*. Paris, Rome, New York. That sort of thing. *The Bicester Weekly* was hardly a font of cultural and consumable wonders.

'My husband picked it because it was close to both Heathrow and Luton. He was a pilot.'

'Oh! Does he still fly?'

'No, love,' Flo's voice turned strangely tight. 'They make them retire at sixty.'

The way she said it made Raven squirmy. As if retirement were akin to a death sentence. Her parents' entire life could be easily described as a battle plan for retirement. It had always sounded like a safe place, retirement. Where there was enough money because you'd saved and enough energy because you'd eaten your five a day and enough time because you'd just sold your pharmacy/newly invented surgical tool/hedge fund/law firm partnership and carved out enough room in your life to start looking after your grand-children who would follow in the same well worn path . . .

Now that she thought of it, retirement didn't seem like the kind of place Flo would like at all. She had more energy in her pinky than Raven had ever had, apart from that one time her sister had actually behaved like a sister and taken her to London to see the Harry Potter plays. Apart from that . . . Raven was more your low-energy variety of teenager. It was safer that way. To fly below the radar. Flo struck her as the type who'd willingly throw herself into the line of fire. A woman who'd fling herself out of an airplane and let photos of her face all stretched out by the wind be plastered all over the shop if it earned a few bob for charity. And also because it would be exhilarating.

'Why don't we put it to Sue as well?' Flo asked. 'The bike ride.

We'll ask her over a glass of this fizz once we've got your bags moved in. If there's anyone out there who needs something fun to work towards, it's that poor girl.'

Raven nodded. 'Sounds good.' Dreams of life at Newcastle Uni definitely kept her tiny torch alight. On top of which, if Sue agreed to go along, maybe Raven could quietly duck out.

Riding a bicycle from the Lake District, along Hadrian's Wall and on to Tynemouth with 'our Kath' from Kath and Kev was decidedly not Raven's cup of tea. Although . . . arriving in Newcastle for a 'well-earned supper' did hold some appeal. As much as she ached to go to uni there, she'd never actually been. An untested nirvana. What if it was a complete nightmare? What if it was everything she'd ever dreamt of?

She considered it more seriously. Imagined herself powering up and then down a hill into Newcastle city centre on a bicycle. Red, preferably. Or aubergine.

Hmmm . . .

Something about arriving via a less beaten trail in a blaze of self-discovery and physically demanding glory seemed strangely fitting.

Most of the characters in the fantasy series she'd been favouring lately were always setting off on epic (usually surprise) journeys. There'd be, like, maximum ten pages of set-up and then kaboom! Time to hit the road. Then, about eight hundred or so pages later? The journey was over, lessons had been learnt, the protagonist was a changed person (usually for the better but mostly because they'd been through the worst) and there'd be about ten more pages of wrapping everything up or . . . kaboom! Another journey would present itself and the protagonist, a little older and a lot wiser would pick up their shoulder bag . . . and off they went on another epic adventure.

She wanted to be that person when she arrived at uni. Wiser to the ways of the world. Unfrightened by other teenagers and their nasty attacks on social media. Not that she'd been a target herself, but . . . why hadn't she reached out to Aisha? Visited her in hospital? At her house once she'd been checked out? Told her no one really believed her parents were going to send her to India to marry an old man to be his slave because she was too dim and too ugly to be married off to anyone else and choose a husband herself like her sisters had. Racist bullshit is what it had been. And yet . . . she'd said nothing. Done nothing, apart from delete all of her own accounts when what she should have done was stand up to the girls who'd started spreading the rumours and told them where to put it.

Insecurity, she supposed.

Fear.

Would it go away if she moved to Newcastle? All those niggly concerns about being too fat, too tall, too weak, too impressionable, too pathetic to stand up to a bunch of bullies she knew were doing the wrong thing. It was awful having all of those frailties roiling round inside of her, vying for supremacy, when what she really wanted to feel was strong. Inside and out. Undaunted. Like Flo seemed to be.

Maybe this trip was exactly what she needed.

It wasn't as if getting off a National Express in front of the student union building had as much of an emotional pow factor as arriving in the wake of one's own spent energy. And maybe she'd even lose a few pounds before she started whatever degree it was she finally decided upon. Yes. Maybe she would go. Maybe it would be her first step into being a woman of the world.

As if Flo had been privy to her entire internal monologue, she gave Raven's knee a bright pat. 'Alright, duck. That's settled then. It's get your bags out time. Just give me a minute and I'll grab one, too. I've got to make a quick call home.'

Raven got out of the car and scanned the street for Sue's house. There it was. A couple of doors down. Number eleven Harworth Lane.

From the outside, it looked perfectly pleasant. As pleasant as a mid-terraced two-up, two-down without a garden on the outskirts of Bicester could in the late February gloaming. Not that Raven had been looking for fancy. Or lush. Or anything at all like the comfortable family home she'd left without so much as a backwards glance because she knew if she'd looked back and seen her mother's tear-streaked face she would've run straight into her arms and begged to be forgiven for having wanted anything other than what they did.

So, yeah. It was fine. It didn't look like somewhere that someone would kill themselves which was, she had to admit, a total relief. (#Don'tTellTheGoths)

What struck Raven the most was how *compact* everything was. Sue-sized. A small wrought iron gate led to a teensy tiny brick path which ran alongside a tidy (small) container for rubbish and an area that could, at best, contain a bicycle (a small one). Four petite squares of glass formed the front window which sported a titchy flower box with a few wax-like cyclamen, some dainty ivy sprigs and two tiny topiaries. Even the front door, painted a lovely shade of pastel blue (lovely if you were into pastels, obvs), seemed Sue-sized. Her sister would've called it bijoux. A term she used regularly because her sister actually was bijoux. Delicately boned, petite features, she was like a little porcelain doll.

At five foot nine, and big boned without the extra weight, Raven was suddenly feeling distinctly super-sized. She should have asked Sue if she could've seen the room before handing over a wad of money that set her back thirty-nine hours in her call centre/Newcastle target. A sudden image of her arms and legs sticking out the windows burst into her head. Oh, Lordy. Would she even fit?

She rehoinked her bag onto her shoulder as it threatened to slide off and tried to knock some positivity into her brain. Her cousin Kalinda, a newly qualified psychiatrist, said fear coloured all first impressions, so . . . given the fact Raven's life was teetering on the precipice of just such a change . . . little wonder everything seemed so little. All of her teenaged hopes and dreams would have to fit into Sue's little house.

Sure. Raven might look as though she was into dark and morbid from the outside, but inside? She was a nineteen-year-old girl moving out of her parents' to pursue a dream that didn't exactly have a well-defined rainbow, let alone a pot of gold at the end of it and to be honest? She was pretty bloody freaked out about it.

'Go on, love. I'll grab this bag and you knock on the door. Oof!' Flo grunted as she tried to stop Raven's second duffel from hitting the wet pavement. 'What've you got in here. A body?'

Books actually. It was a bag full of books. Books from her childhood right up to the huge wrist-benders she poured herself into on a nightly basis, all to escape the ever-encroaching reality that she was going to have to pick what she wanted to do for the rest of her entire life fairly sharpish.

Crumpets and bums. What was she *doing*? Why hadn't she looked for a local law firm to scuttle around for? (*Duh . . . Bicester. Law firm. Parents.*) Was spending money to save money the wisest of things? She'd always been a good saver. It was built into her so she actually had most of the money for the first year. She'd just wanted a buffer to see her into the next. Maybe she should've become a live-in nanny somewhere. An au pair to a family in France who didn't mind a teenager who favoured black lipstick, refused to follow the beaten path and couldn't, for the life of her, understand how everyone else in her family had managed to do it apart from her. They seemed so at ease with themselves. Their bodies. Their lives. Their pre-planned futures. As if everything had, in actual fact, been tailor made for them. How was it she constantly felt so uncomfortable?

Flo clocked the swell of nerves and gave her one of those incredibly practical, but strangely helpful *it'll all be fine* smiles then knocked on an imaginary door. 'It'll be your home too soon enough, duck. Off you pop.'

For what felt like the first time in a long time, Raven did exactly as she was told.

Before her knuckles connected with the door, it swung open. Standing in a small pool of light in the entryway was Sue, anxiety etched into her every feature. 'I'm sorry.' A smile fell from her lips before it had completely begun. 'I'm not sure I can do this.'

Chapter Twenty-Six

Sue was in what her mother would call a right old pickle.

The kind that rattled you to the very core and made you wish you'd never done the thing you did, namely put up a notice to rent out the room she hadn't yet had the courage to enter.

Instead of doing the English thing – offer an abundance of apologies and leave – Flo pulled Sue into a big old hug, ushered Raven in out of the rain with a, 'Course you can, love. You can do anything you want to. It's just nerves, is all.'

She was right, of course.

It was nerves. Nerves and fear and lack of preparation. Having Raven here, duffel bags weighing down her shoulders, had suddenly made everything irreversibly real. As if life had suddenly punched up its colour scheme to Dynamic or Vivid when she'd lived every moment up until now in muted shades of That'll Do. Proof, as if she needed more, that her life had changed forever and would never go back to the steady, reliable, routine-centric existence she'd had just a few short weeks ago. It was *change*. So much change and not any of it wanted. But . . . necessity and all that. She had no money. She'd already taken Raven's. She owed her a roof and a bed and some hospitality.

After an abundance of apologies on her end, a bit of fuss lumping the bags inside, they stood there, the three of them, all crowded into the minuscule entryway, their feet various stages of on and off the shaggy unicorn rug Katie had given her this past Christmas.

It was all quite awkward.

Very awkward in fact. Sue hadn't done a solitary thing to Gary's office. It was difficult to tidy a room when you hadn't yet got the courage to open the door.

She threw Flo a panicked look.

What on earth was she meant to do?

She was perfectly happy to give Raven her own room, but then what would she do? Sleep on the sofa? In the bath? Raven would think her very, very strange. Then again, she was a widow now. Perhaps there was a bit of licence for peculiarity now that Gary had thrown his proverbial spanner into the works. His real spanners were, of course, in his office.

She and Raven shot each other shy looks. The type of looks children who'd been the last two picked for a netball team would share after having been told, actually, the teams were full now so would they mind serving water to the rest of the team and that even though they weren't playing, they were being very, very useful. Maybe they *would* suit each other. Two wallflowers decorating the same interior to very different effect.

Sue looked back to Flo, muted by indecision as to how to proceed. Flo would know what to do. She seemed so capable. So sure of herself. A bit bossy, but not in the dismissive way her mother was, more . . . nurturing. As if she could see the emotional anguish twisting away in Sue's heart and instinctively knew how to make a decision that would help Sue rather than override her as her mother's decisions so often did.

Flo clapped her hands together. 'Let's get Raven's bags up into the room and then I'll make us all a nice cuppa, shall I?' Her practical smile suddenly brightened. 'What am I talking about?' She hoisted up a clinking plastic shopping bag. 'I've got fizz! C'mon girls. The sooner we get things sorted – the sooner we can get a few bubbles in us. There's something I'd like to put to you, Sue. But not until we're all sorted with Raven, here.'

Much to her astonishment, Sue turned, led the two women up the stairs, past the step where Gary's feet had brushed her shoulder as she ran to close the doors against the scene and found herself turning the handle to her own bedroom door.

'Ummm . . .' Raven said after scanning the room. 'This is an en suite.'

'Yes, it's . . .' Sue lunged towards the bed where she'd left a jumper and clutched it to her chest with one hand as she held her other out in an awkward presentation style. 'It's my room actually, I thought you might prefer it to the other room.' She felt Raven and Flo's eyes train on her as if they were actual heat lamps. 'I don't mind going in the other room.'

Gary's.

She wondered if it still smelt of him. All of the things in it had last been touched by him, if you didn't count the gloved forensics team who'd come and gone within a couple of hours. Would she be able to tell? Sense the man who he'd really been instead of the one she thought she'd known?

'You mean my room?' Raven asked. 'The one I was supposed to go into?'

'Yes, umm, but I'm quite happy taking it.' Her arm went into an air-traffic control position towards Gary's door.

Raven shook her head. 'I don't feel right taking your room.'

'Honestly, it's fine!' Sue squeaked. Against her better judgement she pitched back into the master bedroom and pulled open the wardrobe to grab an outfit for tomorrow, inadvertently showing Flo and Raven everything she hadn't done. She hadn't cleared out Gary's clothes. She hadn't moved any of her own, few remaining clothes (the clear out had been rather thorough). She hadn't done anything at all, because in truth she hadn't been able to face up to the fact that the minute Raven walked into her house she would have to accept the truth that her husband was never, ever coming home again.

Flo flew into action. 'If that's what you feel comfortable with, duck? Let's make it happen. Here love,' Flo pointed to Raven's bags. 'Why don't we put these on the bed and help shift Sue's clothes over to the other room?'

Before Sue could protest, throw herself in front of the door and scream *No! I'm not ready!* Flo had swept into the wardrobe, weighted herself with an armful of clothes, strode across the landing and opened the door. Just like that.

Chapter Twenty-Seven

Kath looked up from her quinoa, broccoli and salmon salad, trying to catch Kevin's eye. It happened less and less frequently these days. Meeting one another's eyes over a meal. Astonishing, considering how she used to long to gaze into them. Seek out her fortune in the myriad of blues that kaleidoscoped through his dark-lashed peepers. He'd been the answer to every one of her teenaged hopes and dreams. A performer determined to make it to the top. Now that they'd come true? Most days she couldn't bear to meet her own reflection in them. 'I was having a think,' she finally said.

Kev swallowed noisily and said, 'Were you now?'

She fought the instinct to bristle. She'd set some wheels in motion that she couldn't stop anymore, so it was best to plumb the depths of her diplomacy. Even if her husband chose to speak to her as if it were a rare thing for his wife to come up with a thought on her own. He never used to be like that. Derisive. Then again, she never used to want to be married to someone else, so, she supposed that made them even.

Kev slurped down some rather pricey Chablis she knew for a fact his trainer had told him to avoid.

'Yes.' She forced her voice to stay on-air bright. 'I was thinking about the nip tuck tourism piece you were interested in me doing down in South Africa.'

His eyes flicked to hers, interested. 'Oh, aye?'

She could almost see the self-satisfaction pour in.

'Yes,' she tugged her fork through a lawn of superfood micro greens, then met his gaze again. This was going to take some balls. 'I was wondering how *you* might feel about doing it? You know, bust the myth that women are always the ones who need to change themselves to feel pretty. Like Mickey Rourke.' Kev's eyebrows shot up. Mickey Rourke might not have been the best of examples. She dived in and corrected herself. 'Or Patrick Swayze. You know he looked ever so nice after he . . .' she pulled her own cheeks back a bit and smiled.

Kev's chest puffed up in indignation. 'Patrick Swayze *never.*'

'Course he did. Loads of them did.' She began to rattle off a bunch of names of celebrities she knew had definitely been under the knife. According to her make-up artist, anyway. A font of wisdom, make-up artists.

Kev eventually burst out laughing. 'Come off it, Kath. Out with it. Admit you were wrong. That your . . .' He air scrubbed the area along his own, slightly drooping jawline and grinned. 'You know . . . that you need a bit of refreshing.'

For the first time in her life his smile made her blood run cold. Kevin had just drawn a line between them.

He'd never put it that bluntly before. Not even bothered to be the tiniest bit sympathetic or gentle. As if it were her fault ageing didn't factor well in the ratings.

A shot of courage swept through her. This had gone too far. The competitiveness. The fight for his and hers ratings when, for so many years, it had been *their* ratings and *their* popularity and *their* successes. She didn't feel like his wife any longer. She felt like his employee. An unworthy sidekick about to be sloughed off before he finally bit the bullet and went solo.

She fought the urge to scrape the rest of her salad into the bin, book herself into a hotel for the night and order room service for twenty. But no. This was supposed to be a chance to communicate with her husband. A chance to try and show him what he was doing to her by turning the tables.

It had been Fola's suggestion. She'd told him how, though she didn't want to go, and definitely didn't want a facelift, she was also feeling a strange guilt for refusing a trip many women would've given their right eye for, particularly given the fact what she was doing instead was so much better. So much more . . . real.

But their viewing public didn't really want real, did they? They wanted fantasy. Aspirational, fluffy fantasy. They only liked real if it made them feel better about themselves. Kath and Kev's Kar Krash Marriage. Kath and Kev's Kalamitous Klash.

And what had Kevin done with this chance to add some proper depth to his emotional landscape?

He'd laughed then thrown it right back at her.

She didn't want this. Having to engage in tactical negotiations with her husband – her lifelong partner – to get him to see the way he was treating her wasn't right. Wasn't enough. He was supposed to be the one she could rely on to make her feel better. To comfort her. To make her feel beautiful inside and out . . . the way Fola did.

A heat flickered deep within her as an image of the pair of them looking at one another's reflections in the mirror came to her.

Was she having an affair with him?

No.

Was she falling in love with him?

Yes. The idea of him, anyway.

Did she want her husband to see how much she hurt inside? She was pretending what little self-confidence she had left wasn't being devoured by his constant need to undermine her.

Maybe?

'Fair enough,' she eventually said, though it quite clearly wasn't. 'You know, I think I'll turn in early tonight. Plenty to think about and—' she pipped him to the post, '—of course I'll be needing my beauty sleep, won't I?'

Chapter Twenty-Eight

It was astonishing what three women could do when they put their minds to something.

'There we are, pet.' Flo fluffed up the pillows on the narrow twin bed – Sue's childhood one apparently – and turned on the small unicorn lamp Sue had insisted on shifting from her original room to her new one. The pair of them stood back and gave the room a final inspection. It was more serviceable than inviting, but the room obviously had never been used as anything other than a hold-all for Gary's tools and his mountains of paperwork. 'You'll be fine in here for tonight,' Flo gave Sue a half hug. 'The rest'll sort itself out soon enough.'

Flo wasn't sure she believed anything she was saying, but she had to finish what she'd started, didn't she? Barging in as she had. Rearranging this, moving that, all with Sue making involuntary 'ohh' and 'hmm' noises as she went. Her gut was telling her she'd done the right thing, but it wasn't half hard, watching the poor woman confront her future up close and personal.

When Flo had opened the door to the small room they were now in, she'd never seen blood drain from a woman's face so fast. To the point Flo had almost pulled it shut again. But, that wasn't how progress was made. The poor girl obviously didn't have a solitary soul lending her the emotional support she so obviously needed, so Flo had set about doing what Flo did best. Organising the troops.

She'd set Raven to work changing the bedding in the master bedroom. (She'd not brought her own, the poor love. From the few glimpses that Flo had had while she was unpacking, Raven's entire move looked rather hastily put together. Clothes and books and a couple of sketch pads seemed to be the sum total of her belongs. No favourite pillows, knick-knacks, photos by the bedside. Nothing. She'd investigate later, but . . . *Sue.*) After checking what Sue did and didn't want touched (the desk and the wardrobe were off limits, everything else was fair game) she'd set Sue to work ferrying the remains of her clothes from the wardrobe to a rather beleaguered-looking clothes rack hiding in the corner and a two-drawer filing cabinet that was mysteriously empty. Didn't look touched. Flo couldn't understand why Sue didn't want to tidy things away in the perfectly serviceable wardrobe, and put the piles of papers on Gary's desk in the cabinet, but it wasn't a time to press, so they'd pushed on, with Florence dangling pizza and fizz as prizes at the end of this particular rainbow.

Now, a good two hours later, having made up the bed with a couple of dark throws and unpacked her clothes, Raven was downstairs (as instructed) heating up the oven for the pizzas (one vegetarian, just in case and one gluten free, just in case). Gary's clothes had been tenderly relocated to a miniscule box room (closet really) that housed the hoover, a clothes drying rack and a scarecrow that Sue laughed about, patted then said . . . *Oh, Gary.*

'There's so much of it.' Sue was staring at the Ikea desk, some sort of laminated press wood from the looks of things. It was weighted with three very large cardboard boxes that had, at one time, housed a toilet, a U-bend pipe and a 'sturdy plastic toolbox to suit all of your needs'. In a surprisingly clear hand (Flo didn't know why, but she wouldn't have imagined a plumber having excellent penmanship) they each bore A4 labels. **Bills**, **Invoices** and **Paid**. The first was overflowing and, until about five minutes ago, sent a perpetual flow of paperwork cascading to the floor each time they so much as exhaled. The second was full-ish. And the third, the paid box, was pitiably empty. Next to the boxes was an accounts book. It was filled with endless columns and scribbles and all sorts of indecipherables. She knew because she'd peeked when Sue was out of the room. It'd take more than Google translate to get through that mess. Flo's compassion for Sue deepened.

'I hadn't realised how much paperwork was involved in the plumbing business.' Sue was staring at the boxes with disbelief, as if seeing them for the first time. 'In all of the years I've known him, I never knew Gary to spend more than ten, fifteen minutes in here.'

'So you've not been in here?'

'No, not really.' Sue flushed. 'Gaz used to keep my presents in here. In the wardrobe. He told me I was never to come in unless I wanted to ruin the surprise.' Her eyes flicked to the wardrobe then lingered.

Oh, you poor, silly, gullible girl. The secrets this man has been keeping from you.

She was no detective, or psychiatrist for that matter, but she'd seen enough telly and met enough people to know the unattended paperwork was a likely explanation as to why Sue's husband might have found it all too much. And, Flo suddenly put two and two together, why Sue needed a housemate quite so soon after her husband had taken the darkest route imaginable.

'Do you think we should open it? The wardrobe?' Sue asked.

Oh, god no. Flo didn't. Not tonight anyway.

'I think we've done quite enough for one night, Sue. Why don't we head down for a bite to eat and a bit of a drink after all of this work, eh?'

Sue didn't move. 'It was his father's business to start.' She pointed at the stack of tool boxes at the end of the bed. 'The plumbing.'

'Oh, was it now? And your Gary worked with him, then? Father and son?'

'Yes,' Sue's face softened with a memory. 'Young & Son's Plumbing.' She laughed the first laugh Flo had ever heard from her. 'Gaz used to say his father should've called it Barney Rubble Plumbing with the cack-handed way he went about fixing things. How little he worked. Reg only went out on two or three calls a day. My Gaz could do five or six depending upon the traffic. And supplies of course.' Sue shook her head. Whether it was in awe or disbelief, was difficult to tell.

Sue lifted up a stray pipe wrench they hadn't yet found a home for. 'When his father passed, Gary said he was going to kick things up a notch. Make a proper go of it. And he did, too. Always busy, my Gary. Taking classes to learn more things that the companies put on. You know, jacuzzis and the fancy showers and things. Watching YouTube videos from America to keep up to date. Always helping someone. Good or bad. He was always helping someone.'

A little glow of something Flo had not seen in Sue before appeared. Pride. Pride for the mark her husband had made on the world before he left it. She looked at Flo through glassy eyes, then gave herself a shake as if she suddenly remembered a silent promise not to cry about anything. Not in front of a near stranger anyway.

Raven stuck her head round the doorframe, knocking on it as she did. Her eyes shot to the desk sagging with boxes, the accounts book, the wrench Sue was still wielding. 'Wow. Ummm. Pizza's ready?'

Sue gave the desk a hapless little shrug and said, 'I suppose it's not going anywhere.'

'I can help another time if you like,' Raven surprised everyone by saying. 'If it's simple bookkeeping.'

'Did you study it in college?' Flo asked.

She nodded. 'A bit, but mostly I learnt by helping my parents with the shop.'

'Shop?'

'It's a pharmacy. A small one, so . . .' Her eyes skimmed across the labels on the boxes. 'Small business?'

Sue nodded. 'Plumbing.'

'Any employees?'

155

'No, just Gary.'

Raven chewed on her bottom lip for a minute then said, 'I'll bet you can do most of it on an app if you want.'

Sue's eyebrows lifted. 'He's got this book.' She pointed at the accounts book that looked as if it had been bought around 1952.

Raven pushed her lips out and then gave a 'your call' shrug. 'Pizza?'

'Good idea,' Flo enthused. 'And once we've all got a nice little drink in our hands, how about we put it to Sue about our little adventure, eh, Raven?'

Chapter Twenty-Nine

'Round the country?'

'Oh, god, no love. *Across* it.' Flo's cheeks were pink. Whether it was from the heat or the fizz, Sue wasn't quite sure. Excitement maybe? Raven was staying mysteriously silent, although Flo had assured her Raven loved the idea every bit as much as she did.

A charity cycle ride across the country. She wasn't even sure she knew where Hadrian's Wall was, to be honest. Somewhere up North.

'I've not ridden a bike in years, I don't think. Not since . . .' Her eyes went opaque for a moment then cleared. 'It's been quite a while.'

'It's for a good cause. It's that mental health charity Kath off of Kath and Kev is the ambassador for. LifeTime?'

Sue shook her head. She didn't know it.

'It's a mental health charity, love. She joined up with them when her brother died. He had the depression, didn't he? I thought you might enjoy raising some money for them considering what happened with your Gary.'

Sue took a sip of her drink. She was using coins from her special holiday coin jar to buy food, had accepted money from a stranger who now lived in her bedroom and now Flo wanted her to ride her bicycle across the country to earn money for a charity she had never heard of. She thought of the solitary phone call Gary might have made if he'd known help was available to him.

'How far is it?'

'Two hundred miles.'

Sue's eyes popped open.

'Less. More than one fifty, less than two. And very flat apparently.' She flattened her hand. 'Like a pancake. And you don't do it in one go. It's over about five days.' She suddenly beamed. 'It's camping I think!' Raven choked on her pizza and Flo, without missing a beat, patted her on the back, went to the sink, got her some water and handed it to her all without losing eye contact with Sue.

'Does it cost money? You know, to join?'

Flo's light eyebrows templed. They were blonde, unlike Flo's hair which was a rather lovely silvery grey. It was the type of grey her mother would've preferred to go. A bit more Helen Mirren chic rather than the practical Jamie Lee Curtis she'd ended up with. 'I'm not sure, love. That's a good question. I was just watching Kath talk about it on the telly, but I've not yet looked up the details on the internet. Raven and I were talking about it on the ride over here, weren't we, Raven?' They both turned to Raven who was in the middle of biting into the Big Meaty Deluxe now that she'd recovered from her coughing spell. She waved. '. . . I was saying to her, wouldn't it be fun? And wouldn't it be even more fun if you were to join us.' Raven nodded in agreement.

'Why are you going?' Sue asked.

For the first time that night Flo looked as though she were caught off guard. She took a bite of pizza and made a thoughtful face as if she were finding just the right way to explain her reasons. A hidden tragedy? A personal loss? Mental health problems of her own?

'Oh, I love a new adventure,' Flo finally answered, then with a glint in her eye, added, 'And I can't stand that Kev. This is the first thing Kath's done on her own so far as I can remember and I want to support her. And her charity of course.' She looked down at her piece of pizza then, as if she'd made a decision on a great matter, put it back on the plate and looked Sue square in the eye. 'If I'm being entirely honest, I want to stave off old age as long as humanly possible. I need a bit of va-va-voom in my life. Want to get a little *je ne sais quoi* running through my veins. Riding across the country ought to do it, don't you think, girls?'

Sue and Raven tipped their heads side to side as if the idea were a shiny orb navigating its way through the maze of their minds. Yes. Riding a bicycle across the country would definitely add something to someone's life. Raven looked about as unsure as Sue felt as to what that something would be, but . . . would doing something for someone else help her feel whole again? Useful? Valuable? Sure, she took calls from people seeking help every day at work, but most of the time it didn't feel as though she was actually, genuinely responding. How could she when her responses were pre-scripted? *Oh, god* she needed something to make her feel useful again. 'When is it?'

'Not for a few months yet. May, I think? End of April.' Flo was clearly fibbing. She didn't know. But strangely, Sue didn't mind.

The more time she spent with Flo, the more Sue got the impression this dynamic, vital woman was a big-picture person. A blue-sky thinker who trusted that the details would sort themselves out so long as the intention was pure. Kind. 'They'll want to wait until all of this horrid winter weather's over, won't they?' Flo's question was clearly rhetorical. 'Anyway. What does it matter, so long as we have a good time, right, girls?'

Score one to Sue.

'Right!' Flo wiped her hands briskly together and began tidying things up as if she'd known her way round Sue's kitchen for years now. 'Why don't I leave it with you two girls to talk about, yeah? Tomorrow morning, when you're having your first cuppa, how about you watch Kath together? See if it appeals. Riding a bicycle with a celebrity! Apparently she's bringing along her trainer for "group morale and physio" if anyone needs it. A big strapping lad. Reminds me of Idris Elba, he does. Oh, *girls.*' Flo went the tiniest bit misty. 'We'll be such a merry threesome!' She tipped the rest of her fizz down the sink (*I've got to drive home, haven't I?*), gave them both a tight, reassuring hug, shouldered her large canvas tote (from Vietnam, apparently) then disappeared.

Raven and Sue stared at the closed front door long enough to hear Flo's car grind into gear then tear off down the street. Raven smiled at the door, then at Sue and said, 'She's like Mary Poppins, isn't she?'

'Yes,' Sue smiled as well, feeling a rush of affection for both Raven and Flo. Her new friends. 'So . . . for the morning. Are you a tea or a coffee person?'

'Tea. White and one please,' Raven said, the energy between them still shy, but less anxious. 'If it's all right, I think I'll head up to bed now.'

'Of course,' Sue said, then added, 'You can do what you like. This is your home now.'

Raven turned to head up the stairs then suddenly turned around, pulled Sue into a tight hug, muttered something that sounded like *thank you sosososooo much*, then ran up the stairs and into her room, shutting the door behind her.

Well, thought Sue. *Let the new chapter begin.*

Chapter Thirty

'Can I help you with anything?'

Raven bit back the impulse to correct the shop assistant's grammar because the real answer was no. No he couldn't help her. But throwing shade on someone's grammar first thing in the morning just seemed rude.

She gave him her best 'not really sure' smile and went back to looking at the long row of bicycles, wondering what would happen if she asked him to help her with what she really wanted.

Her parents' support. That was the main thing.

Failing that, she wanted a job that didn't involve people calling in desperate for help she was unable to give, but that paid the same amount and didn't require anything beyond a college education.

She wanted the price tags on these bicycles to be half of what they were.

And world peace.

She wanted that, too. Gandhiji would've approved.

'Are you looking for anything in particular?'

'Ummm . . .' She ran her finger along a set of handlebars hoping the gesture made her look even the slightest bit as if she knew what she was doing. 'I'm just browsing, really.'

'Right.' The clerk went from nice to impatient in a nanosecond. He rolled his eyes in a display of world weariness that the fat, goth girl was considering, but not actually buying something that might

161

help her not be fat anymore. Not that she was paranoid about her weight or anything (she'd eaten an entire pizza last night whilst Sue had picked at a piece or two with her fingertips and Flo had eaten maybe a slice). 'Lemme know if I can help you with anything,' he said by rote as he headed back to the counter where an ultra-fit looking blonde girl around her age was putting mark-down labels on several dozen bottles of anti-freeze.

To be honest, Raven couldn't believe she was in an actual bike store looking at actual bicycles considering signing up for an actual, literal, bicycle trip. Not that they'd one hundred per cent decided they were going or anything, but she wouldn't have believed she'd be living anywhere but her parents' a week ago, so who knew what might happen? They might actually go.

As instructed, she and Sue had watched *Brand New Day* earlier this morning as Sue was getting ready for her early shift. Raven wasn't on until noon but she wasn't really one for lying in and there were all sorts of new noises at Sue's house she wasn't used to, like neighbours. They each admitted they'd seen the show occasionally but clearly not with the regularity Flo had. They'd watched silently as Kath rode on a stationary bicycle that lit up a lightbulb each time she amped up her revs. One watt for each thousand pounds that had been donated. She was up to forty-seven watts so far. They learnt that the ride wasn't for another two and a half months and that each rider would be expected to try and raise five hundred pounds that would also cover their expenses. They'd both drawn in quick, sharp breaths at that news. Fundraising definitely wasn't Raven's bag and, from the looks of things, wasn't exactly Sue's cup of tea, either.

When the segment was over and went on to something about Kev and volleyball and learning how to spike it over the net, they muted the telly, made toast and giggled about Flo's enthusiasm (and a little bit about her bossiness), but in a nice way and it had felt fun, giggling with someone who could totally be her mum but blonde and wasn't even the tiniest bit judgemental. Just . . . nice. Sue, Raven learnt, had trained to be a beauty stylist and, despite not having pursued it, still kept up with the latest hair trends and would happily, if Raven wanted her to, help redo her streaks that had already almost completely disappeared after just a couple of showers. Raven had instantly said yes, not because Sue seemed to be some sort of crazy fashion guru (her overall look erred on the side of girlie), but because Sue was the first person in a very long time to be entirely and completely kind to her. Apart from Flo, of course. She *listened*. When she wasn't spacing out, which, given her circumstances, was completely understandable. Something about her, her fragility perhaps, made Raven want to hug her as she had done last night before tearing up into her room and asking herself over and over again *why did I do that?* because she wasn't, by nature, a hugger. More the kind of girl who shrank away from human interaction, but who knew. Maybe Flo was right. Perhaps moving out and becoming a 'woman of the world' would be the making of her. When Flo had quizzed her about moving out, she had left out the part about it being a self-imposed banishment. Or that her parents had yet to ring her. No messages. No emails. Nothing. Ghosted by her own parents.

'Hey! Raven! 'Sup!'

Raven looked up and there was Dylan, Curry's uniform hidden beneath his thick duffel coat, heading directly towards her. 'Yo, Bryan.' He raised his voice and waved across at the Halford's clerk. 'You still want to check out that bike with me later?'

'Yeah, man. I'm off at six. You?'

'Five-thirty, but I'll come over here and hang.' He grabbed one of the bicycles in front of him and popped it into a wheelie position. 'I'll give one of these babies a run for their money. Can I have a hells to the yeah?'

The hot blonde girl gave him a slow clap then went back to tagging her anti-freeze. She'd clearly been pranced in front of by more than one shopping centre assistant in her day.

'Yo, Bryan. Why aren't you over here helping out Raven?' Dylan's voice went all melodramatic like the man who did film previews, 'The artist with the Magic Eyes. I bet she could do some voodoo shit on you if you don't watch it.'

Raven looked at him. What the actual fuck was he talking about?

Bryan, to be fair, looked equally perplexed.

Dylan started laughing. 'Ah, you guys. You're hilarious. I'm just messing with you. I'm just messing with you.'

Crikey. Dylan needed a hobby or something else to use up his clearly very over-active imagination.

'So what brings you to the finest shopping centre in da hood?' he asked Raven.

She wasn't really inclined to answer whilst he was channelling his inner Kanye. It was weird.

And then, all of a sudden, he became normal, friendly Dylan. 'You looking for a bike? I'm friends with Bryan. I can see if he can use his staff discount for you if you find anything.'

This was so weird. Did he think they were friends?

'Are you getting a new bike? Doing some spring training?' He began jogging in place with his hands on an invisible set of handlebars. When he caught the not-altogether neutral look Raven had shot him, he stopped. 'Sorry. I just ate, like, a whole packet of salted caramel Hobnobs and am riding one *hella* sugar high. I've just come over here to burn some of it off during my break.' His eyes flicked over to where the Curry's was. 'That place is, like, totally dead this time of year. No one wants to buy anything new in March.' He leaned in and said ominously, '*Tax. Time.*'

Dylan was a nutter. A funny nutter, but, Raven looked away. When people were funny with her it made her suspicious. As if the friendly banter was all an elaborate set-up to make her the punchline of a joke she hadn't seen coming.

'So.' He did some display hands across the line of bicycles, taking over Bryan's role with clear relish. 'Which model are you looking at, Madam? Is this for pleasure or for pootling about our lovely Oxfordshire lanes?'

'It's for a charity ride.' *Wot????* Which weird demented spirit made her say that?

'Cool. Cool beans. How long?'

'Just under two hundred miles.' *Seriously???* Shut the actual fuck up, Raven!

'Super cool. In, like, India?'

'Nooo.' Why would she buy a bicycle here to ride in India? 'Hadrian's Wall.' And why was she still talking?

'Nice. Charity ride, hunh?'

'Yeah.' Sweet mother of over-talkative teens. What was going *on* with her? 'LifeTime. It's the—'

'Mental health charity.' They finished together. She met Dylan's eyes and saw a flicker of something she wouldn't have expected to see in there. Recognition. And then it was gone.

'You set up an Insta account yet? I could follow your adventures.'

This caught her cold. She looked away and touched a little girl's bike that had purple sparkly tassels coming off of the handlebars.

'That one might be a bit small,' Dylan joked, then saw she wasn't smiling. 'Hey. You okay?'

'Yeah, yeah. Fine.' She zipped up her coat. 'I'd probably better get going.'

'That's cool. Hey,' Dylan looked over his shoulder to where Bryan appeared to be trying to be helpful to the blonde clerk. 'Top tip? Get one on eBay if you don't really know what you want. Total money saver.' He tapped the side of his nose. 'Take it from a man who's been there, done that.'

Raven scrunched her nose up. Dylan could lurch from persona to persona faster than she could blink.

'Seriously, though,' Dylan said, following her to the door. 'If you want me to help, I go through bikes like that.' He snapped. 'That's why I'm here. Bryan's looking to become a freestyler, like wot I iz and we're going to go see a BMX. Dude went and broke his leg and is giving it up.'

'Wouldn't it be bad luck? Buying someone's bike that they got injured on?' she asked, remembering too late she'd just moved into the house where a man had killed himself.

Dylan looked at her with a dazzling smile. 'Not if you're a better rider than them. Seriously.' He pulled his phone out of his pocket and wiggled it between them. 'You want any help? I'm your man.'

He was obviously a complete and utter idiot. And a nutter. But by the time Raven was halfway to the bus stop, she realised she was smiling too.

Incident No: 627428
Time of Call: 07:27
Call Handler: SUE YOUNG

Call Handler: You're through to the NHS 111 service, my name's Sue and I'm a health advisor. Are you calling about yourself or someone else?

Caller: I'm calling about my daughter.

Call Handler: Can you tell me your daughter's name please?

Caller: It's Lily Vestry.

Call Handler: Lily? That's a lovely name. May I have your—

Caller: Rebecca Hattersby. It's my maiden name.

Call Handler: Very good. And can you please let me know why you're calling about Lily today?

Caller: She's got flu. She's in a wheelchair and has got very special health needs. I have to get to work in an hour, her father's not answering the phone and her carer's going to be late, so can you send a doctor over, please? I'm a bit worried about her temperature and I've not got the time to bring her to the A&E.

Call Handler: Alright.

Caller: Oh, thank god.

Call Handler: No. Sorry, I'm just trying to find . . . Have you tried contacting your G—

Caller: No. We're well past that. Look. Lily's GP isn't all that helpful as her needs are so specialised, but yes, I've gone through the paces. I know the drill. Hang on, darling. I'm just on the phone. Have some of your ice chips, yeah? Look. Sue, was it? I've been through this drill before, love. I've tried calling the GP. They're closed. I've tried calling her useless father. He isn't answering. I've tried calling the hospital. They suggested keeping Lily at home as they've got norovirus concerns. I've tried calling everyone apart from an ambulance which I'm fairly certain she doesn't require, not yet anyway, which is why I'm on the phone with you, hoping you have a brain in your head and aren't relying on that bloody script they supply you with because all I need is for you to send a doctor over, alright?

Call Handler: Right. Okay, well, if we could just run through—

Caller: Please let's not go through this charade, Sue. I need you to send a doctor over.

Call Handler: Can you describe her symptoms please?

Caller: Coughing, congestion, fatigue, chills, fever, aches and pain.

Call Handler: Okay. Hang on just a minute while I—

Caller: Please just send the doctor. I'm not trying to be a bitch. I'm not trying to ruin your day. I sound rude because I haven't slept properly in over a week. Years really. I simply need a doctor to come to my house to take a look at my disabled child before I head off to work so that I'm not panicked she is going to die while

I'm away trying to pay for the roof over our heads and the food on our table.

Call Handler: I'll organise a doctor straight away.

Caller: *Thank* you.

Call Handler: Rebecca?

Caller: [Heavy sigh] Yes, love.

Call Handler: I hope she feels better soon.

Caller: Thank you, love. [Sobbing noise] Oh, god. Shit. Sorry. Thank you for listening. You don't know how rare it is. You've actually made my day.

Call Handler: You're welcome. Do call back if you need anything or her symptoms worsen.

Caller: I will, love. Believe me. I will.

Call Handler: Thank you for calling 111. [Sound of nose being blown] [Call ends] Rachel, sorry? Is it alright if I—? Yes, I'm fine. I'm fine. Something in my eye is all. I won't be a min—

Chapter Thirty-One

Tactics. That's what this situation required. Tactics.

Flo gave Stu's shoulders a rub. 'Alright, darling?'

He gave his hmmmnnn noise which meant he was properly engrossed in his puzzles.

Perfect.

'So, I won't be heading into work today.'

'Oh?'

'No. Not today.'

Hmmnnn.

'I'm off shift for a while now.'

'*Very good. Good. Hmmnnn.*'

There. That was done. Easy peasy.

Right.

Step two.

'What do you think of this, Stu?' Flo brandished her wrist in front of him with a flourish. It was weighted more heavily than it had been during her Fitbit days.

'Oh! You've got yourself a watch, have you? Snazzy.'

Flo rolled her eyes in irritation. It mightn't look like one of those great lunking things the lads who trained for triathlons and Iron Man contests wore, but it was, according to *Cycling Magazine*, the business. GPS, Wi-Fi, ANT+, whatever that was. It was a proper bells and whistles number. She'd ordered it from Amazon two days back after coming home from Sue and Raven's. She'd been so happy that night. Helping the two of them get all set up in Sue's cosy little home. So full of hope. Possibility. Oh, she knew everything wouldn't be roses and rainbows, not with all of that baggage in tow, but Raven had looked less terrified than when Flo had first shooed her out of the car and Sue hadn't collapsed into a sobbing ball of grief when they'd found that mountain of unpaid bills. Not that it would've been a bad thing (better out than in), it just may have made things a bit trickier for Raven.

Saying that, Raven had a few surprising tricks up her sleeve. Volunteering, as she had, to help Sue with going through the papers. It might be easier that way. Having someone emotionally uninvolved work through what looked to be an Everest's worth of discovery. Poor lass. In all fairness, if Stu were to drop dead on the back of plundering their life savings on, oh, a golf club pyramid scheme, say (he'd never do that, he was far too practical, but this was all hypothetical, so . . .), the last people on earth she'd want helping was family. All of that tutting and clucking her daughter was perfecting at far too young an age. So disapproving for someone with so much life ahead of her. Perhaps Jennifer might like to join her— No. She checked the thought. Jennifer's life ran on year planners. Spontaneity didn't factor in. It was one of their 'issues', according to Jennifer. A divergence of life approaches.

She smiled at her watch, brushing her finger over the shiny white face, its features waiting to be taken advantage of. Each of them awash with possibility. Activity-tracking functions, three different satellites it read from, *navigation* capabilities. She could get dropped in Timbuktu and find her way home if she needed to. More so, she supposed, with all of this blasted time on her hands. She squinted at the watch, not entirely sure where to find the time. 'Stu?' She jiggled her wrist in front of him again.

'It looks high-tech. And pricey.' He put down his pen and pushed his puzzles back. 'Is that for Jamie's fortieth? I thought we were going to fly him and the girls over to Portugal.'

Why on earth would she have bought a fuchsia-coloured multi-activity tracking watch for their poor, hen-pecked son? 'No, love. It's for me.'

Stu's eyebrows shot up. 'Oh? Taking up a new hobby are we?' His eyes abruptly brightened as he clapped his hands together and laughed. Delighted. 'Florence Joanne Wilson.' He always called her by her full name when he was tickled about something. 'Does this mean you're finally joining the Algarve Oldies? I thought you'd eventually join in. They really rack up the miles, those girls.'

Flo stopped her lip from curling, forcing it into a twitchy smile. The 'girls' Stu was speaking about were the wives of Stu's golfing buddies down at their gated golf community. They were nice enough women, but astonishingly dull. More so, because they thought they were right fascinating. The lot of them – there were about half a dozen depending upon the time of year and, of course, health scares – considered themselves daring and interesting because sometimes, instead of circumnavigating the pristinely manicured golf course, they sometimes . . . and *only* sometimes . . . rode bicycles into town for a coffee instead of having it, as they usually did, at the club.

'No, darlin'.' She resisted going back to her post behind him to fake strangle him again. Much of her frustration wasn't with him, it was with all this *time* she had.

Faced with a completely blank week, she'd spent Stu's tee-time filling in every waking moment she could. She'd made an appointment at the gym, one with her GP and, of course, she needed to head into the cycle shop a bit later. The only bicycle they had that was vaguely serviceable was Jennifer's old trail bike that she'd left behind when she'd headed for London. Rather than the Halfords down at the shopping centre where the assistants didn't give two figs about properly fitting a bike to the person, she thought she'd check out the adorable little shop on Sheep Street. They used an old-fashioned font on their shopfront that appealed to her. Perhaps she'd get a basket, too.

Then, of course, she'd have to meet up with Sue and Raven. Talk logistics, fundraising, and, of course, if they'd be willing to share a tent with her.

Not that she was sure it was camping or that she'd actually heard from the girls yet. She'd left things with them to marinate, half hoping they'd call her straight after watching *Brand New Day* on the Friday morning. They hadn't. She'd kept herself busy over the weekend (dog walks, googling Hadrian's Wall and, of course, the charity that they would be fundraising for). Now that it was Monday, and she'd not heard a word, she was feeling a bit edgy.

Without work as a means of casually running into them, pressing for information and enthusing them was trickier. Particularly as she'd forgotten to get contact details for either one of them. She could always pop in of course, with a housewarming present or something, but people didn't really pop in anymore unless they were neighbours and even then . . . She'd check Facebook later. Or Instagram. She'd not yet got into the swing of Twitter, but no doubt she'd find them on one thing or another. Surely Raven would be on all of them, being so young.

She removed the watch from her wrist and laid it on top of Stu's Sudoku. 'Take a look. I bet you could navigate a plane with all of the microtechnology in this one.' Flo needed Stu to take an interest. Partly because she'd be tromping in and out of the house with padded bum shorts on over the coming weeks and partly because she hadn't figured out how to work the bloody thing yet. She also had some uncomfortable news to pass on.

'What's this for then?' Stu took on his grandfatherly tone, tipping his glasses down to the end of his nose as he inspected the watch.

'It's for that charity ride I've been telling you I've signed up for. The one with Kath off the morning telly?' She'd only registered on the weekend, but he didn't need to know that. A bit presumptuous on her part seeing as she'd no clue if Raven and Sue were coming, but if it came to it, she supposed she'd be alright on her own. It wasn't as if it would be just her and Kath, would it? That Idris Elba look-a-like'd be there. And, apparently, a bus driver would be bringing all of their luggage from site to site, so at least four of them would be involved. She handed Stu the instruction booklet for the watch. She never read the instructions on anything. That was Stu's job. 'Remember, love? The girls down at the call centre and I signed up for it together.'

Stu's eyebrows dived together. 'Hmm . . . remind me?'

'The one along Hadrian's Wall. For the charity?' She left out mental health, as it was never a concept Stu could wrap his head round. Not in a mean way, he was just so ruddy *logical*, he didn't understand how others could be pulled up short by life.

He began flicking through the booklet, pen making little marks at what he called Points of Interest. 'Would you like me to do the settings for you?'

Flo smiled. This was more like it. Stu's pen went down. Eyebrows furrowed.

Oh, dear.

'Wait now. Hadrian's Wall. Weather's awful there this time of year. When exactly will you be away?'

Exactly when they were meant to be in Portugal for Stu's annual golf tournament with his pilot pals. 'May,' she answered brightly tapping the instruction booklet in front of him. 'Only a week. I'll be back before you know it.'

'But won't we be—'

'Course we'll be going to Portugal, love. I just won't be there during that first week in May is all.'

'Oh, now, I'm not so sure that'll work, darling. Will it? What about Mary and Ray?'

Captain George pawed at the back door.

'What about them? I'm doing something for charity, darling.' Flo crossed to let the dog out for a lollop in the garden.

'But it's their golden wedding anniversary. The table's already booked at the club.'

Irritation cracked through her. For heaven's sake! When had the man become such a slave to monotony! They'd been celebrating Mary and Ray's anniversary since the beginning of time! Hadn't she raised enough glasses to them? They could ring her on one of those video apps if necessary. Pre-record her. She already knew exactly what they'd be talking about anyway. The weather (too sunny or too windy). The golf (Flo never really tuned in to those bits). The tournament dinner (Harold Cookson always won). Stu never won, so it was an exercise in smiling, smiling, smiling until they got through the bland, roast supper, offering a few toasts, had a spin or two round the dance floor as everyone did an hour or so before last orders, then excused themselves to go back to their matching houses on the pristine green to go to sleep only to wake up and do it all over again the next day (bar, of course, the tournament). It was like being a child again. All of this routine.

The dog pressed a muddy paw to the window, woofed, then bounded back down the garden. At least someone had a bit of Spring Fever in them.

'I think Captain George is needing a proper walk, love. Shall we talk about this later?'

Stu gave his head a little disappointed shake. As if she'd told him she was foregoing the anniversary dinner with Mary and Ray to take up pole-dancing classes.

Unexpectedly, her husband smiled at her so lovingly she actually felt its warmth right there in the centre of her heart. He loved her so very much. So purely. Lately, all she felt she did was let him know how impatient she was with him. How frustrated. How could a man love a woman so much and not actually notice her? The real her?

Stu held up the instruction manual. 'I'll have your watch sorted for you by the time you get back, alright?' He looked at her with such hope, such *trust* that she would, in the end, do the right thing. Take up her seat next to him at the club. Applaud for the chaps who'd, once again, wiped the floor with their opponents out on the green. Stuart never once doubted her. Never once believed she was anything other than perfectly content. To the point she could hardly bear it.

And in that instant, she was suddenly torn.

Incident No: 627428
Time of Call: 21:48
Call Handler: SUNITA 'RAVEN' CHAKRABARTI

Call Handler: You're through to the NHS 111 service, my name's Raven and I'm a health advisor. Are you calling about yourself or someone else?

Caller: I'm calling for a friend. Flatmate really, but . . . whatever.

Call Handler: Can you tell me your friend's name please?

Caller: Yeah, um . . . it's Amber, but you're not going to write that down or anything are you? There's not a record of this?

Call Handler: We do record all of our calls for training and quality purposes. Okay. Why did Amber ask you to ring in today?

Caller: She didn't.

Call Handler: No?

Caller: No. I mean, yeah, she totally did. She's just . . . she won't get out of bed.

Call Handler: Would you be able to put that into context for me please?

Caller: I don't understand.

Call Handler: How long has Amber been in bed?

Caller: Four days.

Call Handler: Is she not feeling well?

Caller: No, she's fine. Healthwise. She's depressed.

Call Handler: Has she seen her GP about her symptoms?

Caller: No, that's why I'm calling you. I don't even know if she has one. She does this sometimes. Crawls into bed, doesn't get out for a few days. Loses whatever lame job she's had. It's not what I signed up for when I moved in here. Are you able to section her or put her in hospital anonymously or something?

Call Handler: No, I'm sorry. We're a health advisory service.

Caller: I thought you were the NHS.

Call Handler: We are, but we can only advise you on the best way to treat your situation.

Caller: Uhhh . . . *hello*! Doesn't take a brain surgeon to figure out the girl's depressed. She needs medication or something. Medication she ain't gonna get lying in bed!

Call Handler: Madam, sorry. I did mention these calls are monitored, right?

Caller: I don't give a flying fuck if they're monitored. I want you to help me find a way to help my flatmate and I don't want her screwed-up family finding out because if they do they'll stop paying her rent and they're the ones who signed the lease agreement and I don't have the money to put down a deposit if they take her out and then we'd both be up shit's creek. C'mon. Please. Can you help me out here?

Call Handler: I can offer you the number of a service your friend can call. There's LifeTime which has a number you can ring—

Caller: Have you been listening to a word I've said? She's lying in bed like a zombie. She's not going to call anyone.

Call Handler: Maybe if you rang for her and brought the phone in, she might listen?

Caller: Wow. They've really plumbed the gene pool for staff haven't they?

Call Handler: Madam, I'm only trying to help. LifeTime has seasoned counsellors who—

Caller: I'm twenty-fucking-five. Don't call me Madam. Forget it. Just forget it. You obviously can't help. Buh-bye! Have a nice day! [Call ends]

Chapter Thirty-Two

'. . . and finally, we thought we'd close today with a couple of updates on our upcoming His and Hers adventures.' Kev rubbed his hands together. 'I never knew having a good time could be so competitive, eh, Kath?'

Kath gave Kev a winning smile. She'd been sleeping in the guest room at home for a week now. 'He's not wrong there. Now that you've all seen me sweat just a few buckets as I've been put through my paces, tomorrow our Kev will begin two months of being put through his paces by the various Commonwealth teams here in the UK. Tomorrow? We'll see what Kev got up to over the weekend in Blackpool. Who knew it would be volleyball and not dancing that got him back to our old stomping ground?' She reached out and gave his hand a squeeze. He didn't respond.

She'd already seen some of the VT. It had been ruddy hilarious. Kev out in a windstorm on the beach in Blackpool being absolutely slaughtered by a pair of Amazonian goddesses from Northumberland.

'Ho, ho! Yes. What a laugh. And what will you be offering our viewers over the next few weeks, Kath? More "lightbulb moments"?'

Kev had been quite derisive about her 'light a bulb with a bicycle' fundraising segment. She'd put her foot down though. Literally and figuratively. Viewers were viewers. They needed to see what was happening. They needed to know not only how much money was coming in, but what it was going to do. Plus, Halfords had taken out a string of advertisements to run through the latter half of the show. *Boom!*

'Well, Kev. As you know, our crews will be decamping from the studio up to Hadrian's Wall in just two months' time. Before then, I'll be meeting with a few of the lads and lasses from Team GB's cycling teams—'

Kev's eyebrows lifted a fraction. She'd seen his Commonwealth Games and raised him.

'—Also, the team here at *Brand New Day* thought it would be fun to do a few features on some of the folk game enough to come along on the trip of a LifeTime as well as visit some of the people LifeTime helps. With any luck . . . we'll reach that goal of one hundred thousand pounds in no time. A snip to Comic Relief's millions, but as they say . . .' she patted her non-existent back pocket, '. . . every little helps.'

Kev laughed. 'Oh, Kath. I love your positivity.'

No he didn't. He belittled it. Said she was naive and didn't understand how the real world worked. She knew she lived a privileged life, but she was pretty sure that the fact that she still knew the price of a pint of milk kept her a splash more down to earth than a man who lavished gold flake face cream on his mug every night.

'Thanks, love. It's always so reassuring to know you have my back.' She stiffened at his touch.

'Forever and always.'

They each turned to separate cameras for the sign-off then went to their dressing rooms alone.

'Sorry?' Kath swept the towel Fola handed her across her face.

'I have an idea for your show, Katherine.'

Sigh. How did he make her name sound like poetry?

Fola took her towel, then directed her to a mat he'd just laid out in front of the mirrors she'd grown to cherish instead of resent. He held up a finger, then unfurled a fresh towel on it.

'Fola!' She laughed. 'You make me feel like the queen herself!'

'But you are a queen,' Fola said completely straight faced. 'Just as I am a king.'

'Does that make us a couple then?' She met his eyes, felt a flash of something utterly primal, then instantly looked away. How foolish she was being. He was a vital, thirty-something man of the world. With a girlfriend. He had his whole life in front of him.

She was a middle-aged, married, Northern, lite morning television show host who agreed to let her husband throw cream pies at her.

Fola would never fall for a woman like her. He taught sport to inner-city children who might otherwise be chalked up to the ever-increasing knife crime statistics. She'd not noticed her brother was so mired in depression (and whisky) his liver had stopped functioning.

He was humming with life.

She was a woman whose flirtation skills had rusted back in the early 1980s when Kev had taken her under his wing at the Starlight Dance and Cocktail Lounge just off the main drag of Blackpool's Pleasure Beach.

'Did your mother not raise you to think of yourself as a queen, Katherine?'

She laughed. It didn't tinkle with joy. 'No, I'm afraid my mother raised me to get a job, pay for my own dance lessons and move out as soon as possible.'

Fola looked genuinely aggrieved by this, head shaking as he indicated she should lie down so he could help her stretch out. She dutifully lay down, knees up, one ankle crossed over a knee as he knelt before her. 'My mother raised me to think of myself as a king. Not because of wealth or power or arrogance. She had none of those. No. She raised me to think of myself as a king, because she believed everyone should think of themselves as master of their own destiny. In charge of their own life. Their own future.'

Having a man kneel in front of her, stretching out her glutes and hamstrings, as he told her why he thought of himself as a king was quickly becoming one of the most powerful moments Kath had ever experienced.

'That sounds like wise counsel.'

'She is very wise, my mother. Strong enough to be kind. Strong enough to let go.'

'Of what?'

'Pride.' He leant against her leg, his scent flooding round her like a soft breeze carrying wafts of warm bread in its wake. A personal trainer shouldn't smell of carbs, but by god his aroma made her hungry.

He released the pressure then leant back on his heels while she switched her feet around.

Pride, eh?

Was it pride or love that was motivating her to do this ride?

Loss had been the initial kernel of motivation. Then guilt. A need to make up for the fact she'd not noticed her brother's increasingly rapid descent into alcoholism. They'd led separate lives. He was a late-night raconteur at whatever pub sold the cheapest booze. She was an early morning splash of sunshine for a predominantly female audience setting about their 'ordinary lives' in 'ordinary Britain'. Would she have behaved differently if she'd been raised to think of herself as a benevolent queen of her own destiny?

She squelched the thoughts. What's done was done. The only thing she had control of was her future. 'So, what was this idea of yours?'

'The visits to the riders.' Fola leant in again, his chest against her calf.

She scrunched up her face and tried not to breathe in. 'Sorry?'

'In and out, Katherine,' Fola laughed, drawing his hand up and down the line of his chest. 'In and out.'

She blushed.

Good god. Perhaps she would've been wiser going with a female trainer.

He sat back on his heels again. 'Left leg out, right knee across.' He pressed down on her shin and thigh with his hands. 'I think you should come to school with me.'

She gulped in a deep breath, trying to process what he was saying whilst ignoring the wild fireworks display going hell for leather in her more intimate regions as his hand swept from her buttock to her knee.

'How do you mean? School?' she asked in a high-pitched voice she'd not heard from herself before.

'I thought it could be interesting if you did a segment on me and my kids . . .' She smiled. He always called the boys he trained in football 'his kids'. '. . . People might be more generous.'

'Oh?'

'Most of these boys could do with help from a charity like LifeTime.' Fola released his hold and sat back so she could switch legs again.

He wasn't wrong there. They were the sort of schools that totted up the type of statistics people liked to ignore until, of course, the problem had become 'an epidemic'. Knife crime. Drugs. Poverty. Abuse.

She bit back the instinct to say it sounded a bit too 'BBC' for them. That was how the producers dismissed things as too boring, or too intellectual or too earnest for their target audience of 'busy people wanting a bit of lift rather than a reminder of just how miserable real life actually was'. They didn't need reminders. They lived it. *Oh, that's a tad BeeBeeCeeeee, don't you think, Kath? Why don't we drum up something a bit more fun for the viewer, yeah?*

A fire that had nothing to do with how damn sexy Fola made her feel lit within her.

This ride was for her brother. Her sweet, funny, kid brother who died of alcoholism after serving his country as a soldier for ten years of his adult life, left to mire in the stew of his own, screwed up, PTSD-stricken psyche when they not so gently suggested he hang up his machine gun and find something else to do. He didn't have anything else. Know anything else. He was a servant to Crown and country and had been left to wander round the Midlands with no marketable skills beyond being a class-A sniper. There wasn't much call for snipers in the Black Country. Not yet anyway.

She could already hear the 'no, ta, loves' ring out from round the pitch table at the studio.

She tried to picture herself in an ermine robe and a crown. Not a huge one, something modest. What would Queen Kath do if the chance came to her to do something real? Something that might be out of her comfort zone, but could, with a bit of grist, make a genuine difference in one solitary person's life. She was too late to help her brother. But maybe, just maybe, if she put her pride to the side, humbled herself, she could help someone else's.

'Let's do it.'

Chapter Thirty-Three

'Such an unusual name. Raven.' Sue's mother finished off a bit of roast potato then asked, 'Do they actually have ravens in Pakistan?'

It was all Sue could do not to crawl under Katie's immaculately laid French Oak slab dining room table. What was her family doing? Acting like they'd never spoken to someone of colour before? Mortifying. And, frankly, surprising. Raven was every bit as English as Sue was. Apart from the grandparents who'd come from India, of course, but Raven was a walking, talking, English person. A very brave one, too. She didn't know if she would've agreed to come along to a Sunday lunch at a house full of people she'd never met before. If the roles had been reversed, Sue probably would've hidden in her room and read magazines or snuck downstairs even though she'd been told she had free run of the place and watched a bit of Sunday afternoon telly only to sneak back up before anyone got home. Gary had always been the more social of the two of them.

Perhaps, she was missing her own family and thought being at Sunday lunch would be nice. Or, more likely, Raven didn't like being in the house on her own. What with . . . things.

Either way, Sue was ever so pleased she'd agreed to come. This was her first proper Sunday lunch without Gary beside her to cushion the effects of two to three hours in close proximity with her family.

'It's India, actually. My ethnic heritage is Indian.'

'Oh,' her mother said as if she'd just been told there was an entirely new continent out there she hadn't realised existed. 'So do they have ravens? The Indians?'

Her mother really wasn't letting this go.

'Yes, just like England. But, it's a nickname really. My given name is Sunita.'

Her mother chewed on that for a bit then gave the flat-lipped nod. 'I can see why you went for something a bit more conventional in the end.'

What? Sue and Raven shot one another confused looks. How had Raven gone from being at the unusual end of the name spectrum to conventional? Sue lifted her cloth serviette to her mouth. Gaz would've had a field day with this.

'The Yorkshire puds are first class today, Katie,' Sue's father said.

'Oh, good!' Katie enthused, clearly pleased to have the spotlight back on her. 'I tried out a new recipe today. It called for an extra egg white and it seems to have done just the trick.'

They all nodded and mmm'd and moved their forks and knives along their plates to show their appreciation for all of Katie's efforts. The children, who had been slightly less appreciative, had already disappeared into their rooms after Katie had deemed them impossible to contend with. *Generation Alpha*, she'd intoned as she'd watched them tear up the staircase. *It needs a book writing*. Zac had a 'gaming date' as play dates were apparently too babyish and Jayden said she had a book she wanted to finish but Sue knew she was watching *Gilmore Girls* under her duvet. (Katie didn't 'agree' with *Gilmore Girls*. Something about false expectations and too much caffeine that seemed slightly at odds with her son's freedom to destroy things at will in his video games, but Sue wasn't a parent and, as such, her opinions were generally dismissed.)

After they'd all refused second helpings of Katie's (Marks & Spencer's) lemon tart and Dean had fussed about triple checking no one wanted a coffee or a brandy, Katie did a little dingdingding on her glass and said, 'Announcement time!' She rose and beamed at them all and then, quite specifically, at Sue.

'Suey . . .' she began. 'Dear, sweet, kind, Suey who has been through *soverymuch* these past few weeks. We want you to know, Dean and I . . .' she reached out and gave his shoulder a little fingertip squeeze, '. . . we want you to know that you have our support one hundred per cent.'

Sue's chin quirked to the side like a curious puppy. Support? The last she'd checked they were looking for a peculiar variation on indentured servitude from her.

Katie gave a trill of a laugh. 'Of course, when we – when *I* – took the step to make our offer to you to look after the children *for pay*, we hadn't realised you'd already gone and got yourself a flatmate. *Welcome*, Raven.' Katie pressed a flat hand to her equally flat bosom. '*Welcome* to our home. We have so enjoyed having you as our guest today, but I have to admit we were surprised to hear about you. Nothing to worry about. It only took a tiny bit of the helium out of our well-filled balloon.' She pinched a soupçon of air between her fingers, then looked at Dean and shook her head with a frozen smile that said, *this family of yours simply doesn't know how to stick to a well-laid plan, does it?*

'Aaaaanyway . . .' Katie once again fixed her glow of largesse back on Sue. 'Enough wittering. What Dean and I were thinking, was that, with everything that must be going on with you and the stages of grief still very much in the early phases, we thought perhaps I was a bit quick off the mark to ask you about looking after the kids full-time. Well. Part-time, given that you'd still be at the call centre, but, whatever spin you put on it, you've been a bit hesitant in taking up our offer. I thought you'd pounce on it, but I guess it shows you there's always room in a friendship for mystery. As such, we sat down with our business heads on . . . our recruitment heads . . .' She gave a little helpless shrug as if she and Dean simply couldn't help it, they were born to recruit! 'After a serious round of brainstorming, we decided you might need a bit of a sweetener. Like your mum did.'

Sue threw her mother a confused look. What were they talking about? Katie's mum had been paid to look after the children and Bev had only looked after Jayden and Zac for the Disneyworld trip. There had been quite a bit of mention of Duty Free gin in the lead-up to that trip. Was that what they were suggesting? Giving her some gin to look after their children?? In fact, now that Sue thought of it, the last time the topic had come up, Bev had said she'd rather gnaw her arm off than revisit the 'gory' days of parenting.

'As such,' Katie's smile grew ever brighter, 'we were wondering if you would like to join us and the children for a week in the Canaries!' She sang 'The Canaries' in the way one might sing 'a million pounds'. Sue waited. Katie had a way of putting forward propositions then following them up with the inevitable small print. 'You'll be sharing bunks with Jayden in case she has one of those nightmares she's prone to and Zac'll get the single. There'd only be a night or two when Dean and I would be going out alone and the children would need someone, you know, you, to look after them. Other than that . . . it's a free holiday! We've booked the first week of May. Bought and paid for and just waiting for you to say yes! What do you think Sue?' She gave her shoulders a dramatic little shimmy. 'Have we put the right amount of icing on a pretty nice cake?'

Of all the things Sue disliked, having the spotlight on her was definitely one of them. Particularly when she felt as though someone had already made the decision on her behalf. It was the way her life worked. Perhaps more so now that she didn't have her husband beside her to make up something that would get her out of it. Her future rolled out before her minus the red carpet. She would say yes. Katie and Dean would have an underpaid nanny for life. Raven would most likely move out, because she'd never be home and who wanted to be home alone in a house where a man whose wife didn't know him well enough to prevent his suicide had once lived?

Raven cleared her throat and gave Sue a little nudge. 'Ummm . . . isn't that the week of the cycle ride?'

Sue frowned.

'The charity ride we're going to do?'

'You going on a bike ride, Suey?' Dean looked genuinely interested. 'Cool. What's the charity?' He popped a grape in his mouth, not noticing the daggers Katie was throwing in his direction.

'LifeTime.' She threw a panicked look at Raven who nodded encouragingly. 'It's a mental health charity.'

Raven picked up the baton. 'It's going along Hadrian's Wall. Coast to coast.'

Sue didn't have a clue why she was going along with this. Desperation, she supposed. She had been shoring up her resources to try and find a way to politely tell Flo (and Raven if she'd been waiting for Sue to say something first) that doing the ride really wouldn't be her cup of tea. Today? It felt like a lifeline. A chance to show her family she was capable of making decisions on her own and putting herself on a new course in life. She had to be, really, didn't she? Gary was never ever coming to Sunday lunch with her again.

Bev made a couple of little indecipherable noises then suddenly, 'Is that the one Kath off the telly is doing in memory of that deadbeat brother of hers?'

'He wasn't a deadbeat, love,' Katie's father gently corrected. 'He were a soldier for over ten years. Served his country, he did.'

'Found himself at the bottom of a bottle fairly sharpish if the *Mail* is anything to go by.'

Martin shook his head and gave the table a patpatpat before saying firmly, 'We can't fault him for coming back with a screw or two loose with all of the muck he must've seen.'

Bev made another noise and finished off the rest of her Cabernet.

'Sounds fun, Suey. Go for it!'

Katie glared at Dean. 'Wouldn't coming to the Canaries for a nice relaxing holiday with her family be more fun?'

'Maybe Sue doesn't want to come on a nice relaxing holiday with her family.'

Sue's eyes widened. Was Dean disagreeing with Katie? In front of everyone?

'C'mon, love.' He filled up Katie's wine glass even though her lips were already purple with the cheeky Cab Sav they'd opened after realising they had 'company' rather than plain old family for lunch. 'Maybe we're bulldozing her. We don't want to push you, Suey. It's your decision to make. We were just trying to think outside the box. Let you know we're here for you.' He said this whilst rising, indicating his wife should sit down then murmuring to her that he'd collect the dishes and something Sue couldn't quite make out about the Nordic au pair she'd always talked about wanting.

Gosh.

Katie's two front teeth rested atop of her bottom lip, poised for action, as she worked out how to respond.

Sue rose and also started picking up plates and cutlery.

'I'd support you, Suey,' Sue's father said. 'What do you need? A tenner? Twenty? I could put one of those sheets up down at the council if you like. Bev, how about you talk to the folk down at Asda's and see if—'

Sue's mother shut him down with a look that, shockingly, didn't kill, then hoinked her chair round so she was angled, like a lady in waiting, towards Katie.

'Not to impose, Katie, but I do hate waste and if there's a free ticket going . . .' she cast her eyes down to her hands then back up at Katie, 'I'm always willing to help. I've never been to the Canaries.' She flicked a quick glance at Sue that weirdly translated as, *I've got this*. Not strictly a show of support, but going to the Canaries hadn't exactly been an offer of a free holiday, either, so . . . Sue let natural selection take its course. Granny Nanny was all over this.

Katie ignored them, sending twitchy little signals to Dean to *intervene*. It appeared her well-laid plans were being *kyboshed* by a Bev-shaped spanner. Hmmm. Perhaps Granny Nanny hadn't gone down quite as well as expected in Florida.

Out of the corner of her eye, Sue caught Raven fastidiously finishing the remains of her meal, presumably trying to avoid the awkwardness of it all— No! Raven was covering her mouth with her serviette (cloth, because Katie didn't 'believe' in paper) trying her best not to laugh. And then, just like that, Sue saw the funny side of it all.

The most genuine smile Sue had had in weeks bloomed upon her lips.

Gary would've *loved* this.

She could picture him perfectly, clutching his stomach as he tried and failed and tried again to tell the lads down the pub how Katie's Perfect Plan was left in ruins by Raven and Granny Nanny.

'Well, then.' Dean clapped his hands together. 'That's settled that, then. Mum, you'll be coming to the Canaries and Suey will be on her cycle ride. And while we're at it, were you actually interested in looking after the children after school, Suey, or did you have other plans?'

'Oh, I—' Sue felt the daggers Katie was throwing her way, but all of a sudden, with her mother, father, brother and now Raven having offered these wonderful little gestures of support – her dead husband winking at her from who knew where . . . heaven? – she felt as though she could finally say what she should've said years ago when 'a little favour' turned into something quite different. 'I have other plans actually. If that's okay.'

'Course it is,' Dean said before Katie could say otherwise.

'Now that that's sorted,' Sue's mother was swiftly moving on, 'Katie, if there's any more of that lemon tart left . . .'

Chapter Thirty-Four

'Sometimes I worry you love that dog more than you love me,' Stu laughed, shuffling out of his slippers and folding back a triangle of bedding, as Flo gave her customary evening cuddle to Captain George before he curled up on his mammoth cushion on her side of the bed.

For the first time in her life, Flo lied to her husband.

'Course not, darling. You're my number one.'

For whatever reason, she knew it wasn't true. The dog was. Stu was up there, of course. In the top two. Top four if she counted the children, but really they were their own people now and the closeness so many women spoke of with their adult children simply didn't exist between her and her own offspring. Captain George, though. Captain George wasn't just any old Irish wolfhound. He was special. He played up a loyalty to Stu when she was out, but Flo knew he really loved her most. Didn't judge. Didn't discourage. Didn't force her to sit through another carvery luncheon down the club with the Springfields and the Joneses who were unable to discuss anything beyond their upcoming cruises.

George nuzzled into her neck as if acknowledging the unspoken truth. They were kindred spirits. She'd throw herself in front of a bus for him. A train. Anything really, if it meant prolonging his life. Captain George never said no. Never urged caution. He was a champion of 'yes, yes, yes.'

Stu tapped his wrist, then pointed at Flo's own which was happily weighted with her bells-and-whistles exercise watch.

'How're you going to work in your training with your work schedule? It's an eight to four you're on tomorrow isn't it?' Stu liked to memorise the weekly rota she taped to the fridge. 'You can't head off to the hills of Northumberland with nothing but a handful of dog walks as training.'

Ah. Yes.

She had yet to explain about the work thing. Take the rota down. Flo looked Captain George in the eye then made another split-second decision. 'Oh, it'll all work out. I'll ride in my lunch break. Anyway. As I understand it, there are quite a few flat bits. Along the river and such.'

Stu quirked an eyebrow.

Captain George blinked.

What was this about? Lying to Stu as easily as she made a sandwich. She hadn't even so much as googled the route. Didn't know a thing about it other than that it was up North. A zip of frisson whipped through her nervous system. Who cared? A little white lie wasn't going to make a difference to the foundation of their marriage. She was grabbing life by the horns. Taking control of her future instead of resigning herself to the inevitable.

Stu slipped off his watch and set it on the left-hand side of the lacquerware tray she'd bought him for their twenty-third wedding anniversary (Tokyo-Singapore-London). 'And you're happy with the bicycle you chose?'

'Love it.' She hated it. Was already trying to figure out how to return it, but that lad down at Halfords hadn't half riled her. (Why hadn't she gone local??) When he wasn't flirting with the poor uninterested girl in auto parts, he kept directing her towards those ridiculous adult trikes and electric bicycles. Said they might be more suitable.

Suitable? How on earth did he know what was suitable? He'd

barely spent a quarter of a century on earth! She wasn't a doddery old woman. She was a vital, mostly fit, seventy-two-year-old woman. A vital, mostly fit, seventy-two-year-old woman who refused to be jammed into a demographic. So she'd asked him which of the bikes would be best suited to the Tour de France then bought it. It had been easy enough to pop into the back of the Land Rover, anyway. Light as a feather.

'And you'll set me up with a few meals before you go? Leave instructions and everything?'

'Course, love.' She gave Captain George a look.

Honestly. Her husband, a man capable of flying hundreds of people in an over-sized sardine can across the world's oceans, no longer seemed able to open a tin of soup for himself. He didn't have Alzheimer's. Or any other affliction as far as she knew. He had . . . retirementitis. A slow and invasive erosion of everything that had made him the man she had once ached to marry.

She glanced across at him, all tucked in for the night, cracking open his book to read the solitary chapter he afforded himself before turning in. It would take five to ten minutes and then off went the light, down went Stu's head and he'd be asleep before you could count down from ten. Eight hours later, he'd wake up. The same triangle of bedding he'd just smoothed into place would be folded back so that he could slip his feet into the corduroy slippers he'd wear into the pre-dawn light of yet another day of exactly the same.

Well screw that.

Stu was going to have to up his game. Go to battle with Campbell's cream of tomato. Drive to the shops himself for that matter. Tactics overtook frustration. He could look at feeding himself for a week as a real-life puzzle. A way of keeping his wits intact beyond the morning paper. She loved Stu. Hated watching him disappear into the soft, doughy recesses of pensionville. She wouldn't let him go downhill. Not on her watch. And she wasn't going down without a fight. Bums to Rachel Woolly and her 'not in the best interest to go off script.' This was about lives! The precious commodity of time and how it was spent. The bodies they inhabited and making the most of them. There wasn't a *script* that worked for each and every human. No tried and true prescription for happiness and good health. Everyone was different and, as such, everyone had a different path to follow. Even her and Stu. It didn't mean their love was diminished. Or that it would falter because of a white lie or two. It meant change. And in this case, change was a good thing.

She'd tell him in the morning. About the job. About having to change bicycles. About spreading her arms wide open to whatever the next twenty or so years of their lives had in store.

The time limit hit her like a wrecking ball.

Twenty years if she was lucky. She'd long since whizzed past both of her parents' lifetimes. Her mum passed at fifty-eight (heart attack). Her father at sixty-one (snap). Neither of them had ever set foot outside of England unless you counted an accidental diversion into Wales that lasted, at most, a tense half hour, during which her father executed an impressive U-turn in the middle of a flock of sheep.

George rested his furry chin on her shoulder.

The poor old chap had outlived his 'sell by' date, too. A ripe old ten and a half. Positively ancient for a Wolfhound.

A wash of looming grief doused the flames of excitement. She and Captain George were living on borrowed time. Not Stu, though. His parents had both lived well into their nineties. Died within days of one another, peacefully, in their sleep. Stu had years of puzzle pages ahead of him. Decades.

She gave George a final kiss then climbed into bed, determined to wake up without worrying about when she was going to die. She'd pop into the call centre tomorrow on the way to Halfords. Invent an excuse about trying to find a misplaced jumper in lost property. Accidentally on purpose arrive at break time and have an inspiring chat with Raven and Sue, to ensure they would join her. (Yes, she'd taken a picture of the schedule before she'd left so she knew when they were on next. Mischievous, she knew, but she wasn't going to let Rachel Woolly get one over her.) Once they were on board, she'd pop into that lovely little shop down the village and get herself a proper bicycle and any other accoutrements she might need. She gave Stu a pat on the shoulder then turned off her bedside lamp. She'd not sleep for a while yet, but she had too much to think about to read. Ready or not, Flo was going to ride her bicycle across the country.

Incident No: 38928901
Time of Call: 02:43
Call Handler: SUE YOUNG

Call Handler: You're through to the NHS 111 service, my name's Sue and I'm a health advisor. Are you calling about yourself or someone else?

Caller: I just . . . I was wondering if you were free for a minute?

Call Handler: May I have your name please?

Caller: My name's Becky.

Call Handler: Hello, Becky. My name's Sue. Can you tell me why you're calling tonight?

Caller: Oh, god, I . . .

Call Handler: Are you hurt, Becky?

Caller: No. Not unless you count loneliness.

Call Handler: Oh, well, I – you know we do, Becky. We *do* count loneliness.

Caller: You do? Can you send a doctor?

Call Handler: Are you registered with a local GP?

Caller: Yes. [Muffled swearing] Forget it. You're the same as everyone else. A jobsworth. Don't worry. You won't be able to do anything. Just like the rest of them.

Call Handler: No, Becky, wait. Let's talk for a minute.

Caller: What?

Call Handler: I mean, I can recommend some numbers, where there will be trained people who can talk . . .

Caller: [Bitter laugh] Like I said. You're a jobsworth. What makes you think ringing anyone else will make a difference?

Call Handler: It could. You don't know until you try . . .

Caller: I've tried it all love, believe me. And just so we're clear? I was trying to score. Not to talk. So well done for not succumbing to the ploys of your local crack addict.

Call Handler: I – sorry – hello? Has anyone ever—? She was trying to get drugs. Do you think she meant to ring someone else? Ooop—

Chapter Thirty-Five

Kath would never admit it, but she was absolutely terrified.

'Thirty seconds.'

Her producer gave her a grim nod. Things were not going according to plan.

Kath mouthed 'ready?' to Fola.

He nodded. This meant as much, if not more, to him as it did to her. 'Alright, lads.' His deep voice rang out over the higher pitches of his young football team. 'Everybody gather round and zip it until you're asked a question, yeah?' Astonishingly, the dozen or so jumble of twelve-year-old boys did exactly as they were told. The thirty or so who'd gathered to watch proceedings did not.

Through her earpiece, Kath heard Kev wrapping up his piece on keeping your figure on an all-you-can-eat cruise. 'Note to self . . . avoid the deep-fried Mars bars!' Kev har-har-har'ed, no doubt sharing a fist bump with the perky fitness trainer sitting in her spot on the couch. His voice turned serious. 'But tell me, Kylie. If that dessert bar *is* too tempting to resist, what can our viewers do to make sure they fit into their bikini the next morning by the pool? I know I like to have my cake and be poolside ready, too.'

Oh, good grief. He was flirting. You give a man an inch . . .

Kev loved days like this. Being on his own in the studio. Said it made him feel like the all-powerful Oz. So much so, it sometimes made her wonder why he hadn't tried to wheedle her into retirement rather than plastic surgery. Get someone young and perky like Holly Willoughby to bounce around the studio and give the set that extra zing he was after.

Something in her hardened.

He wanted zing?

She'd give him zing.

'Ten seconds and we're ready for you, Kath.'

It suddenly struck her as odd that Kev had agreed to this segment so easily. It wasn't in the *Brand New Day* remit at all. Normally he would've savaged it at the pitch meeting and yet, when she'd put it forward a few days back, he hadn't put up the slightest bit of a fight.

Kev needed her. That was why. Needed her for the all-important female demographic. The *married* female demographic. Besides, there was no one else idiotic enough to put up with his self-aggrandising, sexist shenanigans but her. She popped on her camera-ready smile.

The producer cued her that they were five seconds out.

'Everyone ready?' She beamed at the camera crew, most of whom had been giving her the evils all morning. A playing field at one of Birmingham's poorest schools wasn't really their thing. She could see where they were coming from. Usually she was over the moon when they attracted a crowd. Today? Not so much.

Fola was trying his best to get the lads to be as quiet as the boys on his team were, but in a matter of seconds he would have the full glare of the *BND* cameras on him as well. Cuffing someone round the ear, if that was his tactic, wasn't really going to curry favour with the viewers.

'Miss! Do you want see my penis?'

'Miss! Miss! Are you going to make me famous, Miss?'

'And now that we're all safe in the knowledge that a couple of sexy cha-cha-chas will burn off that too-good-to-resist banoffee pie—'

Kev's voice needled through her earpiece and constricted round her heart.

'Miss! Are you giving away prizes? I've got no money, Miss. You look minted!'

'. . . let's join our Kath who's gone out into the elements today to drum up some support for her cycle ride. Hello, darling. How is it out there amongst Britain's finest?'

A particularly gritty looking pre-teen began marching in front of the assembled footballers throwing his arm out Hitler style whilst singing 'God Save The Queen'.

Fola had him up and out of there in seconds (scruff of the neck), but not before the cameras had turned red and they were live on air.

The ease with which the story had been approved suddenly made sense.

This was Kev throwing her to the wolves. Watching her drown in her own sea of good intentions.

Kev: One

Kath: Nil

Right then, darling. Bring it on. The scoreboard was about to change.

Incident No: 120912
Time of Call: 11:42
Call Handler: SUNITA 'RAVEN' CHAKRABARTI

Call Handler: You're through to the NHS 111 service, my name's Raven and I'm a health advisor. Are you calling about yourself or someone else?

Caller: I'm calling for myself.

Call Handler: May I have your name please?

Caller: I'd prefer not to.

Call Handler: Umm, okay. It does make it a bit easier if I know your name.

Caller: It's too bleeding embarrassing, alright? Can you handle that? That I feel embarrassed. That it took all my bloody courage to call you and tell you that I've effed up a perfectly gorgeous vagina?

Call Handler: I'm sorry, I – are you calling for yourself?

Caller: No, sorry. I just— [Muted swearing and female voice] I put popping candy up it.

Call Handler: Up . . . ???

Caller: Up her vagina. We were having sex and I thought I'd, you know, spice things up, so I went down on her with a load of popping candy on my tongue and . . . what's that, love? Sorry. She wants me to tell you it's burning with volcanic heat and itching like the world's worst yeast infection. She can't think straight. Can you send a doctor out please? The GP's not open and she says she can't make it to A&E. She's not in a good way.

Call Handler: Could I have her name please?

Caller: No.

Call Handler: I'm afraid I need her name, sir.

Caller: You didn't need mine.

Call Handler: I was trying to get yours, but you started telling me what was wrong with your wife's—

Caller: She's not my bleeding wife, alright? That's why we need the doctor here. Can you understand that? I don't need the fuss of an ambulance. She's refusing to let me take her to the A&E. She's in massive pain, needs a doctor and wants it kept quiet, so could you please just make it happen so I can end this whole sordid— no, love. Not you. You're not sordid. You're— wait! Wait!!! Stephanie, love! I wasn't saying you were sordid! [Call ends]

Chapter Thirty-Six

'It's not like it'll go away if I don't look.' Sue sent Raven a pleading look, willing her to magic life back to the way it had once been. Predictable. Safe.

Raven tilted her head to the side, saying nothing and everything with the small gesture. *You need to confront your reality.*

Which was fair enough. They'd got themselves all psyched up to go bicycle shopping (Halfords, just to get an idea) when Sue remembered she didn't have any money.

'What if it's all invoices?' Raven said after taking a sip of tea. 'Payments owing to you . . . and Gary,' she added. 'That box was pretty full.'

'It could be all bills.'

'There's really only one way to find out.' Raven pointed her finger up at the ceiling. 'I'll do it with you.' She gave her phone a jiggle. 'Easy as one-two-three to download a bookkeeping app.'

Raven was right. Whatever was in those boxes needed looking at. And in all honesty, it would be much, much easier with a friend.

Before she could change her mind, Sue put down her cup of tea and headed for the stairs.

Unpaid. Unpaid. Unpaid and . . . what was . . . hmmm . . . half an invoice with a note to find a receipt for a U-bend. All of it in Gary's excellent penmanship. Sue's heart skipped a beat as her eyes lit on the bottom of yet another tea-mug stained invoice. There was a note to pick up some chicken balls with hot and sour sauce and a fried rice with a heart next to it. Sue felt her heart break as she went back in time to remember the day. They only had chicken balls and sweet and sour sauce when Sue wasn't feeling well. Her 'pick-me-up takeaway', Gary called it.

She ran her finger along the edge of the paper. The date on the invoice was two years old. And just like that, it came to her. Mostly because she didn't get sick that often, but also because of how Gary had made her laugh and laugh, so much so, some fried rice had come out of her nose.

She hadn't been working at the call centre yet. She'd been at a handbag boutique in Bicester Village after her receptionist's job at a dental office had been taken over by the dentist's wife. Her Bicester boss had been a horrid woman. A bully really. Victoria Langham-Smoots. A woman who could not have stuffed more plums in her mouth if she'd tried, Gary used to say. Plummy and impatient. On this particular day, Victoria had sent Sue home when she'd appeared for work red-eyed and pink-nosed with a seasonal cold she'd picked up from her niece and nephew. Victoria had denied her entry to the shop, announcing loudly that she didn't want someone 'filled with contagion infecting the products', as if the handbags had been vulnerable Aboriginals unable to resist chicken pox or measles. Gary had been furious. Threatened to drive across, leaving a power shower job half done to have a word, but Sue had begged him not to (she did hate a fuss) and later that day, Victoria had rung to say she'd found someone more invested in the business and not to worry about coming in again. That night Gary had brought her a pick-me-up takeaway.

She put the paper back in the box and closed her eyes.

This was too much. A bit like going through their wedding photos, but worse, because all of this paperwork, this history, was something they hadn't shared.

'You alright?' Raven asked.

'Sorry, I just—' She shook her head at the piles of paperwork, then gave Raven what she hoped was a grateful smile. 'You're so kind to do this with me.'

'Not a problem,' said Raven, making a pointy gesture at the invoice Sue had just set down. She handed it across, Raven squinted at it, scanned the top of it with her phone, then put it in a different pile.

No more pick-me-up takeaway nights for Sue.

'Sue?' Raven awkwardly crossed her legs into a sort of yogi position. 'Do you want to take a break? Pop the telly on or something?'

'Oh, no. Not at all. Unless you want to. Whatever you want is perfect, but I'm fine. This is fine. It's all fine.' Sue was talking blithering nonsense, of course. She'd actually been feeling as if cement was being poured through her body. Suffocation by insight.

'Would you be happier if your brother was helping you with all of this?'

'What? Dean? No, why would I want Dean to help me?'

'Err . . . because he's an accountant?'

Yes, that was true, but Dean was also married to Katie and Sue wasn't ready for Katie to know about this. Or, god forbid, her mum. *It'll all end in tears, Suey. All end in tears . . .*

Sue bumbled around for an explanation that touched on some sort of truth, 'I mean, you're right in a way. Dean was an accountant, but now he's in accountancy *recruitment*, so . . . this probably isn't his thing.'

Raven chewed on her lip. 'He might have a better idea of what to do. Like, how to get everyone to pay up, or resubmit or something. I don't know if you can invoice for work that's been done years back.'

'Oh, no,' Sue protested. 'You're doing a brilliant job. I never knew you could do so much on a little app.' She was amazed, actually. Ten seconds to find the app, five to download it and off they'd gone. What a difference a clued-in teenager makes.

They'd started out with the tables turned, of course. Sue setting the first box down and giving it a firm look. But when her hand had begun shaking as she lifted the very first invoice written in Gary's handwriting, Raven had taken the lead. Two evenings they'd been at it, now. Absorbing, untangling, filing, trying their best to divine what on earth had been going through her Gary's mind, not just on that last day, but over the last three years. It was how far back the paperwork went. To just about the point where his father had passed.

That had definitely been a rough patch. Reg had been a brilliant father-in-law, but he'd never had a good run of things. Parents gone too early. Straight to work at fifteen. Married young. Divorced young. Gary had moved in with him after his mother had swanned off to Australia with a nouvelle cuisine chef she'd met at Bicester Village back when it first opened. All this and yet Reg, much like his son, had always been one of those chipper chappies. Whistling while he worked. Washing up the mugs from the endless cups of tea his customers made him. Proudly telling everyone he met that his boy was going to take over the business he'd built for him. He'd had such a struggle with his cancer in the end. His second wife, Nadine, falling to bits as he, too, fell to bits. His body betraying him in cruel ways. He'd begged them in the end. Begged Gary and Sue to bring him to the Netherlands or Switzerland. Wherever they could make it all stop. The hospice people had taken over then. It was why Gary had done the 10k for them not even two days after the funeral. He hadn't trained at all. Just signed up and ran. They couldn't have done it without them, those lovely women from the hospice. Managing the physical pain against the emotional.

Anyway.

Sue wasn't ready for her family to know that managing the finances for Young & Son's Plumbing had been quite the problem. Up until he'd died, Reg had always done it, but Sue had presumed they'd done some sort of handover across the years. She'd been sure of it, in fact. The morning her Gary had knelt by his dad's bed tearfully swearing he'd make Young and Son's the best damn plumbing business Britain had ever seen, or Oxfordshire at least, had been a powerful one.

Unfortunately, it appeared Gary hadn't had much of a way with numbers. When they first started going through the paperwork, Raven had gently asked if he had suffered from dyslexia. Sue had said no, dyslexia wasn't really something children had when they were young. Not at their school anyway. They just got on with it. Failed school or passed it. Went to work if it had been the former. Went to college if it had been the latter and then went to work. Indoors, usually. But Gary's future had been laid out for him. He was a born plumber. End of.

Sue watched as Raven tucked a blue carbon sheet under the next invoice and re-totted up yet another set of Gary's mismatched numbers before putting the real figures into the app. (The dyslexia diagnosis was seeming more and more likely if Sue was being honest.)

She caught herself smiling at the book. Then frowning. The duplicate invoice booklet was one of a dozen or so that had a) clearly lived in the footwell of Gary's work van and b) been bought back when Reg ran the business.

Sue remembered Reg crowing about bulk buying them when the stationer on the high street went out of business some . . . gosh . . . was it ten years back? Reg had always loved a bargain. When they'd lost him three years ago it had been a blow and a release. A blow because he'd truly been loved. A release because, though he'd never put words to it, her Gary had never felt a proper man with his father 'running the show' and Reg was not the type to retire. Gary'd never been grumbly about it, but Sue knew he had been chomping at the bit to make his own mark in the world. Prove her parents wrong. Get them to finally treat him with the same respect as they did 'our Katie'.

Had Gary taken his life because the man he'd hoped to be and the man he'd turned out to be hadn't matched? It surely, surely couldn't have been over a bit of ketchup.

Sue shoved the thought straight back into the increasingly full cupboard of questions she lacked the fortitude to ask and gave her shoulders a little shake. Today was about facts and figures. Not speculation.

Raven readjusted her reading specs, pushed her lips forward in a dark lippy moue and stuffed a pencil in her messy topknot. She was looking very official. More steampunk than the goth look she tended to favour. Perhaps it was the absence of eyeshadow. She'd gone for simple eyeliner with flicks at the corners today. The look leant her an added maturity. It was that or the businesslike manner with which she'd approached their task. Wise beyond her nineteen years. Her parents must be so very proud of her.

She held her phone over the recalculated invoice, waited until it had been scanned then raised her eyebrows. 'That's over twenty grand he's owed so far.'

The breath left Sue's body.

'And how much do we owe the vendors?'

Vendors. She'd never used that word before yesterday afternoon. Raven was full of them. Vendors, payees, accounts receivable, accounts owing. Learnt them all at her mother's elbow, she said. Helping at the pharmacy since she was young. The most Sue's mother had taught her was that marriage was nothing more than a disappointment unless, of course, you were ambitious like Katie and Dean.

Raven thumbed across a couple of pages on her phone. 'About four grand. You're owed about twenty going three or four years back if you include the bills from when your father-in-law got sick. And you owe about four which, if everyone pays . . . would leave you with sixteen. There's the VAT returns to do as well if he was VAT registered. Do you know if he was?'

Sue shook her head. 'Why would he have needed that?' She'd never really talked to him about the nuts and bolts of his business. Only the funny stories, really. Like the time he'd saved a squirrel blocking someone's toilet. They'd giggled about that for ages. The smile faded from her lips as she began to tune back into what Raven was saying.

'. . . although it's not obligatory if it's under, you have to be VAT registered if you earn over eighty-five thousand—' She stopped when she saw Sue's face crumple. Gary definitely wouldn't have needed to register for VAT.

All of which meant, if everyone paid up, Sue would have sixteen thousand pounds.

And then a few more pieces shifted into place.

Sixteen thousand pounds was what their joint savings had been. An account they'd been scraping together for their retirement or a house upgrade (whichever came first). He must've been using it to pay off the bills to protect her from the fact he was falling behind on the paperwork and then when that had run out and the money owing began building up . . .

Sue tried swallowing against the lump in her throat but couldn't. Her poor, lovely, kind, sweet Gary. Not wanting her to worry.

Snippets of conversations they'd had over the years came back to her as, systematically, Sue and Raven got back to work sorting through the piles of paperwork

'*GarBear?*' She used to call him GarBear when he was in a grump about something. Her own little grizzly. '*What's all of the swearing for up there? Anything I can help with?*'

'*No, Suey. You're all right. Let's pop out for a film shall we? Or a drink down The Oak? I've done more than enough scribbling for one night.*'

'*Gaz?*' He was Gaz if she was concerned but didn't want him to know. '*Everything alright? Need a cuppa?*'

'*Right as rain. I might head down to the pub and watch the footie with the lads. Finish this lot of paperwork up after. That alright?*'

She shivered as her skin remembered the touch of his calloused hands after he'd slide down the banister and pull her into a hug. No. *No.* She wasn't ready for this. She wasn't ready at all.

'Why don't we pop the telly on and watch something silly, eh? *Celebrity Bake Off's* on.' Sue loved *Bake Off*. It was so gentle and sweet. People getting into a sweat over their mille feuille. It was adorable.

'But – we've barely started,' Raven pointed at the stacks of papers Sue had refused to let her decant from the boxes.

'That's enough for today,' Sue said, suddenly desperately wishing they'd left the boxes exactly where they were. 'You know,' she said, flicking on the telly even though Raven didn't seem keen. 'Now that we're getting such a large amount of money, why don't you call that friend of yours? Dylan, was it? The one who can get the deal on the bikes. The least I could do after all of this is get your bicycle. It's March already and if we're going to support Flo, we've got to get training.'

'Ummm . . .' Raven looked down at the notepad she'd been using to make notes in and began sketching something out with one of her coloured pencils as a flush crept onto her cheeks. 'Sue,' she said, eyes still glued to her notebook. 'You know you have to ask people for the money, right? That it won't just . . . you know . . . go into your bank account.'

Sue laughed a silly, girlish laugh. 'Course I do!' She laughed again, hoping it would mask the terror consuming her. Grow a spine or face bankruptcy. The choice was hers. 'Course I do.'

Raven ripped the piece of paper out of her notebook and handed it to Sue.

'Oh,' Sue said, then sobbed, 'A flower. No one's ever given me flowers before except— Thank you, Raven. It's a beautiful rose. I don't think I've ever seen one this colour.'

'Coral,' said Raven.

'Any particular reason you chose it?' It really was quite an extraordinary rendition of a rose. Complete with dew drops. She leant down towards the paper, fully expecting to smell it.

Raven shrugged, still unable to meet Sue's eye. 'It stands for a couple of things. Friendship . . .' her eyes lifted to meet Sue's. 'And sympathy.'

'Oh. I see,' said Sue, bursts of joy and pain colliding in her heart. Then she did what she always did when she had absolutely no idea how she'd get through another day. Turned, walked into the kitchen, and popped on the kettle.

Chapter Thirty-Seven

'For Christ's *sake*, Mother. How bloody long is this ride meant to be?'

'Not long, darling. Just a couple more miles.' Flo ground her legs round again, discreetly shifting the cycle up a gear. When would this interminable ride ever end?

'I think we should turn around. This is too long for the children and Captain George will be exhausted by now.'

'Nonsense! The children are loving it,' Flo protested. 'And George has plenty of life in him yet, don't you, Captain?' She gave him a smile then made a train noise for a reason she couldn't entirely fathom, but matter and mind were having a bit of a tug of war for supremacy at the moment.

As pleasant as it was to see her daughter and grandchildren, Flo wished Stu hadn't greased up everyone's old bikes and sent them all out together. She'd done three rather long miles along the canal yesterday as a trial run on her *new* new bike and was feeling it. Not that she'd admit as much, but her bum was hurting far more than she'd anticipated and if she wasn't mistaken her knees had made a rather peculiar crunching noise when she'd run upstairs to fetch a hot water bottle for seven-year-old Lily who had a cold which she would, no doubt, transfer to Stu, who didn't seem to be able to resist his grandchildren's various contagions in even the best of scenarios – i.e. absence.

'Is this bicycle working out well, then?' Jennifer grunted as they rode up a rise that looked easy until they were peddling up it. 'Dad told me about the racing bike debacle.'

'He called it a debacle, did he?' Flo tried and failed to avoid using her snippy voice. Was she not allowed to make mistakes now? She didn't want to bring up the calamity that had been the handsfree scooter tour in Cancun, but he could be assured she would if cornered about this.

Jennifer made one of those noises indicating there would've been no need to call it a debacle, if it hadn't been. Such a daddy's girl.

Flo stuffed a bit of hair sticking to her forehead back under her ridiculous helmet, intensely annoyed that her husband had said anything whatsoever to Jennifer, a woman intent on taking a parental caretaker role *decades* earlier than necessity warranted.

'Mum? Are you sure Captain George is up to this?'

'Don't be ridiculous. I know that dog better than I know myself.' A familiar raft of irritability clanked through her. Jennifer and Stu were always questioning her. *Are you sure you checked this? What did the instructions say about that?*

What her husband and her daughter failed to understand about her was that Flo was logical. Sensible, even. Down to earth. Being raised in an unheated house where neither parent was functioning at full capacity did that to a girl. Sure. She liked pretty things. She liked whimsy. She liked fun! But despite what anyone said, being a flight attendant took a lot more than an ability to smile and pour hot coffee at ten thousand feet. It took tenacity. Epic amounts of patience. And courage. She never talked about it, but the time she'd strapped into the emergency harness at the bottom of the plane so she could drop a smoking laptop battery out of the hatch and into the Pacific midway between Los Angeles and Hawaii had been one of the most exhilarating in her life. The harness had been so strong there'd been zero chance of being sucked out of the plane, but even so . . . that adrenaline rush had never been equalled. The passenger who'd owned the laptop had been particularly irritating, so it had been a double pleasure. And there had been the time with the terrorist, of course. A bipolar man who'd forgotten to take his meds it turned out, but at the time they'd all thought he'd been a terrorist including Flo who, without even thinking, had leapt upon him and taken away his weapon. She generally left out the part about how it had been a Pez dispenser rather than a detonator, but either way, the passengers had been alright and the plane had landed safely in Houston where she'd enjoyed margaritas on the house for the entire three-day layover.

'Most bikes have at least eighteen gears these days,' Jennifer said, eyes glued to Flo's handlebars.

'Pothole,' Flo pointed out a bit too late for her daughter to notice, and then, 'Nonsense.' She was well aware she could have chosen an eighteen or even a twenty-seven geared bike seeing as the one she'd returned (with Stu's help) had had every single bell and whistle apart, of course, from an actual bell or whistle. 'Seven's plenty. I grew up on three.'

'And rode fifty miles to the coal mines and back in all weather,' Jennifer sighed (her one nod towards melodrama). 'I know, Mum. I'm only pointing it out because you're making life harder for your-self if you're really going to do this.'

Flo shot her a quick look. 'Why on earth wouldn't I do it? It's for charity!'

Jennifer pretended to be interested in her children, this sort of conversational impasse being all-too-familiar terrain for the pair of them.

A surge of outrage roared up in Flo. Why wouldn't everyone stop picking on her? She had a brain. A body that functioned very well for a seventy-two-year-old woman, thank you very much. The GP had told her, her heart age was fifty-seven! So what if she didn't have all the bicycle gears the universe had to offer? Mabel (her bicycle was definitely a Mabel) had seven of them.

'The chap down the cycling shop said Mabel was perfect for riding round country lanes and in town.' Flo had checked the Hadrian's Wall route online the other day and they'd be out in the country alright. That and riding straight through the heart of Newcastle. So there you were, town and country. Mabel was also, the chap had said, *excellent* for hills. So. Seven gears it was. A bouncy leather seat, a basket on the front and a tingy bell she'd already used twice. It was perfect. Apart from the seat not being quite as comfy today as it had been during her two minute trial ride.

'Why Mabel?' Jennifer pursed her lips betraying the onset of a couple of lines.

'I thought it sounded fun.'

'Fun?'

'Yes, you know that thing that sometimes happens when you're not trying to talk your mother out of doing something for charity.'

Jennifer sighed again, then pushed ahead to instruct her son to zip up his waterproof because it looked like it might rain in the next forty-eight hours. She didn't even notice the floods of daffodils coming up all along the towpath. Jennifer had loved daffodils when she was little. They'd made her utterly giddy with delight. Where had all of that glee gone? The wonder?

Flo shifted on her seat again wondering, as her posterior announced its discomfort, if her own mule-like tendencies were, in fact, hand-me-downs to Jennifer. After she'd returned the racing bike (to a different Halfords, there was no chance she was going to have that reedy, spotty boy give her a knowing, *I get it, you're old*, look) and gone to the lovely little village cycle shop, she had point blank refused to buy any of the padded lycra shorts despite strong encouragement to do so. While Stuart had embarked on a lengthy discussion about the durability of something or other in Mabel, Flo had tried on a pair, but it had felt like having nappies on, so no thank you very much my good man, but she'd do this the old-fashioned way. With her own natural cushioning.

Cushioning, it was becoming clear, that wasn't entirely up to the task.

'Mum?' Jennifer pulled to a stop. 'It's time to stop. The children have had it and I really don't think Captain George is looking right.'

'Honestly, Jennifer—' Flo stopped and turned back to see Captain George doing his best to keep up but there was something decidedly out of kilter in his gait. She dropped the bike and as she went to him, he collapsed to the ground.

A phone call to Stu, a silent car ride and three hours of pacing in the waiting room of the vet's later, Jennifer was as livid with rage as Flo was hollowed out with grief. She'd hurt her baby. Over-stressed his raging joints and ligaments until – snap! His right cruciate ligament had gone.

'It's so typical of you,' Jennifer was saying. She didn't even wait for Flo to reply before continuing her lecture. 'Pushing and pushing beyond what is actually enjoyable all for your own benefit.'

'The vet said George would make a full recovery.' A very expensive recovery, but cruciate ligament surgeries really were on a different level these days, he'd said. George would be enjoying the same technological advances as Alan Shearer had.

'He's *old*, Mum. He shouldn't have been out running that long. Just as the children shouldn't have been out for such a long ride in this bloody awful weather. Lily's properly ill now. Dad's going to get sick because you know he won't leave her side. And Jake.'

'Jake wasn't sick when we left.' According to Stu, he was happily watching a documentary on killer whales after a hot bowl of soup.

Jennifer gave a brittle laugh. 'Believe me, Mum. He will be by the time we get back.'

'And it's all my fault, is it?'

'It usually is, Mum,' Jennifer said with uncharacteristic venom. (Normally it was world weariness that accompanied her slights.)

Flo shifted in her chair so she could face her daughter. 'Now what's that supposed to mean?'

'Oh come on. You know you're always pushing when it's obvious no one else wants to take part.' Jennifer's eyes were lit bright with anger.

'Really?'

Again, the hard laugh filled the empty, easily moppable waiting room.

'Mum.' Jennifer fixed her with a look of sheer disbelief. 'Do you remember anything about our childhoods?'

Of course she did. Jennifer was being ridiculous.

'All of the "adventures"? They all ended in disaster.' She began to tick things off her fingers. 'The ski trip when Jamie broke his leg after the instructor told you it was too icy to take out a beginner? The walking tour of The Great Wall when Dad had a chest infection that took six months to clear because you insisted we see it through? My broken arm after that stupid muddy not-so-fun run you made us all do in Snowdonia?'

'Adventure comes with risk, darling. No one died,' Flo said trying to pin down exactly why these things were her fault and to block out the fact the vet had said putting Captain George under at his advanced age did come with added risks.

'They weren't fun, Mum,' Jennifer ground out. 'Not in any way. None of us enjoyed being dragged around so you could get an adrenaline rush. Not me. Not Jamie. Not Dad. You never saw it though. The nanny, or should I say nann*ies,* saw it. The cleaners saw it! Dad saw it. But not you. Oblivious Flo intent on doing things her way, no matter the consequences!'

'Jennifer, you're being ridiculous. I'm hardly a tyrant!'

'No,' Jennifer said after a moment's breathing (counting down from ten as instructed in some team-building exercise no doubt). 'You weren't a tyrant. You were just selfish.'

Jennifer gave her *a look* then began to study a packet of weight loss food for cats with a concentrated fury.

'If you'll remember, Jennifer, I'm doing this ride for charity.'

Flo didn't feel on stable ground here. Even less so when Jennifer barked a ha! Then asked, 'Which one?'

'LifeTime.'

'Okay, okay,' she nodded intently as if trying to explain to a simpleton why having an excess of middle-management positions was a bad thing, '. . . so who's the person you're doing it for? And don't you dare say Dad, because where I'm sitting, he's the only sane one of the two of you.'

'Oh, I uh—' She'd not really got that far.

Jennifer's eyebrows went up and her grim expression turned a bit too self-satisfied for Flo's liking. 'You're doing it for yourself, aren't you?'

'I'm doing it for people who need comfort dogs,' Flo said, a bit more majestically than intended. She wasn't, but the walls were covered in pictures of people hugging their successfully healed cats and dogs and it was the first thing that had come to mind.

'Comfort dogs?' Jennifer clearly wasn't going to let this fly. 'Who do you know who uses a comfort dog, Mum?'

'I – well – your father, for one. Your father loves Captain—'

'No, Mum,' Jennifer cut in. '*You* love Captain George. Dad loves cats.'

What?

'But did you even for a second consider getting him a cat? No. Because you wanted your precious Wolfhounds. So as usual, Dad didn't say anything to make you happy because he knew you loved the dogs more than you ever loved us. You exhaust us, Mum. Squeeze us dry. Why the hell do you think Jamie lives in Australia?'

'Jennifer! That's not – of course, I—' And then, with unsettling clarity, Flo realised Jennifer was right. But not for the reasons she thought. Children were so . . . needy! And dismissive. They'd always preferred a cuddle in Stu's comfortable lap to hers. His storytelling. The way he cut apples. Jennifer had always been so disapproving. Even as a little girl. Honestly, who cared if a sandwich was cut into triangles or rectangles? George didn't. But Jennifer? Oh, Jennifer cared. Whereas Captain George . . . the love they shared was completely based on mutual admiration.

Before she could come up with a proper line of self-defence, Flo's phone vibrated in the pocket of her cycling jersey (her one concession to cycling wear). 'Work call,' Flo mouthed, making a show of putting on a very serious face as she took it. She had yet to tell Jennifer or Stu her 'rota blip' at the 111 centre was permanent. 'Florence Wilson,' she said.

'Flo?' A timorous female voice asked.

'Yes.'

'It's Sue, here. Sue Young from the call centre?'

'Sue! Yes. Hello, *Sue*. What can I do for you?' Flo asked pointedly, making it clear to Jennifer that despite having been tarred and feathered as Britain's very own Joan Crawford, she was actually, an exceedingly thoughtful and helpful person who many people relied upon.

'I was ringing to see whether or not we might meet.'

'Yes, duck, yes, of course.' Flo covered the mouthpiece of the phone and whispered, 'This poor woman. Her husband hanged himself a few weeks ago.'

Jennifer's jaw tightened as if to say 'There's always someone more interesting than me.'

'Raven and I were hoping to talk to you about the charity ride.'

'The cycle ride for LifeTime? Which I am riding in aid of people who require therapy dogs?' She gave Jennifer a pointed look she hoped translated as *See? Not so selfish after all.*

'We'd like to go but, we just had a few questions before, you know, committing.'

'Brilliant. Wonderful. *Such* a good cause. Why don't we meet for coffee?' Oh, this was cracking good news. Now she had an actual reason for going on the ride. As a support to Sue and Raven who were clearly going through complicated emotional issues far beyond the realms of angry adult children throwing a childlike sense of adventure and delight in your face.

After they had decided upon the where and when, the vet appeared with a wobbly Captain George wearing a support sling. Unlike Jennifer when she'd appeared from behind the A&E curtain with a freshly plastered arm, George began to wag his tail and grin in his lovely, toothsome way. Flo dropped to her knees and gave him a cuddle, ignoring the 'where Flo goes, trouble follows' looks she knew her daughter was sending her as she told him again and again just how very much she loved him.

Chapter Thirty-Eight

Raven held her phone out at arm's length. 'Here . . . tip your head a bit more . . .' Sue's blonde head bobbed into view, out again and then, after she scooched her bike a bit closer to Raven's, became fully visible. 'There we are. One . . . two . . . three . . . ping! All done.' She scrolled for Flo's number, then sent the picture along with a 'Hope there are bikes in Portugal!' message.

'Shall we head down that way?' Sue pointed along the canal towpath. 'I think it heads into the woods and then circles back. It's maybe . . . seven miles?'

'Sounds good.' Sounded long. She tried to cover up her grunt as she climbed on her bike with a satirical whoop. Sue gave her a confused look, then a thumbs up and climbed on her own bike.

'So . . .' Raven nodded at Sue's sky-blue bicycle after a few minutes. 'What do you think?'

Sue patted the bike's handlebars, wobbled for a second, gripped the bars until her knuckles were white then shot Raven a giddy grin. 'I love it. Dylan really knows how to find a bargain.'

Raven gave a proud smile, as if it were entirely down to her that Dylan was, indeed, a bargain-bagging eBay savant. When it came to cycle stuff, anyway. And he knew some crazy sick cycle tricks as well. His humble bragging about cycle parkour – an insane way of riding a bicycle on the tops of walls and rooftops and jumping *with* the bike on and off of just about anything – was genuinely, honest to goodness, humble. He could pop himself and his bicycle . . . *from a standstill* . . . onto the top of a bin and then carry on riding it as if he'd done nothing more than dodge a puddle. She looked down the cycle path they were on and tried to imagine how Dylan would ride up or down or fly over all of it with a little cocky flick of the wheel this way or that. Just thinking about it made her exhausted. The boy was as full of energy as she was of teenaged disdain for her fellow teenagers. Dylan excepted, obvs.

'Thanks for coming out with me,' Sue said after a bit of silent pedalling.

'Absolutely. No problem.' Raven swallowed back the guilty apology that should have followed. Sue had actually been quite diligent about going out, even if only for a bit, the entire ten days since they'd made their purchases. She invited Raven every single time and never once moaned or cajoled or rebuked her when she made her excuses. The truth was, she'd hit a bit of an emotional snag of her own and was afraid if they had alone time without the telly, everything she'd been spilling her guts to the work therapist about would come flying out in a torrent of woe that she really didn't deserve to feel. Not when Sue was going through the actual death of an actual loved one who had mired her in substantial debt and then topped himself rather than face up to what he'd done. Not that she was judging, but . . . effing hell. She hoped there was some mahoosive apology letter buried somewhere amidst all of those receipts and things. Boxes and boxes, he'd left. She didn't know how Sue got up in the morning. Not that Gary had left her much choice. Anyway . . . she'd not met the man. Not her place to judge.

'How many miles do you think Kath does a day?' Sue asked. 'She looks pretty fit.'

Raven shook her head. She didn't know. 'I suspect her trainer sees to that.'

'Maybe we should've hired Dylan,' Sue said in a way that suggested she might think Raven and Dylan were a thing.

To put her well off that track because – *No,* Raven barked a not-ruddy-likely laugh then asked, 'Have you rung the production office back?'

'The *Brand New Day* people?'

'Yeah.'

Sue shook her head. 'I thought we'd better speak to Flo, because it sounded like they thought we were all still working at the call centre and I didn't feel it was my place to – you know—'

'. . . tell her about The Rachel Incident?'

Sue crinkled her nose. 'Yeah. I wish they'd have her back. The place feels a bit . . .'

'Boring?' Raven offered.

'Quieter,' Sue countered in that politic way of hers.

'Maybe they will. If Flo, you know, apologised. It's not like people are exactly banging the doors down to work there.'

'What do you think you'll say?' Sue asked, the tone of her voice making it clear she'd drifted off somewhere entirely different.

'When?'

'When they come to interview us?'

'Oh, god. I don't know. I was just presuming Flo would do all the talking and I would stand there like a berk, then it would all be over and that would be that.'

'But . . .' Sue made a weird chewing motion as if she was trying to taste the perfect way to explain what she'd actually meant. 'I don't really want to do it. I'm probably more shy than you are – not that it's a contest,' she quickly added. 'It's more that . . . I was just thinking.'

'What?'

'Well? It's not just any old bike ride is it? It's a bike ride for a charity that helps people who are going through a tough time and . . . I don't know. It seems important to make sure people know that we support that as well as the people who ring in and the people who volunteer, and Kath who is making it all happen.'

Raven nodded. All good points. She felt a bit squeamy, now. To have been so blithe about it. She, after all, was going through her own things and probably could've done with someone neutral to bounce ideas off of before she did stuff like move out of the family home to prove a point she wasn't entirely sure was worth proving.

'Are you going to . . .' Oh crap. She'd just started a sentence she didn't really know how to finish.

'. . . talk about Gary?' Sue quietly finished for her.

'Yeah.'

'I'm not really sure it's something they want on television.'

'Kath talked about it. What her brother did.'

Sue's lips disappeared into her mouth with an *mmm*.

'I'm sure they'd help you. You know, how to phrase things.'

'What about you?' Sue deflected. 'What would you want to talk about?'

'How to be brave,' Raven blurted.

'You'd be good at that,' Sue said, clearly missing the fact Raven had meant it as a wisecrack, a filler to cover for the fact that the last thing she wanted to do was appear on television, let alone *Brand New Day*. Hello? Total opportunity to be mocked.

But where?

She wasn't on social media anymore. If people did say things about her, what did it matter? Sticks and stones and all that . . . So . . . why not? Maybe growing a pair was what she needed to talk about. Bravery wasn't painting your face blue, waggling a sword in the air and shouting oaths of loyalty. Bravery came in all shapes and forms. She thought Sue was brave for getting out of bed every morning. She thought Flo was brave for not acting like an old person. Could bravery come in the form of a chubby, Indian, goth girl who froze when life threw 'fix it now' moments at her? Maybe.

They rode along the canal towpath and into a woodland, dappled with early spring sunlight, the idea growing in her along with the spring flowers poking out here and there . . . like little fragile promises of good things to come.

Chapter Thirty-Nine

ONE MONTH LATER

'Well I know *I'll* be racing down to get one!'

Kath turned away from her husband who was pretending to drive a car and then crash it. She put on her brightest smile for camera three. 'A ten-pound voucher for an MOT? Amazing!' She let her astonished smile soften. 'Now, as part of our popular new series where we meet the riders who'll be joining me and my trainer Fola in four short weeks for our Trip of a LifeTime, today we're off to Bicester—'

'Wanting some bargain designer wear, are you, love?' Kev cut in. 'I thought it was all lycra and padded bums for you and your crew these days.'

Kath oh-ho-ho-ho'd, as she checked the monitors and saw that Kev had indeed signalled for them to open the camera angle up to a two-shot. He'd been doing that a lot lately. Not letting her have one on one 'chats' with the viewers. *People want crazy Kath. They want fun Kath. Not all of this bloody, earnest bullshit you keep on about. It's getting right tedious it is.*

Actually it had proved very popular. Particularly, and rather astonishingly, in the wake of Fola marching the 'scrubby ASBO waiting to happen' off of live television.

'About time someone dealt with the little heathens properly,' said one caller. 'I'd have done far worse,' said another. 'Disrespecting Kath like that.'

Since then, viewing figures regularly peaked when the segments about the people joining Kath on the charity ride aired. It turned out people didn't want jolly jolly all of the time. In between the cream pies in faces and ice bucket challenges, they also liked discovering they weren't the only ones going through tough times and, against the odds, finding a way to survive them. Make a difference, even.

'Actually, Kev, whilst you're not wrong—'

'Am I ever wrong?'

Oh, ho-ho-ho. A voice in Kath's ear told her camera two was on a one shot. 'What the team here at *Brand New Day* hadn't bargained on was finding not one, but *three* women within a few miles of one another who are in training to join us.'

'Three? Crikey. What's in the water in Bicester, I wonder?'

'Kindness?' Kath suggested with an impish smile. 'Generosity? That was my take, anyway, when I went down there with a crew yesterday afternoon. I will warn you. You'll see a side of me you don't often see.'

'The back side?'

'Oh, ho ho ho . . . you're just full of 'em today, aren't you, Kev? Why don't we take a look at the first of our Three Amazing Women of Bicester mini-films.' She gave a nod and the taped segment began to play.

Kev pulled off his mic and stormed off set, muttering something about the balance of the show being out of sync. Funny that. Kath could say hand on heart it didn't feel comfortable . . . but it did feel right. So, unlike her husband, she sat back and watched as the segment played.

The first shot was of Florence Wilson riding her bicycle along a canal. It cut to her waving to Sue and Sunita, or Raven as she liked to be called.

Kath's nose crinkled as her own voiceover rang through the studio.

All these years and she still hadn't got used to the sound of it. This time however . . . this time she sounded properly invested.

'Florence Wilson isn't your average seventy-two-year-old grand-mother. She lives here, in a sleepy village just a few miles outside of Bicester. Flo, as she prefers to be called, has travelled the world not once, but hundreds of times in her role as a flight attendant with British Airways. While she may have retired from the friendly skies, she has far from retired from life. Together with friends Sue Young and Raven Chakrabarti, she will be joining us at the end of May for our Trip of a LifeTime.'

The segment cut to Florence waving goodbye to Sue and Raven as they carried on down the towpath. Then it showed Florence putting a poultice on an Irish Wolfhound's leg, Florence waving goodbye to her husband, getting in her car and then, through the magic of television, arriving at work all in a quick ten-second edit.

Kath's voiceover continued, 'By day, Florence works for the NHS 111 call service taking calls from all over Oxfordshire and Bedfordshire.'

Kath smiled as a two shot of the pair of them appeared on the monitor. She'd really liked Flo. A proper can-do woman with extra bags of verve in tow.

'So this is where it all happens, is it, Flo?' she watched herself ask.

'Absolutely.' Florence made a grand gesture with her arm. 'This is where hundreds of calls a day are taken, all helping the good people of Britain.'

On-screen Kath made a *forgive me for putting it this way*, but . . . 'Many women your age would be quite happy to put their feet up. What is it that keeps you so active?'

'I like to live life to the full, really. Seize the day! As they say, you're a long time dead, so why not make the most of the time we have here on— Sorry, do you mind if we just . . . yes . . . there we go . . . just over here.'

Kath's brow furrowed as she watched the next bit. At the time, she'd not thought a thing of Flo moving her to the far side of the forecourt outside the call centre, but now that she watched it again, they were practically in the hedge by the time the officious-looking brunette dipped in and out of shot. Her line manager, Kath thought. Maybe she'd not asked permission to film. Kath tuned back in as Flo explained what had inspired her to do the ride: '—and, of course, your enthusiasm to raise money for such an important charity was inspiring. In fact, they have a call centre for LifeTime, don't they? Oh. You wouldn't mind just taking one more step this way, would you? Out of security's way is always best.'

Flo threw a naughty wink at the camera.

'You're not a trouble maker at work, are you, Flo?' She definitely was a woman in possession of a wicked laugh. A wicked laugh she wasn't using right now.

'Not at all. I tried – try – to do my very best for the callers. Anyway, back to what you were saying about LifeTime. What sorts of hours can people ring in?'

Kath smiled. Flo was born to do television. 'You're an excellent prompt for a very important point I was hoping to make, Flo. Yes. LifeTime does have a dedicated hotline staffed entirely by volunteers. [Looks directly to camera.] I promise you viewers, this was completely unrehearsed, but it is important for all Britons to know that when they think there is no one out there who can understand what they're going through . . . there is. LifeTime has dedicated, twenty-four-hour listening lines open to anyone who feels they might need a friendly ear.'

'What type of qualifications do the helpline folk need?'

'Flo, if I didn't know better it'd sound like you're in the market for another job!'

Kath crossed her arms. Maybe that explained the funny business with the line manager.

Kath continued for a bit about how LifeTime was always looking for volunteers, that there was training, but the main thing they were looking for in the volunteers was an ability to listen, really listen, and not just trot out the same truisms everyone knew.

Flo gave an earnest nod, then jumped in. 'So what you're saying is that people want a *personal* touch. Not a scripted response to a genuine problem that is specific to the caller. Who wants someone plodding through a script by rote when you're at your darkest moment? No one! That's who! Just because two people take milk in their coffee doesn't mean they want the same amount, does it? Or coughs! One might have whooping cough. One might have pneumonia. It pays to take an interest, doesn't it? Going off script doesn't mean you're daft. It means you're *interested*.'

'Absolutely,' onscreen Kath agreed. 'What it also—'

'In fact I would say it's *critical* that the volunteers have a mind of their own. If someone out there were to call me, for example, I can pledge, hand on heart, I'd be willing to listen for as long as you needed. We'd pour a proverbial cuppa, sit down and hash it out. Ten minutes, an hour, all night long. Whatever it takes.'

Kath nodded along as her onscreen persona said, 'I know I'd like you to be on the end of the phone in my hour of need.' She would as well. Maybe she could carve out a little Kath and Flo time on the ride.

'I'd do that for you, Kath.' Flo had taken her hand at this point. 'If you needed it. I'd be there for you. No judgement. No script. Just you and me talking about the things that really matter.'

Kath's throat grew itchy as she watched her eyes glass over on the monitor. The editors had said they'd cut this bit out if she wanted, but if she wanted their viewers to know the real her then she couldn't edit out the tough bits. The vulnerable bits. 'Ooo! You caught me there.' She waved her hand in front of her face as if it was a cure-all for an unexpected attack of emotion. 'Blimey! I just got hit by — ooof.'

'You alright, love?' Flo asked.

'Yes, I just . . . [Shakes head] Goodness! Forgive me. I'm obviously feeling a bit emotional today.' A sob escaped her throat.

'Better out than in, darlin'.' Flo pulled her into a half hug.

Kath tried to shake herself out of it. She'd be back on air soon. But she was riveted as she watched herself say, 'I just wish my brother was here to see how amazing you all are. I wish he'd known there were people like you he could've called for support.'

The make-up girl, Bridie, scurried into place as a tear streaked down her cheek as her onscreen self properly succumbed to the tears. 'I should've been there for him.'

Flo rubbed her back, "S all right, duck. We all should have done a lot of things.'

Flo gave her a tissue, Kath gave Flo a hug. It had all been about a million times more moving than she'd thought, but . . . she hadn't really thought of her brother speaking to an actual person before. She stuffed down all of the feelings again, watched the onscreen notice telling people the LifeTime number if they'd been affected by the content of the segment and then, mercifully, they cut for a commercial break.

'Alright, Raven? Put it here, yeah? Before you're too famous to remember me.'

Raven looked up from her drawing, surprised to see Dylan standing in front of her, his hand curled into a loose fist waiting for a bump. She gave it an awkward tap with her fist after flipping her phone face down on the table, weirdly embarrassed at having been caught looking at uni specs in Costa. 'Sorry, umm . . . what are you talking about?'

'I saw you on telly yesterday, didn't I?' He mouth trumpeted the opening tune to *Brand New Day* then put his hot drink on her table and gave her a double thumbs up. 'You sounded really smart, like.' He did a little re-enactment playing both Kath and Raven which was weird because he gave her a voice like the Queen and Kath sounded like Sporty Spice.

After her face had stopped burning, her interview with Kath had actually been pretty cool. She had a way of listening that made you feel as if she was *actually* listening. And she'd stuck to the plan, unlike Kev, who always seemed to be springing things on people as if he loved catching them out. Thank god he was going to Cape Town.

'I loved that bit about social justice. You was like, all up in the cyber bullies' grill. "Keep your mitts off of my social media and shit, yeah?"'

Raven frowned. She didn't remember everything she'd said, but she was pretty certain she hadn't said that. Rather than talk about exactly the truth – her complete shame and horror that she'd stood by while an innocent girl was driven to the point of complete despair – she'd talked *near* the truth. Cyber bullying was a big enough tabloid issue she'd been confident she could keep her actual emotional investment in it vague. But venturing into the realms of social justice? Not so much.

She examined Dylan's eyes for red lines. Nope. Clear and . . . oh! Sparkly sea-blue, a bit like Bradley Cooper's, not that she fancied Bradley Cooper because he was like, bleurgh, old, but . . . Dylan's eyes were nice.

'I liked the part where you said teenagers needed to take charge of their own lives because they were practically grown-ups anyhow and the future was their future so they might as well own it.'

'Yeah, well . . .' She was no Greta Thunberg. She gave a single shoulder shrug hoping she looked as if it had been pre-planned because all of it had actually been born out of sheer panic. Sue had been asked to go and had been terrified so Raven had said she'd go with her only to figure out she too was terrified until she thought about talking about cyber bullying and then it was like a whole different person had come out of her. Someone articulate and strong who could shrug off trolls and shamers. Someone who could stand up to her parents and refuse to go to uni straight out of college, move in with a newly widowed colleague and agree to go on a 174-mile bicycle ride for a mental health charity. So . . . she was discovering herself, really. And her superpowers. Like an ability to step up and do things even if there were people out there who thought you were a fat, brown, goth slag. Even fat, brown, goth slags could step up for people. For Aisha Laghari, for example.

'I especially liked the part where you were all, *I don't need social media if all it's doing is tearing people down*. An online community should be like – an online *community*, proper like – where we build people up, not tear people down, innit?'

'But you're on Instagram,' she reminded him. 'Keeping your peeps happy.'

He laughed, then sobered and said, 'Nah.'

'What? I saw you.'

'Nah.' He looked over his shoulder then back at her, head tucked low. 'They're just selfies I send to my mum.'

Her forehead shot up. 'Oh?'

'She's got anxiety and depression and shit and when I'm at work she kinda freaks, so . . .' He threw a lame pose.

Raven never thought her heart could ache for Dylan, but at that moment it did.

'Anyway,' he said, drawing back up to his full height. 'I just thought you said some cool shit.'

'Thanks.'

She'd tried to catch the segment on the work telly but had been stuck on a call from a man experiencing chest pains. Whilst her colleagues gathered round the coffee area and watched the interview, she was busy trying to persuade him an ambulance was the wiser choice over waiting for the doctor even if the ambulance service was staffed by 'foreign muck'. The 'foreign muck' were better placed to help him as he was displaying signs of an actual heart attack which could kill him and yes, they would know how to speak English and work the automated external defibrillator (AED).

As the staff clapped and walked back to their stations, giving her little pats of encouragement and popping coins and the odd fiver into the tin she and Sue had placed on the counter where everyone who did charity walks or runs or rides did, she'd smiled actual smiles and mouthed thank you whilst ignoring the barrage of racist slurs from Mr Heartattack as she transferred him to the ambulance service.

'Your parents must think you're the shit,' Dylan said.

'Uh – yeah, not so much.'

He looked genuinely shocked. 'Why not? You've got a kick-ass job. You do stuff for charity. You're on telly.'

She barked out a laugh. Her parents would've been horrified to discover the entire world knew their daughter was taking *gasp!* a gap year. Gandhiji, after all, would never ever have taken a gap year. (Nor would he have invested in Pharma tech, but that was another story.)

'They're pretty busy,' she said, hoping that was enough.

Dylan pulled out a chair and sat down across from her. 'My mum watches it and we were having a cuppa before I went off to work and she was like, is that one of your mates and I was like, it sure is Mums, and she was like, she's brave riding all that way, and I was like, double hella brave Mum. Then I told her about your friend and the . . .' he mimed being hanged by a noose, '. . . and how that really, like, hurt me that someone could be so low and how I helped you get your bikes – mega deal! – and then she wanted to follow your Insta site and we couldn't find it so . . .' He wiggled his ever-present phone in between them. 'Wot's the secret identity, Raven?'

Ah. This had been a sticky point at work as well. Everyone wanting to follow her Instajourney. It was like she, Flo and Sue were celebrities at work now. 'I don't have one.'

Dylan did a double take. 'Are you for real?'

She made a weird smiley apology face. 'I deleted all of my accounts.'

He ha ha ha'd and then did a double take when her expression remained unchanged. 'Nah, c'mon. For real?'

She pressed a button on her phone and showed him. Just the factory pre-set apps plus a cycling one Flo had downloaded for her and the accounting one she and Sue used for Young & Son.

'Man, you got balls!'

Raven laughed. Brave definitely wasn't one of the adjectives she would've ascribed to herself. Cowardly, fearful, ashamed. There were more, but . . . lately she'd been feeling other things, too. Helpful. Proactive. Involved. On a micro-level, obvs, but lately, all of the things that she'd thought had been happening to her were actually things she had made happen.

'You're turning your weakness into your strength, aint'cha? Showing the dickheads where they can shove it.'

There was something about the way Dylan spoke – an emotional rawness – that told Raven he knew *exactly* what big dickheads people could be. And then she remembered Halfords and the way the shop assistant had been so dismissive of him. His gazillions of selfies that turned out to be for his depressed mother. The fact he spoke to her. In public.

'How's work?' she asked.

'Ah, yeah, that didn't pan out so good.'

'What do you mean?'

'I left.' He glanced over his shoulder then dipped down to say, 'Got fired, actually.'

'Why? I thought you loved it there.'

'I did, but . . .' again he looked over his shoulder then down at the table where he traced something into a water ring. 'Sometimes I have to stay up late with my mum, you know, to keep the demons at bay and I fell asleep on shift.'

'That doesn't seem so bad. They could've just woken you up.'

'I was out on the floor. A customer found me.'

'Ah.'

'So, if they've got any jobs going at the call centre . . .' He flashed her a grin and then said, 'Nah. I don't think I'd be any good at that.'

'I'm sure you would, but it's not everyone's thing. What *do* you think you'd be good at?'

'See?' Dylan smiled his almost Bradley Cooper smile. 'You know how to ask the real questions, don't you?'

Errr . . . it was kind of an obvious one, but . . . maybe that was the problem with life these days. No one asked the obvious questions hovering between them like, *how are you?*

'So . . . ? What are you good at?'

'Computers. That's pretty much my area of expertise. Total techno geek if I'm being honest.'

'Right. Well, if I hear of anything . . .'

'Cool, cool.' He tapped the table with his fingers then said, 'I think we should conduct a social experiment.'

'Sorry?'

He took her phone, then looked up at her, 'I think the world of Instagram needs a new star.'

Raven stiffened as he downloaded the app she had very specifically deleted.

'Right,' Dylan began to cackle. 'Who would you most like all those crackhead cyber bullies to have a smackdown with?'

Raven was about to protest and then thought of her superpowers. The ones that had given her the strength to move out of her house and in with Sue. The ones that kept her calm when angry, racist men were having heart attacks and refusing medical treatment. The ones she should've used when Aisha Laghari was lying on the bathroom floor at college. She thought for a while. Trawled through the things that had brought her genuine, proper joy over the past few months. Helping Sue. Meeting Flo. Getting rid of that unicorn rug in Sue's entryway. Brown Goth Pinterest boards full of take-no-prisoners-chock-full-of-attitude women saying, *Damn straight, I'm a girl of colour. Yeah, I like black lipstick. Too right I have a resting bitch face. And I'm pretty on top of it.* All with a healthy dash of *you can't troll me now – I own everything you want to shame me with.* 'Got it,' she said to Dylan as he started taking snaps of her with his phone. 'What do you think of this?'

*

'Ooo la la! Look who's here! It's the winner of the Tour de France!' Dean crowed as he opened the door to Sue. She put the kickstand down on her bicycle and took off her helmet. She smiled at Dean and accepted the half hug he pulled her into, enjoying the new-found, yet entirely unspoken closeness she'd felt with him since Sunday Lunchgate as he'd now taken to calling The Day Someone Said No to Katie. The children ran down the stairs, shyly waved and 'Hi Auntie Sue'd' her before heading back to the kitchen to 'Muuum? When's lunch ready?'

Dean flicked his thumb to the spot where the children had just been. 'They wanted to see the resident movie star.'

Sue flushed. 'I'm hardly that.'

'You've been on telly. More than any of us have.'

'Actually, Dean,' Katie swept from the kitchen through to the dining room holding a very large roast in front of her as if it were a crown. 'I was on the telly back before I met you.'

'It's all been downhill since then, hasn't it, love?' When she disappeared, Dean dropped Sue a wink. 'Totes jelly!'

Sue swatted at him then took off her reflective jacket and cycling shoes.

'Look at you and all of your fancy kit!'

They both looked down at Sue's outfit. Padded shorts, a shirt with a back pocket in it for her house keys. Shoes with a two-bolt clip to go with her hybrid pedals. All things she'd never known existed before Dylan, Raven's friend, had explained them to her and showed her the best places to get them off of eBay. *There is like, thousands of offers on things that have only been worn once,* he'd said. He'd been right. She'd spent just over a hundred pounds on everything including the bike. Far less than Flo had spent, judging from her blinky expression when she and Raven had showed up for their first ride together, unable to resist telling Flo about the deals they'd found.

'With all of those donations coming in you can gold plate them if you like.' Dean nudged her shoes.

'No! Dean, I – oh, no, I just—' A swell of nausea rolled through her as she pictured the spike in donations after her segment had run on *Brand New Day*. As if she were the charity case. She were the one to be pitied. That wasn't the case at all! It was Gary they should be thinking about. Gary and the fact that he hadn't felt there was anyone in the world he could open up to. Not even his wife. The one person in the world he should have been able to count on and she had been absolutely oblivious.

'Bad joke. Bad joke.' Dean swiped his hand across his face. 'I know you wouldn't do anything like that.'

'I couldn't even if I wanted to which, of course, I wouldn't.' Sue said hotly, fighting back a rush of unwanted emotion. She'd been so proud of how she'd held it together on the telly. Explaining to Kath how she was doing the ride in the memory of her husband so that no one else had to go through what he'd gone through. Raven and Flo had come along to lend their support, rightly guessing Sue would try to back out of her interview. Flo had suggested she pretend she was the woman in the Scottish Widows advert and Raven had said as long as she remembered it was for LifeTime it would make it easier. Both of them had been right. Kath had also been incredibly kind and open. Even lovelier than she seemed on the telly. So much so that once they had started talking, telling each other stories about Kath's brother who had apparently been a brilliant mimic and Gary who could get the whole pub laughing with his long, drawn-out jokes, it had almost been as if the cameras had disappeared. Except for the big microphone waving above them.

'Don't you worry, Suey. You've got the biggest heart in the whole of the UK. You deserve every penny of it.'

'It's not for *me*,' Sue shook his arm off of her shoulder. 'It's for LifeTime.'

'They're sending in the donations because of your story,' Dean insisted. 'For what you've been through.'

What Gary had been through was a million times worse than

anything she'd been through so no way was she going to accept any of this as a compliment.

'*Ooeeeoo*. Look who's bothered to show up.' Bev appeared from the kitchen with a large tray of cauliflower cheese in her oven-mitted hands.

'Sorry, I was just . . .' Sue was about to explain how the ride had taken longer than she'd thought when her mother briskly turned and headed to the dining room where she heard some sort of self-righteous exchange about *some* people deigning themselves to be above *helping* with the *family* meal.

'Don't worry about her. Mum's just jealous.'

'What?'

'Of you being on telly.'

'No, she's not.'

Dean grinned, 'Wanna bet? She's spent the past half hour going on about everyone at work asking how to get on your Instagram site and wanting to contribute to your fundraising site.'

'I don't have a fundraising site. It's all part of *Brand New Day*.'

'Give us your phone.'

Sue unzipped the pocket of her mostly all-weather jacket and handed it to him. Dean gave it a couple of taps. 'Don't you have a passcode for this?'

'No. Gary's the only other person who looked at it and I'd nothing to hide, so . . .'

Dean's eyes flicked over to meet hers. He cricked his neck then asked, 'What do you want as your password?'

'Garyboberry,' she said without thinking. It had been her password for the past fifteen years for just about everything. Garyboberry1999 when they required numbers. Garyboberry1999! for when you needed a symbol.

Dean tapped in the password. 'Put your helmet on,' he directed. 'Now smile.'

She gave him a confused smile.

Dean did a few more swishes and flicks on the screen then handed the phone back to her. 'There. Now you have an Insta account linked to the *Brand New Day* donations page.' He dropped her a cheeky wink. 'I've put fifty quid in in Mum's name.' His phone rang, interrupting one of the first complicit moments they'd shared as brother and sister since they'd been children.

His face went sombre as he listened then began nodding along, 'Yeah, yeah. No, I get it. I'll make some calls, but . . .' he swept his hand across his face. 'Shit. Yeah. Can you tell Katie I'm going to have to sit this one out? Lunch, I mean.'

'What's wrong?'

'Ohhhh . . . Suey . . .' Dean went into a mode she was all too familiar with. The 'you wouldn't understand' mode. 'Just some staffing problems. Our IT guy decided to go walkies.'

'In tax season?'

Dean's chin jutted out as he scrubbed it. 'It happens. Separates the boys from the men, tax season does.'

'I know someone,' Sue said. 'He's a computer guy.'

Dean started to laugh and then stopped, as if he'd given himself a lecture about actually listening to Sue rather than blowing her off as was the usual family remit. 'Who's that then?'

'His name's Dylan. He's young, but . . . from what I understand, he knows his way around a computer.'

A phone call to Raven and then to Dylan later, Dean had a smile back on his face.

'Suey?' Dean tapped at his phone for a few furious seconds. 'You're a bloody marvel.' He wiggled the phone in front of her face. He was moving it too quickly to read but it looked like it was the donation page he'd just set up. 'Let's just say the tax year just got a little bit brighter for me and for LifeTime.' Then he crooked an arm round her neck and led her towards the dining room. 'Time to see if we can saw through Katie's yorkies.' And just like that, she felt closer to her brother than she ever had.

Chapter Forty

'Today, campers,' Raven whispered to her phone under her tented covers, '. . . Big Boned Goth Girl is hitting the road. And yes, I did just talk about myself in the third person.' She smirked. 'I think that's enough Kanye action for one day, don't you? Back to Owning My Fears . . . So, today's bit of Too Much Information, or, as I like to call it, *honesty*: Today I am scared utterly shitless of what lies ahead. And what is that exactly? That's fifty-three miles in one day. On a bicycle. Where there are hills, a nuclear power station, and the promise of rain. Which will all be very interesting, considering I've not really been riding my bike much.'

She did one of those silent laughs that let her viewers know she knew she'd put herself in a tricky situation and was *well aware* of the consequences, but . . . hopefully it would be a mind over matter thing. It better be, anyway. Particularly seeing as she'd made it very clear she found being hot and sweaty as a result of exercise completely revolting. It seemed a lot of other people thought so too, and as such, she now had almost a thousand followers, including seventy-two in Argentina. She was pretty sure Dylan and his way with hashtags had something to do with that. #GothGirlsGotBack Ha! Priceless. The look on his face when she'd actually twerked. Hi*llllar*-ious.

She hadn't had this much fun in actual years. Hanging out with Dylan was like having a real mate.

Not boyfriend/girlfriend style, just . . . fun.

When actual strangers began following her, it was a proper shocker. It had also made the knot in her stomach tighter because at some point she was going to have to tell Dylan and her followers and probably Kath about Aisha and the truckload of guilt and panic and, let's face it, fear, that had all but turned her inside out exactly when she should've been doing something helpful, but that day had been an epic TIFU day if ever there was one, just like the day when the cutter had rung her and had obviously hit an artery and just like that, the self-doubt monkeys began swirling round her brain— zip! Zip it up. And breathe.

Right now, right here, in this moment, she was enjoying being Big Boned Goth Girl. A self-styled, too tall, heavily proportioned, geeky goth of colour who hated exercise and loved learning weird facts about just about anything, including the fact that it was possible to become a knight by buying a round of drinks in the pub at Piel Island.

Being a geek and making a berk out of herself weren't the only things that had helped boost the numbers. They'd been tactical. They'd tagged in *Brand New Day*, obvs. Trip of a LifeTime. Again, obvs. Cycling stuff. Whatever was trending that day, including musicians, actors and politicians being idiots because the only people they thought about were the old voters who weren't thinking about the young people and the apocalypse of a planet earth they were going to be living in sooner rather than later, but . . . whatever. Noel Fielding. *Bake Off*. Make-up. She'd tagged tonnes of make-up brands. Amazing goth clothing she'd never be able to afford to wear in a million years. Dylan had suggested she start writing mock lyrics to songs about being a goth geek and loving it, but she had a voice like a donkey and there were limits to just how far she was prepared to go to make the point that you should be free to be who you wanted to be on social media without fear of being bullied. All of which meant she needed to get her head back in the right place and do this thing before she climbed onto her bicycle and began what could only be fifty-three miles of horror. She propped herself up on her elbow, making sure the covers were still over her head and shifted the camera a bit.

'As discussed, they don't make much in the way of cool cycling gear for big girls like me. Particularly ones on a budget. That being the case and the "team T-shirt" being mandatory . . . I am forced to accessorise.' She pulled another face to let her viewers know she was being ironic. Of *course* she was going to accessorise. That's what Big Boned Goth Girl did. Particularly today, given she'd already caught a glimpse of the T-shirts they were being forced to wear. A rather startling shade of yellow. YELLOW! Who suited yellow? No one apart from maybe Michelle Obama, that's who. 'After great amounts of reflection and limited make-up supplies, today's eyes will feature . . . flames of glory! If you look the part, it's easier to become the part. That's your top tip for today. But, shhhhh.' She flicked back the covers to reveal the dark guesthouse room. 'We have to be very, very quiet.'

She tip-toed past a lightly snoring Flo and a curled-up Sue who looked more like a kitten than a full-grown woman. Raven quietly closed the bathroom door behind her and put her phone on the little shelf above the sink in the teensy-tiny attic toilet that was more slanted ceiling than room.

Raven grinned at her phone and brandished her favourite eyeliner. 'As ever . . . once the false eyelashes are on, we start with my favourite colour . . . black.'

Chapter Forty-One

'It's here, Sue!' Flo made large pointy gestures at the continental buffet. 'That yoghurt you were after.' She was surprised how quickly the dining room where riders were gathering for a 'team spirit breakfast' was filling up. For some reason, she'd only pictured herself, Sue, Raven and Kath riding along, Fola weaving between the four of them, cheerfully calling out encouragement.

But no. By her latest headcount, there were at least fifty of them. The small coastal hotel had only been big enough to fit Kath and her rather vast television crew overnight, so the rest of them – the riders – had been parcelled out amongst the guesthouses dappled along the one and a bit streets that made up Ravenglass. (Raven, naturally, had been thrilled by the name and that the smattering of buildings made up a hamlet rather than a village because both Hamlet and Ophelia were apparently 'proper goth icons'. That girl could put two and two together and come up with seventeen.)

'Sue?' Flo held up the bowl of fruity yoghurt pots when Sue failed to rise. 'They hadn't put it out yet. Apparently there's only the one poor girl on today.' Raven leant in from beside her and made a *can't quite hear you* face so Flo took matters into her own hands and brought the entire bowl over. Sue quietly thanked her as she selected a raspberry flavoured one from the handful of pots resting in ice then fastidiously went about opening and decanting it into her bowl.

Flo frowned. Sue was very quiet this morning. Nerves, most likely.

She was feeling them too, but they were obviously manifesting themselves differently. Whenever she was nervous, she got very 'helpy'. After she'd woken to the sound of Raven talking to herself in the loo, Flo sorted herself out in her usual expeditious fashion and in a matter of minutes had busied herself out on the street directing folk to the main hotel, back to the dining room, pointing out the long row of bicycles they'd be assigned after breakfast (no one was allowed to bring their own for some strange health and safety reason she hadn't quite grasped) and all sorts of other things she would've imagined the 'team organisers' would've been all over but weren't. All in all it had been a very busy morning. For her and the poor girl at the front desk, anyway.

'I'm loving that eye make-up, Raven.' Flo tapped the side of her own, more modestly adorned eyes, wondering if she'd gone with her more natural look a bit too soon in life. 'You look like Cleopatra as one of those Marvel Superheroes.'

'Cleopatra would've been an epic goth,' Raven grinned a surprisingly toothy black-lipped smile as she dug into her bowl of Frosties.

Flo basked for a minute. A smile from Raven was one of those truly rewarding smiles. Rare. Like sightings of a white hippo. Perhaps not the best of similes and one she certainly wouldn't share, but they were rare and lovely and Flo was pleased to have elicited one. Endorphins, she was guessing. The thrill of something new? Whatever it was, Raven had been quite the cheery little goth lately. Lovely to see. Just lovely.

It was just what she'd needed to see as, over the past week or so, Flo had been increasingly worried she'd bullied the pair of them onto the ride. She'd long had a habit of cajoling her fellow cabin crew into 'little adventures' away from the pool at the crew hotel. Adventures which eventually got her the nickname Fearless Flo. She'd taken it as a compliment at the time, but now that Jennifer had schooled her otherwise as regards her family adventures, she wondered if, in actual fact there hadn't been a bit of an edge to it.

A note of warning. 'Join fearless Flo at your peril!' As if it were her fault the tyres blew on the bus bringing them back from the rather excellent elephant polo match some forty miles outside of Delhi three hours before call.

As she watched Sue and Raven, cycling clothes on, exchanging quiet observations about their fellow riders, Flo was gripped with a desperate need for this to have been the right decision. Convincing Sue and Raven to ride with her. More than anything she hoped they were here by choice. Not force, or obligation or, even worse, guilt. She'd be horrified to discover they'd only come because they didn't want the jobless, busybody old woman who'd all but commandeered their lives over the past couple of months, to feel bad. They'd been like the perfect economy passengers for weeks now. Riding, collecting donations, doing the interviews with Kath though they'd both recoiled at the first mention of it. They'd proverbially accepted that they were getting sour cream and cheese pretzels rather than dry roasted peanuts and a glass of real champagne from the off. Not at all fussy like the Premium Economy passengers. Inventing allergies to Prosecco that didn't extend to the champagne they happened to know was available in the First Class Cabin. Asking for a duvet from Business because they were feeling unwell. A baby to stop crying.

She'd found the door-to-door debt collecting quite fun. The second they answered the door Flo could assign the person to their cabin, their pre-booked dietary needs, their utter helplessness now that they were strapped into a seat ten thousand miles above sea level. Her favourites were the cheery sort who tended to sit back near the loo, flicking through *Heat* and *Grazia* and having a bit of a laugh, settling in to watch the latest romantic comedies, eyes glittering with excitement when she pulled up with her trolley, whether or not she'd run out of the green peppercorn steak. They were the types who made sure they said something lovely about Gary. Who made Sue's eyes glitter with tears of pride.

Feeling too restless to sit, Flo carried the yoghurts round to the other early bird cyclists already eating their Wheaties or Bran Flakes or tapping the table impatiently waiting for coffees or hot breakfasts that clearly wouldn't be arriving anytime soon if the recent arrival of the chef and the queue at reception were anything to go by.

Honestly. All of these people and only the one poor girl running between reception and the kitchen like a headless chicken. Why wasn't anyone helping her?

'They've put you to work, have they?'

'Oh, hello there, Trevor.' He was a fifty-something chap Flo had met at the pub last night during the 'Riders' Social' now looking the tiniest bit worse for wear. Silly man. Downing pints like water the night before their big ride. She'd met him a thousand times over on the airlines. Economy exit row-type who never slept. Not even on the long hauls. Always awake, always hungry and always knew something about everything. Regularly offering little titbits about their destination – *I'll bet I know something about Buenos Aires you don't.* (It was founded twice and yes, she had known.) – or, worse, the airplane. *Did you know the Boeing 737—* Yes. She did. She flew on one for a living.

'Need something nourishing to take on the world?' Flo jiggled the two yoghurt pots she was holding.

Trevor laughed a loud attention-grabbing laugh. 'Watch how you go, love! People will think you're flirting with me and if I'm not mistaken, you're a married woman.'

Flo's smile froze a little. The reminder made her heart cinch more that it normally did at mentions of Stu. Like the stalwart he was, Stuart had driven her and the girls (and Captain George who still wasn't his usual self) to the studio in Birmingham yesterday after weighing their bags on the bathroom scales (no more than 15kg each), checking their helmets for cracks, noting down their emergency numbers and, of course, blood types (O+ for Sue, B- for Raven, both of whom had donated at a recent, in-house drive at the call centre). He'd also given each of them a set of pocket hand warmers 'just in case.' All of which had driven her to distraction until Stu, Captain George by his side, along with the other riders' families, had waved them off until they'd disappeared from sight, at which point she'd missed them more than she could have ever imagined possible. Missing Stu in this way simply wasn't like her. Throughout their entire married life, they had spent countless nights apart, what with her flying to one end of the world and Stu flying to the other, tag teaming one another for school runs, the electrician/plumber/builders coming at nine, the telly man fixing the aerial on Sunday as a special favour, making sure the milk wasn't rancid before pouring it into the children's cereal because another trip to A&E for food poisoning was out of the question. No, this felt more like a separation. As if the lies she'd been telling him about heading off to work these past few weeks had driven a wedge between them only she could see. Stu, you see, wasn't a liar. He was the most loyal, reliable, honest man she'd ever met. Up until now, Flo had been the occasional bender of truth, more to expedite things than to actually deceive, but this was different. A slippery slope of deceit Stu didn't deserve to be a part of.

She stared at Trevor, vaguely tuning in as he asked 'did she know' that there was genuine quicksand out on the beach which, by the way, was a tidal *estuary* composed of three *rivers*, not the *sea* as most people thought. Right now Flo didn't care what most people thought. She only cared about Stu, no doubt innocently sitting at home finishing his puzzles, perfectly satisfied that his wife would never ever tell him anything that wasn't true. A complicated knot of regret and frustration formed in her throat. If she'd been honest in the beginning she'd most likely be in Portugal now, with Stu, preparing for another sunny day of avoiding the speed-walking golf widows and their decaf coffee mornings.

A surge of injustice rushed through her. Why did it feel brazen to want to participate in life despite the fact she had to take joint supplements? The Paralympics was all about triumphing over adversity. Ageing should be the same. Judged on a case-by-case basis. It wasn't as if David Attenborough was being forced to hang up his hat despite an inability to yomp through the jungles of the Amazon anymore. Quite the opposite in fact. The world was desperate to squeeze as much out of him, Judi Dench, Maggie Smith and Clint Eastwood as possible! No one was jamming them into cabbage scented care homes in a pair of adult nappies. She was exactly the same as she had been ten years ago. Better if she had any say in it. So! It was *society's* fault she'd had to lie to Stu. Not hers. She'd been doing her very best to be a contributing member of the United Kingdom's economy and door after door was being slammed in her face. Despite some rather heroic efforts down the local library and even, on one particularly bleak day, the job centre, it became remark-ably clear that no one wanted to hire a seventy-two-year-old woman who'd just been fired from their call centre position for using plain old common sense. No one apart from mobile care centres looking for 'paid companions for the elderly' – a job she would never take in a million years because a) old people and b) it was plain wrong to be paid to chat nonsense with someone over a cup of lukewarm tea and a packet of Rich Teas when they should have family there to talk and reminisce. All of which made her wonder if her own children would come back home and talk to her when she didn't have teeth and could no longer remember the name of the Prime Minister. Jennifer might. Jennifer always liked being right.

Anyway. It was all much of a muchness now. She'd come clean to Stu when she got back. That, or start volunteering down at the local RSPCA centre and slip it into conversation as if she'd been working there for ages and Stu was the one who didn't remember.

She primly readjusted the yoghurts. 'Well, if you're not interested in the yoghurt Trevor, perhaps you'd like something from the cold buffet.'

'Trying to get yourself a job, are you?'

'Ha!' She sniffed and turned, making a dramatic display of

pouring herself a bowl of muesli and milk before returning to her seat by Sue and Raven. A few minutes later when she couldn't bear watching that poor girl from reception who was now also trying to be the waitress run herself ragged, she wrangled the two of them into helping her serve the hot dishes whilst the girl took the rest of the orders. Whenever she passed Trevor, she pretended she was hard of hearing. For him, the cold buffet would simply have to do.

Chapter Forty-Two

Don't panic. Don't panic. Don't panic. Don't panic.

Sue was definitely beginning to panic. What had so recently been an out-of-focus, out there, never-really-going-to-happen adventure, was suddenly a very real, very scary thing.

'You sure you're going to be alright in that?' the man standing next to her asked when the first of what looked set to be a number of raindrops began to fall. Trevor, was it? She vaguely remembered him telling her something about Hadrian's Wall last night. Or was it about bird migration? Perhaps it had simply been about the weather. There had been so many facts flying about the pub they'd all melded into one big indecipherable blob of information she simply couldn't digest, so she had adopted her Sunday lunch face, a smile and a nod combo, until Flo finally agreed it was time to turn in. Raven, who was not one for group activities, hadn't needed any convincing.

'You know, the forecast isn't looking very clever,' Maybe Trevor said.

Sue looked at her light, allegedly waterproof jacket. 'I should be alright?'

'Doesn't look hydrophobic to me.' He tweaked a bit of the electric-orange fabric on his own jacket. 'Keeps *everything* out, it does.' He began to list the elements: wind, rain, sleet, hail . . .

'Lucky you!'

'It's not luck, love.' He tapped the side of his head, his expression turning schoolmastery. 'It's research. You don't know what life's going to throw at you, so it's best to be prepared.'

'Oh, okay. Well . . .' She was fairly certain he didn't mean finding your husband dangling in the stairwell. 'Thank you?'

He gave her an *I see you* nod and clacked away in his nylon and fibreglass shoes which, Sue now knew, had a two-way adjustment dial-closing system because he had been detailing the merits of his road shoes over her eBay'd trail shoes for the last few minutes. Trevor's shoes didn't let water in. Hers, with a simple two-bolt system, definitely would. Wet feet spelt foot rot and without feet you were useless as a cyclist. Every good rider knew that. All this whilst she'd been silently trying to talk herself out of running to the train station and leaping on the first one, regardless of destination.

She tried to channel her fears into a single question. *What was it that scared her the most?*

The riding?

No.

Being on television?

Not really.

Kath had been so lovely to talk with, it had been less painful than she thought to admit to the whole of Britain that her husband had killed himself and left her in debt because he couldn't run his own business. She'd couched it differently, of course, but . . . facts, she was learning on an increasingly regular basis, were facts.

Many of Gary's customers had, thanks to Flo and Raven, paid up now. The surprise had been when even more people, having heard her story on *Brand New Day*, had tracked her down and sent in cheques or PayPal donations to cover those who wouldn't. Those funds, she sent directly to LifeTime.

What scared her most, she realised, was for the ride to be over.

Between work and the 'training/debt collecting' sessions and shopping for bum-friendly cycling shorts and watching an entire boxset of Tim Burton films with Raven (*Frankenweenie* being their joint favourite), Sue had been busy and focused and completely bereft of time to think about the fact that when she got home, Gary wouldn't be there to hear about any of this. Not the daily mileage. Not the poor choice of weatherproof gear. Not Trevor. A man Gary would've absolutely loved to mimic. But Gary would never mimic anyone, or laugh appreciatively, or give her a warm hug of congratulations ever again. And for that reason, she was absolutely dreading getting on her bike and beginning a journey that would conclude with the inevitable . . . acceptance.

She scanned the area for Raven and Flo. Hopefully they were meeting people filled with slightly cheerier tales and a more relaxed approach to cycling gear.

The more she looked, the more she worried she was the only one who'd used Primark as her main outfitter. She had one pair of padded shorts, a reflective vest and one cycling top with a pocket in the back, but the rest was really just leggings and T-shirts.

All around her, the fifty-odd riders were wearing lycra leggings, reflective, weatherproof, wind-resistant, breathable jackets, the cleats on their far-more-serious-looking shoes clacking on the ground as they leant into some rather severe-looking stretching positions.

Suddenly her decision-making process – such as it was – seemed absolutely ridiculous. No wonder her mother had thought her completely mad for choosing this over a free trip to Tenerife with Katie, Dean and the kids. That world, she was familiar with. That world, whilst not entirely pleasant, was safe.

What on earth had she been thinking? Going on telly. Telling the entire world she'd been so useless her husband had – well – had had nowhere to turn? Astonishingly, her uselessness as a wife had already garnered her quite a few Instagram followers even though she'd only put three pictures on so far. (Sticky toffee pudding, their helmets and her bag on the bathroom scales at Flo's.) She didn't have as many followers as Raven, who had informed them over breakfast that her numbers had already topped a thousand.

'Can we have all of the riders over here please!'

A red-haired woman about the same age as Sue was beckoning everyone over to the long row of bicycles just outside the two guest-houses where many of them had spent the night. The woman was wearing an orange version of the brightly coloured LifeTime T-shirts they'd been handed at the group meal last night as they were given their room assignments (Sue, Flo and Raven were given a family room with a set of bunkbeds and a double bed which they'd drawn straws for). When the woman turned around, Sue saw she had BECKY printed on the shirt and SUPPORT TEAM.

Flo, who was on the phone with her husband discussing how to apply Captain George's poultice, signalled to Raven and Sue that they should go on over. She'd catch up in a minute.

Raven, who looked quite different in her riding shorts and bright yellow T-shirt, was beginning to look as nervous as Sue felt. Little wonder considering the poor thing hadn't really done all that much riding apart from their twice-weekly 'debt collecting' rides. Numerous times, Sue had invited her to ride into work with her, but she'd always declined for one reason or another.

'If I could get everyone's attention, please! Great. Excellent.' Becky waved them all in closer. 'I'm Becky Harris, part of your cycle support team from Newcastle's very own Pedal Power!' She whacked an arm around Kath. 'Thanks to Kath here and her passion for LifeTime, you all are about to do an amazing, but very difficult ride. That's why, so far, you all have raised over two hundred and twenty-three THOUSAND pounds!'

Everyone cheered.

'How about we double or even triple that by the time you cycle into Tynemouth?'

Another cheer.

'Okay. Now that that's sorted, let's talk facts.'

Sue looked at Raven who made a scared face and pretended to bite all of her nails off. Despite her nerves, Sue giggled. Riding with Raven looked set to be as natural as living together had been.

Becky put her hands into a film director square. 'Big picture? All you have to do today is get on your bike and ride. There's some lovely coastal bits, some beautiful country lanes and even some hill work for those of you who like a bit of a challenge.'

Sue hid a smile when Flo arrived just in time to roll her eyes as Trevor shouted out, 'The more hills the merrier!'

'That bloody man will drive us mad by the time this is through,' Flo intoned as she pulled her windproof fleece zipper up to her chin.

'That's the spirit,' Becky gave everyone the thumbs up. 'Right. The small print. We have an advance party van. It is manned by this lovely young woman to my left, KC and her trusty companion Dean-O. Give everyone a wave, you two.' A pretty blonde girl who looked as if she were an outdoor-wear model waved, as did the hipster-type beside her. 'Do not – I repeat – do not try to keep up with them. This is not the Tour de France. They'll have tea, coffees, biccies, oranges, all the good stuff you need to keep your energy levels up at the twenty-mile marker and the forty-mile marker. Lunch will be picnic style and will be on the piers at the lovely seaside town of Maryport. For those of you who are extra speedy, there is an aquarium that is well worth a look. They have kindly extended complimentary tickets to our riders who arrive early.'

Whilst the group applauded, Raven threw Sue a look that said all she needed to know. They'd be missing out on the aquarium.

Becky clapped her hands together and gave them a rub. 'Today is the longest day, but also one of the flattest.'

Murmurs of relief rippled through the crowd.

'But! Your health and safety are paramount, isn't that right, Kath?' Kath nodded. 'If you need a rest, if you are in any pain, if you need something from your bag – just look to the back of the peloton –

you'll be riding in formation, am I right???' She didn't pause to find out, 'I'll be there for you in this big old van, yeah?'

Someone began to hum the theme song from *Friends*.

Becky laughed. 'Alright, that's enough from me. How about we have a quick hip-hip for the brilliant Kath Fuller who's got a live spot coming up with Kev and then we all hit the road!'

Ready or not, thought Sue, as she hip-hip-hoorayed along with the rest of the riders . . . *here I come.*

Chapter Forty-Three

'Do you mind if I touch you from behind?'

As it happened, Kath didn't mind in the least if Fola touched her from behind. Or the front. Her body, as usual, had sprung to high alert when he'd approached her through the crowd of cyclists pulling on their jackets and readjusting their shoes out here on the blustery green in front of the hotel. The truth was, she'd been tingly ever since Fola had boarded the large touring bus they'd all taken from Birmingham. Since then the feeling had only grown. It reminded her of being thirteen and falling deeply in crush with David Langham, a Jack the lad who regularly ignored her until one day one of her mates had pushed her towards him and their teenaged bodies had collided in a whirl of heat and hormones. It was days before they could get a moment alone to see if the frisson buzzing between them was real. It hadn't been in the end, but, oh, that electric feeling of anticipation . . . Bliss. This trip had been much the same. Last night had been all bustle. Meeting and greeting the riders as they checked into the small coastal hotel where they'd set up a temporary headquarters. Going over scripts with her producer. Checking that Kev had arrived in South Africa with his crew. Going to bed on her own, spreading her hand out on the cool sheet beside her wondering what it might be like to have someone else's body that wasn't Kevin's beside her . . . and then remembering that the entire reason she'd made this whole thing happen was to honour the life of her brother, not flirt with a desperately gorgeous and kind man fifteen years her junior, who would very likely be horrified to discover just how much she had the hots for him.

This morning, after her usual plate of scrambled eggs and avocado with hot sauce and a rare foray into the magical world of toast (mmmm, *carbs*), she was crackly with anticipation. This – the bikes, the crowd, the charity logo everywhere, her brother's picture on the back of her shirt – it all felt *real*. As if everything she'd done in her life, the good choices and the bad had led her here . . . to the start of a Northern yellow brick road she hoped would deliver her to a place of self-forgiveness and peace and resolution about her brother. It was that, or be haunted by a genuine fear that all she'd done with her life was forsake her family in the single-minded pursuit of dance followed by an empty life in the limelight that looked glittery and nice but was, in fact, entirely forgettable. She wanted to make a difference. A real, genuine, difference. If Oprah suddenly up and died (god forbid, she was completely Kath's hero), the world would notice. Millions would fall into a collective grief as they reflected upon the remarkable life of a sexually abused girl from the wrong side of the tracks who had helped so very many people along the way and, in the process, sold squillions of other people's inspirational self-help books. If Kath were to disappear . . . maybe a column inch or two in *The Sun*? A chance for the station to reboot the morning programme? A new model bride for Kev? That'd be about it. Unless she took this chance to truly change, no matter the consequences.

Fola, clad in his usual workout gear – trainers, loose fitting T-shirt that showed off his broad shoulders, and slimline tracky bottoms – walked behind her. 'If you really want to get the most out of this quad stretch, Katherine, you want to bend from here.' She felt his fingers slip into the crease between her thighs and hips. 'Lean forward, pushing your glutes back and your chest forward . . . Yeah. That's right. Are you feeling it now?'

Oh, she was feeling it alright. Feeling all sorts of tingly, heated glitter bombs going off like popping candy in her 'treasure chest' as Kev liked to call it. Not that he'd gone on any treasure hunts lately. A thought which immediately made the feelings go away. Oprah wouldn't lust after her trainer. Fola's fingers shifted to her hips, causing her to twitch in all sorts of wicked ways. Oprah would probably have a female trainer anyway. A girl who'd won gold in a 800-metre race, barefoot, against the odds, wearing nothing but a hand-me-down tracksuit she'd been given by the Red Cross after her entire village had been swept away in a tsunami.

Kath stood up and took a couple of steps back from Fola. This had to stop. Unless it was actually love she was feeling.

Was it? She stared at him, willing his expression to tell her. He looked at her, confused. Not really the lovestruck expression she was after. More likely her feelings were the complicated, meno-pausal, rat's nest of complexity all leading to one inevitable endgame: admitting that her marriage to Kevin had been a mistake.

'Alright, Katherine?'

'Yes. Wonderful,' she lied, looking into his eyes again, desperate to see something, anything, that mirrored her experience. The flickers of heat when their hands brushed. The tightness in her chest when their eyes caught and meshed. The bone-deep ache for change.

'I'll just go help some of the others if that's alright?'

Ah ha ha ha, she weird laughed. 'You don't have to ask my permission.'

He gave her a lightly perplexed look that said, I know that. I wasn't asking your permission, I was just being polite.

Ah ha ha ha ha.

Quicksand, take me now.

She pulled her arm across her chest and pressed it flat with her other hand, feigning nonchalance. 'Cool. Cool beans. I'll just catch up with the crew and see you in ten for take-off?'

Fola squinted at her in the way a mother might examine their child before pressing a hand to their forehead to check for a fever.

'Alright, Katherine. Maybe do a couple of calf stretches as well, okay?' He stroked one of his very long-fingered hands along his calf, evoking a ripple of goose pimples along Kath's belly.

'Excellent suggestion. I'll get on that.' She made a show of lifting her heel to her bum and tugging on it, realising, too late, that she was not doing a calf stretch at all, but she'd already made a complete div of herself so why not commit? She pulled up her other foot and gave that a stretch, too. Balance, she reminded herself from countless yoga sessions, balance was everything.

Right then and there she vowed not to speak to Fola unless it was absolutely necessary. Doing anything else would be ridiculous. She didn't want to have an affair. She wanted to make a difference. The way Oprah did. And Oprah did not get to where she was in life by crushing on her PT. So! It was time to put on the blinkers and go full steam ahead Oprah.

Her crush would go away, she would raise loads of money for LifeTime and hopefully, somewhere along the next one hundred and seventy-four miles she would get a sign from her brother that she hadn't been all bad. It was that or carry on being a jowly, middle-aged, almost has-been on the brink of seeing both her marriage and her career swan dive into the forgettable depths of lite entertainment television.

'Kath?' Her producer signalled that the lines were up between South Africa and Ravenglass. 'Kev wants a word. Says the shirt you're wearing makes you look like you have yellow fever. Any chance of switching into something a bit more flattering? His words, not mine.'

Kath took in a deep breath and counted to ten. It was going to be a long week. And she wasn't talking about the cycling.

Chapter Forty-Four

'So it's goodbye from us here at the studio . . .' Kev waved at the camera.

'. . . and hello from . . .' Kath twirled her hands into a magician's assistant position as, through the magic of television she and Kev were transported to:

'Cape Town!'

'And the Lake District!'

Kath waved again, her body catching unnaturally as if she were filled with shattered glass. Telling Kev she would be happier married to a pygmy hadn't really been the best of farewells. Not to mention entirely politically incorrect. For all she knew, pygmies might have a reputation as fabulous spouses. Unlike Liverpudlian disco dancers desperately clinging to the embers of their morning television career.

'You're looking well rested, Kath!'

Oh, ha ha ha. Marinating in Kev's parting shot had kept the bouncing sheep at bay. *You're making a spectacle of yourself, Kath. Humiliating yourself. No one cares about a dead drunk. You making a show of it is doing about as much good as your brother ever did.* It had been a particularly low blow. Even for Kev, who tended to shoot from the hip, not below it.

Kev, who could clearly see his monitor, began whistling the

opening measures to 'Singin' In the Rain'. 'It looks as though the heavens have decided to smile down upon one of us.'

Kath wrestled her umbrella back into submission. 'I'm feeling a bit more like Mary Poppins than Debbie Reynolds today!'

She grimaced. What percentage of their viewers would even know who Debbie Reynolds was? Should she throw in a Carrie Fisher reference or would that just confuse people further? Buggeration. Three hours sleep was taking its toll and she had fifty-three miles ahead of her today.

'Good to see the bank holiday British weather can be relied upon to put us in our place. Some of us, anyway!'

Oh, he really was going for it today, her Kev.

She blinked away some raindrops and tried to pretend she was in *The Notebook*, but a little less sexy. Fuck Kevin and his bloody ratings. This was important. Her brother had been important. All she had to do was keep walking that tightrope between entertaining telly and heart on her sleeve and the advertisers would stay happy. 'It'll be like riding through a facial, Kev. That's what I'm going to tell myself anyway.' Urgh. Amping up her beauty regime. Way to relate to the punters. 'I can't see my monitor, but I'm guessing things are a bit sunnier where you are.'

Blah. What are you on about?

'Quite literally, Kath!'

She sang through a few bars of 'Singin' in the Rain'. Most of their viewers would be about to head out into this, so best to make the most of the sympathy card.

'Tell me, Kath,' Kev cut in, 'will you be doing any riding yourself, or will you be getting your trainer to do it for you?'

Oh, ho ho ho ho.

Apparently, one of Kath's many flaws (Kev had quite the list), was that she . . . let's see . . . how did it go? . . . ah yes. She 'delegated to deleterious effect.'

In case she hadn't understood what he'd meant, Kev had clarified.

(This, whilst tapping out a series of texts to his assistant about what she should pack for him.) Kath, apparently, 'lacked the spine to see anything important through.' Getting her brother into rehab? Fail. Keeping her appearance up to snuff? Fail. Championing Kev, the true star of *Brand New Day*? Epic fail – particularly when she kept insisting on throwing his sage advice back in his face and turning the spotlight on her bloody, useless, drunk, dead brother instead of focusing on something fun, which was all the viewers were after anyway. Did he really, after all these years, and all he'd taught her, have to continue to do everything for her as if she were that same clueless Geordie he'd met at Butlins where she'd no doubt still be if he hadn't taken pity on her?

A flame lit deep in the morass of darkness that verbal lashing had carved out inside of her. Kev was full of horse shit. She *was* talented. Relatable. A damn fine dancer, presenter and now, an inspiration to others to not hide their pain. She'd *earned* her spot in the limelight every bit as much as Kev had. More so, now that the advertisers seemed to have perked up since she'd announced her ride.

With that in mind, she decided it was time to start sticking the screw in.

'As you well know, Kev, while you're down there enjoying a bit of beach blanket bingo, I'm going to be riding every single mile along with our LifeTime riders. I think most of them will agree, the physical journey will be short compared to the emotional journey most of our riders have taken to get here. Looking out at them now, knowing the heartache some of them have endured, makes my heart want to burst. We've got one hundred and seventy-four long miles ahead of us.'

'I'd say you'd need those miles to burn off calories from all of that sticky toffee pudding you lot got stuck into yesterday.'

He probably needed them too, if his road producer's report on the number of G&Ts he drank on the plane to Cape Town was anything to go by.

'It was certainly a fun way to start off the trip, Kev. What better way to bond than getting a tour of Cartmel's very own sticky toffee pudding headquarters? We'll show you that exclusive inside glimpse after we set off, but as you can see we've got quite a few riders keen to get on the road to earn some more money for LifeTime.' She pointed at the crowd of people behind her who waved and cheered. A gust of wind caught her brolly and tugged it out of her grasp. A crew member bounded out to get it and as he ran back towards her she did a 'Melania flick' as they'd come to call the tight hand gesture meaning he should stay out of shot. A gesture, it should be noted, usually reserved for Kev.

'Blimey, Kath. There's someone out there who doesn't want you to have a good time. We're slathering on our factor fifty down here, aren't we, girls?'

Kath glanced at the repositioned monitor and saw a group of female athletes towering behind Kev, all geared up in their Commonwealth Games kit, volleyball nets beyond them and the ocean just beyond again. She pictured a shark roaring out of the surf and gobbling up her husband.

'You know us Brits, Kev. We always love a challenge.'

'You're not jokin'.' Kev flicked his thumb at the team of highly respected athletes. 'The girls here have challenged me to a game later. I don't fancy my chances.' He beamed at the camera, gave it a knowing wink and, if she wasn't mistaken, she saw the tiniest twitch of panic flicker across his face.

A whisper of something she hadn't felt for her husband threaded through her. Pity. Somewhere beneath that fame-hungry bon vivant was an incredibly insecure man so desperate to keep his place in the world, he'd belittle a woman, his wife, on the brink of doing a charity ride for her dead, ex-soldier brother who'd cried out for them to help, only to receive a deposit in his bank account so that he'd take his sorrows elsewhere.

'What do you want from your trip, Kev?'

He blinked at her. This wasn't scripted and even she was surprised to hear the genuine interest in her voice.

'Good tan, good fun, an arm-wrestling match with a lion,' he answered with his usual Jack the lad panache. 'Why? What do you want from your trip?'

'Peace, I suppose.'

'Well you won't be getting that, Kath. Not with what the weather man has in store for you. I'm guessing sore knees are a more likely option. Let's all of us cross our fingers that Kath makes it across the finish line intact, shall we?'

He held up his fingers and then made a face as if to say, *she won't make it, but . . . bless her for trying.*

And just like that, she knew Kev's next raft of veiled insults would bounce off her like water on Gore-tex. He was acting like a right plonker. Oblivious to the fact that her LifeTime campaign had unearthed a more caring viewership. Fans who, whilst still keen to watch Kath and Kev make complete idiots out of themselves, also had sorrow and fear and pain in their lives and felt comfort in the knowledge that 'even the likes of Kath and Kev' had to search for silver linings as they ugly cried their way through life's challenges.

Her producer gave her a wrap-it-up twirl of the finger.

'Well you enjoy your beach blanket, Kev. Just a quick note to any of our viewers who live along the route today . . . the graphic should be popping up – yes – there it is on your screens. Don't be shy about giving us a wave of support as we ride past or even join us for a mile or fifty-three. The number, if you'd like to donate is on the bottom of the screen and on our website . . .' She turned to the group and cupped a hand to her mouth. 'Are you ready to get on yer bikes for the trip of a LifeTime?'

A roar of cheers and whoops erupted around her as not only the riders, but a large crowd she hadn't noticed gathering joined in, waving them off as she mounted her bicycle, rode about ten metres down the road only to discover that the first part of the

Coast to Coast path entailed dismounting and walking for three hundred metres.

This, she thought as a dawning recognition rose within her, must've been what it felt like for her brother each and every morning. Elation that he'd made it to another day, despair that it would never be easy.

Chapter Forty-Five

'And so it begins, O Happy Instagrammers. The Epic Journey of Discovery. I won't lie. I'm feeling like an oversized Frodo . . . ready to set off where no Big Boned Goth Girl has gone before . . . the Cumbrian Coastline. In shorts. On a bike. In the rain. Not feeling remotely miserable at all.'

[Camera pans to Sue who is chatting earnestly with Flo and a beardy guy who, by the looks of things, is totally dominating the conversation.]

'These are my trusty, yet unlikely, companions, ready to take on the challenges of the Epic Journey that will end in . . .drumroll please . . . NEWCASTLE UNIVERSITY where I will discover the answer to life, the universe and everything . . . or, at the very least, the lure of the jello shot.' (Off-camera fake crowd noises.) 'Then off to Tynemouth where the journey actually ends, but what sort of epic journey would it be without the inevitable, illuminating side journey?'

Camera pans to Kath Fuller beckoning everyone into formation then back to an EXTREME CLOSE-UP.

'There's our chirpy leader. And now . . . See this? It's my happy face. See this? It's my scared-as-shit face. See this? It's my too-late-to-back-out-now face. Hasta la vista, world. We're off.'

The sooner Flo got some wi-fi the better. She wanted to FaceTime Captain George. See how he was getting on. And, she tersely

267

reminded herself, Stu as well. She'd left him quite a detailed list of George's after care, but couldn't shake the niggling feeling that he'd think pre-warming George's favourite blanket before bedtime wasn't necessary. He'd not seen the look in George's eyes the first time she'd done it. Pure love, was what it had been. Disbelief, in fact, that he should have someone in his life who knew him so very well.

She glanced at her odometer (irksomely configured in metric despite Stu knowing full well she still worked in imperial but she'd been so guilt ridden about him having to nurse poor Captain George in her absence, she'd not insisted he change it as she normally would have done).

Humph. Not quite so far along as she'd hoped two hours of pedalling would have advanced her.

Flo tried to speed up but the gears appeared to be working against her. All twenty-seven of the ridiculous things. Complete excess, when the seven on her own bike had been perfectly fine. These were clacking far more dramatically than hers did. Plus the handlebars were all wrong. And there was no basket.

Clacketyclacketyclack.

She shifted gears again, looked up and saw that Raven, who'd just been beside her, was already halfway up the slope, pedalling away as if she had some sort of in-built rocket launcher powering her up the hill. That, or one too many coffees at breakfast.

She'd learn.

Flo began to hum 'Bicycle Race' by Queen then stopped as the slope most definitely turned into a hill.

Sue picked up the rest of the song, fat-bottomed lyrics and all, for her.

'Great song, isn't it?' Flo said, happy for the distraction from some rather clunky internal gear changes. This was, most assuredly, no Bicycle Race. Bicycle slog more like. Her knees, for some reason, weren't playing ball with the rest of her. Sympathy, no doubt, for Captain George and his poor, snapped cruciate ligament.

A Bicycle Built for Sue

'Mmm . . .' Sue crinkled her nose. 'Who was it by again?'

'Queen, darling.' *Queen!* The anthem makers of Flo's twenties and thirties. She'd absolutely loved them. The charged lyrics. The way they spoke directly to her, championing those who chose to march to the beat of a different drummer. Oh how she'd wept when she'd heard Freddy Mercury had died. So much so, Stu had (fleetingly) been convinced they'd been on friendly terms.

'Queen, yes, that's right.' Sue nodded beneath her helmet, her expression turning wistful. 'Gaz took me for my birthday.'

'To see Queen?' Impossible. She'd have been about nine.

'The movie. *Bohemian Rhapsody*? With the actor from . . .' she hmmed a moment and then, 'I can't remember. One of those shows Gary just loves.'

'Film?' Flo asked instead of commenting on the tense Sue had used about her husband.

'It was ever so good. It was a biography really, about the singer . . . what was his—

'Freddy Mercury.'

'Yes, that's right.'

Of course it was. Flo had been what they now call a super fan. Not obsessive or stalky or anything, but when Queen went on a world tour, Flo had never been more insistent about having a say in her roster. Twelve times, she saw them. Six in Europe, five in the US and one bitterly cold day in Toronto. But she'd been there, just like the postman. Come rain or shine. Whipping out her lighter at a moment's notice. Singing and swaying along with the rest of the crowd. It was at a Queen concert – December 1st, Madison Square Gardens – when she'd finally decided she could, and would, marry Stu. The crowd was at fever pitch when, with characteristic showmanship, Freddy had hushed them all into a silence so taut all twenty thousand fans must've been holding their breath. He sat down at his piano, waited, then began to sing the opening words of 'Love of My Life'.

Stu, whom she had dumped an hour earlier when he'd refused to wave sparklers about on the grounds of health and safety, had somehow found her again and, with his characteristic understatement, slipped his hand into hers, along with a different type of sparkler. The type that came in a little eggshell-blue box.

She'd said yes instantly, and it was right there, amongst the thousands of drunk and stoned and tripping Queen fans, that they shared their first public kiss. It had even involved tongues and, if memory served, Stu's hand up a garish satin top she'd favoured at the time. The next morning was the only time Stu had ever been late for crew call. Five minutes, but still . . . she'd loved wielding that power over him, even if had only been the once.

Behind her she heard voices. She took a glance back, a sharp pain lancing between her thigh and buttock as she did. Crumbs. She'd forgotten it. Her bouncy, luxurious gel seat cover. She could picture it perfectly, sitting on her dressing table so she wouldn't forget – forgotten because of a small whimper she thought she'd heard when Stu was shifting Captain George from the kitchen to his favourite outpost, the conservatory sofa. *To prevent saddle soreness*, Stu had said when he'd given the seat to her with that sensible look of his. Then he'd handed her a small pot of Happy Bottom Bum Butter. A purchase, no doubt, that had caused his bank manager some alarm. She shifted back into place with a grimace. It'd be fine. She could put up with anything for four days. Particularly now that she'd finally succumbed to the lure of padded shorts. Shorts, Stu had assured her, specifically designed for longer rides. Hopefully an Unhappy Bottom wouldn't be a problem. She perked an ear at the sound of voices. 'Competitive oldies on your five o'clock,' she stage whispered to Sue.

Sue wobbled as she looked over her shoulder, just as the two other 'silver surfers' of the group rode up alongside them.

Whilst Flo considered herself an open-minded friendly sort, even to the 'Trevors' of the world, these were the type of people who, particularly in the last few years of flying, irked her the most. The

A Bicycle Built for Sue

lean, wiry type of senior traveller Flo often saw eating homemade granola bars in the middle rows of economy (bliss! After all of that by-choice roughing it they'd endured out on Macchu Picchu or the bus down from Everest or wherever it was people who didn't worry about their knees went). Their skin was always leathery, but with the healthy glow of someone who, without too much encouragement, would sign up for a triathlon 'just to see how they got on.' She and a couple of the other more seasoned flight attendants had taken to calling them 'meerkats', as they were forever hunting about for the whereabouts of the cabin crew. This was where they differed from the Trevors. They didn't want to give information. They wanted to receive it. In high volume. Tailwind speeds. Pronunciation guide for near-extinct tribal peoples. Best kept teppanyaki stand hidden in Tokyo's cavernous subway system. Insatiable, they were. If there was any reading material to back up whatever it was you'd just told them, so much the better. They were exhausting. The lot of them.

Flo tensed as the pair of them rode up alongside her and Sue, their expressions alight with interest as they pointed out flowers on the bankside, cumulonimbus clouds scudding along the horizon (now that the rain had moved east) and the call of a female black-bird. They looked as though they were on holiday rather than an arduous cycle ride raising money for a mental health charity. Didn't look as though they had a care in the world.

'Blustery today,' said one as if they'd all just won the lottery.

'Interesting how strong the wind is,' said the other, 'particularly if you take into account what Trevor said, about the Helm Wind.'

Sue, bless her, made the mistake of asking, 'What's a helm wind?'

The meerkats launched into an astonished retelling of Trevor's 'did you know' all of which, Flo was gratified to note, slowed them down as they reached the hill's ascent so that she could keep up. For some reason, having to get off of her bike and push in front of these two would've been an ego blow she wasn't ready for. Not on Day One, anyway.

'It's Flo, isn't it?' asked Meerkat Two.

Like a few of the other riders – not all – Sue, Raven and Flo had gained a bit of notoriety from their bit on the telly. She tapped her helmet and said, 'I'm surprised you recognised me with this on.'

'Oh, no. It wasn't that, it was more . . .' Meerkat Two put her fingerless gloved hand to her dried apple face and laughed, 'You look a bit different in real life is all.'

Old, thought Flo, grimly. She was going to say *old*.

'Well! Lovely to meet you. See you at the first biscuit stop.'

Meerkat One, mercifully, took that as her cue to push on ahead to see if she and Meerkat Two couldn't buy a little time to bird watch when the route hit the beach again.

Flo, aching from trying to keep up with the lot of them, changed gear.

A stubbly chinned thirty-something man rode up alongside Sue just as the narrow country lane opened, rather miraculously, straight out onto the seafront. He was wearing the 'full kit and caboodle' as Flo liked to say. He had on the yellow shirt, of course, but underneath it was some sort of 'second skin' type top that seemed quite popular amongst the impressively large turn-out of middle-aged men. Cycling shorts, clip-on shoes, reflective, polarised glasses, helmet complete with blinking light on the back and his water bottle was filled with a coloured energy drink. 'Nice day for it,' said the man.

Sue heaved a sigh of relief. At last. Someone to talk with. She'd lost Flo somewhere along the way. A 'comfort stop' that Flo hadn't wanted her to stick around for. She hadn't spotted Raven for a while either. Early on in the ride, it became apparent that Raven's riding pattern was . . . erratic. Powering up a hill one moment, stopping to talk to her phone the next, coasting down a hill sticking her feet out and squealing *wheeeeee!* the next. Not at all the girl who had quietly and diligently helped Sue sort through hundreds of invoices, knocked on dozens of doors and, at the end of each evening, made hot chocolate for the pair of them before slipping off for 'an early night and a read.' It was like meeting an entirely different person. The inverse, she supposed, of discovering her cheery, contented husband was actually spiralling ever downwards into the depths of despair.

Raven, it appeared, had a fun side.

Being an up and coming Instagram star 'on her terms and her terms only' had lit something up in her. She'd never have painted flames onto her eyes before now. It was as if she'd found some spark of joy either from the ride or Instagram or that quirky lad Dylan that she'd not managed to find living with a forty-two-year-old, recently widowed, 111 call handler who didn't quite know what to do with herself beyond tidying their perfectly clean house and watching re-runs of *Bake Off*. She certainly seemed to have more on her mind than 'just pedalling'. A remit Sue had taken to heart until she realised 'just pedalling' left her with quite the surplus of thinking time.

'We're lucky the rain cleared up,' said Sue, happy to escape the rabbit hole of too much personal contemplation.

The man laughed, Sue's reflection catching in the polarised lenses of his glasses. 'It'll be back soon enough.'

'Oh?'

'I'm from Newcastle, like Kath,' he said as an explanation for his authority on the matter. 'The weather goes through all four seasons at least once an hour here Ooop North.'

'Good thing I hadn't planned on coming back with a tan,' Sue quipped from an arsenal of chit-chat she didn't realise she had.

'Charlie,' he said with a little wave.

'Sue,' she said, swerving to avoid a puddle.

'First charity ride?'

'Does it show?'

'No,' he said, amiably. 'Not in the least. This is my third,' he volunteered.

'Oh?' That seemed . . . committed.

'What made you choose this particular ride?' Charlie asked, pulling his reflective sunglasses off to reveal a pair of warm brown eyes.

'Oh. . . .' Sue had really rather hoped everyone had seen her piece on the show and that she'd never have to talk about it again. Kath had been the one to actually explain about Gary and his . . . decision. She'd not had to say a word except, of course, that she was really pleased to be going on the ride and to be part of such a good cause.

'I'm on the ride because of my mum,' Charlie volunteered.

'Oh, I'm – sorry?' It was difficult to know how to respond to a statement like that.

'Not to worry. Chemical imbalances are what they are, but . . . she's getting help now, that's the main thing. For her bipolar,' Charlie explained when Sue threw him a questioning look.

'Gosh,' said Sue. 'That's sounds complicated.'

Charlie nodded. 'Can be. Especially when she stops taking her meds. There're only so many times you can explain away picking up your mum from the police station for an ASBO.' He laughed as if he'd just told Sue his mother was regularly being caught talking too loudly at the library. 'But! Single working mum, good person at heart – these things happen. It's my turn to look after her. Anyway, she seems to have resigned herself to the fact that if she wants to participate in so-called normal life, she's going to have to take her meds.'

Sue nodded, feeling an unexpected prickling of tears. Maybe if Gaz had said something, to his doctor even, they might've given him happy pills to get through his rough patch.

'But enough of my hard luck story,' Charlie waved it away.

'No,' Sue cut in before he could ask her about her story again. 'I'm interested. Please. Go on.'

Marijuana, booze and . . . Raven was no expert . . . but she was pretty sure this latest group of young men were smoking crack. Not that they were openly smoking it, but they definitely saw her coming and were definitely behaving strangely. Excellent life choices, peeps! Not.

It turned out that when they weren't on country lanes the cycle route took them 'off road' onto some pretty amazing cycle/pedestrian routes, many of which were regularly used by dog walkers, joggers, walkers, all sorts. There were also a healthy array of benches with plaques on. *To Doris. To Harold. For The Beckermet Birders Who First Spotted the Long-Billed Dowitcher.* She couldn't blame the folk who stopped and took a pew for a while. Some of the nature-y bits were lush. Happening upon the ultra-urban looking lads in a beautiful woodland was a bit weirdy, though. On a par with riding her bicycle along the coast, only to round a corner and see a vast nuclear power plant looming above reams of chain-linked fencing, coiled razor wire and machine-gun-wielding police officers. It was like happening upon a surreal, post-apocalypse film set. There were big signs everywhere warning about the danger of entering, no drones (as if she carried one of those around in her back pocket) and, amusingly, a sign recommending cycle path users give way to passing trains. Errr. Okay?

She looked away as she passed the bench full of men – they looked older up close – sitting, legs spread wide apart, staring out at the valley below as they were bathed in a burst of unexpected late-morning sunshine.

How depressing. She hoped brain annihilation wasn't what she was doing by turning down her place at uni, moving out of her parents', and ignoring their increasingly irate once-a-week messages about how disappointing a daughter she was (this week's was a corker) all to pursue hopes and dreams even she couldn't pin down.

All she knew was what she didn't want. Which didn't really seem a brilliant starting point. Then again, deduction narrowed the field of choices, so . . .

'Hello, there!'

Much to her shock, Raven turned to see Kath Fuller ride up alongside her without, miracle of miracles, her ever-present camera crew in tow.

'How're you getting on?' Kath asked as she easily met Raven's pace.

'Good. Yeah. Fine. Just . . .' she shifted a bit on her cycling seat. 'You know. Finding my groove.'

'I saw your Insta post during tea break.'

'Oh?'

Ruh-roh.

'I love your honesty,' Kath said.

Raven winced. She'd not really minced words when it came to her thoughts on celebrities participating in charity events to up their popularity. She hadn't cited Kath by name, but it was pretty clear the post had been inspired by her. Raven had made the post after she saw Kath stopping to sign some autographs for a group of women outside a coffee shop just a few miles into the ride, camera crew in tow. It had seemed so self-serving, particularly as she'd been banging on about doing the ride for her brother. It hadn't felt an entirely fair assessment seeing as she had yet to divulge why she was on the ride, but . . .

'It made me think,' Kath said, as if putting oneself under the spotlight was a good thing.

'Oh?'

'Absolutely. The last thing my brother would've cared about was a bunch of people in lycra riding across the country to raise money for a charity.'

'What would he have wanted?'

'To be listened to.'

Raven nodded. She got that. If her parents had ever, like, for one minute even, sat down and asked, what do you think/want/believe, she might not be here right now.

'Did you see those lads back there?' Kath asked.

grateful to see a town in her entire life.
most peculiarly, of tinned spaghetti. Just
m the end of her ride, the smooth pave-
nd her gratitude evaporated. Her bum
n reminders that she was mortal, thank
l her eyes on the end of the street where
ders chatting, drinking energy drinks
they'd had an absolutely brilliant time
n reminder that she was mortal. Finally,
dismounted her bicycle with little to

ut there?'

rse smile as Becky, one of the group
out of her hands and wheeled it into
I—'

there on one of these things,' Becky

e ran a hand the length of her body.
e.'

t away. 'Honestly. It's why I do the
eeping up with you lot.'
Which did beg the question, how

ing her as she pulled up next to
er. Had it really taken her five

ng things beyond their limits
aptain George lying in his bed,
fully thin without his coat of

ad her cheer elsewhere. If she

'Yeah.' She did her utmost best to keep a neutral face because she wasn't quite sure where Kath was going with this.

'They remind me of my brother.'

'Oh?' Gosh.

'Ex-military, if their tats are anything to go by.'

Raven made a yeah, yeah, obvs nod. What the hell? Kath Fuller, down with the ins and outs of military tats. Who knew?

All of a sudden Kath applied her brakes and threw her thumb over her shoulder. 'Want to go back and have a chat with them with me?'

'Ummm . . .' *Not really, they were drug addicts?*

'I promise you it'll be interesting.'

Freaky was what it would be. Like Dorothy encountering a talking scarecrow or . . . She shrugged. Who was she kidding? It wouldn't be any freakier than finding out Dylan was normal beneath all of his street talk and selfie obsessions or moving in with a woman whose husband decided to end it all out of nowhere.

Kath smiled as she rolled to a halt, unclipped her shoes from her pedals and studied Raven in a way that didn't make her squirmy. Which was little short of a miracle, as being under anyone's scrutiny tended to make her squirmy. 'C'mon. It'll be interesting. Particularly for someone with flame eyes who likes to champion the underdog.'

Ack. Now she did feel squirmy.

In her head she definitely did. In reality? Not such a great track record on that front. Although . . . she had sort of helped Dylan get a job. Well, Dean's brother Sue had really, but she'd been the go-between. By all accounts he was loving it. Said Dean let him wear anything he wanted to work so long as the computers stayed pukka.

Raven glanced back at the lads then thought, *fuck it.* I'm with Kath of Kath and Kev. They'll stick two fingers up at us, tell us where to stuff it, then we can carry on riding.

Twenty minutes later, Raven was utterly gobsmacked. The men she'd thought were smoking crack told Kath they were actually ex-soldiers doing art therapy. Kath had rightly recognised one of their tattoos and they were astonishingly easy to mine for information. Maybe it was Kath being famous that made them so chatty. Maybe it was meeting a Big Boned Goth Girl with flames shooting out of her eyes and wearing lycra. Maybe they were just lonely. None of them could find a job. All of them were desperate to be listened to. To be heard. Desperate to figure out how to live in their small towns with their small lives making absolutely no difference whatsoever when they'd been programmed to put their own lives at stake for a bigger cause: a country that had, effectively, turned its back on them when they'd come home. They'd eventually pulled the notebooks Raven had mistaken for gear out of their jackets and showed them the mask templates they'd each been given to draw their emotions on.

Fucking harrowing came to mind when the first one reluctantly pulled out his drawing. *Lonely* for another. *Savaged* for the third. They gave her a template when she mentioned she liked to draw. She put it in her pocket wondering what her 'inside face' would look like if she let it out.

'Is it helping you, chaps?' Kath asked. 'The therapy?'

'Better than sitting round doing nothing,' said one.

'Yeah, definitely,' said the one who'd drawn a face that made *The Scream* look like a cheery yodeller. 'Takes what's in here,' he tapped his head, 'and gets it out. At least for a while.'

'Thanks for stopping,' said the third. 'It . . . it makes a difference. To be listened to. Properly.'

Kath's eyes got all leaky with tears as she hugged them all and promised to send a shout out on the next morning's show for 'taking the ride to another level'.

As Raven and Kath pedalled away, Raven began to craft a re traction for her previous Insta post. Kath wasn't a do-gooder givi face time to a charity she kept at arm's length. She was a wom actively making amends.

Flo had never been mor
Even a town that smelt,
a few hundred metres fro
ment turned to cobbles a
had had more than enoug
you very much. She traine
she could see dozens of r
and generally looking as if
versus having endured a grin
mercifully, she arrived and
no panache.

'Alright, love? Good day o
Flo forced on a yes, of cou
support team, took her bicycle
a long row of cycles. 'Yes, fine
'You wouldn't catch me out
interjected chirpily.
'Oh?'

'Wouldn't last five minutes.' Sh
'This was not built for enduranc
'No? I'm sure you could—'
Becky waved Flo's feeble protes
van. Makes me feel athletic just k
'But . . . you drive at the back.'
had she got there before Flo?

A vague memory of a van pass
the seaside hotel came back to h
minutes just to get off her bicycle?
Jennifer's warnings about pushi
sprang to mind, as did an image of C
his shaved leg and hip looking pai
shaggy fur.

She willed Becky to move on, spre

were to take one step her weaknesses would be as exposed as George's were.

'Fola's doing stretches in the hotel ballroom if you need a bit of a cool down.'

'Oh, I'm fine.' Flo lifted one foot and pretended to do a little stretch. A move that unleashed an unexpected rush of emotion. She'd felt incredibly alone today in a way she hadn't felt since before she'd been married. Alone and guilty and desperate for news on Captain George which she daren't ask for because hearing Stu's calm, steady voice would only add to the guilt and longing for his familiarity she was already feeling.

'Are you doing the ride on your own?'

'No, I . . .' Flo scanned the crowd for Sue and Raven, and came up empty. Little wonder as Raven had, with her encouragement, ridden ahead much earlier in the day and set off from the tea breaks near enough when Flo arrived.

Sue had ridden ahead as well, occasionally falling back to check that Flo was alright, but, again with Flo's encouragement, had pushed ahead, clearly enjoying listening to everyone and the stories that had brought them on the ride.

'Well, let's get you inside for a nice hot cuppa before teatime, shall we?' Becky pointed towards the hotel entrance where, to Flo's delight, Raven and Sue were scanning the crowd. She waved, they waved, Flo excused herself from Becky and all of her positivity, gratefully accepting the ginger biscuit and cup of tea Sue handed her as they entered the hotel where they would regroup, sleep, then find a way to do it all over again.

Kath closed her eyes, lifted up her chin and let the sea air buffet her. It had been a long, emotional day but strangely curative. As if taking these baby steps towards marrying her public persona with her private self were helping her tap back into the person she never realised she wanted to be: a listener. Of course she listened to people on the telly.

But she also had a producer's voice in her ear, Kev's expressions to read, her own reeling thoughts trying to keep herself a few seconds ahead of what was actually happening right this very moment, so . . . this was new. Listening and receiving without a plan.

'Katherine?'

She blinked her eyes open and jumped straight into TV hostess mode. 'Fola! Hello. How did you get on today?'

'Good,' he nodded earnestly. 'Really good. Lots of thinking time.'

'Oh? Did you not ride along with anyone today? It seemed a pretty chatty group,' she added to cover the fact she'd been tactically ignoring him hoping that, because he was so gregarious and beautiful, he would have met people on his own.

'Yes, absolutely. I chatted with many people, but I also had a lot of time to think.'

Six hours and thirty-seven minutes, if anyone was asking.

'It is amazing meeting all of these people who—' he looked out to the sea, searching for the right words. 'People who have known such loss. Who are so honest about how they feel. How they got to where they are in life. I find it very humbling.'

'You? Fola, you're a total saint. I think you don't have anything to worry about on that front.'

Fola shook his head. 'No, I am no saint and it's never a bad thing to be humbled.'

He said it in exactly the same way the Dalai Lama would've said it. Come to think of it, the Dalai Lama was a pretty humble guy.

'Oh, come on. You're one of the kindest, nicest, most helpful people I have ever met.' She touched his arm. He looked at the spot her hand had vacated and then looked her in the eye with an electric intensity.

'Katherine. I have a confession to make.'

Oh, please no. Don't let him confess that he loved her. Not now that, after her own six hours and thirty-seven minutes of contemplation, she'd finally come to terms with the fact that loving him was completely mad. Seeing those soldiers today . . . it had been . . . beyond real. They didn't have a solitary second spare in their lives to live on cloud cuckoo land because they were too busy dealing with the reality of it.

So, no. She didn't love Fola. She loved the *idea* of him.

This little fiction she'd been carrying around – this secret romance – it was so much lovelier to dream about than face the reality that she didn't love her husband anymore.

She was a textbook menopausal mid-life crisis.

Her thoughts pinged back to the ex-soldiers and how grateful they'd been to have been seen, to have been heard. Now that had been humbling. Maybe instead of Fola she should fall in love with a combat veteran – No! She returned to the mantra she'd been repeating over and over with each turn of her pedals today: What would Oprah do? How would she SuperSoul this?

Oprah would look it in the face and call it what it was. A time to decide what kind of person she, Kath Fuller, actually wanted to be.

Oprah did not fill emotional voids with deeply gorgeous, incredibly compassionate personal trainers. Oprah did not pretend she was happy in a relationship she didn't want to be in anymore. No, Oprah dug deep. Right into her soul. Fearlessly. Unafraid to admit she had, in her time, felt bad about herself whether she was fat or thin. That being rich didn't take away the hurt that came from people having told her she was ugly as a pre-teen. That fame came at a price . . . a vulnerability to public opinion. Opinion Kath had tried to keep entirely positive whilst stuffing secret after secret into her closet. Oprah kept it real. Which made opening up the closet to the rest of the world a pain-free exercise. There was nothing to hide.

'My girlfriend and I were talking—' Fola began.

'Oh?' Her smile stayed bright, but she saw instantly that his 'confession' was tactical. He knew she fancied him and was finding the kindest, gentlest way of letting her down which made her feel worse than she already did, but . . . alas alack, served her right for having believed a life in the limelight with Kev would make her feel whole.

'Yes, we were talking and I said to her, I have learned a lesson today.'

Kath's brow furrowed. 'Really?'

'Yes. I learnt that you are made of much more strength than you think you are.' Fola smiled that sweet smile of his and despite herself, she blushed.

'Don't be ridiculous. I'm no different to any of the other riders.'

'That's what makes you strong,' Fola said.

'I don't follow.'

'I've never really seen you interact with other people and I thought—'

Oh, god. He'd thought she was a spoilt princess.

'I was impressed today,' he said, instead of spelling out what they both knew. She *had* been a spoiled princess, and then her brother had died and the scales had dropped. Or whatever it was that happened when you realized, too late, giving money to someone who was asking for your time was perhaps more cruel than pretending you'd never received the call.

It was too late, of course, to truly make amends to her brother, but . . . she could spend the rest of her life trying. 'Thank you, Fola.'

He gave her shoulder a squeeze then scanned her in a way that she saw now, was entirely professional. A physio looking for faults. Not a future lover looking for clues about the intimacies they might one day share.

'You're off the clock, actually,' she said, giving her hands a swift rub and her feet a quick stomp. 'You should go get a drink. Eat a family pack of Oreos or whatever it is trainers do to indulge themselves.'

Fola laughed then. A proper, full belly laugh. 'You know what I do?'

'No.' She hadn't a clue. Much to her shame, she had never once thought about Fola's real life. Just the fictional one they might live if they ran away from her troubles and her stresses into a future dappled with rainbows and unicorns . . . Now that she thought about it, she knew next to nothing about Fola Onaberi other than that he was gorgeous, kind, funny, smart, proactive, and obviously in love with his girlfriend who she hoped to god appreciated what a lucky woman she was.

'I watch your show.'

'What? No you don't.'

'Honestly, I do. You make me laugh. You make everyone laugh. Your heart is kind.'

'What? Because I know how to take a cream pie in the face?'

That month where Kev had lobbed a pie at her every time a politician got one in the gob had been a cracker. Not.

Fola shook his head, disappointed that was the first place she went. 'No, because you do it knowing you'll look foolish but do it anyway because it makes other people happy.' Fola gave a few rich chortles as he pictured her with cream pie on her face, then waved his hands between them as if erasing the cream and returning her to her normal face. He took her hands in his. 'You are a very kind woman, Katherine Fuller. You change lives.'

She pulled her hands out of his because it felt too nice, too intimate, and laughed her own, more cynical laugh. 'That's very sweet of you, Fola, but now I think you're stretching it a bit.'

'You changed my life.'

She smirked. 'I doubt that, somehow.'

'You were the first person who hired me to be their personal trainer.'

'No, that's not true.' She thought back to the list of references she'd had for him and came up blank. 'I had – someone must've—'

Fola threw her the first sheepish look she'd ever seen from him. 'I made up all of the names of all of the clients I had.'

'What? No. You were—'

'—desperate.' He filled in for her. 'No one would hire me.'

'So you fibbed?'

His grin turned apologetic. 'I thought that was how it worked in the magical world of showbiz.' He did some jazz hands. 'And I definitely didn't think you'd hire me if I didn't have some famous names on my roster.'

Kath thought for a minute and then burst out laughing. Hilarious. Absolutely completely hilarious. 'So you never made Cheryl's bum—' she made a gesture that she hoped signified absolutely perfect.

'Never met her in my life.'

She laughed some more, throwing out more names she vaguely remembered from the list, each and every single one getting a 'no, not them either' shrug from Fola.

When she'd calmed down and had assured him it was in absolutely no way a problem that he'd faked it till he made it, they walked back to the hotel in a companionable silence. In the large lounge where many of the cyclists had gathered, Raven was drawing on the back of a T-shirt, a queue of people behind her.

'What's this?' Kath asked as she took in the large flower Raven was drawing on the back of her shirt.

'An aster,' she said then pointed towards an older woman – ah it was Flo! – who seemed intent on attracting Fola's attention. 'Flo's had a hard day,' Raven said in a way that made it perfectly plausible that an aster was the only solution for it.

'That's kind. Any particular reason you chose the aster?' asked Kath.

'It means patience and a love of variety,' smiled Raven. Her brightly coloured flame eyes had, from sweat most likely, faded and pooled in tear drop splodges of colour along her jawline.

'I'm going for the daisy,' volunteered a dark, curly haired woman watching Raven with hawklike intensity. Rachel? Rachel who, if Kath wasn't mistaken, had suffered from severe post-partum depression

'Yeah.' She did her utmost best to keep a neutral face because she wasn't quite sure where Kath was going with this.

'They remind me of my brother.'

'Oh?' Gosh.

'Ex-military, if their tats are anything to go by.'

Raven made a yeah, yeah, obvs nod. What the hell? Kath Fuller, down with the ins and outs of military tats. Who knew?

All of a sudden Kath applied her brakes and threw her thumb over her shoulder. 'Want to go back and have a chat with them with me?'

'Ummm . . .' *Not really, they were drug addicts?*

'I promise you it'll be interesting.'

Freaky was what it would be. Like Dorothy encountering a talking scarecrow or . . . She shrugged. Who was she kidding? It wouldn't be any freakier than finding out Dylan was normal beneath all of his street talk and selfie obsessions or moving in with a woman whose husband decided to end it all out of nowhere.

Kath smiled as she rolled to a halt, unclipped her shoes from her pedals and studied Raven in a way that didn't make her squirmy. Which was little short of a miracle, as being under anyone's scrutiny tended to make her squirmy. 'C'mon. It'll be interesting. Particularly for someone with flame eyes who likes to champion the underdog.'

Ack. Now she did feel squirmy.

In her head she definitely did. In reality? Not such a great track record on that front. Although . . . she had sort of helped Dylan get a job. Well, Dean's brother Sue had really, but she'd been the go-between. By all accounts he was loving it. Said Dean let him wear anything he wanted to work so long as the computers stayed pukka.

Raven glanced back at the lads then thought, *fuck it.* I'm with Kath of Kath and Kev. They'll stick two fingers up at us, tell us where to stuff it, then we can carry on riding.

Twenty minutes later, Raven was utterly gobsmacked. The men she'd thought were smoking crack told Kath they were actually ex-soldiers doing art therapy. Kath had rightly recognised one of their tattoos and they were astonishingly easy to mine for information. Maybe it was Kath being famous that made them so chatty. Maybe it was meeting a Big Boned Goth Girl with flames shooting out of her eyes and wearing lycra. Maybe they were just lonely. None of them could find a job. All of them were desperate to be listened to. To be heard. Desperate to figure out how to live in their small towns with their small lives making absolutely no difference whatsoever when they'd been programmed to put their own lives at stake for a bigger cause: a country that had, effectively, turned its back on them when they'd come home. They'd eventually pulled the notebooks Raven had mistaken for gear out of their jackets and showed them the mask templates they'd each been given to draw their emotions on.

Fucking harrowing came to mind when the first one reluctantly pulled out his drawing. *Lonely* for another. *Savaged* for the third. They gave her a template when she mentioned she liked to draw. She put it in her pocket wondering what her 'inside face' would look like if she let it out.

'Is it helping you, chaps?' Kath asked. 'The therapy?'

'Better than sitting round doing nothing,' said one.

'Yeah, definitely,' said the one who'd drawn a face that made *The Scream* look like a cheery yodeller. 'Takes what's in here,' he tapped his head, 'and gets it out. At least for a while.'

'Thanks for stopping,' said the third. 'It . . . it makes a difference. To be listened to. Properly.'

Kath's eyes got all leaky with tears as she hugged them all and promised to send a shout out on the next morning's show for 'taking the ride to another level'.

As Raven and Kath pedalled away, Raven began to craft a retraction for her previous Insta post. Kath wasn't a do-gooder giving face time to a charity she kept at arm's length. She was a woman actively making amends.

Chapter Forty-Six

10 SECOND INTERSTITIAL: BRAND NEW DAY

VISUAL: Sue Young

GRAPHIC: Sue Young, Fundraiser for LifeTime

AUDIO TRANSCRIPT:

SUE YOUNG: I can't believe it.

Off-camera question: What can't you believe?

SUE YOUNG: That I just rode my bike fifty-three miles.

Off-camera question: Have you not done that before?

SUE YOUNG: No. Nothing like it. It's such a sense of . . . of . . . achievement, you know? Doing something you thought you never could.

GRAPHIC: BRAND NEW DAY: Bringing out the Best in Britons Everywhere

Flo had never been more grateful to see a town in her entire life. Even a town that smelt, most peculiarly, of tinned spaghetti. Just a few hundred metres from the end of her ride, the smooth pavement turned to cobbles and her gratitude evaporated. Her bum had had more than enough reminders that she was mortal, thank you very much. She trained her eyes on the end of the street where she could see dozens of riders chatting, drinking energy drinks and generally looking as if they'd had an absolutely brilliant time versus having endured a grim reminder that she was mortal. Finally, mercifully, she arrived and dismounted her bicycle with little to no panache.

'Alright, love? Good day out there?'

Flo forced on a yes, of course smile as Becky, one of the group support team, took her bicycle out of her hands and wheeled it into a long row of cycles. 'Yes, fine, I—'

'You wouldn't catch me out there on one of these things,' Becky interjected chirpily.

'Oh?'

'Wouldn't last five minutes.' She ran a hand the length of her body. 'This was not built for endurance.'

'No? I'm sure you could—'

Becky waved Flo's feeble protest away. 'Honestly. It's why I do the van. Makes me feel athletic just keeping up with you lot.'

'But . . . you drive at the back.' Which did beg the question, how had she got there before Flo?

A vague memory of a van passing her as she pulled up next to the seaside hotel came back to her. Had it really taken her five minutes just to get off her bicycle?

Jennifer's warnings about pushing things beyond their limits sprang to mind, as did an image of Captain George lying in his bed, his shaved leg and hip looking painfully thin without his coat of shaggy fur.

She willed Becky to move on, spread her cheer elsewhere. If she were to take one step her weaknesses would be as exposed as George's were.

'Fola's doing stretches in the hotel ballroom if you need a bit of a cool down.'

'Oh, I'm fine.' Flo lifted one foot and pretended to do a little stretch. A move that unleashed an unexpected rush of emotion. She'd felt incredibly alone today in a way she hadn't felt since before she'd been married. Alone and guilty and desperate for news on Captain George which she daren't ask for because hearing Stu's calm, steady voice would only add to the guilt and longing for his familiarity she was already feeling.

'Are you doing the ride on your own?'

'No, I . . .' Flo scanned the crowd for Sue and Raven, and came up empty. Little wonder as Raven had, with her encouragement, ridden ahead much earlier in the day and set off from the tea breaks near enough when Flo arrived.

Sue had ridden ahead as well, occasionally falling back to check that Flo was alright, but, again with Flo's encouragement, had pushed ahead, clearly enjoying listening to everyone and the stories that had brought them on the ride.

'Well, let's get you inside for a nice hot cuppa before teatime, shall we?' Becky pointed towards the hotel entrance where, to Flo's delight, Raven and Sue were scanning the crowd. She waved, they waved, Flo excused herself from Becky and all of her positivity, gratefully accepting the ginger biscuit and cup of tea Sue handed her as they entered the hotel where they would regroup, sleep, then find a way to do it all over again.

Kath closed her eyes, lifted up her chin and let the sea air buffet her. It had been a long, emotional day but strangely curative. As if taking these baby steps towards marrying her public persona with her private self were helping her tap back into the person she never realised she wanted to be: a listener. Of course she listened to people on the telly.

But she also had a producer's voice in her ear, Kev's expressions to read, her own reeling thoughts trying to keep herself a few seconds ahead of what was actually happening right this very moment, so . . . this was new. Listening and receiving without a plan.

'Katherine?'

She blinked her eyes open and jumped straight into TV hostess mode. 'Fola! Hello. How did you get on today?'

'Good,' he nodded earnestly. 'Really good. Lots of thinking time.'

'Oh? Did you not ride along with anyone today? It seemed a pretty chatty group,' she added to cover the fact she'd been tactically ignoring him hoping that, because he was so gregarious and beautiful, he would have met people on his own.

'Yes, absolutely. I chatted with many people, but I also had a lot of time to think.'

Six hours and thirty-seven minutes, if anyone was asking.

'It is amazing meeting all of these people who—' he looked out to the sea, searching for the right words. 'People who have known such loss. Who are so honest about how they feel. How they got to where they are in life. I find it very humbling.'

'You? Fola, you're a total saint. I think you don't have anything to worry about on that front.'

Fola shook his head. 'No, I am no saint and it's never a bad thing to be humbled.'

He said it in exactly the same way the Dalai Lama would've said it. Come to think of it, the Dalai Lama was a pretty humble guy.

'Oh, come on. You're one of the kindest, nicest, most helpful people I have ever met.' She touched his arm. He looked at the spot her hand had vacated and then looked her in the eye with an electric intensity.

'Katherine. I have a confession to make.'

Oh, please no. Don't let him confess that he loved her. Not now that, after her own six hours and thirty-seven minutes of contemplation, she'd finally come to terms with the fact that loving him was completely mad. Seeing those soldiers today . . . it had been . . . beyond real. They didn't have a solitary second spare in their lives to live on cloud cuckoo land because they were too busy dealing with the reality of it.

So, no. She didn't love Fola. She loved the *idea* of him.

This little fiction she'd been carrying around – this secret romance – it was so much lovelier to dream about than face the reality that she didn't love her husband anymore.

She was a textbook menopausal mid-life crisis.

Her thoughts pinged back to the ex-soldiers and how grateful they'd been to have been seen, to have been heard. Now that had been humbling. Maybe instead of Fola she should fall in love with a combat veteran – No! She returned to the mantra she'd been repeating over and over with each turn of her pedals today: What would Oprah do? How would she SuperSoul this?

Oprah would look it in the face and call it what it was. A time to decide what kind of person she, Kath Fuller, actually wanted to be.

Oprah did not fill emotional voids with deeply gorgeous, incredibly compassionate personal trainers. Oprah did not pretend she was happy in a relationship she didn't want to be in anymore. No, Oprah dug deep. Right into her soul. Fearlessly. Unafraid to admit she had, in her time, felt bad about herself whether she was fat or thin. That being rich didn't take away the hurt that came from people having told her she was ugly as a pre-teen. That fame came at a price . . . a vulnerability to public opinion. Opinion Kath had tried to keep entirely positive whilst stuffing secret after secret into her closet. Oprah kept it real. Which made opening up the closet to the rest of the world a pain-free exercise. There was nothing to hide.

'My girlfriend and I were talking—' Fola began.

'Oh?' Her smile stayed bright, but she saw instantly that his 'confession' was tactical. He knew she fancied him and was finding the kindest, gentlest way of letting her down which made her feel worse than she already did, but . . . alas alack, served her right for having believed a life in the limelight with Kev would make her feel whole.

'Yes, we were talking and I said to her, I have learned a lesson today.'

Kath's brow furrowed. 'Really?'

'Yes. I learnt that you are made of much more strength than you think you are.' Fola smiled that sweet smile of his and despite herself, she blushed.

'Don't be ridiculous. I'm no different to any of the other riders.'

'That's what makes you strong,' Fola said.

'I don't follow.'

'I've never really seen you interact with other people and I thought—'

Oh, god. He'd thought she was a spoilt princess.

'I was impressed today,' he said, instead of spelling out what they both knew. She *had* been a spoiled princess, and then her brother had died and the scales had dropped. Or whatever it was that happened when you realized, too late, giving money to someone who was asking for your time was perhaps more cruel than pretending you'd never received the call.

It was too late, of course, to truly make amends to her brother, but . . . she could spend the rest of her life trying. 'Thank you, Fola.'

He gave her shoulder a squeeze then scanned her in a way that she saw now, was entirely professional. A physio looking for faults. Not a future lover looking for clues about the intimacies they might one day share.

'You're off the clock, actually,' she said, giving her hands a swift rub and her feet a quick stomp. 'You should go get a drink. Eat a family pack of Oreos or whatever it is trainers do to indulge themselves.'

Fola laughed then. A proper, full belly laugh. 'You know what I do?'

'No.' She hadn't a clue. Much to her shame, she had never once thought about Fola's real life. Just the fictional one they might live if they ran away from her troubles and her stresses into a future dappled with rainbows and unicorns . . . Now that she thought about it, she knew next to nothing about Fola Onaberi other than that he was gorgeous, kind, funny, smart, proactive, and obviously in love with his girlfriend who she hoped to god appreciated what a lucky woman she was.

'I watch your show.'

'What? No you don't.'

'Honestly, I do. You make me laugh. You make everyone laugh. Your heart is kind.'

'What? Because I know how to take a cream pie in the face?'

That month where Kev had lobbed a pie at her every time a politician got one in the gob had been a cracker. Not.

Fola shook his head, disappointed that was the first place she went. 'No, because you do it knowing you'll look foolish but do it anyway because it makes other people happy.' Fola gave a few rich chortles as he pictured her with cream pie on her face, then waved his hands between them as if erasing the cream and returning her to her normal face. He took her hands in his. 'You are a very kind woman, Katherine Fuller. You change lives.'

She pulled her hands out of his because it felt too nice, too intimate, and laughed her own, more cynical laugh. 'That's very sweet of you, Fola, but now I think you're stretching it a bit.'

'You changed my life.'

She smirked. 'I doubt that, somehow.'

'You were the first person who hired me to be their personal trainer.'

'No, that's not true.' She thought back to the list of references she'd had for him and came up blank. 'I had – someone must've—'

Fola threw her the first sheepish look she'd ever seen from him. 'I made up all of the names of all of the clients I had.'

285

'What? No. You were—'

'—desperate.' He filled in for her. 'No one would hire me.'

'So you fibbed?'

His grin turned apologetic. 'I thought that was how it worked in the magical world of showbiz.' He did some jazz hands. 'And I definitely didn't think you'd hire me if I didn't have some famous names on my roster.'

Kath thought for a minute and then burst out laughing. Hilarious. Absolutely completely hilarious. 'So you never made Cheryl's bum—' she made a gesture that she hoped signified absolutely perfect.

'Never met her in my life.'

She laughed some more, throwing out more names she vaguely remembered from the list, each and every single one getting a 'no, not them either' shrug from Fola.

When she'd calmed down and had assured him it was in absolutely no way a problem that he'd faked it till he made it, they walked back to the hotel in a companionable silence. In the large lounge where many of the cyclists had gathered, Raven was drawing on the back of a T-shirt, a queue of people behind her.

'What's this?' Kath asked as she took in the large flower Raven was drawing on the back of her shirt.

'An aster,' she said then pointed towards an older woman – ah it was Flo! – who seemed intent on attracting Fola's attention. 'Flo's had a hard day,' Raven said in a way that made it perfectly plausible that an aster was the only solution for it.

'That's kind. Any particular reason you chose the aster?' asked Kath.

'It means patience and a love of variety,' smiled Raven. Her brightly coloured flame eyes had, from sweat most likely, faded and pooled in tear drop splodges of colour along her jawline.

'I'm going for the daisy,' volunteered a dark, curly haired woman watching Raven with hawklike intensity. Rachel? Rachel who, if Kath wasn't mistaken, had suffered from severe post-partum depression a few years back. She'd made a life-changing phone call to LifeTime when her mother-in-law came to visit her and her colicky baby twins. She'd let herself in, then run up the stairs when she'd realised the house was quiet. Too quiet. It had been. Rachel had been holding a pillow over their faces for just a moment's peace. The twins were eight now and the loves of her life. 'It stands for family,' she said proudly, then teared up, which the chap next to her saw and pulled her into a hug with a 'there, there, we're all in this together, aren't we, love?' And just like that, Kath knew she was in the right place, at the right time and her life, whichever way it was meant to go, should be guided by exactly this.

Sue took a sip of her soda water, wincing as she discovered stretching her legs out was much more difficult than it had been a couple of hours earlier when they'd sat down for supper. Maybe she should've followed Flo's lead and been 'ex-Fola-ated' – a Flo-term which Sue was pretty sure meant get a massage or kneaded or cracked or whatever it was physios did to make people like Kath so fit and full of beans and people like Flo walk with more comfort. The poor woman. She'd never seen such a production getting out of an armchair. Flo had laughed it off, of course, but . . . Flo laughed about most things. Didn't mean there wasn't something buried beneath that smile of hers. Not in a million years would Sue forget the kindness with which she'd handled her telephone call all of those weeks ago. But it was difficult to burrow beneath all of that . . . efficiency.

'Well, hello there. I wondered where you'd got to.'

Sue looked up and saw Charlie standing there, a half-drunk pint in his hand.

'I was just watching the artist at work,' she said.

They both looked over and watched as Raven put the finishing touches on what appeared to be a sunflower.

'Feeling alright? It wasn't too bad today,' said Charlie. 'Long, but . . .'

'No, absolutely. I'm good. Well . . . a bit crickly.'

'Is that a technical term?' Charlie laughed. 'Crickly?'

'Yes. I learned it from Fola.' She hadn't. She'd just made it up, but the joke obviously didn't have wings.

'Oh,' Charlie blew out a solitary, low-toned whistle, pointing at the empty chair beside her before sitting down. 'Been seen by the big man, have you?'

'No.' She nodded towards the lobby where Flo had disappeared right after supper with two plastic bags of ice she'd bewitched from the bartender. 'He saw my friend, Flo? Her knees are giving her gyp.' Sue said the last part in a low voice even though Flo was two entire floors away in their room lying on the first of three single beds the hotel had somehow levered into the room. They had to walk sideways between them! Anyway. It was for charity.

'Flo?'

'She's umm . . .' Sue tapped her chin. She never really liked describing people. It felt . . . well in Flo's case it felt unfair because she was the oldest one on the tour, possibly bar the two women she'd taken to calling 'the meerkats' and Sue was pretty sure the last way Flo would've liked to be described was 'old'.

'She's a bit more mature than me? She's the one who convinced Raven and me to join her, actually. Great laugh, tall-ish? She's a really kind woman.'

Charlie did one of those circular nods. The type that said he really didn't have a clue who she was talking about.

'Come across anything interesting today?' he asked after taking a sip of his pint.

'I petted a cow,' Sue said, brightening at the memory. It had been early on in the ride when most of the middle-aged men had hacked off at a competitive pace and slowly, but surely, everyone had spread out until they all realised it genuinely wasn't a competition and there would be tea and biscuits for everyone no matter what time you arrived at the comfort break tent.

'A cow,' nodded Charlie. 'Impressive.'

She'd thought so. It was one of many firsts she'd experienced today. Walking past a nuclear power plant. Pushing her bike up a hill. Braking down a hill. Talking to people who openly admitted to being depressed or anxious or, in one case, a terrible mother. It might not sound like much to someone who was more worldly, like Charlie seemed to be, but for her? It had been a difficult, exhilarating, scary and eye-opening day.

'You know what struck me the most?' she asked Charlie.

'Tell me,' Charlie leant in.

'All of the people.'

Charlie's brow furrowed. 'Sorry, I—'

'I know, I know – it sounds ridiculous, but . . . I just couldn't get over the fact that there were all of these *people* everywhere. Going to the shops, driving their cars, heading to and from work, sitting on benches, walking their dogs. They're everywhere!'

'People . . .' Charlie's laugh was kind, but it was clear he wasn't understanding her. 'I guess they all can't be in London.'

Urgh. That wasn't what she meant. In fairness to Charlie, *she* didn't know what she meant, but what she'd thought as she'd ridden her bicycle past all of those lives – lives in full flow – was . . . *I hope they all have someone to love them.*

Across the large hotel lounge, she could hear Raven 'closing up shop' amidst a sea of protests.

'Honestly,' Sue said to Charlie. 'She's been at it for ages. They've barely left her alone during teatime.' Raven's chicken Kiev had gone cold as people kept pushing phones in her face and asking for this flower or that to be drawn onto their shirts. She supposed she could blame Kath, who'd magicked up a brand new set of Sharpies when Raven's own pen set had died.

The woman who'd just had hers done started singing, 'Lucky me! Lucky me! Now I've got the lucky Chakrabarti Charm!' The riders had all cheered and applauded as she grandly made her way to the lift wearing her newly decorated T-shirt as a cape.

Raven caught Sue's eye, rolled her own then crossed over to her table with a decidedly jauntier gait than she'd ever shown. In public, anyway. 'Here you are, Sue.'

Sue's heart felt fit to burst as Raven unfurled a T-shirt now emblazoned with a coral rose on the back and handed it to her. 'Oh, Raven. That's lovely. Thank you.' She admired it a bit more, then carefully folded the T-shirt in her lap before remembering they weren't alone. 'Have you met Charlie?'

Raven gave a waist-height wave. 'Hey. I'm Raven.'

'Charlie. Bipolar mother.'

Raven frowned.

'Sorry,' Charlie laughed. 'Being here feels a bit like being in Alcoholics Anonymous, you know?'

Sue looked to Raven. No. She hadn't made that link either.

'Apologies,' Charlie held up his hands. 'It's my way of coping. TMI at the best of times. I just figure, if everyone knows I'm Charlie "Bipolar Mum" Stanton, then we get to avoid a whole lot of awkward questions. It's just out there.'

'I see,' said Sue, not at all ready to introduce herself as Sue, Wife of Gary who committed— Nope. No. She wasn't ready. Not without an avalanche of terrifying feelings following in its wake. 'You know?' she began, instead of saying what she should have which was, *I am so sorry you're going through what you're going through and I hope participating in this ride brings you some peace.* 'I think I need to turn in.'

In the lift (Charlie had joined another group), Raven asked, 'Are you alright?'

'Yes, absolutely. You?'

'Yeah, I just thought you might've been a bit freaked with . . .' she tipped her head down to indicate the lounge.

'With what?'

'With that guy flirting with you.'

Sue's eyes popped open wide. 'He wasn't flirting.'

'Okay,' Raven said, which made Sue think, was he? And then, as she did with all things she couldn't cope with thinking about, she shut the idea down. As soon as they got to the room, she curled up in her bed and, just as she did every night since he'd gone, she pretended Gary's arms were around her and everything was exactly as it had always been, apart from today, she had petted a cow.

Chapter Forty-Seven

10 SECOND INTERSTITIAL: BRAND NEW DAY

VISUAL: Florence Wilson in cycling gear about to start off for DAY TWO of Hadrian's Wall ride

AUDIO TRANSCRIPT:

FLORENCE: Although LifeTime doesn't directly provide them, I'm sure they would agree with me in saying that a therapy dog really can change a life.

Off-camera question: Do you have one?

FLORENCE: I believe all dogs are therapy dogs, in their own way. Captain George, my Irish wolfhound is . . . excuse me . . . ooo . . . apologies . . . Yes, thank you, love. Silly me, forgetting to pack tissues. Anyway, what I meant to say . . . it's difficult being away from him.

Off-camera question: And your husband? You must be missing him as well. Is he proud?

FLORENCE: My husband? Yes. He, umm . . . Stu is definitely . . . well look at this watch for example. He can track all of my journey on it. So, yes. Proud. That's my Stuart. Proud and very, very good at making things work.

Off-camera question: Is there anything you'd like to say to him before you set off today?'

FLORENCE: Yes, of course. Remember darling, the vet said to make sure you change the dressing twice a day and I put Captain George's medicine in with a bit of tuna. Second cupboard to the right of the fridge, top shelf. And, Stu, I . . . I – oh dear, could you . . . yes thank you, love. Just one of those two-tissue days I guess. Anyway, Stu, just a quick byline to say I'm not actually working at III anymore and please make sure everyone down at the club donates because my bum is bloody sore. You were right about the padded shorts. You were right about a lot of things.

GRAPHIC: BRAND NEW DAY: Bringing out the Best in Britons Everywhere

'. . . and surprise, surprise! They trounced me,' Kev beamed, his face a darker shade of shoe leather than the 'fawn' it had been before he'd left. Looks like someone ignored the beauty therapist about using the factor 50, then.

Kath smiled at the camera.

'Sounds like an incredible time, Kev. And those meerkats? Adorable! You watch yourself tomorrow. A wine and segway tour? Sounds dangerous! Now, as Kev had such an exciting report – I've not got much time, but I know our riders will be wanting to hit the road for Brampton via Carlisle. First things first? I want to send a really loud shout out to the lads from the Sixth Armoured Division. One of our young riders and I – the self-titled @BigBonedGothGirl if you follow Instagram – met and chatted with former servicemen yesterday. They're a pretty amazing trio who put their lives on the line in Afghanistan, Iraq and Syria to keep us safe. I hope any of you in the Maryport area who have jobs going will consider them. I know finding a job was one of my brother's biggest struggles and . . . oh, jeezypeeps. This is harder than I thought. Apologies, ladies and gentlemen. I just— Have you ever felt like you let someone down?'

Kath's producer's voice came through her earpiece. 'Where exactly is this going, Kath?'

Any bloody direction I want it to, Kath thought.

She took a step closer to the camera as the producer tightly announced one minute left before they cut to commercial. She was supposed to have had a three-minute segment but Kev, his beach volleyballers and his meerkats had run over.

'The truth is, I let my brother down. He came to me for help and all I gave him was money. Money helped, a bit. To buy alcohol. What I should've given him was my time. My contacts. My ear. He needed a job. He needed his sense of pride back. He needed someone to listen to him because the world he left when he joined the army as a sixteen-year-old Newkie lad was not the world he came back to as a forty-year-old ex-soldier. All of which is to say . . . viewers, maybe it's time we all started listening a bit more. To the brothers of the Sixth and all the rest of you serving and retired army, navy, air force heroes? Even a few minutes of being heard could make such a diff—'

'That's thirty seconds, Kath.'

'Right . . .' she pulled out a cheat sheet and cleared her throat, 'Time for a few shout outs to our riders from their loved ones.'

'Jason and Jeff Woodland want their mummy to know they think she is extra special and that they are riding their bikes round the park today as a show of support.'

A teary Rachel blew the camera a kiss and said, 'I love you, babies.'

Kath zipped through a few more, each one touching the heart of the recipient, all of which made her own heart stretch and ache and squeeze tight. They interacted with their viewers via Twitter all of the time but this? This was different. More powerful, because the viewers could actually see the impact of people taking time out to say, I see you, I hear you, I want to help.

'Time for sign off,' the studio producer announced. 'Kev? Three seconds to you before we cut away from Cape Town and wrap with Kath.'

'That's it from me here on the Gold Coast. You enjoy making all of those new friends up there, Kath.'

A glimmer of possibility that Kev finally got why she was doing this lit within her. 'I will,' she enthused as the producer told Kev he was a wrap. 'It astonishes me how resilient everyone here is. Depression, anxiety, PTSD, suicide – these are just a few of the issues everyone here is riding for. With any luck, we can pass our goal of five hundred thousand pounds and really make a difference.'

'Struth! I'd give you the difference right now to get you to talk about something a bit cheerier. Makes me want to kill myself just listening—' The monitor went blank, then fuzzed with static, then an apology message about the signal came up for a moment before cutting to a commercial. Kath's skin went prickly. Kev had said that on air. He'd thought his mic was off and . . . oh, boy. Some several hundred miles away, Kath could already hear the complaint lines begin to ring.

Raven stared into the phone lens desperately trying to think of something beyond the fact that she was completely and utterly miserable. As big a draw as her so-called 'authentic angst' seemed to have been . . . self-imposed alone time had found her swan diving into the darker realms of her psyche. Realms she wasn't entirely sure she wanted the Insta-sphere to have access to.

She'd long since told Sue, who was impressively fit, to ride ahead. Flo had insisted upon staying close to Becky because 'she was worried about her being all alone back there' even though Becky's job was to ride at the back, but, whatever. Raven had been sending out her

'I'm quite happy riding alone thank you very much' vibes and, as such had spent rather a lengthy spell of alone time.

Alone with her Insta fanbase, which had increased by fifty per cent overnight. Apparently the world liked self-deprecating, overweight, Indian goth girls openly sharing their misery with a japey flair. Or maybe it was all the tags for 'Chakrabarti Flower Power' Kath had sent out. Kath was far more popular than Raven had thought. Stupid, she knew, considering Kath had been on television for like, a hundred years, but it would never once have occurred to her to join Kath's FOUR MILLION-plus followers. Then again, now that she'd met her, she could see the draw. She was super nice. It was good to support super nice people. Especially when they were married to a major dick. And now, thanks to her largesse, Raven had heaps more followers.

All that said, for the first time in, like, ever, the alone time she'd sought was morphing into deeply reflective time and she didn't like the direction it was going.

She missed her mum and dad. The ding-a-ling of the bell as customers entered their shop. The racket her mother made clanking pans around the kitchen as she pressed the phone to one ear instructing one relative or another on how to live their life as she whipped up a 'light' supper (usually, like, five different dishes, all of which were totally yum).

She missed her bossy sister.

And her goofy brother.

Their kids, their pets, their habits, their smell. She missed it all. And something about missing them made their lives appear like a pop-up book in her mind, but a pop-up book written by someone who could only see the good in them. Her parents' shop filled with people grateful to have a chemist who remembered their name, their prescriptions, their GP. Her sister's lightning-fast way with numbers that had made ploughing through algebra and calculus about a gazillion times easier. Her brother's gentle way of handling conflict or an upset toddler which made it really really easy to see why he'd become a paediatrician. They'd all followed their actual paths, not The Dictated Path. All of which culminated in the dawning realisation that maybe her parents thought she would genuinely be a good lawyer and were merely encouraging her to do what suited her best? Or, perhaps, just like her, they weren't really sure what she'd be good at so went with what was familiar?

That, or she was now officially hallucinating from the undignified trauma of her derriere being rubbed raw. Or, even more simply, perhaps absence really did make the heart grow fonder.

Down the M1 and left a bit had never felt so very far away.

She dispiritedly wiped the rain off of her odometer and gave it a squint. Ten miles down. Thirty-seven more to go.

Sweet mother of fuck. If ever there was any time to be prone to dramatics, now fitted the bill. It wasn't like there were any witnesses or anything. If you didn't count sheep.

She jabbed at her phone and began talking, not entirely certain whether or not she was actually recording. She blithered on about how riding in the rain yesterday had been fun. Well. Tolerable. She wasn't so into this exercise gig that the words 'fun', 'cycling' and 'rain' necessarily went hand in hand. That said, yesterday the rain hadn't physically hurt when it landed on her. Yesterday she hadn't had a bum that needed a new layer of epidermis. 'Let's be honest, friends,' she said (she'd taken to calling her viewers friends as it seemed, well, friendlier), 'one of the biggest challenges I'm facing today is finding a place to wee. Wot? you might ask. But you're in the great out of doors! The wilderness! Surely there's somewhere out there in the wilds of Britain for a discreet wee. Well, let me tell you – Britain's country lanes are not quite as rich in secret spots as one might think. Someone's always going past. If it isn't another cyclist, it's a Land Rover. If it isn't a tractor, it's a herd of cows, a tour bus, a community bus, a bus I would rather be riding on to find a toilet somewhere that's warm and dry because peeling off all of this exercise malarkey in the pouring rain, only to have a nettle present itself to my backside is all I need to inform you, dear friend, that camping will never be my jam. And then there's pulling it all back on again— Ah! There's a spot. *Finally!*'

'Hey there!' A thirty-something woman Raven hadn't spoken to yet rode up alongside her. She glanced at her phone. *See? See? Proof I am wise and all knowing. There is nowhere in Britain to privately have a wee.*

'Nice day for it, eh?' said the woman, who looked very much as though she made her own granola.

Raven gave her camera the side eye, then pocketed it in the one place that was vaguely waterproof, her sports bra.

'Hi,' she said. 'Raven.'

'Yeah, I know. Molly,' she said. 'I've been following your Insta feed.'

'Oh?'

'Yeah. You've got some fun perspective on the human condition.'

Raven glanced at Molly, too startled by the comment to act cool. 'Really? What do you mean?'

'Oh, you know,' Molly began, which was a ridiculous way to begin because Raven had literally just said she didn't understand. 'I believe a lot of kids your age don't think about other people and their perspective and how they are absorbing the world. You know – a minute in another man's shoes theory? Anyway, all of this me me me malarkey has made Western civilisation – at the very least – the epic shithole that we see today.'

'So . . . I take it you're from the Optimists' Society?'

Molly laughed. 'No. No. I'm a shrink. Well. School shrink slash guidance counsellor. Gummy bear?' She held out a soggy packet.

Wet, glommy and misshapen, it was just about the best gummy bear Raven had ever had.

Right there and then, Raven decided that if she ever were to see a shrink, she would see one like Molly, granola-aura notwithstanding. She finished chewing, took a swig of the energy drink Sue had mixed up for her this morning then asked, 'Do you generally counsel people that the world is an epic shithole destined for ultimate destruction?'

'Ah!' Molly brightened. 'I didn't say anything about ultimate destruction. Interesting path you took, there.'

'I didn't—' Raven stopped. 'So . . . does the fact I think the world is an epic shithole destined for destruction mean I also think there is no opportunity for salvation?'

Molly grinned. 'Ah, well . . . now that's the big question, isn't it?'

Raven slowed and pointed up ahead. 'Cattle grid.'

'You don't ride over them?' Molly asked.

'Errr . . . no.' They were totally bumpy and her tyres could fall through them and the assault on her arse wasn't even worth contemplating.

'Why not?' Molly wasn't slowing down.

'Because, they're a hazard.'

'Really? Or are they a perceived hazard? A risk worth taking?'

What school of counselling did this woman come from? She most likely had an internet degree or was lying and was actually a Scientologist on a secret recruitment mission. Was it Tom Cruise in disguise? Would she pull her face off for a big reveal when Raven decided to convert?

'C'mon, let's ride across it together,' Molly encouraged. 'I bet you'll surprise yourself.'

Raven glanced at her, the cattle grid, the pouring rain, desperately trying to remember the contents of the first-aid kit she'd stuffed in her CamelBak (thanks Mum and Dad). There were plenty of bandages in there. Bandages that would have to swaddle her huge helmet head, because on the off chance she suffered a massive brain injury that put her in a coma forever, they would have to leave it on until emergency services arrived. Maybe there weren't enough bandages. She should walk. On the other hand, if she rode and took the optimist's view of massive cerebral injuries courtesy of the cattle grid and/or the tarmac, a brain bleed would a) very likely put an end to this conversation,

b) mean she'd never have to pick what she was going to study at uni and c) allow her to live out the rest of her life in a nice quiet ICU ward with, hopefully, her parents keening by her side lamenting the fact that they'd ever suggested she work with Uncle Ravi forcing her to leave the family home armed only with a duffel bag full of fantasy books and another full of black clothes and a lifetime's supply of eyeliner. She would also get to ride in Becky's warm, dry van until the ambulance came (air ambulance if the injury was truly traumatic).

'Okay,' Raven decided about a metre from the grid. 'Let's do it.' From there everything turned slow-motion. She actually felt her heart stop beating as she held her breath, heard the individual plippity-plop of rain drops on her helmet, vibrated with the whirr of rubber on tarmac as she pedal pedal pedalled and then . . . oh! You *could* ride over a cattle grid and survive.

'See? Perceived hazard.' Molly looked smug, but the happy kind of smug that came from proving to someone they were capable of overcoming something that terrified them, all of which meant . . . was Molly not a Scientologist at all, and actually an imaginary angel sent to teach her a valuable lesson about fear? She thought about taking her photo to see if she was actually hallucinating her and then thought better of it. This was a moment to live in, not record for posterity.

'Why are *you* on the ride?' Raven asked. 'Are you building up your client list?'

'Ha!' Molly smiled, her grey/brown plaits swishing across her shoulders, 'I suppose you could say it's pretty good feeding ground for people who are interested. But no. I'm riding for my kids.'

'You have children?'

'No. I couldn't have kids,' she said, then pointed at her womb. 'Barren as the Sahara.'

'Oh, I'm sorry.'

'Not your fault.'

'No, but I – I can feel badly for you.'

'True . . .' Molly said, then. 'How 'bout you? What's your plan? Kids? Uni? Digging a hole somewhere to prepare for Armageddon?'

'If I believed Armageddon was coming, I'd probably prefer a cave . . . a cave on a mountain top.'

'So you could see it all coming?'

'Exactly,' Raven grinned. She was beginning to like this Molly.

'So what is it you didn't see coming?'

This whole entire situation for one. Not living at her parents' for another. Being so dithery about what to do with her future. Living with Sue. Realising how many gazillions of people lived with mental health issues and called into 111 for reassurance that they weren't going completely mad. The epidemic of loneliness that seemed to be seizing the country. Exhausted parents, middle-aged men having heart attacks, people googling their symptoms and refusing to accept the worst-case scenario might not actually be the scenario at all. There was a little bit of her now linked to every single one of her callers and, now, her Instagram followers. She didn't really know how to deal with all of their pain, let alone understand her own. There was also the fact that *she* might've been the one to break the link with her parents, not the other way round, and, as such, she might never have her mum's pakoras again, or worse, never make them proud. The more she thought, the scratchier her throat got.

And just like that, Raven began to weep. Weep and talk. Things she didn't even know she'd been worried about or frightened of poured out. Aisha, her family, her grades, her spot at Oxford (which she did, a little bit actually, kind of want), her Uncle Ravi, the time her brother's little girl threw up on the floor and Raven had just left it there waiting for someone else to discover. By the time her verbal well ran dry, her tears had stopped and the biscuit and tea tent appeared on the horizon, Molly pointed at her odometer and said, 'Look at that. See how far you've come?'

*

'You know it was *Europeans* who built Hadrian's Wall – not just the Romans.'

Flo squawked out a short scream, horrified to discover Trevor pedalling alongside her. More so when he appeared completely oblivious to the spray he was sending her way as he ploughed through the endless puddles. 'How did you get here?'

'Didn't you see me ride past?' He pinched a bit of his startlingly reflective waterproof jacket. 'I rode past you about ten minutes ago on my way to get this from Becky. The other one was soaked through.'

Hmm. No. She hadn't seen him at all. Or noticed Becky stopping even though Stuart had put a rearview mirror on her helmet. And a blinking light. Not that the blinking light would've helped, but – ooo, this wasn't good. Hello, Alzheimer's, farewell sweet youth. She willed her aching joints to play ball just until Trevor had bored of her more . . . oh, god . . . her more senior pace.

'I wonder if Hadrian had his lads out in this weather or if they had a union. Ha!'

Hmmm. It could be some time. Perhaps he'd already bored everyone else silly and was here to torture her until the next so-called comfort break.

'That's right,' said Trevor as if she were a willing participant in this conversation. 'Syrians, Romanians, Romans – of course – always the Romans, the Spanish . . . from the North of Spain of course, so they wouldn't have considered themselves Spanish in the way modern Spaniards do although, if you follow the papers, even that's up for question, borders being the negligible things they are these days. Perspective, isn't it?'

'Mmmm.' Flo wasn't really up for snippets of historical and topical insight today. Then again, it might be a good chance to try and remember things to prove she hadn't lost her marbles. Plus Stu might find them interesting and she owed him a call. Yesterday she'd been so tired she'd fallen asleep before her head had hit the pillow. She'd woken up to a darling picture of Captain George nestled on the settee on her phone and two melted ice packets tied to her knees with socks, now hanging on the back of one of the seats in Becky's van because she knew she'd need them again tonight and she was damned if she was going to tie wet socks to her already aching knees.

Flo breathed into another sharp pain (as recommended by Fola) while Trevor waxed lyrical about the definition of a Roman mile (a thousand paces or 5,000 feet as opposed to the modern mile which was 5,280 feet thus making the modern mile longer than the—). Oh dear god, this trip wasn't at all what she'd imagined it would be. For some reason she thought she'd be feeling much more triumphant. Inspiring poor, shy, grief-stricken Sue out of her humdrum, miserable life up to the wild Cumbrian coastline to confront her grief and then embrace a future happiness. For Raven she'd imagined . . . well . . . she wasn't quite sure what she'd imagined for Raven. A bit of weight loss? A desire to wear brighter colours? It certainly hadn't been an ever-increasing Instagram following and a crowd of people begging her to draw flowers on their shirts (even though Flo had to say, the one Raven had drawn for her was rather fabulous). Then it came to her. She'd wanted to be the hero. The amazing woman who'd seen the despair and woe in these poor women's lives and changed it by pushing them both out of their comfort zones and into a place of unexpected bliss and discovery. Elements of it were coming true. Not because of Flo, though, but because of what Sue and Raven had been carrying in their own emotional arsenals. They were both made of sturdier stuff than she'd given them credit for. Sue had ridden ahead ages back after checking several times that Flo would be alright on her own, but she'd promised one of the women – Rachel? Marianne? – one of them, anyway, that they could have a talk about grief counsellors. And then off she'd pedalled, riding her bicycle as if she'd never heard of joint pain or arthritis. Raven, too had powered off after checking that Flo would be okay. She didn't seem to need human company quite as much as Flo did.

Despite the fact she knew Raven had hardly ridden her bicycle at all prior to the ride, Flo, it seemed, was the only weak link.

'. . . and did you know that Hadrian's Wall is not just a wall?'

'What? No. No, Trevor. I did not know that,' Flo snapped, hoping her tone would spur him to ride on and fill some other poor sod in on the inner machinations of empire building. He did not. Rather, he kept expectantly looking at her until finally, she broke and asked, 'What is it if it is not a wall?'

'More like an obstacle course!'

'An insurmountable one, presumably?'

'Well, no. I think history proved that wasn't the case, particularly as only ten per cent of the wall is visible now, unlike the viaducts the Romans built that still stand today, but as you will no doubt see for yourself, there are the ditches – or vallums—' Trevor droned on and on as if he'd committed the entire shelf of Hadrian's Wall history books to memory.

'Trevor!' Flo finally erupted. 'What exactly is it you're trying to achieve by passing on all of these endless, boring, tedious facts about the past! I did not come up here to learn about history!'

Trevor, much to her horror, looked genuinely wounded by her outburst which, to be fair, had not come out in a remotely friendly fashion. 'Why did you come?'

It was a very good question. So good, she actually forgot about her aching knees and burning thighs and sore buttocks as she contemplated an answer. 'I suppose I wanted to prove I still had a bit of life in me.'

'How do you mean?'

'I just . . . everyone around me is getting old. Getting old and grey and achy and dying or fussing about the fact that I should be behaving more like one of them.'

'One of whom?'

'The old, grey, dying people.'

'It sounds nice.'

'What?'

'Having people to fuss about you.'

She hadn't really thought about it like that before.

'It means they care, doesn't it?' Trevor asked. 'It means you have people who love you.'

Yes. Yes, she supposed it did. And somewhere along the line she'd led herself to believe that that type of love was suffocating, when in actual fact, Trevor here saw it as a comfort.

'Do you have family?' she asked.

He shook his head. 'Sadly, no. My parents both passed a while back and I never managed to tempt anyone to be my lawfully wedded . . . so . . .'

A wash of shame flushed through her. Poor Trevor. He was a kind, lonely man trying his best in a world that didn't take to people who didn't conform. She'd been incredibly rude and unforgivably thoughtless. It was quite uncomfortable to confront the reality that, despite having always considered herself a kind, friendly, selfless woman, what she actually was, was . . . ha! Jennifer would love this. She was actually a selfish, myopic, insensitive know-it-all who briskly put people in their place all to serve her quest to prove to the world little Florence Pringle (yes, she'd dumped the maiden name sharpish) . . . that little Florence Pringle was interesting. Interesting despite the fact her parents had lived a small, insular, incurious life on the outskirts of Birmingham. They'd always said they were perfectly happy as they were but she'd found it impossible to believe them. How could they be happy without having tried a croissant from a proper boulangerie in Paris? How could they be happy having never stood with twenty thousand people singing along with one of the world's greatest ever superstars? How could they have been happy in that square mile of city they never once expressed an interest in leaving?

They just had been. They'd had their friends, their families, and, of course, they'd had each other. Now that she really thought about it, her mother and father had genuinely adored one another's company. Fussing about this or that, reading bits out from the neighbourhood rag to one another then discussing it. Clipping it out, putting it in an envelope because they thought a brother, sister, aunt or uncle might find it interesting, too.

How could she have mistaken contentedness for colourlessness? Maybe facts made Trevor happy. Perhaps that was his reality. Facts = fun! It didn't have to be her reality. Perhaps the question she should've been asking herself all these years wasn't about *what* people were interested in, but *why*.

'Tell me, Trevor,' Flo asked, 'How is it that you know all of these interesting things about Hadrian's Wall?'

His wounded look stayed put as he warily answered, 'I attend lectures through University of the Third Age.'

'Oh?' She bet the two meerkats went there, too. She made a note to make sure their paths crossed during the next biscuit and tea break. 'Sounds interesting.'

'Yes, there really are some interesting talks.' Trevor's voice brightened, 'In fact I attended one the other day detailing the history of the ukulele which, I was shocked to learn, didn't originate in Hawaii as popularly believed. In actual fact—' He stopped himself and threw Flo an apologetic look. 'Sorry, I do rabbit on endlessly. I doubt you're interested.'

'No, no,' Flo protested, her insides beginning to crumble in despair and not about the idea of being given a second-hand lecture on the origins of the ukulele. No, her despair was tapping into something much deeper. Trevor's self-imposed editing was her fault. A thought that horrified her, considering if someone did the same to her she would rail against it with all of her might. Worse, there was a frighteningly familiar ring to this scenario. Not the bikes and the rain and geriatric knee joints. It was the feeling of closing someone down. Something she realised she had done over the course of her married life again and again and again. Stu loved facts. Loved passing them on. Loved dazzling her and the children (who also loved facts) with little nuggets of insight into how the world as they knew it had been put together. Because of Stuart she knew there were approximately sixty thousand fasteners holding a Boeing 777 together. (It tortured him that he didn't know the exact number.) Because of Stuart she knew the Cambodians had 'lost' Angkor Wat for nearly five hundred years. She knew tomatoes originated in the Andes and not Spain or Italy. That chocolate came from the Amazon and that Warren Buffet could lay claim to having the most expensively traded stock of all time unless you counted the tulip bulb craze in Holland between 1634 and 1637. All of these things she knew because of her husband. How much more would she know if she hadn't shut him down? Hadn't hurt his feelings. Hadn't cajoled, pushed, and pressed him and the children to stop reciting boring old facts and *do* something. Do something *interesting* when all along Jennifer, Jamie and Stuart had been quite happy as they were. Everything Jennifer had said about her was true. She had been selfish. She had prioritied her version of life over theirs, preferring the love of a dog to her own family which, until this very moment, had made perfect sense. She should have cherished them more, valued them more, made them feel proud of their passions and interests. She would do all this and more when she got home. Lavish them with the same love and attention she gave Captain George without, of course, compromising the love and attention she gave Captain George. There were, after all, limits to how much one could change.

'Tell me, Trevor,' Flo said in a tone she hoped carried a thick layer of apology, 'How did the Scots respond when Hadrian showed up with all of these workmen of his?'

'Ah!' Trevor's eyes lit up. 'Now that's an interesting story.'

And for the next hour he talked and talked and talked, during which time Flo had plenty of time to reflect on how she might have been a better mother, a better wife and whether or not knee surgery might lend itself to Zumba Gold and, heaven help her, decaf coffee with 'the girls'.

'I owe you an apology.'

Sue started. She'd been so lost in thought she hadn't even noticed Kath riding up alongside her. 'Sorry, I— Why do you owe me an apology?'

'Kevin,' Kath said, her expression a shade of grim Sue didn't think she'd ever seen on TV's Kath Fuller before.

'Oh,' said Sue. 'Yes, well . . .' She'd not actually heard what Kev had said herself as Kath was the only one who could hear him and, of course, the crew, and everyone watching television which was how word began circulating that Kevin was now being flown home under a cloak of shame and Ben Fogle was being left behind to do something on rhinos or hippos and then, of course, have a go at playing the beach volleyball team. 'I think,' she began, fighting against the discomfort of talking about it, '. . . not everyone has experienced what I have so I'm sure he didn't mean to be insensitive—'

'No, please,' Kath waved a fingerless gloved hand. 'What Kevin said was completely reprehensible. Your husband died by suicide. To make a joke of it, as if suicide was a way to escape a conversation you didn't want to have, was inexcusable.'

Sue almost said she hadn't tried to have a conversation one way or another with Gary, let alone a difficult one, so perhaps there was some merit in the crass statement. It got people talking. There were a thousand things she could have asked her husband that day and all the days before. But no. They had their routine and they'd stuck to it. For the rest of her life she'd have to live with the fact that the last thing she'd said to him was to leave her to it, she had things handled and that she'd let him know when supper was ready. She had, in effect, told him he wasn't necessary. Having replayed the evening over and over again, she was quite certain he'd not heard the part about it being toad-in-the-hole, which could've been the problem right there because as her mother was fond of saying, the devil was in the detail and it was a detail she was desperate to get right. She considered asking Kath what she thought but she appeared to be on a bit of a roll so Sue didn't say a word. As usual.

'He'll be reprimanded of course,' Kath was saying. 'I'd be shocked if some of the advertisers didn't pull their support. It'll be all over the papers. Who knows? They might even cancel the show. And make no mistake – he'd deserve it. *I'd* deserve it for having set up a situation where he could say such a horrid, horrid thing.'

'Oh, no. Please, no. *Brand New Day* is an institution, I doubt they would—'

Kath barrelled on, 'It was a tactless, insensitive, vile thing to say. Especially considering you are out here, just a handful of months after enduring such a painful, senseless tragedy, helping to raise money for people who hopefully won't ever have to go through what you did. Suicide is a plague right now in the country. Did you know thousands of men a year take their own lives? Young men, middle-aged, *teenagers* all reaching rock bottom and seeing absolutely no light at the end of the—'

'Please!' Sue heard herself beg. 'Please stop!'

Kath not only stopped talking but also stopped her bicycle and, to her surprise, so did Sue whose face wasn't wet with rain, but tears and snot and all of the other ugly things she hadn't let herself show since her darling, sweet, loveable Gar-bear took a ten-metre length of sailing rope and hung it from their loft beam.

They stared at one another until Kath dropped her bike, strode to Sue and fiercely pulled her into her arms, bicycle and all. She held her so tight and close she could actually feel Kath's heart pounding against her own. 'I'm sorry,' she said. And then, 'I'm sorry, I'm sorry, I'm sorry, I'm sorry,' until she too was weeping and ugly crying and making animal noises that normally would've terrified Sue to the point that all she would've wanted to do was find Gary who would make her laugh and make all of her fears disappear, only Gary wasn't here anymore. It was only Sue. Sue and her tears and a talk show hostess who would probably be out of a job by the morning if what she'd just been saying about the sponsors was anything to go by and none of that was very comforting. She didn't know what would be comforting. Maybe nothing at all. 'Nothing's going to take it away, is it?' Sue sobbed. 'Nothing's going to fix the pain.'

'No,' wept Kath, angrily waving on a cyclist who was slowing to approach them. 'I thought it would go away with time, but if anything it's worse.'

'Don't say that,' Sue wailed. 'I don't have the strength. There are all of those stages!'

'What stages?'

'The grief stages.' Her words were coming out in solitary huffs and then as one big long sentence. 'And the scariest thing is I don't think I'm even at the first stage yet.'

'What? Denial?'

'YES!' Sue shouted, no longer able to say anything without pushing it into the realms of hyperbole, as if all of the feelings she'd contained over the past few months were finally coming out in a series of FULL CAPS and PLOSIVES and LANGUAGE that described the most extreme states of existence like ANGUISH and TORMENT and HEARTBREAK. Heartbreak was EXACTLY what she had been try-ing not to feel since the beginning of February and PRECISELY, SEARINGLY PAINFULLY what she was feeling right this very second because no matter how hard she pedalled, or how many donations she raised for LifeTime, her beloved Gary wouldn't, in two days' time, be there at the finish line. He wouldn't be holding a banner or a sign or a ridiculous bunch of unicorn balloons or even, as he sometimes did, a solitary rose. All that was waiting for her was several hundred miles away. A family who treated her like a spinster Auntie, even when she'd been married, and three more boxes of invoices that may or may not explain why her husband was dead.

'He was supposed to be there,' she said to Kath.

'Who?'

'Gary. He was supposed to be there when I finished. I don't know if I want to finish now.'

'You can. You will,' said Kath in a way that sounded as if she was also trying to convince herself.

'But how do you know?'

'Because we don't have any other choice.'

Sue let her bike fall to the ground. Then sat down herself, right there on the roadside, too exhausted at the prospect of having to face the whole rest of her life on her own. Kath knelt down beside her, took one of her hands, but said nothing. So many of Sue's life choices had been dictated to her. Her schooling. Her training (hairdressing had been her mother's idea, not hers). Her role as N'auntie Sue. Neither a nanny nor an Aunt. But she had been a wife. And that had been by choice. Her one solitary choice and look how that had turned out. How could she trust anything she chose to do now? Even this. This so-called do-goodery. It wasn't making her feel any better. If anything it was making her feel worse.

'Go away,' Kath yelled when her camera crew pulled up alongside them, 'We're having a moment here and I don't want it fucking televised!'

They drove off rather sharpish.

Someone must've walkie talkied someone else because other riders did go past – but at a respectful distance, eyes on the ground or straight ahead – diligently sticking to the course that had been laid out before them while Sue and Kath remained glued to the ground, the weight of it all too much to bear on something as flimsy as a bicycle.

Sat there, in the rain, they talked and talked. Asking all of the questions out loud they had been too frightened to ask anyone else. Was it my fault? Could I have changed his mind? Was there anything I could have done to make him happy?

No. Maybe. Not really, because happiness came from within.

All of which led them to the one thing neither of them would ever know for sure. The reality was, they would spend the rest of their lives with unanswered questions, broken hearts and having absolutely no idea if they could or couldn't have helped their loved ones because their loved ones had taken matters into their own hands.

'Saying that,' said Kath who'd now reached a more philosophical place, 'I'm convinced Rob would've chosen something far sexier than choking on his own vomit.'

'I don't know,' ventured Sue. 'It sounds like something a rock star might do. You said he was super cool.'

'Yeah, but . . .' Kath tipped her head up, the rain falling more like a mist now. 'I think he would've preferred to go a bit more by choice, you know.'

Yes, thought Sue. She did know. She'd never once thought of Gary's choice as an act of empowerment. Maybe if he'd been in a cult or a monk living in an oppressive country, but . . . he was a plumber. An excellent plumber who had a wife who loved him and a football team full of men who he'd played with since he was eight and a local pub where they knew his drink without even asking.

'Either way,' said Kath. 'I should've been there for him. I should've been there for him and I left him fucking hanging by a— Sorry. Jesus!' She went to slap herself on the forehead and bonked her helmet instead which threw her head back in a weird snapping motion. 'Sorry, it was an analogy, I – shitfuckingbullocks I wazzocked that up, didn't I?' And then all of the sudden the pair of them were laughing. Laughing like a pair of hyenas. 'Thank Christ Kevin didn't hear that,' Kath snorted. 'I'd never hear the end of it. Forgive me?'

'Of course I do,' Sue said. 'There's nothing to forgive.'

'I suppose there will always be things people say that end up hurting.'

Sue nodded and then looked up at the sound of Big Ben chiming. 'Sorry. Sorry.' Kath pulled her phone out of a little plastic wallet hanging round her neck. 'Bums.' She held up the phone. 'Dean-O.'

Sue raised her eyebrows. She'd not really seen much of Dean-O. He rode at the head of the pack with the men who had skinny legs and muscled calves and, strangely, pot bellies.

'Really? Seven more? Blimey. That's quite a lot. Can we get Becky to . . . right. I see. Okay, we'll let everyone know in Carlisle over lunch and I guess we'll take it from there.' She clicked off the call and put it back in her waterproof wallet.

'Everything okay?'

Kath made a not-so-much face. 'Depends upon how much you're enjoying today's ride, I guess.' Kath popped on the smile Sue was much more familiar with. The 'uh-oh, here comes trouble' smile that usually preceded Kev pulling some sort of prank on her. Maybe she used to like it, the pranks. Perhaps she'd adored the thrill of the unknown. Loved it right up until the thrill changed into something else. A nightmare. 'There are seven more miles on today's route than we thought.'

'Gosh.' Sue had only mentally prepared herself for forty-seven miles.

'And apparently the last seven miles are pretty hilly. And by pretty I mean—' She put her arm up at a ninety-degree angle.

'Ah.'

'Never mind, Sue,' Kath said, looking strangely bolstered by the news. 'What is it they say? Pray for the best, prepare for the worst and expect the unexpected?'

'They can't do that. Just change the itinerary.' Flo knew she was being churlish and that she should be putting on her sunshiney 'of course you can sit in an upright position for ten hours even though it's the same position they use for torture' smile, but she was in the depths of a very exclusive pity party and had no idea how to yank herself out of it. 'That's not what they said. We are meant to stay in Brampton.'

'You'll be fine,' Sue insisted. 'You know, Trevor was saying Gilsland is where Sir Walter Scott met his wife.' She frowned. 'Or perhaps that was Brampton. Gilsland sounds like somewhere in one of the *Hobbit* books, doesn't it?' She made a rabbit face as a stand-in for a Hobbit face, then smiled one of her dear sweet Sue smiles. 'Don't you think, Raven?'

Sue was quickly realising she needed someone else's support in her 'look on the bright side' campaign. Flo, as things stood, was unwilling to be cajoled into smiling, let alone riding seven extra miles.

Raven nodded, but didn't respond as she had a mouth full of baguette.

Fuelling. That was smart. Flo didn't have the energy to fuel. Not anymore. Not now she knew she was a selfish, overpowering, control freak who was single-handedly responsible for the fact her husband no longer had any energy to do anything beyond the puzzle page and her children rarely ever visited except when Stu was around. And then it hit her. This was exactly the sort of thing Jennifer would've hated. A turn of events that Flo would've insisted was an adventure and forced everyone into no matter how miserable or broken they were. And they always came. Into the souks of Morocco where they'd become terrifically lost. Jamie had somehow lost a shoe and Jennifer, with her blonde hair, had been pulled into a carpet shop without her even noticing. (Stu had bought her back, along with an exorbitantly overpriced cushion cover they'd ended up donating to charity in the end.) They'd all trudged into the Ethiopian restaurant she'd insisted would be delicious. They'd all hated it (even Flo, but she was hardly going to admit that to her whining, why-can't-we-have-fish-and-chips-like-everyone-else children). They weren't like everyone else, Flo had insisted. That was the point. To be unique. To be someone to envy. But did people envy her? Not really. Did they invite her to join them in their adventures? No. She was the one who cajoled and pushed and busy-bodied around folk until all they could do was relent. Even her poor, darling Captain George who had run and run alongside her when she'd insisted upon doing that ridiculous canal loop. All these people so willing to please and what had she shown them in return?

Nothing but disdain.

Flo had never felt more disappointed in herself in her entire life. She was no better than Linda Hooper and her capfuls of bleach down the village hall.

'Seven extra miles,' Sue was saying as if seven (modern day) miles were akin to a trip down to the corner shop. 'You've done that several times already today, Flo . . .' she tapped her fingers along her chin, thinking.

'Five times,' Raven filled in for her. 'We've done thirty-five from Silloth. Then it's twelve to Brampton and another seven to Gilsland.'

A dull throbbing pain presented itself so profoundly in Flo's knees, she barely heard as Raven talked her through the rest of the route. A bit of river this, a bit of undulating countryside that, a market town that had hosted Charles Stuart for one night during the Jacobite rising. The fact caught her attention.

'How on earth did you know that?' Flo asked.

Raven scanned the crowd and pointed at, surprise surprise, Trevor. 'Cool dude. He's like a walking talking Google.' Raven opened her mouth to take another bite of her baguette and then looked at Flo. Really looked at her. 'You know, if your knees are hurting too much you could always ride in the bus with Becky. That's what it's for. Support.'

'No!'

The vehemence of her response surprised all three of them. She might be a selfish, thoughtless, excuse of a mother who'd pushed her husband and children into doing all sorts of things they'd never wanted to do, but she was *not* going to do this charity ride on the bus. She'd tapped far too many pilots' wives for money to only partially complete the trip. That . . . and she felt she owed it to Stu and the children. A penance for all she'd put them through. She'd crawl if she had to, which, considering how difficult it was going to be to stand up from the picnic table again, might very well be a possibility.

'I might just be a bit slower than usual is all. But I will do this. I will ride all of the miles. Roman or otherwise.'

Sue began nodding and saying alright, alright, so what would we advise someone if they were to ring in with sore knees?

'RICE.' All three of them said in tandem. And then, with the efficiency of a trauma team, Sue and Raven went to work getting ice packs, cool gels, Fola and, to her surprise, Kath.

'Alright there, Flo?'

Such a simple question. And yet . . . it felt like a game changer.

Flo had a choice to make. Lie through her teeth to keep up appearances as any self-respecting British woman of a certain age might, or be honest.

Everyone was looking at her. Raven, Sue and Fola who really did have magic hands. The man should be copyrighted. Or cloned. If she were home she could imagine Stu insisting upon seeing to Flo's knees. She closed her eyes and pictured the chair he would park her in, the sounds as he meticulously went through the medicine cupboard (Stu liked to be prepared) and the steady, assured way he would knead away her aches and pains.

As the heat from Fola's hands transferred deep into her knees, she began to understand what Stu and her children meant to her. They were her foundation. They made her strong. They were the reason she'd spent the past thirty-plus years showing off just how fabulous she could be. Desperate to prove she was interesting, fun and the life of the party. Desperate to prove Stu had made the right choice and that her children had the most interesting parents. What a fool she'd been. They'd wanted someone to love them. Someone who would love them back with the same fierce loyalty they'd shown her.

Her throat went scratchy. She was going to have to earn it back. Their love. Their respect. She'd certainly lost Jennifer's. Jamie? Hard to say, but the poor boy had gone from her domineering household straight into the arms of another bossy, controlling woman, so . . . And Stu? God above, she hoped Stu still loved her. Respected her. 'You know, Kath,' she finally said, her voice sounding smaller than she had ever believed it could. 'This is much, much harder than I thought it would be. What a silly moo I've been. Thinking I could just hop on my bicycle and ride across the country. And at my age!'

Fola made a tsk tsk sound with his tongue, then slipped away saying something about finding compression bandages.

Flo reached out her hands to Raven and Sue, both of whom were soaked through, stiffly shifting from foot to foot and, in Sue's case, really quite muddy. 'I'm so sorry I dragged you into this. We should've just had a cake sale. Sue, you make such lovely cakes. Have I told you that? How very much I love your cakes?'

Sue clasped Flo's hand in both of hers. 'You didn't drag anyone! And you're not old. You're . . .' Sue floundered for a moment because the truth was, yes, she was old unless you were counting the queen. 'You're an inspiration. You encouraged us. Me anyway. And Raven.' She gave Raven's arm a squeeze and Raven, who Flo had noticed wasn't really a toucher, pulled little Sue under her arm and gave her a quick hug. Sue squatted down (with some difficulty) and looked Flo straight in the eye. 'I never in a million years would've thought to come on a ride like this.' She grinned up at Kath. 'Especially with someone famous. I never would've asked people to donate money. I never would've believed I could've done anything like this at all—' her words jammed in her throat and a sob erupted where Flo guessed she might have said 'without my husband.' When she'd swept away some tears, Sue continued, 'I'm glad I'm here. I've ridden over eighty miles on a bicycle. Little Sue Young from Bicester. Little Sue Green who never finished anything in her entire life. I'm not finished yet. And neither are you.'

Creakily, Flo stood up. 'We're going to do this, aren't we?'

'Yes we are,' Sue said.

Little smiles and giggles rippled through the four of them as Kath pulled them all into a group hug that felt very much like a pre-game huddle as they each said again and again with growing conviction, 'We're going to do this, we're going to do this, we're going to do this.'

I think I can, I think I can, I think I can, I think I can.

'Alright Sue?'

Sue gave Dean-O a thumbs up. Talking wasn't part of the plan. Pedalling was. Pedalling was all there was.

I think I can, I think I can, I think I can, I think I can.

'Nice to see you up here with the Tour boys,' Dean-O grinned, cycling up the hill as if he were being pulled up it by some invisible string. 'You're motoring. Way to pull it out of the bag! Must've been holding back for your friends.'

No. That hadn't been it. When she hadn't been weeping by the side of the road over the husband she would never see again, she'd been riding at a natural pace. Finding out about the extra seven miles had been a kick in the stomach she hadn't needed, but . . . seeing Flo so down had made her heart ache. It was the first and only time she'd seen her look properly frail. There'd been a part of her that would've been quite happy to get on the bus with her and Becky, but when that 'NO' had come out of Flo so forcefully – as if she'd pulled it up and out of herself from the very centre of the earth – she knew she had to finish the day's ride as well. So she'd drunk an entire Coca-Cola, eaten a Snickers and then sucked down a gel pack Fola was handing round in order to encourage Flo to get her electrolytes back in balance.

She had never felt so zippy. So much so she was considering doing the same again before Sunday lunches with her family. That way when Raven moved on, which she inevitably would, and Flo went back to her life, which she inevitably would, Sue might have the fortitude to stand up to her mother and Katie who, no doubt, would make it very clear for years to come how ridiculous she'd been to choose the cycle ride over a 'holiday' in the Canaries.

Although . . . some of that vroom vroom was fading away now that they were approaching Gilsland which, true to Flo's elevation watch, was quite the uphill journey.

I think I can, I think . . . I can, I . . . think . . . I . . . can, IIIII think IIIIII caaaaaaan.

Hmmm.

Those gel packs weren't quite the cure-alls she'd originally thought.

'Heading back to see your friends? That's the spirit. Remember . . .' Dean-O tapped his Gore-Tex covered heart. 'Now that you know you've got it in here, to get up there . . .' He pointed to the top of the hill, '. . . you know you can do anything.' He gave her a wave and then, though she felt she was pedalling as hard as she could, first one, then another, then another cyclist passed her until a grim-faced Raven, and a strapped-up Flo were flanking her as if she had been the one needing their support all along. One step forward, a thousand back. But perhaps not quite as alone as she'd thought.

I think I can, I think I can, I think I can, I think I can.

'And you're getting on alright? With food and waterproofs and everything? How's that watch working out for you?'

For the first time in their lives, Stuart was the one propping up the conversation. Florence simply didn't know what to say to him. No idea whatsoever as to how to confront the fact she'd bulldozed into his lovely, contented life and then commandeered the rest of it for her own pleasure.

'I've been enjoying all of those ready meals you put in the freezer for me,' Stu said. Flo could hear him pat-pat-pat his belly, the sound so familiar and dear to her she almost burst into tears. There was so much she had to say to him, so many things to apologise for but each time she tried the words lodged in her throat like undercooked porridge.

'How about you? Are they feeding you well? With all of that weather you're having, I'm surprised they haven't called the thing off. Good job it wasn't camping as you'd originally thought, eh?'

'Oh, you know . . . it's the British way isn't it? Stiff upper lip and all that,' she said, hoping Stu couldn't hear her stomach grumble. Everyone had gone to supper now. She simply hadn't been able to face the large, increasingly motley crew at the pub crowing about mileage and near misses with tractors as they zipped up and down the extraordinarily steep hills on the way to Gilsland. That Hadrian must've been made of adrenaline. On her watch, the elevation had read like a heart rate monitor – the graph lurching upwards and downwards like someone suffering tachycardia. Peak and trough and peak and trough. Sue and Raven had very, very kindly pushed their bikes up alongside Flo as Becky shouted out encouragement and sang along to her 'happy mix' which she had played at full volume, windows down, despite the ever- present rain. Becky and the crew were off at the pub feasting upon hamburgers which were, apparently, a gift brought to Britain from the Romans if Trevor's latest recitation was anything to go by. He'd told her this when he'd tapped on her door to present her with a spare banana and a slightly worse-for-wear packet of crisps when he'd heard she wouldn't be joining everyone for supper. She'd humiliated herself by weeping when he'd handed them over. Whether it was from the pain of sitting up, or the idea that she'd have to walk the five steps back to her bed, or from the sheer generosity of his gesture, she didn't know. All three most likely. Today had taken all of the energy she'd possessed. She hadn't the slightest idea how she would complete tomorrow's ride which, whilst mercifully shorter, featured the steepest hills of the entire coast-to-coast journey. It would make or break her. If this was the Grand National and she saw herself behind the starting gates, she would place her bets elsewhere. It would serve her right, she supposed. Being wheelchair bound from here on out. A victim of her own foolhardiness.

'Stu, darling?'

'Yes, love?'

'You wouldn't mind, awfully, putting Captain George on, would you?'

'Of course not, love. He's just here, right by my side.'

Wise old pooch.

She waited until she could hear Stu's chair shifting across the tiles and the rustle of fur against phone before whispering, 'Hello, my darling George. I'm so sorry I hurt you. I hurt you and abandoned you, but you know you're in good hands, don't you? Better hands than mine, anyway. Stuart is . . . Stuart's the very best man I know. We're both lucky to have him. He's . . . please don't take this the wrong way, because I love you so very much, but . . . Stuart's the love of my life. He'll look after you, my darling boy. Just as he's looked after me.'

She was seized with a strange desire to howl but only managed to achieve a sort of low keening noise. Her body's way of saying, *enough.*

She stopped when she heard the chair rasp against the tiles again.

'Alright there, darling? Me again.' Stuart's voice sounded a bit choked, as if he needed to clear his throat but was waiting until he got off the phone because he knew how much Flo hated the noise. *An old person's noise,* she'd snipped at him. *Save it for your eighties.* 'How are you getting on, Florence? Really?'

'It's – I . . . I'm finding elements of it a bit more challenging than I thought.' It was the closest she had come to being entirely honest with him on any of their calls. 'Two more days. And it's for such a good cause.'

'Absolutely. We'll be cheering you on, George and I. And the children, of course.'

'Thank you, darling.'

'Night night, then. Rest well.'

They ended their call and in the ensuing silence Florence sank into a dark abyss, having never felt more alone.

Raven tip-toed through the darkened bedroom and into the loo. After carefully pulling her pants out and away from her derriere as opposed to stripping them downwards as she'd made the critical mistake of doing when they'd finally reached the B&B, she slowly lowered herself onto the toilet seat. Oh*wow*thathurt. Stingy where she'd never been stingy. Raw where . . . well . . . frankly . . . bum blisters weren't really de rigueur in your average teen's life, were they? She wished her mum was here. Her mum would help her. If she weren't too stubborn to admit to her mother she'd been mortal and made a mistake. Raven panted through the most torturous wee she'd ever had then sort of slithered down to the bathroom floor. She pulled all of the towels she could reach over her, tucked a face cloth beneath her cheek, and closed her eyes. A return journey to her bed was beyond the realms of possibility. Her entire body was being savaged by lactic acid. Those final seven miles had utterly slaughtered the remains of her bum skin, not to mention . . . other bits . . . *down there*. Tomorrow was going to be a loooooong day.

Chapter Forty-Eight

10 SECOND INTERSTITIAL: BRAND NEW DAY

VISUAL: Sunita 'Raven' Chakrabarti

AUDIO TRANSCRIPT:

RAVEN: It's amazing, yeah. To be part of something bigger than myself. It shows you how good people really are beneath, you know, whatever their personal armour is. Mine is obviously make-up.

Off-camera question: Who taught you how to do it?

RAVEN: Who taught me? YouTube. There isn't a Brown Goth Vlogger I couldn't name. Ha. Hmm . . . It was my sister actually. For her wedding. She was such a Bridezil— sorry – she was very *exacting* about how she wanted everyone's make-up to be because she wanted a traditional Indian wedding even though we were born and raised here, but . . . you know . . . it was her wedding and I was her little sister – keen to please – so I used to lock myself in my room and practise and practise and practise, until – voila! I can do an eyeliner flick with the best of them.

Off-camera question: Your parents must be proud of you.

RAVEN: My parents? Well . . . you know. They work hard in their shop. Their pharmacy. To be honest – that's my new thing, bald honesty on hashtag Big Boned Goth Girl – I spent the night on the bathroom floor wishing my mum was there. I knew exactly what she'd do. She'd grab one of her weird salves and begin dabbing me with it while telling me off for being such an idiot, letting my bum get as sore as it is. Who knew it would take blisters on my booty to finally realise that micromanaging me is her version of love. She does it to all of her customers. Telling off Mrs Caplan for not picking up her prescription before the last one is out. Calling the Saunters' grandkids so that they'll come get Mr Saunter's heart pills because he can't walk very far anymore. They know *everything* about their customers. So, yeah . . . I guess, it's me who's proud of them, really. Doing what LifeTime does on their own street corner, because that's where kindness begins, if you're lucky. At home. Sorry, I – does that answer your question?

GRAPHIC: BRAND NEW DAY: Bringing out the Best in Britons Everywhere

'Well that's it for the shout outs this morning. I'm glad we had time to get all of them in today. And an extra thank you to the Toes Up Energy Drink company for sending along a case of their carrot and ginger power shots! I think we'll all be needing one of those today, especially with the weather. I thought it was April showers that were supposed to bring May flowers!' Kath smiled, then frowned. She still had three minutes. Five if she asked them not to run the piece on wine tours outside of Cape Town which, all things considered, she thought was for the best. Kev was being flown back to the UK, allegedly to apologise, but she had her doubts. Apology was not one of Kev's fortes. Her producer had advised her to proceed as normal, no acknowledgement of what happened, business as usual. The advertisers were all being busily and adamantly assured that something like that would never, ever, happen again.

Kath didn't think Kev should be given a chance to prove them right or wrong.

She pointed up to her right, as instructed, knowing the team back at the studio would be filling the spot in with a *Horrible Histories*-esque graphic. 'We'll be riding a modest twenty-seven miles today – about thirteen of them up hill and over dale until we arrive at the historic market town of Hexham which, if our resident brainbox Trevor is to be believed, has Britain's best bread pudding at the refectory cafe, right in the heart of Hexham Abbey.'

Witter, witter, witter.

This was ridiculous. What was she doing acting all bright and chirpy when their entire viewing audience was no doubt quivering in anticipation for her to . . . what exactly? Fall to bits? Take a hit for her husband as she had so many times throughout the years? Smile, smile, smile?

Or was this the time to take a page out of Fola's book? Pack her bags and try something new? He might not be rich. He might not be famous. But he could look at himself in the mirror every morning.

She squeezed her eyes tight even though she knew there'd be wrinkles and tried to summon a picture of her brother. He came to her, laughing. Lolloping about with her on his back. He used to love doing that once he'd grown taller than her. He'd hunch down, have her jump on, fingers woven together round his neck, choking him no doubt, then he'd race and race and race around the house, her mother screaming *no you'll be the death of her* and her father saying *put that girl down* and Kath laughing and clinging to him but not having a care in the world because she'd known without a shadow of a doubt that when she was with him, there was no safer place in the world to be.

'You know what?' Kath opened her eyes, looked into the camera, and for the first time ever felt as though she was genuinely speaking directly to her viewers, 'I was supposed to cut to a lovely little feature we did about a brilliant retiree from Codley Gate who lives his day-to-day life like one of Hadrian's legionaries. He is a legend. Painstakingly restores a portion of the wall he inherited as part of his father's sheep farm. Hats off to him for showing such fortitude, but if it's alright with you, we'll save that for later.' She could feel the cyclists behind her lean in as her voice grew less morning show host and a bit more . . . Oprah. 'The truth is, I'm finding it difficult to carry on as if absolutely nothing happened yesterday.'

Her producer took a step towards her, clipboard in hand, head shaking back and forth in that *no, no, no this isn't happening* way of his, but she put on the blinkers and carried on talking. The real Kath. The one with everyday aches and pains, sorrows and joys. A lapsed Catholic with thirty years of confession to beg forgiveness for. 'I owe you all an apology. Well, Kev owes you an apology more than I owe you an apology, because what he said yesterday was one of the most reprehensible, insensitive, and cruel things a man could say. The last thing a person going through a tunnel of darkness needs is to be mocked, so for that, I hope he gets down on his knees and begs for your forgiveness. The reason *I* owe you an apology – is because over the years, I enabled him to think saying those sorts of things was okay. I let myself be the butt end of his jokes, the recipient of his cream pies, the silly goose to his clever alpha male when in actual fact, I've come to realise my husband is a weak, weak man. No better than a schoolyard bully. Power and prestige and money and fame doesn't make him a better person. Kindness does. And he doesn't seem to understand that. As such, I wanted you, our viewers and supporters to know I will be filing divorce papers. I don't know what this means for the show, his future, or my future. But what I do know, is that when I get on my bicycle today, I will be able to look each and every one of these courageous, incredible riders in the eye and say thank you. Thank you for showing me your hearts

– raw and tarnished and beautiful – because they have given me strength at this, my darkest hour.' She popped on a smile. 'Don't forget, after the commercial break our mystery celebrity chef will be giving us a foolproof way to keep our pavlovas crunchy on the outside and gooey on the inside . . . a bit like I used to think our Kev was. Join us tomorrow as we reach Tynemouth and celebrate, what we hope, is *Brand New Day*'s first record-breaking fundraiser. From all of us here in Gilsland . . . we wish you an *epic* one until the *next* one . . . which we hope will be even better. See you again at six. Bye for now!'

Kath smiled brightly at her producer, her body feeling tingly and light, as if all that honesty had filled her with helium. 'Well!' she said when she'd closed the space between them. 'I guess I'd better be looking for a new job then.'

'There's no need to ride with me,' Flo griped.

'We're not leaving.'

'Well, I wish you would,' she said, lacking the emotional elasticity to stop being so bloody unpleasant. Most of the group was well on their way (including Trevor who'd apologised but said he really did want to push on so he could spend some quality time at the fort-lets up by Vindolanda which Flo had been crushed to learn wasn't a wine-tasting stop). Unable to convince them to press on as well, Sue and Raven were riding too close for comfort. For Flo's comfort anyway. She was achy and grumpy, and, courtesy of the rain ham-mering down on the roof all night, exhausted from a poor night's sleep. Their B&B hostess had been absolutely brilliant, deftly ignoring the fact that a seventy-odd-year-old woman had sulked throughout her elaborate breakfast. Alongside the full English and hot, buttery croissants, she'd made big bowls of the creamiest porridge Flo had ever had. One spoonful in and she had been reminded too much of Stu who also made a mean bowl of porridge. Thinking of Stu, made her miss Captain George which, of course, made her think of

Jennifer and all of the well-aimed accusations her daughter had pelted her with all those weeks ago. It had felt like a lifetime and yet, the time and distance had provided no buffer from the plain fact that her daughter disliked her. And not just as a mother. As a person. *If we'd met on the street,* Jennifer had said on the car ride home from the vets, *I don't think we'd ever be friends.*

'You two go on ahead.'

Flo wanted zero witnesses to her physical dilapidation. No one to bear witness to the emotional mangle she was being fed through at her own hand. Alone apart from Becky who would, annoyingly, be crawling along behind her in that ruddy van of hers.

'We're not leaving you on your own,' Sue said.

'Sorry,' Raven confirmed. 'The buddy system is a system for a reason.'

Flo glowered. 'I can tell you right now, there will be walking.'

'Then we'll walk,' said Sue, giving a little nudge to Raven who instantly said yes, yes, they both loved walking and were very happy to walk. All twenty-seven miles if necessary. In fact, did she know that it was possible to walk a marathon in around eight hours? You could do it in six, really, but she'd added in a couple of hours to account for the hills.

Raven, it came to pass, had had three carrot and ginger power shots in the course of receiving a sponsorship offer from the Toes Up Energy Drink company for her Instagram site. She'd told them she would think about it.

Ten minutes later, having arrived at the foot of their first hill, via a flooded cycle path that had the three of them plunging their pedals into ankle-deep water, they were walking.

Flo thought her misery had peaked yesterday, but it turned out she had been wrong. Quite wrong in fact.

Today's fun little fact was that despite the ice packs, the Deep Heat, two knee supports and some rather peculiar tape Fola had put on her calves, her body wasn't strong enough to get her to the end of this wretched trip. Wasn't strong enough to get her home.

She was going to die out here.

Die in front of increasingly resilient Sue. Die in front of Raven who had seemed so fragile when she'd met her in the New Year, but, if Big Boned Goth Girl was anything to go by, would bounce back from this. Her death.

From where Flo was standing (pedalling), the only person who might really be upset at her demise was Flo.

She would never hold Captain George in her arms again but he'd be more than alright in Stu's care. Never heat up a tin of soup for Stu again (neither tomato nor his beloved chicken noodle). She'd never get to tell her daughter what a fool she'd been or try and make up for the years of parenting that had driven her daughter to become a brittle, rule-loving, efficiency expert who barely noticed the daffodils. Or Jamie. She missed him, too, but under Cynthia's care he'd very likely turn out fine either way, until, she supposed, Cynthia turned seventy and decided to do a cycle ride across the Australian Desert or climb Uluru in the dark or whatever it was Asian-Australians did to prove to themselves the hearts beating in their chests beat for more than just their own pleasure. He'd get a bit of breathing room then. A bit of time to reflect. Her sweet, dear boy. A bit of a pushover, but . . . the world couldn't all be Stu's.

She tipped her face up to the rain, letting the sensation of it wash through her because, after today, she'd never feel it again. What a waste, she thought, relieved, for the very first time, that her parents couldn't see her now. What a waste.

'Did you know,' began Sue—

'—I'm sorry, Sue,' Flo interrupted, '. . . but if you're going to tell me one more thing about bloody Hadrian's bloody Wall I am going to stuff my head into this hedge until you stop.'

Sue, much to her surprise, did not feel hurt by this or any of the other little barbed snippets Flo had been sending out like poison darts all morning.

She knew it wasn't personal. That Flo was going through what they all were: battling demons they'd not thought they'd encounter courtesy of all of this thinking time.

Shepherds, Sue thought, must be very, very peaceful people. Old ones anyway. The young ones probably listened to podcasts or Radio 2.

For some reason this struck her as incredibly funny and, as if cued by the heavens, a flock of sheep ran up to the low hedge to encourage her with their bleats and baas.

She smiled at them and gave them a courtly wave, feeling quite a different woman to the one she'd been yesterday.

It was as if the tears she had shed had cleared the way for someone new: the elusive New Sue who had flickered and flared quite a lot in the early days after Gary had – after Gary had killed himself. New Sue had all but disappeared as she stumbled through the aftermath of the trauma she never once imagined herself having to survive. But now it seemed she was back. And Sue kind of liked her.

So who was this woman?

The New Sue.

Someone who would no longer try and break awkward silences with the phrase 'Did you know . . .' That was for sure.

Which did lend itself to the question . . . what *would* the New Sue do? She'd already done crumpling to the ground to sob and sob in the pouring rain until eventually all of those tears had to turn to laughter, because, truth be told, she didn't think she could face the future if it was going to be entirely miserable. Gary would've been pretty annoyed if she walked round with her 'sad clown' face as Raven called it.

She glanced across at Flo, whose eyes were glued to the road about a metre in front of her as instructed by Fola, who said there was no point in looking up ahead when what really mattered was the next step she took. And the next. She'd sent him on his way fairly sharpish after that, but it seemed some of what he said had stuck.

Sue tried to think of a joke, something, anything to lighten the mood hunkering around them like the misty cloudscape they were cycling towards. The only joke she could remember was one Dean had told her back when they were about six. It went something along the lines of what was black and white and red all over but she couldn't remember if a newspaper or a frog in a blender was the answer, so . . .

'And will you turn that bloody music off!' Flo bellowed at Becky who had been trying and failing to hit just the right note with a Sia anthem that, Sue presumed, was meant to be inspiring.

They heard the van screech and then, rather terrifyingly, it surged towards them, sending the three of them flying into the streaming ditches to avoid getting hit by Becky, one of the most generous and kind women any of them had ever met who, it now seemed, was trying to kill them?

Sue pulled herself out of the ditch, wishing Flo's mood hadn't gone quite so dark. It was one thing to snipe at her, but at Becky? Really?

'Everyone alright?' Raven asked, taking special care to help Flo who was, unsurprisingly, furious.

Sue looked ahead to where the van had skidded to a halt at a cross angle in the small country lane. This was definitely not the way Becky parked, or drove for that matter.

She left her bike in the ditch and ran up to the van.

Becky was sat in the front seat, ashen faced, covered in sweat, arms crossed tightly over her chest.

'Becky? Is everything—'

'Sorry, sorry, sorry. My chest. It's just. God. Sorry. My arm started hurting and then my other one and now I—' she broke off, sweat pouring down from her temples. 'I think I— oh, god, I think I'm going to be sick.'

She pushed the door open, sending Sue flying, but had forgotten to take her seat belt off so hung there, wretching onto the step that she had bounced on and off of throughout the journey, happy as a lark.

'Is everything okay—' Raven ran up to the van, quickly taking in the scene. 'Becky!' She unbuckled her and somehow managed to hoist/carry her out of the van onto the side of the road. 'Do you have food poisoning? Did you drink something last night?'

'No – I . . .' Becky doubled over, wretching so hard her entire body shook.

When she'd recovered, she began to whimper in short, sharp breaths.

'She's having a heart attack.'

Sue and Raven turned to see Flo looking very much like old Flo. Efficient, capable, ready to tackle a challenge.

'Sue, you ring 999. Raven, lay her out flat in the back of the van, find a blanket or something – we don't want her out here in the wet.' Flo pulled open the side door of the van. 'I'll try to find some aspirin.'

Sue pulled off her backpack, dug into the zippy bag she'd stored her phone in then dialled 999. Nothing. She dialled it again. Nothing.

'I can't get any signal,' Sue hit her phone against her leg as if that would suddenly cause all five bars to pop into life.

Nothing.

She glared at the phone. No. This was not going to happen. Not on her watch.

'Where's your phone, Raven?'

Raven pointed to the camelbak still on her back. Sue dug round until she found it. Same thing. No signal.

Flo came round the corner with a bottle of aspirin, tipping one into her hand and instructing Becky, 'Here you are darling. You've got to chew it. It'll be disgusting but you must do it. Raven, can you get a bottle of water for the lass, please?'

'Flo, we need your phone.'

Flo dipped into the pocket of her waterproof jacket and pulled it out. The front glass was fogged and the touch screen refused to respond. They all looked at one another in despair. 'It must've got soaked when I went into the ditch.' Her voice held no accusations. It was just a fact. Becky had begun to have a heart attack and they'd all fallen in the ditch and now they were out here in the middle of a deserted country lane on a miserable Sunday morning with absolutely no one about and no phone signal and a woman's life entirely dependent upon them.

'Oh, shit.' Raven sagged as Becky went limp. 'She passed out.'

They all shifted her into place in the back of the van. Flo clambered in and shook Becky by her shoulders, then rubbed her knuckles hard against her chest.

'Stop! Don't, please,' cried Sue. 'You'll hurt her.'

'It's a sternum rub,' Flo said matter of factly. 'Painful stimuli determines whether or not she's fainted or is unconscious.'

Becky didn't respond at all which meant '. . . CPR,' they all said.

Sue shook her shoulders and bounced up and down on the balls of her feet. If anyone was well equipped to save a woman from a heart attack it was three 111 call operators, one of whom had also been a flight attendant.

'Start the van,' Raven said to Sue. 'Find her iPod and put on "Staying Alive".'

Flo gave a quick nod of approval but Sue remained motionless. 'This is hardly the time to listen to music.'

'It's the beat at which you're meant to do the compressions,' Raven reminded her.

'Shouldn't we be trying to bring her to hospital?' Sue asked, her voice growing more and more high pitched as Flo began ripping open the many layers of Becky's earth mother ensemble.

Flo stared at her for a moment and then solidly said, 'Yes. Head to Hexham, follow the signs. There are plenty of them. If you see a village hall or an old phone box with an AED on it – stop there first. Raven and I will take turns doing compressions.'

Sue, an uncertain driver at the best of times, climbed over the vomit and into the driver's seat and turned on the van. She gave Raven the iPod as, from the rearview mirror, Sue could see Flo begin to give compressions.

After a couple of false starts and horrified apologies they were on their way. Sue's mind reeled with ways to get Becky the help she needed as fast as possible. She would sound the horn if another car came by. She put on the flashing lights. She drove in the middle of the small country lane until she pictured getting hit by an oncoming car so lurched the van to the side and drove so close to the hedge Raven instructed her to drive in the middle of the road again. Raven, in times of stress, had an incredibly solid, commanding voice. Sue drove up and down and up and down until she rammed on the brakes, the road in front of them completely flooded. It was possible to pass on a nearby footbridge if you were, say, on a bicycle . . . but in a van? No chance. If they'd bothered bringing their bicycles with them they could've . . . what? Propped Becky between them on the central support bars and pedalled her to Hexham?

Sue clenched her jaw, stared into the rearview mirror, trying to keep her mother's leering, jeering voice out of her head, but all she could hear was, 'It'll all end in tears, Suey. It'll all end in tears.'

Not today it wouldn't.

Sue jammed the van's long gear shaft into reverse. There was simply no chance she was going to let her mother be right. Not about this, anyway.

She drove, in reverse, forcing herself to tune into Raven and Flo who were timing how long they'd been doing compressions.

'What are you doing?' Flo asked when she noticed they were going in reverse.

'The road is flooded. We can't get through. I'm going to see if there are any turn offs.'

Flo started tapping at her watch, swiping and pinching and flicking her fingers along the screen. 'There aren't any. Not that lead to Hexham anyway.'

'What about Gilsland? Is there a hospital there?'

'No. Maybe Brampton but that'll take at least twenty minutes. Maybe half an hour and—'

They all stared at one another as the bleak reality of their situation sank in. Unless they found a way to make an AED out of the jumper cables . . . Becky might die.

'Don't stop!' Sue shouted, realising Raven had fallen into the same motionless stupor she had.

'Sorry, sorry,' Raven returned to the syncopated pulses as Sue painstakingly drove backwards until, mercifully, the lane widened enough to do a tortuously jerky seven-point turn until, at long last, they could drive forward.

'Oh my god, my arms!' Raven screamed in frustration. 'Flo, we've got to switch. My arms have gone numb. Sue? What the actual fuck? Why aren't you driving?'

'I—' Why wasn't she driving? She had a life to save. An actual life that was barely being kept afloat in the back of a muddy, cold, industrial van.

This wasn't the way Becky's life should come to an end. Becky's life shouldn't come to an end at all.

In the back Raven and Flo began bickering about how long they should keep up compressions.

'Thirty minutes,' Sue said.

No one acknowledged her.

The bickering continued.

A force she had never known she possessed surged through her like lava. 'Thirty minutes!' she said, jamming the van into gear. 'Now think of solutions! Actual solutions!'

Flo and Raven stared at her, jaws agape.

'Why aren't you doing compressions?'

Raven took over again as Flo continued to stare at Sue as if she'd never properly seen her before.

'What would you do on the aeroplane, Flo?' Sue demanded.

'We have an AED kit and we'd call for a doctor on board. There's almost always a doctor on board.'

Flo and Raven threw helpless little looks around the grey, misty landscape as if one might emerge from the elements in this, their hour of need.

'There is something that Trevor said,' Raven began.

'Oh, dear god, no,' Flo immediately began to dismiss.

'Let. Her. Speak,' Sue ground out.

'It's a real thing,' Raven said, looking both terrified and intensely keen to prove Trevor's nugget of information just might be their saving grace. 'I looked it up after. A guy was having a heart attack in an ambulance in Chicago and he was dying and they couldn't get him back, not even with the AED, and they were speeding along and hit an epic pothole and kablam!' She raised her hands which Flo promptly grabbed and put back on Becky's chest. 'The pothole saved his life.'

'So . . . I need to hit a pothole?' Sue's eyes darted between the road and Raven.

'You need to hit an *epic* pothole. And as far as I can remember, there weren't any on the road here.'

'Do you want me to do it?' Sue asked.

Raven and Flo both shouted 'no' which Flo felt a bit bad about, but Sue's driving was erratic at the best of times and they didn't need to turn an already bad situation into four fatalities.

'So . . . what exactly do I need to do?' Sue's eyes connected with Raven's.

'You need to find some uneven ground. But not the flooded bits of the road. And then when you see a sleeping policeman or a pothole or whatever . . . cane it. Cane it until Becky's heart starts again.'

'Okay,' said Sue. 'Got it.'

She gripped the steering wheel so hard her hands felt as though they were melded to it, then set off at a speed no one would have recommended on these slim, wet, country lanes. Gary would've whooped with admiration. Gary would've said, 'I knew you were made of fire, Suey! No one else ever believed me when I told them, that girl's made of fire, but I always knew it!'

But Gary wasn't here anymore. It was Becky's life that needed saving today. Becky, who had been with them throughout this long, difficult journey. Always encouraging. Always supporting. Never once letting any of the exhausted (Raven), grumpy (Flo), or dispirited (Sue), riders dim her smile.

Sue crested a hill and what she saw ahead spread out before her made her heart sink. The banks of the creek they'd been riding along had burst and at the bottom of the steep hill . . . a lake sprawled out where the road had once been.

She looked to her left.

Woodland.

She looked to her right.

A sheep field awash with rocky outcrops and a load of sheep.

A few metres down there was an open field gate. Sue gunned it, yanked the van into the field, pressed her foot as hard as she could, weaving in and out of clusters of startled sheep, silently telling them there was a life at risk and that they would be okay. With steely eyed determination, she pressed down on the accelerator, aiming the van towards a rocky looking bit further up the hill. A hill which may or may not end on a cliff. She didn't know. She couldn't see. She felt like Thelma *and* Louise, but not with a death wish. More like, a life wish. Full, rich, complicated life wishes for her, for Becky, for Flo, for Raven – for everyone. She pressed her entire bodyweight onto the accelerator pedal, praying to everything that was good in the world, that this would work. 'Hold on, girls!!!!!!' They crested the hill and as Sue felt the tyres lose their connection with the earth, Flo shouted, 'I've got a signal!'

OPENING SEQUENCE: BRAND NEW DAY

GRAPHIC: HADRIAN'S WALL SPECIAL WITH *BRAND NEW DAY*'S KATH FULLER

VISUAL: Kath riding her bicycle, Kath talking to riders, Kath hugging Sue, Kath holding up Flo's arm in an ambulance as if she'd won a gold medal, Kath giving a foil-blanket-wrapped Raven a fist bump, interior shot of a pale, but smiling Becky receiving a bouquet of flowers from Kath, Sue, Raven and Flo with doctors applauding in the background.

VOICEOVER: When I first came up with the idea of riding my bicycle along Hadrian's Wall in support of LifeTime, I thought it would be a doddle. A bit of a laugh. Something most of our viewers would mute until my husband Kev's pieces from South Africa aired. After all, who wouldn't want a holiday in one of the world's top ten destinations? Wine, sun, sand, sea and hot beach volleyball players . . . I thought this was something I would do alone.

CUT TO:

KATH: (helmet under arm) But you proved me wrong.

CUT TO: Exterior: Kath outside Hexham Abbey

KATH: You joined us on our coast-to-coast journey and did so in spades. (Blows viewers a kiss) Thank you. From here. (Presses hands to heart) Truly. Thank you. What I learned about our viewers shouldn't

338

have come as a surprise, but let me tell you this . . . I think you're *amazing*. Amazingly kind, amazingly generous, amazingly sensitive. To date, we have raised over *four* hundred thousand pounds for LifeTime, a charity that is there for you. All of you. LifeTime volunteers can advise, support, but mostly, they're there to listen. I want you to know I am, too. Saying that, I would like you to be the first to know that when we reach the end of our journey this afternoon – it will also be the conclusion of my journey with *Brand New Day*. From the weekend, I will be . . . considering my options. But for now! Join us live as our riders prepare to set off for their last epic one . . . until the next one – which I hope will be even better.

Chapter Forty-Nine

'And if everyone could lean into the stretch . . . ahhh . . . that's it . . . well done everybody.'

As lovely as Fola was, there wasn't a chance in hell Flo was going to be able to cajole her quadriceps into doing anything beyond what they damn well pleased today.

'How was your interview?' Sue asked, her head bent towards her knee like the astonishingly flexible thing she was.

'Fine, yes.' Quick was what it had been. She hadn't felt right taking credit for saving Becky Harris's life. It had very much been a group effort so she'd said as much and then asked the cameraman if she could go now because she had a date with a roll of kinesiology tape. 'I understand Raven's got another sponsor wanting to cash in on her Insta-fame.'

Sue laughed, switching legs. 'Yes. Yes, she has. The most reluctant Instagram star in the world, our Raven, but . . . she seems intent on saying no to sponsorship and yes to keeping it real. Right!' She stood up and clapped her hands. 'I'm going to fill up my water bottles. Can I get you anything?'

A younger body. A gel seat. A journey that was entirely downhill and ended at a fish and chips shack. 'No, I'm fine. You go on. See you in Tynemouth, love.'

'You're alright to ride on your own?'

'Happy as,' said Flo.

Happy as a what or who, she thought as Sue gave her a quick, tight hug, then wandered off into the crowd of cyclists all buzzing with excitement that they'd made it this far and only had thirty-seven more miles to go.

Thirty-seven modern miles.

She sent her bicycle a hooded look, its frame sparkling in the morning sun as if it couldn't think of a better thing to do than hit the road again. After all. That's what its job was. A ludicrous stab of envy shot through her. Why couldn't her life be as simple? Her destiny so straightforward?

She screwed her eyes shut tight and reminded herself she could very easily be lying dead in a morgue if Becky's van had ploughed over rather than through them.

She gave her cycle a pat.

One more day. One more day of riding and this insane journey would be over. Flo checked her attitude. Given how dark things had turned yesterday, it wasn't that awful, but . . . creak creak creak. Despite Fola's ministrations and that rather lovely EMT's topical pain medication (he'd slipped her the entire tube when the camera crews had left), she was genuinely worried her old bones weren't up to it. Stuart was right. She needed to retire. Properly. Spend more time with her increasingly distant children. The grandchildren she barely knew. Make friends with the silver surfers and drink decaf coffee. Learn to play . . . oh dear lord . . . learn to play bridge.

But it made sense. Particularly after she'd tried to press life back into poor Becky's heart and failed. Thousands of compressions she'd done, along with Raven, of course. That girl . . . that girl was someone you wanted by your side in a crisis. 111 didn't know what they had in her. A shoe-in to replace Rachel Woolley if the woman ever left the call centre which, if Flo were in charge, would've happened some time ago.

She and Trevor had been right in the end, about the pothole. Sue had gunned that huge old van up a hill until it took flight and when it had landed with an almighty slam . . . Becky had blinked up at the two of them as if she were a newborn kitten. A middle-aged, slightly overweight newborn kitten, but there had been an expression of such innocence on her face . . . such joy . . . as if the only thing she needed in life was air. She'd looked Flo right in the eye and said, 'Ginny?' Then she'd sucked in an almighty breath and passed out again. They'd had quite a palaver determining whether or not they needed to carry on with the compressions or look for another pothole, but two of the tyres had burst and, of course, the mud had begun to absorb the two that hadn't, but mercifully they had signal by then and a 999 call operator on the other end of the line giving instructions and continual assurances that, as the rain was clearing, an air ambulance was on its way. Perhaps she'd apply for a position on their team—

'Flo?' Sue touched her arm and pointed towards the other side of the market square (cobbled!!!) where riders had gathered for their 'Brand New Stretch' as they'd taken to calling Fola's pre-ride sessions. 'Isn't that your Stuart?'

And so it was. Her Stuart. Heart hammering every bit as much as it had when she walked down the aisle some forty-odd years ago, she hobbled over to him trying not to betray just how stiff she was. 'Stu?' she said, and then, 'What have you done with Captain George?' And that's when she saw what Stu had done. Next to him was a bright red, electric bicycle built for two with a tented trailer attachment inside of which, on his favourite blanket and with his favourite toy, was Captain George.

'I thought you might like a bit of company for this last bit,' Stu said.

Flo threw herself at her husband, hugging him so tightly he eventually wheezed a plea for her to loosen her grip.

'You saw?' she asked, hoping he knew she meant the clips on the news from Raven's Instagram feed of her dragging herself up the hill and then bouncing around the countryside with Becky, the

A Bicycle Built for Sue

CPR, the helicopter, but most of all the shame that she'd felt for being so daft as to think a ride like this would be a piece of cake. It had been so very hard, and for a thousand different reasons than she would've thought. She loved her husband. She needed him. And at exactly the moment she needed him most, here he was, helping her complete a journey she hadn't realised she needed to make. And she wasn't talking about Hexham to Tynemouth.

He nodded. 'I saw.'

'You came.'

He nodded again, clearly bemused at the astonishment in her voice. 'Of course I came. You're my Maypole, aren't you?'

What? No. Stuart was *her* maypole. Oh, she chided him for it, the fussing, the bothering, the endless delays until they read the instruction manual properly, but . . . everyone needed someone in their lives to read the manual, didn't they? Guidelines existed for a reason. They were, more often than not, very helpful.

'We haven't really known what to do with ourselves, George and I,' Stu said, leading Flo over to George so she could have a proper cuddle. 'When we saw everything you'd been through, well . . .' He pointed at the tandem. 'We thought you might like a bit of company.'

'But how did you organise all of this? It was only on the news last night. And when I rang . . .'

'When you rang we were already on the road.'

'What?'

'We spent the night in Harrogate and got up extra early. Didn't we, George? Woke up early this morning and hit the ground running . . . well . . . in the car anyway.'

'But Stu? How did you find an electric tandem bicycle after six o'clock in the evening?'

Stuart's expression turned sheepish. 'I got it the day you left. About two hours after being in the house alone. George and I couldn't stand it, could we, lad?' He reached back and gave the dog's head a gentle stroke.

'But . . . but you're home all the time,' Flo said. 'On your own.'

'Aye, but . . . love,' Stuart's eyes unexpectedly glassed over as he reached out to take her hand in his. 'Those times we always knew you were coming back.'

An intense, life-affirming rush of love coursed through her so hard and fast, Flo felt positively light-headed.

'I love you, Florence Wilson,' Stuart said. 'You're the light of my life and I'd like to keep you round as long as possible.' Then he leant towards her, and for the third time in his life, kissed Flo in public.

The closer Raven got to Newcastle, the more uncomfortable she felt. And not just because her bum bandages were shifting beneath her four remaining pairs of underwear, two sets of cycling shorts and an outer layer of leggings which were meant to be holding it all in place. No . . . it wasn't that. It was fear. Fear that she'd put the wrong Oz at the end of her yellow brick gap year.

It had been eleven months since she'd left college. Eleven long months to focus, earn and hunker down. Fine tune exactly what it was she wanted to do for the rest of her life – or at least university. And did she feel any closer to knowing what that was? Nope. Not a clue. Unless T-shirt flower painter was a thing. Was there a degree in Instagramming? Probably not. She glanced at her odometer. Twenty-odd miles to figure out what she wanted to do with the rest of her entire life or admit that she had, in fact, been a complete idiot not to follow her parents' advice from the off and that all of this, the jobs, the moving out, the bike ride, had all been a complete and utter waste of a year. Awesome.

'Hey! Raven! Fancy a couple of ride-along friends?'

Raven turned and saw Molly, the school counsellor and a freshly shaven Trevor riding up alongside her.

'Course,' said Raven, unusually grateful for the break in her alone time.

'So!' began Molly as if she'd rehearsed a little speech. 'How *are* you?'

'You mean after yesterday?'

'Yes,' nodded Molly. 'And . . . you know . . . the other days before that.'

Raven went wide-eyed. Was Molly really asking her to talk about the meltdown she'd had the other day? In front of *Trevor*? She was about to say something like, yeah fine but it was intense, then reminded herself that she had been Instagramming her deepest darkest thoughts to total strangers for the past few days and that she had received nothing but support in return. More than that, really. She'd received actual sponsorship offers. Which she'd totally turned down because, durrrr, look at the Kardashians.

She glanced over at Molly who looked genuinely interested, and Trevor who had unwittingly enabled her to save a woman's life and thought . . . maybe it's time to try something new. Owning her feelings in front of actual people. So she began to talk. And talk and talk and talk about uni and her parents and how she knew they meant well and that whilst the idea of being a lawyer wasn't completely reprehensible, it wasn't really the float to her boat, not like her art was, which, to be honest, she knew was alright, but not exemplary or groundbreaking like Van Gogh or Picasso or Banksy all of which, weirdly, made her think of Dylan who, no, wasn't her boyfriend but an actual mate, maybe even her first mate ever, like *genuine* mate, because so often in school you thought someone was your friend who wasn't really your friend and of course she had considered herself to be one of Aisha's friends but actually what they had been was loners who had recognised a pot and a kettle and then not done anything about it even when Aisha had totally needed her to call the kettle black which wasn't really the analogy she was going for, but they got what she meant, right? She should've stepped up. She should've stepped up and she hadn't and even though things hadn't turned out completely brilliantly for Aisha at least she was alive and knew she was loved by her family which was something she was beginning to understand about her own family all of which made her extra conscious that when she made friends in the future she would definitely step up when necessary even if it did scare the absolute crapola out of her but, to be honest, after yesterday, fewer things than she thought scared the crapola out of her, except, of course, disappointing her parents which was really the biggest fear she had because even letting Gandhiji down felt less awful than the idea that her parents would never be proud of her which, now that she had had a lot of time to think about it, really was her worst fear. Worse even than climate change which was also ranked right up there in the realm of things that were too freaky to think about, so instead she nattered on about her parents, their shop, their customers, her siblings, their children and everything she hoped they would do together as a family like ride alongside this beautiful river, through incredible parklands like these – look! – did they see the wild ponies? – and maybe, one day, she and her family would be like one of these families walking their dogs and jogging and yes, even cycling, although she wasn't so sure her father would really like the cycling but maybe they could do something else so that they could do whatever it was together, and she began to run through the options of activities her father might enjoy until first Trevor and then eventually Molly, excused themselves and Raven was once again riding on her own looking at the world around her as if seeing it for the very first time which, she realized, as a fizzy burbly excitement effervesced through her, she was. This *was* a Brand New Day. And it *was* epic. Whether or not Newcastle was her destiny suddenly didn't matter anymore because somewhere, somehow along this journey, a kernel of self-belief had begun to form and grow within her and whichever way her future panned out, she knew she would come out smiling.

'Alright if I come in?'

'Sue! What are you doing here?' Becky pushed herself up against the mountain of pillows and pointed at the small television screen opposite her bed. 'I thought I just watched all of you head off down the road!'

'I thought I'd take a little detour before setting off.'

'Don't you want to hit the finish line with the rest of the group?'

'Oh, I'll catch up.' Sue dodged a lurching bouquet of heart-shaped balloons as she walked into the room. 'Dean-O promised me there'd be an extra-long comfort break outside the museum at Wallsend for—'

'Trevor,' they both said and laughed together.

Sue looked round the room. 'Gosh! It's like a florist's shop in here.'

Becky sank back into her pillows with a smile. 'Who knew it would take a quadruple heart bypass to feel like an Interflora van driver, eh?'

'We're all ever so happy you made it,' Sue gave her hand a light squeeze, mindful of the drip taped into the back of her hand, the snaking of tubes and monitors attached to her chest. 'Did they find your daughter? Ginny?'

Becky blinked at her and then, as if as a strong wind had been holding her features in place, the wind dropped away and her expression crumpled.

'Oh! Becky, I'm so sorry. Did I say the wrong thing?'

'No, no,' said Becky. 'I'm ever so grateful for everything you did. So *very* grateful, but . . .'

'But, what? Were they not able to get in touch with her? I am more than happy to make some calls.' Sue stopped talking when fat tears began to form then trickle down Becky's lovely, kind, but incredibly pale, face.

'Ginny died, Sue.'

Sue gasped. 'Oh, my god! Becky! Yesterday?' She floundered and stuttered until Becky eventually took her hand in both of hers and gave it soft strokes as if soothing a puppy.

'Ginny died about fifteen years ago. Fifteen years, two months and five days to be exact.'

'I'm sorry, I don't understand. You always spoke about her as if—'

'—as if she were alive, I know.' Tears slid silently down Becky's face as she explained. 'She died in a car accident. A ridiculous one, really. Can you believe it? She was hit by lightning. It went straight through the windscreen and poof! My little girl was gone.' She pinched her hands together then opened them up so that all that was between them was air. 'I thought maybe yesterday it had finally come.'

'What had come?'

'My chance to be with her.'

A wave of nausea swept through Sue. Never, even when that dreadful red velvet curtain had closed as Gary's casket slid back towards the bowels of the crematorium had she ever wished herself dead. 'No. Becky. You don't mean that. You are so kind and full of life and such a wonderful person. You couldn't possibly want to be—'

'—with my daughter?' Becky finished for her. 'Yes. Yes I could. Not that I was willing myself to have a heart attack and nearly take you lot with me, but . . . it's all I've been doing these last fifteen years. Wishing I was with her. Trying to experience everything my Ginny couldn't. Stupid, wasn't it?'

Sue made a vague noise. She was beyond judgement when it came to grief.

'Fifteen years,' Becky sighed, grating her lips against her teeth, the blood returning ever so slowly as they plumped back out again. 'Fifteen years of ruining my marriage, my friendships, everything really, all to try and live a life that was never mine to live.'

'I wish I had something incredibly wise to say. Something that could help.'

'You could tell me what I'm going to do now,' Becky said, laughing the most forlorn, watery laugh Sue had ever heard.

Sue forced herself not to answer straight away. She, of all people, knew trotting out the standard *there, there's* and *it'll be alrights* and *time heals all wounds* placations were really ways of getting a grief-stricken person to stop talking because, the plain truth of the matter was, being around someone who was so very sad was unbelievably uncomfortable. People just wanted it to stop. People like her mother. Her sister-in-law. And, maybe, her Gary – who must've kept everything that had been troubling him from her because he had never been able to bear it when she cried. Even if it was at a Christmas advert. He used to flee the room, squealing – *squealing!* – no, Suey, no! Please. Don't cry. Please don't cry. Then he'd return and pour chocolates and tissues and takeaway menus – whatever he could gather into his arms to make her tears disappear because, Sue finally saw, bearing someone else's pain on top of your own, could sometimes be too much to handle. So much so, that for some people, the only solution was to end it all.

She pulled a chair up to the side of Becky's bed. 'Why don't you tell me about all of the things you're interested in?'

Becky pulled a face. 'Go on, Sue. You'll be missing the rest of the ride.' She glanced at the wall clock. 'You don't have time.'

'Yes, I do,' said Sue. 'I have all the time in the world.'

Because some things simply had to be staged, the crew had stopped all of the cyclists, including Kath, at the newly redeveloped North Shield docks – a lovely area that had been completely transformed since Kath had left the area some forty years back. Whoever had waved their magic wand over the rundown fishing port had struck a perfect note between yesteryear charm and modern comforts. Like food. There were so many delicious restaurants to choose from serving oysters to fish and chips to sushi and back again. The air smelt of chips and spices and burnt sugar. Everything she'd been avoiding eating since she'd been about twelve years old.

'Who wants an ice cream,' she asked the small group of men who had regularly led the charge throughout the week. 'I'm paying.' Much to her delight – they all did. As each cyclist pulled up, their faces lit at the sight of all of the double and triple scooped cones being handed out to everyone in a bright yellow T-shirt.

About an hour later, the last of the riders pulled up to the group. First Flo, then Raven and finally, Sue. Kath didn't know why, but the three women's arrival seemed to bring with it a lovely sensation of quiet, but utterly beautiful achievement to the group. A calm she'd not felt before.

Her producer came up and touched her elbow. 'Ready?'

'Absolutely.' And she was. After a few quick instructions about riding the additional mile along the beachfront and then – yes, she was very sorry – up one last hill to the Tynemouth castle, there would be refreshments and medals and an announcement about the fundraising and, with any luck, a bit of a crowd to cheer them in, but! as much as she would've loved it to be the whole of Britain cheering them in, it was best to remember it was Friday lunchtime. Not everyone who was a morning telly fan would be able to get out of work and join them, but as she knew everyone would be heading off to be with their loved ones after the ride – she hoped the ice cream cones and medals would serve as the heartfelt thanks she owed each and every one of them for putting LifeTime on Britain's headlines, and raising so much money because, as they all knew, every little bit did actually help.

Then she got on her bicycle, and began to ride. Yes, to the castle, but after that? Not a single solitary clue what her future held in store and for the first time in her life . . . the possibilities felt exhilarating.

'Well, would you look at that, Flo! Your Kath got it wrong, didn't she?'

Flo couldn't stop grinning. Riding up that bloody great hill to the castle had been a doddle with the electric bike. Even with Captain George on the back. And to see not only that Kath had been wrong about the crowd, but that she had been wildly wrong, made all of the aches and pains she thought she'd never forget just . . . disappear.

Together she and Stu collected her medal which, of course, was immediately given to George to wear and he looked very proud indeed, nose poking out of his covered tent, happily receiving all of the pets and cuddles just some of the actual thousands of people who had turned out to cheer them in were doling out like lollies.

'Ah! There they are,' Stu said. Most unexpectedly seeing as Flo hadn't expected to see Stu, let alone anyone else she knew today. She scanned the crowd, a jumble of cyclists and families and banners and mobile food trucks dotted about the place, handing out free snacks and LifeTime stickers. There was even a massage tent which Flo would've imagined herself plopping down in and never leaving until her eyes lit on the one person she never in a million years would've imagined being here.

Jennifer. Jennifer and her husband, Andrew, and their two gorgeous little children all waving LifeTime flags with her name on one, Mum on another and Nanna Flo on the other two.

'Oh, my darlings!' Flo ran over and pulled them all into her arms laughing and crying the happiest of tears wondering how on earth she'd been so blessed as to have such a loving, forgiving family.

'I think I owe you an apology,' she whispered into her daughter's ear.

The expression on Jennifer's face was hard to read.

'More than one?'

Jennifer tipped her head back and forth clearly weighing up just how many apologies Flo owed her, then tipped her thinky frown into a smile. 'Probably about as many thank yous as I owe you.'

'Thank yous? Whatever for?'

'For making life interesting,' Jennifer said, hooking her arm in Flo's as they followed behind Andrew who was walking behind Stu who had one grandchild on the back of the tandem and one in with Captain George, all of them gabbling about which fish and chip shop would be the best one to have their first ever seaside fish and chips from.

Once they'd eaten and Flo had somehow, miraculously, found Raven and Sue to hug goodbye and promise to see again soon but perhaps in a coffee shop this time, Stu set about securing the tandem to the top of the Discovery (along with the hazard flags) and tucking George (with some help from Jennifer and Andrew) into the backseat (with a special doggy sling to keep him safe). Though it took ages and at least three consultations with the instructions, Stu's thinning hair and intense focus on exactly what he was doing didn't seem quite so troublesome as it once had and Flo didn't feel the slightest urge to strangle him. Not even when they climbed in the car only to have to climb out again so he could check the oil, the windscreen washing fluid levels, and full beam lights. Twice. When Stuart finally climbed back up into the car he turned to Flo with a bright smile. 'Where to, Madam? With the weather forecast looking so nice, I thought perhaps we could head up to Scotland! Have a ride round the lochs. Or perhaps head down into the Yorkshire moors. I understand the wildflowers are rather extraordinary this time of year. Of course, if Yorkshire isn't your cup of tea—'

'Stu?'

'Wales? The Johnsons showed me a clip of some lovely waterfalls and with all of the rain we've been having, they might be really splendid.'

'Stuart, darling—'

'We could head south. The Cornish coast is meant to be quite spectacular—'

'Stuart, love!' Flo pressed her fingertips to his dear, sweet mouth. 'Could we please just go home?'

He looked at her a moment, startled, then took her hand in his and gave her knuckles a kiss. 'Of course, darling. Anything you like.' He began driving in his slow steady way down the high street, past the cyclists and their families, stopping for a mother manhandling a pram across the road where she shouldn't be, ignoring the impatient pips of the driver behind him, taking the moment to pop on Radio 3 with a

'I hear they're going to play Barber's *Adagio* later this afternoon.' And then, 'Why don't you sit back, relax and think about something new for this summer, shall we? Perhaps give Portugal a miss?'

And that, of course, was when Flo understood that Stu had been with her on every journey, every adventure, every flight of fancy all along. The love of her life who knew her so much better than she had ever known him.

Raven wasn't entirely sure how, maybe it was Trevor shouting do it, do it, do it as she pedalled about as slowly as any human could without falling off up the final, excruciatingly steep hill up to the castle, but she did it. And when she got there it was like arriving at a party she'd never known she wanted to go to. A party where she wouldn't have to press herself against the wall and pretend that's where she liked standing. A party where she didn't try to start up conversations with some of the cool kids only to realise the only reason they were talking to her was to wait for a gap in a much cooler kid's conversation. Not that she was a party expert or anything.

'Raven! Raven over here!' She looked up and saw someone waving a huge sign emblazoned with the Big Boned Goth Girl logo she'd posted a few days back. Wait. There were four more signs being jigged around behind Dylan's. Sweet mother of Holy Ganges rivers. Was that her – 'Mum? Dad?'

Shyly beaming, Dylan ushered her parents towards her, cemented as she was to the spot, her bicycle serving as a security blanket (something she'd never had in real life because, derrr . . . Gandhiji wouldn't have wandered round with a stinking blankie and his thumb in his mouth, would he?). And then her sister appeared, not so much as a single thread of a power suit in sight. Then her brother, a child hanging onto each leg as he Frankenstein Daddy stepped towards her. And then all of a sudden they were all talking and laughing and yes, blubbering a little bit because it was like, totally emotional.

'We're so proud of you, Sunita. Raven,' her mother corrected herself. 'We can't believe what a beacon of hope you've become to young people.'

'Sorry. What?'

Her sister gave her a smirk. 'We've all been following your Insta feed.'

'How did you know about that?'

Every member of her family began looking round until their eyes landed on Dylan who was standing by a petite woman with mousy hair and a slightly timorous, but distinctly happy smile. Dylan gave her a thumbs up and said, 'Peace out, Raves. Soz, but I had to let your fam-damily know you were like, a total star.'

'But how did you even know who they were?'

He looked at her like she was an idiot. 'I get my mum's stuff from your parents, innit?'

A whole series of little lightbulbs went off. Yes, she'd seen him at school, but only because she'd seen him a whole lot more at her parents' pharmacy.

Citalopram had been the first prescription. Then Prozac. That hadn't worked. It had given her headaches. Then Paxil, Tritellix, Viibryd, then Lexapro.

She looked at Dylan's mum. 'Thank you.'

'For what, love?'

'Raising such a brilliant son.'

She flushed and went a bit glossy eyed as Dylan tucked her under his teenaged arm with a 'who's the best mum in the world, eh?' He flicked an apologetic look at Raven's mum. 'Present company excepted, Prof.'

Prof? He called her mum Prof?

Dylan nodded at her mum and then her dad. 'They saved my mum's life.'

Her dad began to do that little wobbly head shake of his that suggested the details weren't exactly right. 'We just noticed some discrepancies was all.'

'Yeah, but – she could have died, innit? You saved her life.' Dylan was refusing to let whatever this was slide. He turned to Raven and began to explain in a way that suggested Raven would see sense. Raven would be the one who understood and it made her want to hug Dylan so hard but that would be interrupting and if she'd learnt anything over the course of this trip, it was that listening, really listening to someone was one of the finest forms of friendship.

'Her doctor, right?' Dylan was saying. 'Her doctor went on holiday and my mum went for a check-up with a locum and that doctor wasn't paying attention to what my mum was telling him and he gave her a new prescription to take with her old one and the two together?' He made a kaboom noise.

'Maybe not quite so bad as that, but . . .' Her father's head tipped from one shoulder to the other and then said, 'We're just pleased we could help.'

'Sunita,' her mother began in an all-too-familiar voice. 'I think you're looking a bit peaky. When's the last time you ate? Stick out your tongue. Ohmygod, Sunil! Would you look at your daughter's tongue? She's dehydrated. Come, come. There's a drinks stand some-where. Vineeta? You push your sister's bicycle, she must be exhausted. Sanjay, take your jacket off and give it to her. We can't have her catching a chill? Not after riding all that way.'

Raven, for the first time in her life, happily complied as layers were tugged off, the state of her body was discussed in great detail, where they would eat, what they would eat, why they shouldn't have fish and chips like all of these other people because a fatty diet after such strenuous exercise would make her feel bloated and who wanted to feel bloated when they had such a long journey home?

Home.

Raven pictured an amalgam of her room at Sue's and her child-hood room, not entirely sure where she fitted anymore, but not in a bad way. More in a way that signalled another transition was on the horizon. Another change. But this time, a good one.

As she was being shuttled off towards the High Street where her brother said he had spotted not one, but three restaurants that would fit their mother's criteria, she caught eyes with Sue who was surrounded by her family and a whole lot of other people she hadn't seen before.

Dylan gave Dean a big old wave. 'Alright, boss?' Dean did one of the weird surfing hand things that Dylan regularly did in his selfies. Selfies he sent to his mum. Damn, that boy was cool. Talk about learning not to judge a book by its cover . . .

She gave Sue a wave and then made an 'I'll call you' gesture with her hand standing in for a phone. Sue nodded, her own expression looking every bit as dazed as hers no doubt was.

Sue was shell-shocked.

They were all here.

Every last person she had expected at Gary's wake.

His football mates. His pub mates. His step-mum. Her entire family. Even Katie. Which was very peculiar, because they were all meant to be in the Canaries. When she had crested the hill and pulled into the square in front of the castle she had felt elation and relief at finally having finished the ride but also a strange sense of hollowness. As if a chapter had closed in her life and she'd not yet found a way to turn the page for the next one. She had a job to go back to, a house to go unlock the front door to, but . . . she didn't think she wanted those things anymore. The ride, the talks with Kath, the terrifying incident with Becky, the talk she'd had this morning in hospital . . . they were all game changers. And why do something like this if she wasn't going to finally start listening to what the universe was saying to her?

Her eyes scanned all of the beaming faces, their voices and congratulations all blurring into one happy buzz.

It's your choice.

It's your future.

As she was showered with flowers, and was instructed to read all of the banners and silly signs (*We believe in U Sue! She's a SUEnami! Watch out life! We're going to SUE you!*), Sue felt a strange sense of calm come over her. There was no need to feel uncomfortable or awkward or unworthy. She had earned this. Literally by the seat of her padded pants, she had earned this.

Flo barged through the lot of them at one point, pulling her into a fierce hug, whispering promises to bring her bicycle to the nearest metal merchant so they could all watch it be crushed into nothing and to please never let her talk Sue into anything quite so ridiculous ever again. Sue gave her a kiss, unable to put into words how very grateful she was that Flo had talked her into it. This ride had changed her life. Her perspective on it anyway.

Later, after her mother who had been none too subtly trying to wangle an introduction to Kath, had met and lavished her with adoration, Sue caught eyes with Raven and Dylan – both of whom gave her big old fat waves, their faces happy as could be.

'He's a good lad.'

Sue turned to see Dean also returning a wave.

'Is he still at the agency?'

'Absolutely. He's a bright young man. Works hard. I've offered him a full-time job.'

'Oh?'

'Would've been a fool not to. He knows things about computers I could only dream about knowing. Thanks for the intro, Suey.' Dean's face went a bit funny and he scrubbed his jaw and pushed his lips out as if he were trying to hold in something he wasn't entirely comfortable saying and then, finally, as if someone had turned a key in his back, he said, 'Sue, I owe you an apology.'

'What? Why?'

He glanced at Katie, who was squeezing Bev for the entirety of her conversation with Kath, then steered Sue away from the crowd to a bench. 'Gary came to me.'

Sue's heart went still – suspended in the centre of her chest as Dean continued.

'He came to me a few times after his dad died, asking for help.'

'What kind of help?'

'With the accounts.'

Her heart lurched up into her throat but she still managed to ask, 'And did you? Did you help him?'

Dean pushed his chin out and looked away, a gesture which told her all she needed to know.

'I'm so sorry, Suey. I hadn't realised it was that bad.'

'How do you mean? How do you even know it was bad?'

'Dylan told me.'

'What?'

'Don't be mad. Raven told him about you and the boxes and all of Gary's invoices and he suggested that – whilst you were away – he bring the ones you hadn't been through into the office so we could have a look.'

Sue tried to swallow and couldn't.

'He's owed a lot of money, Suey. He owes some, too, but . . .' Dean finally met her eyes again. 'I fucked up. I've got four of my best freelancers on it but I'm overseeing it all. We're putting a proper set of accounts together. Sending out invoices. Talking to all of the vendors. We're getting it sorted, alright? You're not to worry about money, little sister. You're going to be okay.'

A week ago, Sue would never have believed him. A week ago she would've wondered what he wanted. More babysitting. A cake to be made for his staff. A run round the lounge with the hoover before Katie got back. But there was something about the way Dean looked at her now – as if she were an actual, real person – that made her believe him. And whilst, yes, more than anything in the world she would've preferred to be up to her neck in debt and have her Gary by her side, that wasn't the case. It never would be the case.

Dean pulled an envelope out of the inside of his jacket pocket (a jacket Katie must've made him wear because it was royal blue and she knew for a fact Dean couldn't bear royal blue, but people did things for the people they loved even if they didn't always make sense, didn't they? Though she'd never once admitted it, Sue couldn't bear toad-in-the-hole. But she made it, because of the way her Gary's eyes lit up . . .).

'I found this in one of the boxes.'

'What is it?'

He glanced over her shoulder to where her family were all standing in a group, their faces lit with expectant smiles. 'I'll get them to a restaurant. You stay here. Have a read. Join us after.'

She took the pale pink envelope in her hand, surprised not to see the telltale shake.

And then, once Dean had left, she opened it and pulled out a huge, over-the-top Valentine's Day card featuring an enormous unicorn dressed like Cupid.

She ignored the tears falling down her face and made herself open it.

Dear Suey –

Happy Valentine's Day, love! Happy Valentine's Day for this and all of the Valentines yet to come because if you've found this card, then you know I'm not here anymore. I'm so sorry, but I just can't anymore. I'm too close to dragging you down the rabbit hole with me. If there is one thing I meant from the bottom of my heart it was my marriage vow to you to always, always protect and care for you. This is the best way, love. I know it might not seem like it now, but I promise you, it's the best way.

Things took a different turn than I thought they would with the business. With Dad gone . . . oh, Sue. I'm not good with numbers. Bills. All of that stuff I was desperate to be a part of. Dad was right. I was wrong. Cancer took him too soon and now that I've cocked just about everything up beyond repair, I've decided it's best to take myself out of the equation. Know this – I love you. Always have. With all of my heart, Suey, I love you.

And I'm sorry. I'm so incredibly sorry I have chosen to do what I am about to do, but for me it will be a release. I hope, one day, you will see it that way, too. None of this is your fault. Quite the opposite. Besides my dad, you were the only one who ever believed in me. That makes you the strongest woman I've ever known. You stood up to everyone when you married me. You stood up in front of the world and said, I believe in this man even though he is pants at Maths, and Biology, and all of those other subjects I should've done at school that you were brilliant at. You changed your life to be with me. I may not have told you, but I thanked Heaven every single day that I had such a brilliant, loving girl by my side. Now I will be free and I hope you grow to feel the same way. You can do anything you want to. Put the unicorns in the bin and live the life you want to.

Love, your Gary

TWO YEARS LATER

'Fifteen seconds to air, Kath.'

Kath gave her spine a little wriggle. Two years it had taken to get to this point. Two years of staring every single one of her life's failures in the face, hugging them, thanking them for making her the person she was today, then bidding them farewell.

Bidding farewell to Kev had, surprise surprise, been relatively easy. Why would she want to spend the rest of her life with someone who treated her as though she was inferior to him? Worthy of ridicule? There had been some hellos as well. Things with her children were good. Really good. They'd rekindled their relationship as adults and it was a comfort knowing they'd always pick up the phone to her now when she rang. The run on *Strictly* had been brilliant as well. She'd not won, but the public had really been behind her and Claudia Winkleman was a friend now, as was Bruno. The love. Him and his saucy Cha cha cha.

'Ten seconds.'

She gave her audience the thumbs up. Women mostly, but there were some men out there, too. Ever since the cycle ride, they'd begun popping up on her Twitter following as well. In all honestly, she could hardly believe they'd filled the two-hundred seat auditorium. And the buzz! The energy crackling through the place made it feel as though she was about to open the *Strictly* season.

She glanced at the side stage where her 'secret' guest gave her a *here we go* smile.

'And we're live in five, four, three . . .' Kath's eyes slid to the producer's fingers, just below the studio camera, then up to the lens as . . .

'Hello and good afternoon Britain! I'm Kath Fuller. I hope you've all got a nice warm drink and are sitting comfortably, because we have got an incredible woman here to talk to us today on this – my brand new show – *I'm Listening*.'

Kath walked to the front of the small stage in the regional television studio wondering whether anyone beyond the people in this room would see the show. She stared at the camera and saw the autocue roll into place.

She was meant to launch into a deep and meaningful, but artfully crafted, monologue about the ethos of the show, how it had been born from a void she'd felt not only in herself, but in society. How her entire life had changed when, amongst other things, her marriage fell apart on live television. Her weaknesses had been made public. But, despite all of the shame and embarrassment and pain that had followed she had risen, like the Phoenix from the flame, to host her own television show again.

But she didn't want to. The monologue was too . . . it was too beige for what had actually happened. The truth was, even with the incredible amount of support she'd received from the public, she'd lost her job and no one else had swooped in to capitalise on her time in the limelight. She'd felt ugly and old and unwanted. Particularly when Kev had been offered a job before she had. It'd fallen through in the end, but he was hosting some sort of radio show in the Midlands these days and had, by all accounts, a very loyal following. She wanted to tell them how soul destroying it had been when she'd gone to see her children. Their first response to her tearful pleas for forgiveness was to shake their heads and say, no Mum. It's too late for anything like that. She'd considered turning to drink, before remembering all of the wheels that had been set in motion had been for a dead alcoholic so she took a long hard look in the mirror, stripped everything back to the 'essential Kath' and began to volunteer at LifeTime.

The calls she'd taken had yanked her out of her one-woman pity party. Particularly the overnight shifts. The number of men she'd spoken to who reminded her of her brother had been staggering. She wanted to tell them all of this and how it had led her to take an eye-opening pilgrimage across America to be an audience member in chat show after chat show until, at long last, she'd reached California, where baring one's soul seemed to be an entry requirement. All of which had led her back here to Newcastle, to this stage, in front of this audience who were waiting for her to say something. Anything really.

So she did the only thing she felt they deserved: stepped to the side, held her hand out to the side of the stage and said, 'Ladies and gentlemen, I am proud and humbled to introduce to you my mentor and, I can't believe I'm saying this – my friend, Oprah Winfrey! Let's show her what a Newcastle welcome is all about!!!!!'

It was less than a five-minute spot, of course. And they'd only managed to make that happen because Oprah was already over in the UK doing one of her SuperSoul roadshows. But she'd come to Kath's out-of-the-way studio in Newcastle. She'd sat down and listened to Kath's story, along with the audience. Nodded and absorbed just how low Kath had had to go before she realised that she had a chance to make a difference, a *real* difference in people's lives and that the only way to do that was to own everything she was which was why, when Oprah had come out on stage, she'd been carrying a birthday cake with sixty candles on it. All of which Kath blew out in a oner. And now that Oprah was gone and the cake had been shared amongst the audience and the crew she had just a bit more unfinished business to see to.

'That's ten seconds to final commercial, Kath,' said the voice in her ear.

'. . . that's all we have time for today from Newcastle, but I want you to know that when you tune in tomorrow – and I really hope you will – I'll be here . . . and I'll be listening.'

TWO AND A HALF YEARS LATER

'It's hill climb time!'

Flo stood up on her stationary bicycle, loving the expressions on everyone's faces as her students tried and largely failed to heave themselves up to standing on their pedals. It was the trying that mattered. The journey.

'Remember! No matter what you achieve – you've achieved a personal best! Because by walking through that door – by choosing Golden Soul Cycle – you have made a decision to love yourself! Can I have a yes, Flo!'

She'd stolen this end bit from *MasterChef*. She'd actually stolen quite a few of her inspirational lines from *MasterChef*, but so long as it worked, she figured a bit of verbal plagiarism wasn't going to land her in the clink. After all, who would want to arrest a poor, grey-haired old dear from Portugal's finest golf and retirement community?

The motley, mis-matched crew of geriatrics pedalled and sang and 'Yes Flo'd' every Tuesday and Thursday when she and Stu were down here in the Algarve. This time they'd be staying a bit longer so she could train one of the younger girls who ran the pilates class. The leisure centre wanted to run it full time now that it had proved such a hit. The class was completely full today. Full of oldies. Some with dyed hair, some with gunmetal grey, or, like her now that she'd grown it out, shock white. Right in the centre of them all, her Stu was pedalling away, singing rock and pop songs she never knew he knew the lyrics to (he had helped with the playlist), and, of course, cheering the other riders on.

After the students had sweated and groaned and begged Flo to give them all a break, she turned off the disco ball, leaving the room in a soft, restorative light and pressed the song on her playlist they all knew signalled cool down. 'Everyone get your lighters ready!'

There was all sorts of fiddling with phones (Stu had helped everyone download the app because real lighters were forbidden . . . health and safety), and then, as the flickering artificial lights began to fill the dark room, that same rush of joy she'd felt all of those years ago in a stadium filled with crazed fans rose within her.

'Time to dial back the resistance,' she said. 'Put a towel round your neck. That's right. Beatrice, take a drink of water, you look a bit flushed. That's right, everybody. Slow your tempo down . . . nice and easy.' And then, just as she did every single time the lyrics began to wrap round her, reminding her just how close she'd come to throwing it all away, she looked her husband in the eye and began to sing along with Freddie, 'Love of My Life'.

THREE YEARS LATER

Raven watched as the eighteen-year-old in front of her shifted and, as she had done so many times when she had been asked to talk to someone about what was troubling her, avoided eye contact.

She pushed the box of felt and scissors and glue towards her.

She'd just shown her how to make emoji-shaped elbow patches. If she wanted to do it, great. If she didn't? Not a problem. Crafting or drawing or etching out squares and triangles were all ways of letting the brain process whatever it was they really wanted to say.

'It's like getting into Oxford wasn't enough, you know?' Alexandra's voice was filled with an all-too-familiar fury. 'It's like, whatever I do, it won't be enough unless it is *exactly* what they'd planned for me.'

Raven nodded. Even though she'd been taught not to nod at the training sessions, she'd learnt from experience that if you were really listening to someone, you couldn't help but nod. It was a biochemical reaction or something. She'd have to check on that. She was only three years into her psychiatry degree so she still had quite a way to go before she understood all of the whys and wherefores, but she was pretty comfortable when it came to this terrain. The 'please your parents' turf. She asked, 'What do you think it is they want you to do?'

'Oh, you know,' huffed Alexandra, 'Graduate with honours, then get a masters or a PhD and make loads of money so that they can brag to everyone about what brilliant parents they are.'

'I know this might sound weird, but do you think it's their way of keeping you safe?' Raven began to doodle, a crayoned flower appearing amidst the spirals and swirls and other shapes that covered the piece of paper she probably should've been taking notes on, but had decided her 'counselees' should see. Feeling as if you were being inspected, when what you really wanted was to be heard, was annoying. So, she listened. Listened and doodled and pushed bits of felt and coloured pens around and, sometimes when she had a bit of extra money because her mum had filled her freezer with loads of homemade food, glitter. She had a weakness for glitter.

'I dunno. I suppose if you wanted to look at things that way, you could.'

Raven tapped the table and drew Alexandra's eyeliner-rimmed eyes up to her own. 'They're probably a bit freaked.'

'What? Why?'

'You know. They've been looking after you for eighteen years – like a job. And now all of a sudden – they don't wield the power they used to. It must be freaky.'

'Oh,' Alexandra laughed a dry, angry laugh. 'They're not letting go of the reins that easily. Let me assure you.'

Raven pushed a few crayons in Alexandra's direction. This might take a few more sessions. Who knew? Maybe they'd meet all year. The student-to-student counselling sessions were cool like that. Flexible. A lot like Raven had become after her ride when everything changed all over again.

She had moved back into her parents' a couple of weeks after they'd got back from Northumberland and, much to her delight, so had Sue. Little, timorous, lovely Sue had put her house on the market and applied to Oxford-Brookes to retrain as a paramedic. Raven had somehow managed to convince Oxford University she really actually did want to go there, but she'd been taking some time out to 'fine tune her academic wants and needs' which, much to her surprise, took the form of training to become an art therapist. She was going to become a proper shrink so she could write prescriptions if necessary, but if her parents' pharmacy was anything to go by, it was a path she would try and avoid. Why take drugs to mask what you were feeling if you didn't have to? Yeah, facing some of life's hurdles was painful, but . . . realising you could leap over them? Fucking epic.

THREE YEARS AND ONE WEEK LATER

'Well, would you look at that,' Sue's father cleared his throat and began a weird nodding thing that Sue expected was keeping some tears at bay. 'It fits like a glove. Well. A hat glove. As if it was made for you, anyway.'

'Do you think?' Sue couldn't wipe the smile off of her face. Little Sue Green, wearing a mortar board and gown.

'You look ever so clever, Suey.' Bev genuinely did look proud. She threw a look back at Katie. 'Doesn't she look clever, Katie. Our Suey?'

'Mmm,' said Katie, still a bit miffed that Sue's graduation had fallen in the midst of the children's half term when she had been hoping to take them sand dune surfing in Germany. Flo had recommended it apparently. For core strengthening. But Dean had overruled her and insisted they stay here.

'Here she is!!!!' Flo bustled up to the group, Captain George walking alongside her without so much as a limp. 'Stu! Stu get over here.' She leant into Sue and said conspiratorially, 'He keeps bossing me round, telling me how to train the new puppy, so I thought I'd give him a go and let him see what it was like handling a mad thing.'

Sue thought Stuart had probably had more than enough experience with mad things, but was too happy to tease Flo about it. 'Thanks so much for coming. I can't believe you're here after having just been in Australia.'

'What? We wouldn't have missed it for the world! Besides. What better way to knock the jet lag out of our system, eh? Bit of sunshine, an inspirational story. Hey. Do you think they'd let an oldie like me in the back of your ambu—'

Flo laughed hysterically before Sue could find a kind way to say *not really, no.* 'Only joshing you, love. I'm quite busy enough with the new pup and you'll never guess. Stu's teaching me how to golf! We'll most likely need you to dog-sit again if you're free in about four weeks' time?'

Sue laughed and smiled. She loved dog-sitting at the Wilsons'. Especially in the autumn when Flo gave her free rein to fill up their freezer with all of the cakes she made alongside *Bake Off*.

There was a call on the tannoy for all of the graduates to make their way to the front of the outdoor seating area.

'Sue!' Raven ran up, her parents in tow. 'We made it!'

Sue pulled them all into a huge hug. They'd been such a help over the past few years. She had lived with them right up until she'd got her place at Oxford-Brookes when she had decided perhaps a bit of time living on her own might be good for her. At forty-two years of age, she had never done it. She loved her little, sunny studio to this day. It looked out on some lovely fields and was just over a mile from campus. Instead of melting down her bicycle as promised, Flo had given it to Sue with a promise to keep her up to date on her studies in person or via email as she and Stu were doing a bit more travelling these days. *A bit of a second honeymoon we're having*, she'd stage-whispered well aware Stuart could hear them perfectly well even though he was busy with his Sudoku.

When the head of her department handed her her diploma, Sue's smile actually hit ear to ear. Gary would've absolutely loved this. Would've rented out the function room at the Royal Oak and this time . . . this time she would've filled it. She couldn't believe how her life had changed. Would she have preferred Gary to be a part of it? Of course she would have. So she pictured him sometimes, standing at the far side of a restaurant or up at the pub bar, giving her one of his cheeky winks or one of those crooked smiles he'd once told her he reserved specifically for her, and then she made herself tune in, be present in whatever it was she was doing, and live her life, for that, after all, was what he had wished most for her. And now, thanks to having known and loved him, she knew the life she would lead from here on out would be so much the richer for having loved a man who had loved her every bit as much in return.

'Suey!' Dean clapped his hands together after they had finished the requisite family photos. 'We were thinking we'd like to take you out tonight. Have a slap-up meal somewhere. What do you say? Indian? Pub grub? Something a bit more swish? Your call.'

She gave him a hug (they hugged a lot more these days). 'Thanks, big brother. I'm afraid I'm busy.'

'Oh?' His eyebrows did that 'tell all' thing they did whenever he was trying to live vicariously through her life (he had recently expanded the business, with Dylan's help, into IT recruitment).

'Would you take a rain check?' It was something she never would've dared ask someone before, least of all Dean but, she was a different person now. She could deliver babies. Help burn victims. Stop heart attacks (with the proper equipment or without). A myriad of things to help take away the pain when people needed someone most.

And, of course, tonight she would be doing more of the same. But not in her shiny new reflective gear. No. Tonight was something even more special than climbing out of an ambulance, gurney and run bag at the ready. This was her gift to Gary. Her gift to life.

Incident No – 1309
TIME: 21:47
Call Handler: SUE YOUNG

Call Handler: Hello, you've reached LifeTime. My name is Sue. I'm a suicide widow, a paramedic and I'm here to help. What would you like to talk about today?

Caller: How much time have you got?

Call Handler: For you? All the time in the world.

Author's note

In order to make this book as realistic as I could for the charity cycle ride, I decided I wanted to ride my bicycle along the same route Sue, Raven, Flo and Kath took. So I did. Were there flaws in my plan? Most assuredly. But was I pleased it went the way it did? Definitely.

Let me caution you: Think twice before not riding your bicycle for two years then embarking on a 174-mile journey from Ravenglass to Tynemouth. In October. During a week where the wind and rain are relentless. And it's cold. And you told your husband you didn't want to be tempted by his warm, cosy car if he was riding along as a support driver. So he went to Scotland instead. Which, for three rainsoaked hours you can actually see, as you round the corner from Anthorn to Bowness-on-Solway. I'd thought it was Brigadoon until a septuagenarian travelling alongside me for half an hour on his electric bicycle set me right.

Silver linings? I learnt a lot about what pushing yourself to the physical limit can do to your emotional state. It is long and hard and sometimes scary because much more of the journey was on actual roads than I had thought. There were far more hills than I'd anticipated (my planning could've been a lot better). And riding at the tail end of 'the season' meant there was A LOT of time on my own. Without headphones or podcasts or anything apart from my thoughts to keep me busy. Most of which went like this: *I think I can, I think I can, I think I can.*

Little nuggets that ended up in the book: Yes . . . my bum was sore. Insanely sore. Turns out it's really, really hard to pull up not one, but three pairs of lycra shorts when they are saturated. It is also difficult to find a hedge to hide behind that isn't knee deep in mud (that time of year) where the lorries can't see you. No offence to the lovely Cumbrian town of Silloth, but for some strange reason, you smelt of tinned spaghetti to me. Which, frankly, had the chicken burger not been available, I would've gladly eaten a tin of. I ate sticky toffee pudding for dessert. Every night. I was in my bed and asleep by 8pm. Every night. I was also up at 6am and riding by 7am every morning. The longest day was the first, at fifty-four miles, and the shortest was the last but that was mostly because I can't add. They all ended up being the same amount of hours long because someone didn't inform Hadrian that putting a wall on a hill meant the ride wasn't going to be carefree and whimsical.

There were heaps of blackberries in the hedges so if I needed a bonus snack I had one. The folk who ran the B&Bs were insanely kind. A particular shout out to the Tourist Information Centre in Brampton which is staffed entirely by volunteers and run on £1000 per year (plus any donations from saturated passers-by who are given a cup of tea!). They sheltered me from the rain, gave me a hot cup of tea and called a B&B, the Hollies on the Wall, and explained I had reached my physical limit for the day (I had. There were tears), and could they please come get me. Which they did. (I was three miles downhill from them and would've arrived under nightfall if I had continued.) Upon arrival, they stuffed my saturated cycle shoes with newspaper, let me play with their dog and gave me the best breakfast of the ride. (I hasten to add the breakfast at the Hallbank Guesthouse in Hexham was also tremendous and the hospitality was fabulous.)

It was really hard and it was also unbelievably satisfying to achieve. In a weird way, I was grateful for all of the bonus 'hardships' I had to manoeuvre as it helped me to understand all of the emotional turmoil each of my characters was going through. Pushing your bicycle through shin-deep water for healthy chunks of the ride brings out the philosopher in a person. And the calf muscles!

I did some fundraising for the charity Mind and a lot of people donated. It was truly humbling. If you fancy leaving a donation for them or Samaritans (or volunteering to help), here's how you do it:

https://www.mind.org.uk
https://www.samaritans.org

If you know someone you are frightened for, you can also ring the charities and they will advise you on ways to help. Well done, you. xx

Acknowledgements

Big thanks to Chacha for answering a thousand million questions about 111. Gratitude to the wonderfully generous Debbie Macom'er for her endless supply of valuable advice and introducing me to chocolate-covered bacon. RIDICULOUS. And lovely. To Jackie for reading and reading and reading. Jackie (still you) and Pam and Christine for reading in that final week when I thought I wouldn't finish. Your cheerleading ensured that I did. Janet, Alison, Kate, Ruth, Jeev & Immi for being a wonderfully supportive trampoline of friendship and suppliers of hilarious gifs.

Big juicy love to my spectacular husband for offering to drive alongside me during the cycle ride and not taking it too badly when I said no, but being proud of me when I finished and taking me out for sticky toffee pudding before I set off. For everyone who cheered me on during that ride. It was bloody difficult, so thank you for being there. To all of the amazing people who ran the B&Bs where I stayed because you were so nice. I was filthy, and bedraggled and not entirely charming upon my arrivals, but you always made sure my tum tum was full and I had a smile on my face when I set off in the pouring rain each day. To Pedal Power cycle holidays for supplying me with a bicycle and picking me up at the end (and letting me use your name in the book). Hearing your story made me even more determined to write mine.

Thanks to my agent, Jo, for being fabulous and introducing me to Go Away Doctor juice. That is some magic carrot and ginger potion. Ditto on the thanks (mental and health) to Sophia Bartleet (friend extraordinaire), Natasha Hogben (snap), and Chantal Prince, friend and all-important osteopath, for making sure my shoulder and arm remained in working order and that my knees weren't paralysed after riding along Hadrian's Wall. Deep, happy belly thanks to Matt, Mich, JP and Andy for all of the Friday night suppers. Yum. Your friendship means the world to me. To Sue and Stu for your fabulous positivity (and unbelievably enviable allotment plot). Amazing.

Heartfelt thanks to my editor Kate for trusting me to take Sue on the right journey and shepherding me back in when I went off on whatever is smaller than a B road.

I do, or, sadly, have known, several people who have ended their lives. The holes left in their wake . . . all I can say is, if you think you've had enough, please, please, think again. There is someone, someone you might not even know yet, who can help.